Praise for Alice C̶l̶a̶y̶t̶o̶n̶
New York Times bestselling Hudson Valley series

CREAM OF THE CROP

"Emotionally ripe with bold dialogue, strong characterization, steamy sex scenes and Clayton's trademark wacky humor, the author builds a delectable, opposites-attract romance."

—*RT Book Reviews* (4 star review)

"A titillating story with plenty of happy endings."

—*Library Journal* (in a starred review)

NUTS

"Small towns are filled with different personalities and *Nuts* is simply that, chock-full of so many special nuts you won't want to leave."

—*Heroes and Heartbreakers*

Praise for Alice Clayton's laugh-out-loud sexy Cocktail series

LAST CALL

"Witty dialogue, engaging scenes and the ever-present smoking-hot chemistry once again prove that Clayton is a master at her trade."

—*RT Book Reviews*

"The hilarious conclusion to a series that made me laugh until I cried, swoon until I sighed, and reminded us all that there's always time for one *Last Call*."

—*New York Times* bestselling author Colleen Hoover

MAI TAI'D UP

"Clayton's trademark charm and comical wit saturates the storyline, which features engaging dialogue, eccentric characters and a couple who defines the word 'adorable.'"

—*RT Book Reviews*

"Alice Clayton is a genius! *Mai Tai'd Up* is sexy, steamy, and totally hilarious! A must read that I didn't want to end."

—*New York Times* and *USA Today*
bestselling author Emma Chase

SCREWDRIVERED

"Cheers to Alice Clayton! *Screwdrivered* is a hilarious cocktail of crackling banter, heady sexual tension, and pop-your-cork love scenes. The heroine is brisk and lively (can we be friends, Viv?) and the hot librarian hero seduced me with his barely restrained sensuality. I've never wanted a nerd more."

—*New York Times* and *USA Today*
bestselling author Kresley Cole

"*Screwdrivered* has sexual tension, romantic longing, and fantastic chemistry."

—*Fresh Fiction*

RUSTY NAILED

"We want to bask in the afterglow: giddy, blushing, and utterly in love with this book."

—*New York Times* and *USA Today*
bestselling author Christina Lauren

"Clayton's trademark wit and general zaniness shine through in abundance as readers get an intimate view of the insecurities one faces while in a serious relationship. Steamy playful sex scenes and incorrigible friends make this a wonderful continuation of Wallbanger and Nightie Girl's journey to their happily ever after."

—*RT Book Reviews*

"For fun, sex, and strudel, make sure to spend some time with these wallbangers."

—*Heroes and Heartbreakers*

WALLBANGER

"Sultry, seXXXy, super-awesome . . . we LOVE it!"

—Perez Hilton

"An instant classic, with plenty of laugh-out-loud moments and riveting characters."

—Jennifer Probst, *New York Times* bestselling
author of *Searching for Perfect*

"Fun and frothy, with a bawdy undercurrent and a hero guaranteed to make your knees wobbly . . . The perfect blend of sex, romance, and baked goods."

—Ruthie Knox, bestselling author of *About Last Night*

"Alice Clayton strikes again, seducing me with her real woman sex appeal, unparalleled wit and addicting snark; leaving me laughing, blushing, and craving knock-all-the-paintings-off-the-wall sex of my very own."

—Humor blogger Brittany Gibbons

"A funny, madcap, smexy romantic contemporary . . . Fast pacing and a smooth flowing storyline will keep you in stitches. . . ."

—*Smexy Books*

And for her acclaimed Redhead series

"Zany and smoking-hot romance [that] will keep readers in stitches . . ."

—*RT Book Reviews*

"I adore Grace and Jack. They have such amazing chemistry. The love that flows between them scorches the pages."

—*Smexy Books*

"Steamy romance, witty characters and a barrel full of laughs . . ."

—*The Book Vixen*

"Laugh-out-loud funny."

—*Smokin Hot Books*

BUNS

Alice Clayton

GALLERY BOOKS

NEW YORK   LONDON   TORONTO   SYDNEY   NEW DELHI

G

Gallery Books
An Imprint of Simon & Schuster, Inc.
1230 Avenue of the Americas
New York, NY 10020

First Gallery Books trade paperback edition May 2017

GALLERY BOOKS and colophon are registered trademarks of Simon & Schuster, Inc.

For information about special discounts for bulk purchases, please contact Simon & Schuster Special Sales at 1-866-506-1949 or business@simonandschuster.com.

The Simon & Schuster Speakers Bureau can bring authors to your live event. For more information or to book an event, contact the Simon & Schuster Speakers Bureau at 1-866-248-3049 or visit our website at www.simonspeakers.com.

Manufactured in the United States of America

10 9 8 7 6 5 4 3 2 1

Library of Congress Cataloging-in-Publication Data

Names: Clayton, Alice, author.
Title: Buns / Alice Clayton.
Description: First Gallery Books trade paperback edition | New York : Gallery
    Books, 2017. | Series: Hudson Valley series ; 3
Identifiers: LCCN 20 16053077 (print) | LCCN 2017004583 (ebook) | ISBN
    9781501118173 (paperback) | ISBN 9781501118197 (ebook)
Subjects: LCSH: Man-woman relationships—Fiction. | BISAC: FICTION /
    Romance / Contemporary. | FICTION / Contemporary Women. | GSAFD: Love
    stories.
Classification: LCC PS3603.L3968 B86 2017 (print) | LCC PS3603.L3968
    (ebook) | DDC 813/.6—dc23
LC record available at https://lccn.loc.gov/2016053077

ISBN 978-1-5011-1817-3
ISBN 978-1-5011-1819-7 (ebook)

To Mohonk Mountain House,
where inspiration became reality

Acknowledgments

As I sit writing this, I'm staring out a hotel window, gazing at the Sydney Opera House. How is this my life? How did I get here? How in the world did a woman managing a day spa in St. Louis, Missouri, end up on the other side of the world at a book signing (signing books she herself actually wrote, but you knew that)?

The answer is you. Simply put, it's you, you gorgeous reader you. You came along with me on this wild ride from the moment I hit publish on the first chapter of *The Unidentified Redhead*, back when it was nothing more than a little-known piece of fan fiction.

I love this community more than I can ever say. There's something so magical about women reading romance, and recommending romance, and loving romance as much as we all do. And as grateful as I am as an author who gets to participate, I'm even more grateful as a reader for the genre itself. In this very strange world we're living in right now, to be able to spend the last few moments of my day, every single day by the way, in bed with an incredible piece of romantic fiction is exactly what we all need.

But now specifically about this book, the *Buns* that you're currently squeezing. This book was inspired entirely by a trip I took to Mohonk Mountain House in New Paltz, New York. This hotel is like a peek into a different world. It's beautiful, it's peaceful, it's like a giant hug on top of a mountain. I can't say enough about this piece of heaven on earth except to say that while Bryant Mountain House inspired Mohonk, creative license was required to invent this fictional world because there is nothing, NOT A THING, about the real resort that would ever require someone like Clara to come along and update it. Mohonk is, quite literally, perfection. It's become one of my favorite places on the planet. And to anyone who lives a train ride away from the Hudson Valley, figure out a way to go spend a weekend up there. And if you don't live close by, go anyway. Make the trip. It will change your life.

I must thank my usual suspects, Nina Bocci, Jessica Royer-Ocken, Marla Daniels, and while she is my new editor I've admired her for years now, Lauren McKenna. Thank you all for always pushing and expecting better. I couldn't have done it without you.

And thank you again to everyone who came along on this journey with me. I'm not entirely sure where we're going next, but I hope you'll be along for the ride.

Alice

xoxo

BUNS

Chapter 1

"Partner?"

"Partner."

"Partner?"

"Partner."

"Partner?"

"Not if you continue to have this newly developed comprehension problem, but yes, Clara. Partner."

Whoa.

I sat across three feet of mahogany desk from inarguably my favorite adult in the entire world, who happened to also be my boss, and she just told me that if I was able to knock this next job out of the park, I'd be promoted to partner.

I breathed in, then out. In, then out. This was one of those moments—the kind you read about, the kind you remember later on in life when you reminisce about the good old days and you point to it as though it were a blue ribbon, plucking this day out of all the others and festooning it with colors and sparkles and maybe a unicorn. One day I'd look back and say *that was the day my life changed. That all the hard work and hours and weekends spent in the office and missed dates and skipped parties and blood and sweat and tears became worth it because I'd arrived here, in this space and time, and I'd finally carved out a place in this world that was* mine.

Barbara smiled, watching me take it all in, likely being able to see my wheels turning. She hired me five and a half years ago, took me under her wing and mentored me every step of the way. And now she was handing me the keys to the kingdom. Partner in one of the most well-known and well-respected branding agencies in the country. If . . .

"So Bryant Mountain House leaps into the twenty-first century, and I get to see my name on the letterhead?"

She nodded. "That's the deal, kiddo."

I breathed in, then out. In, then out.

I smiled. "I'll head down there tomorrow."

I didn't own a car. Not that uncommon when you consider I'm on the road nearly 80 percent of the year, and when I was home in Boston I pretty much walked everywhere I needed to go. The nightmare traffic in Boston was enough to make me change the channel the few times I'd actually paused to watch a car commercial, wondering if I should part with some of my hard-earned dollars and finally bite the bullet.

I did love to drive, though, and took any excuse to head out onto the open road whenever a long-term job opened up. And let's face it, long-term jobs basically described my entire life.

But now I was about to be, maybe, possibly, made partner in this career I loved so much. Was this real? Was this happening? Was this—

"Just make sure she's full of gas, okay?"

I snapped back into the present at the Hertz rental car lot on the edge of town. I'd been daydreaming while this kid had been lecturing me on my full-tank options.

"Sure, sure, gas. Full of it. You got it." I patted the roof of my rental, a beige four-door Corolla. Solid. Safe. Dependable. Utterly boring. "Am I good to go?" I was anxious to get on the road. It was only four hours to Bryant Mountain House, but I wanted to make sure I had time to scope things out before dinner.

"Yep, where ya headed?"

"Catskills, upstate New York . . ." I trailed off as a car inched forward out of the car wash, catching my eye. Early spring in the Northeast, when everything was sullen and gray, muddy and cold, was one of the earth's uglier moments. But when this beautiful convertible, shiny and red and all kinds of pretty, rolled out and reminded the world what summer looked like, I couldn't stop staring. It was bold, brash, braggy, and wholly unnecessary.

And eight kinds of fun.

The kid followed my gaze, raising an eyebrow in appreciation.

I pointed. "How much is that one?"

"Niiiiice," he replied, his estimation of me going up a few notches. Born seven weeks premature, I've always been on the teeny side. Dressed in black leggings, black wellies that practically swallowed me whole even though they were the smallest size in stock, and a black rain slicker to keep the intermittent drizzle off me, I looked like I belonged in a beige four-door Corolla.

But underneath that rain slicker was a cherry-red clingy T-shirt. And underneath the leggings were cherry-red silk panties. And as I took off my ball cap and ran my hands through my hair, turning my pixie cut into short little blond spikes, I spoke through cherry-red painted lips.

"Yeah, I'm gonna need that one."

Twenty minutes later I blazed out of Boston in my wholly unnecessary, determined to knock this job so far out of the park I might just buy one of these for my cherry-red collection, sweet-ass ride.

A partner deserved something a little special, right?

A partner should also know better than to take a sports car on twisty, windy roads still crusted with salt and ice and potholes. This is why I rarely if ever made spur-of-the-moment decisions, rarely if ever flew by the seat of my pants. I preferred to Keep It Simple, Stupid, and leave the crazytown to my best friend Natalie Grayson, and even to some extent my other best friend Roxie Callahan, who could serve up her own brand of crazy when needed.

Natalie and Roxie. The three of us had met years ago when we all wound up at a culinary school in California, all eighteen and ready for big-time changes. Roxie was the only one who actually had any real culinary skills, and while I'd enjoyed the year I spent in California, I realized early on cooking was never going to be more than a hobby, and hightailed it back to New England. Natalie was similarly disillusioned with cooking as a career, and she also headed back to her home, the island of Manhattan, which she was pretty sure belonged only to her.

Roxie stayed, made her mark in California as a private chef to the stars, and only found herself back in her tiny hometown of Bailey Falls, New York, when her career imploded over an ill-timed whipped cream turning into butter. This very butter is what changed the course of her life and made her truly appreciate her hometown, a hometown that had welcomed Leo

Maxwell in the time she'd been gone, the man who was currently rocking her world.

The town's next victim into its black hole of charm and sweet was Natalie, a city girl if there ever was one. Officially she lived in Manhattan. Unofficially she was fooling no one as she'd recently begun spending weeknights ninety miles north of her island in the company of one Oscar Mendoza, owner of Bailey Falls Creamery and the only man who could make her set one toe north of the Bronx.

And here I was, heading toward that same town, which was also home to Bryant Mountain House, the old hotel I'd been hired to rebrand, reshape, and get back in the black.

Roxie and Natalie were thrilled, convinced that once I spent some time in the quaint town, I'd fall just as in love with it as they did and decide to stay.

I never stayed. Anywhere. I loved being on the road, meeting new people, hanging my hat somewhere just long enough to sink my teeth into something that used to be incredible and needed to be brought back to life. And once that was done, it was off to the next project.

I had an apartment. I had things in it. I had my name on the mail slot.

I did not have a home.

"Keep your bags packed, kid, you're not gonna be here long . . ."

I blinked up at her, the sunlight behind her turning her head into an eclipse of sorts, unable to make out individual features of her face but knowing somehow that her expression would be one of tired resignation. I was just one more kid in a houseful of others. With their own never-truly-unpacked bags . . .

I shook my head to clear it, squeezing the steering wheel. Partners in shiny convertibles didn't think about the past, they thought about the future. I pulled over to grab a coffee for the road, thumbed through my travel playlist, and cued up some Fleetwood Mac.

"You can go your own way . . ."

That's for damn sure.

∾

Three hours later I turned off the interstate and onto the state highway that would take me into Bailey Falls and up to Bryant Mountain House. Turning off the tunes, I began to put my game face on.

This was where I needed to think, to ruminate, to imagine what it must be like to have your entire family's history potentially subjected to a wrecking ball. When I took on a job, that is what I took on. It wasn't just a few months of work, it was a way of life. And not just for the family but for all of the employees whose lives were typically just as tied into the history as those whose names were on the letterhead. The Bryant family was small in actual name but large by proxy. And I'd be working to save jobs for more than just the family.

The Bryants had owned this property for almost one hundred and fifty years. And like so many other family-run hotels, they'd relied too much on "but this is how it's always been done," which simply doesn't work anymore in this modern age. With Yelp and TripAdvisor helping everyone make their vacation plans, reviews could make or break a place. And they'd had their share of bad reviews in the last few years. Couple that with the recent economic crisis and belt-tightening across the board for vacationers, and they were in danger of losing their beautiful hotel.

Unless . . .

* CUE TRUMPETS *

. . . they had *me*. Which they did. I rolled my neck, cracked my shoulders a bit, and settled in for the final leg.

I had a hotel to save.

* CUE A SECOND BUT EQUALLY IMPRESSIVE ROUND OF TRUMPETS *

"Melanie Bixby, arriving guest," I said, leaning out of the driver's-side window at the guard shack at the edge of the property. I didn't even blink anymore when I used my pseudonym, it was second nature at this point. When I checked in under my real name, I never got the true sense of what was going on at a hotel. Clara Morgan was given the red-carpet treatment, Clara Morgan was upgraded, complimentary champagne was sent up almost without fail, and literally every single parking attendant/busboy/junior housekeeper went out of their way to bid good morning/afternoon/evening to Clara Morgan.

Melanie Bixby, however, was just your average guest, and always got the real story.

"Bixby, Bixby, oh sure, there you are, Ms. Bixby. Let me just grab your parking slip." After a moment inside, he returned with a pass that he set just inside on the dashboard for me. "Now you keep that there while you're with us, that's how we tell the overnight guests from the ones who are just here on a day pass."

"Day pass?" I played dumb.

"Yes, ma'am, Bryant Mountain House has some of the best hiking and biking trails around. For thirty-five dollars folks can come spend the entire day in the woods. No access to the main house, but there's a nice enough snack shack on the edge of the property for refreshments."

"Do you get many day-passers up here? I mean, in the off-season?"

The attendant looked skyward, scratching at his beard as though divining the answer. "Not really, ma'am, no. Summertime sure, but it's getting harder and harder to get people up here when it's cold and rainy. Like today. We had a storm a few weeks ago that would—now would you look at that? Me running my mouth off, when you've got places to get to! You just stay to the right, this road will take you right on up to the resort." He smiled companionably, his eyes crinkling at the corners as he waved me on.

"Thank you!" I called out as I rolled my window up against the chilly spring rain that had begun to fall. Heavy and sloppy, it'd be slushy ice by nightfall if it kept up.

I stayed to the right as directed and began to wind my way up up up. The road twisted and turned to the top of the mountain underneath the late-afternoon sky, which was thickening with storm clouds and an ever-increasing gloom. On my left the hillside was covered in trees and thick brambles that'd be bursting with green in a month or so. On the other side the road fell off sharply, the trees giving way every so often to showcase fallen boulders, craggy and rough. I spied a trailhead, clearly marked for guests of Bryant Mountain House, winding into the forest.

The hiking must be incredible up here.

Making a mental note to investigate the off-season trails, I continued up the hill, which at this point was quickly becoming the *Mountain* in *Bryant Mountain House*. Turning my wipers up another notch against the now-steady rainfall, I turned around the final bend and there, finally, was the resort.

At least, there was part of it. The enormity of this single

structure was too great to be captured in just the windshield of my tiny, impractical, and *wholly unsuited for mountain terrain* sports car. But what I could see was impressive as hell.

I drove under a stand of weeping willows planted along the road like soldiers, arching across and creating a tunnel effect that in summertime must be stunning. At the ass-end of winter and the equally-as-ugly beginning of spring, the bare limbs feathered together, slick with slush and almost gnarled. Not entirely welcoming.

Shivering slightly, I continued through the archway, getting my next peek at the resort. Rising high into the air, the east wing loomed up suddenly—the real money shot being either the mountain view to the west or the lake view to the east. Six, no, seven stories climbed against the wintry sky. I slowed to a stop to appreciate the architecture—fieldstone mixed with deeply burnished redwood, green shutters, soaring high gray stone chimneys. I whistled as I hit the gas again, once more twisting into the dark woods that surrounded the property. I passed several barns, the stables, the summer garden, and glimpsed just the edge of the championship golf course.

And then the road swung me back around to the front of the resort and the edge of the parking lot. One look at how fast the rain was falling and I immediately opted for valet and gunned it for the covered entryway.

Gunning it in a rain that's bordering on icy sleet isn't wise in a boring beige Corolla, and it is for damn sure not recommended in a shiny red sports car with rear-wheel drive. I spun out on the last turn, my back end slipping wildly as I clutched the wheel and tried to straighten out. I overcorrected, swung wide, and out of the corner of my eye I caught a man dressed in a green slicker and matching hat gesturing, holding out his hands and yelling.

"Look out!" I cried.

"Stop!" he cried.

I thumped the curb and by mere inches missed hitting the rain-slicker guy, who threw himself to the side at the last second, tumbling into a large shrub.

"Oh my God," I whispered to myself, everything suddenly quiet. I looked through the wipers and saw galoshes kicking in the air, the shrub branches thrashing wildly as the man I'd nearly hit fought to climb back out. "Oh my God!"

I jumped out of the car, ran over to the shrub just as he was pulling himself loose. "I'm so sorry, oh no, are you okay? I'm so sorry!"

His raincoat, emblazoned with the words BRYANT MOUNTAIN HOUSE, was caught on a limb, his hat was hanging off the back of his head by the string, and one of his galoshes had come loose.

"Oh, for pity's sake!" he exclaimed, tugging at the branch.

"Can I help you?" I asked, reaching for the tangled limb.

"No no, I think you've done enough," he snapped.

"Well, let me at least see if I can—"

"It's fine, don't do that—"

"I think I found where it's stuck, just—"

"Don't do that, it's going to tear, it's really fine, it's—watch out!"

The branch tore free, taking with it half of the raincoat, thwapping him upside the head as it rustled and resettled back into the bush.

"Wow, I can't believe that just . . . I'm so sorry."

"It's. Fine." He spoke through gritted teeth.

The two of us stared at each other. I felt terrible. He looked frustrated.

I clasped my hands behind my back, looked around, then tried to smile. "So, where do I check in?"

Chapter 2

Turns out the man I'd tried to hit with my car was the bellman tasked with assisting me inside.

"You're Ms. Bixby, yes?" he asked, once he'd brushed himself off.

"How did you . . . ah. They called up from the guard shack?" I asked.

"Indeed," he replied drily.

Just then another attendant dressed in a similar rain jacket came running out. "Sorry about that, Mr.— Whoa . . . what happened here?"

"Ms. Bixby had a little trouble navigating that last turn," the guy from the bushes said, walking over to the car and turning it off, tossing the keys to the other attendant. As I watched, he seemed to compose himself, straighten up, and put his game face back on. "I'll just retrieve your bags from the trunk and we'll see about getting you checked in, shall we?"

"Yes. Please." I nodded, wanting to stay out of his way and not cause any more problems.

I followed him into the lobby, catching my first glimpse of the opulence in this great old hotel. A graceful staircase made of thin spindles and sturdy oak stretched up several floors and down at least one from what I could see, bisecting a large receiving room. Conversational chairs and love seats were grouped around one, two, no three fireplaces, all roaring and chasing away the outside chill. Each fireplace was unique with mantels carved of dark woods and flanked by ceramic bricks in deep greens and golden yellows. Victorian through and through, it was beautiful, though somewhat . . . fussy? No, *dated* was a better word for it.

"It's beautiful, isn't it?"

"Hmm?" I asked, turning toward the bellman who'd been watching me, taking in my reaction. "Oh yes, it's lovely."

"Those were found on-site when they dug the original foundation," he said as we passed by five enormous amethyst-colored crystals displayed above another enormous fireplace, this one made of stacked stone.

"Really?" I asked, nodding in appreciation. "And when was that?"

A look of pride came over his face, as though he'd been the one to dig that first shovel of dirt. "1872. In fact, right where you're standing was where the original boardinghouse kitchen was."

He smiled then, the kind of smile that makes you want to invest in toothpaste and sunshine. I found myself unable to resist offering my own pearly whites back in response. If all the employees took as much pride in Bryant Mountain House as the bellman, we were in better shape than I thought.

I followed him toward the check-in desk, noticing his black wingtips, his crisply ironed tan chinos paired with a forest-green fleece with the resort name emblazoned on the back. Little bit of a mishmash for an employee uniform, but on a rainy afternoon like this, I certainly wasn't going to stand on formality.

"Hello, Trish, this is Ms. Bixby, checking in."

"Of course," a pretty blonde behind the desk chirped, and just as I went to pick up my tote bag, the bellman reached for it at the same time. I don't know which one of us tipped it over, but the entire contents of my bag spilled out all over the carpet.

"Must be something in the air today, sorry about that, let me help you," he said, kneeling next to me as I began stuffing everything back in—notebooks, pencils, iPad, wallet, my planner . . . hey wait, where was my planner? I looked left and there was the bellman, studying my planner with a strange look on his face.

I coughed pointedly, and his eyes snapped up to mine.

"Here you go," he said, smoothing the engraved cover and handing it back.

"Thanks. I'd lose my head if this ever went missing," I said with a laugh, popping it back into my bag. Not just my head but anything and everything about whatever job I was currently working on. Filled to bursting with newspaper clippings, photographs, red-lined spreadsheets, and handwritten notes, my planner was the single most important item in my tote bag. Setting aside the practical aspect, it was also sentimental to me. Barbara had given it to me the day I went out on my own, working a job in Colorado.

"Here you go, kiddo, this'll help keep all those plates in the air a bit longer," she'd said, handing me the leather-bound planner. Embossed on the front cover was my name in silver letters.

"Barbara, you spoil me," I replied, running my fingers over my name. "Thank you, it's very sweet."

"I'm protecting my investment." She laughed. "It's in my best interest that you stay focused out there on the road."

And on the road I'd been ever since, planner of grand ideas by my side.

Speaking of by my side, my bellman was studying my face with an appraising expression. I couldn't help but do the same.

Now that we were out of the rain, I could really see him. Auburn hair, closely cropped but threatening to wave and curl given the chance. Tall, slim build, sharply cut cheekbones and a strongly chiseled jawline. A sprinkling of freckles across his nose and sun-kissed cheekbones hinted at someone who enjoyed the outdoors, even in the wintertime.

He wore tortoiseshell-rimmed glasses, the tones mimicking the reddish-blond hues in his hair, and his eyes were the deepest blue I'd ever seen, almost ink-like. Eyes that searched mine as though looking for something, and then widened when he found whatever it was he was looking for.

The left corner of his mouth turned up, and he flashed me an easy grin.

"Ready to go upstairs?"

"Sure?" I replied, realizing as he grinned again he knew exactly how cheeky he was being. I rolled my eyes, slinging my tote over my shoulder and silently berating myself for flirting with a bellman not five minutes after arriving.

Never. Get. Involved. That was a rule that was as firm as the buns this guy likely had under those perfectly ironed chinos.

Pocketing the honest to goodness actual gold key to my room, I resisted the urge to give him my own cheeky grin. "Lead the way."

It was quiet, so very quiet when we reached the sixth floor and made our way down the hallway. It was almost too quiet. The hotel, like many old hotels, had been added on to over the years, creating a bit of a rabbit-warren feeling. A few steps up at the end of this hall, a turn at the end of that one, another few steps back down, the hallway went on forever!

"Good lord, I'm going to need a map to get back to the

lobby," I said, after our fourth turn. "Why'd they stick me all the way down here?"

He looked casually back at me over his shoulder. "They gave you one of the best rooms in this wing. Very private."

I'd heard nothing coming from any of the rooms I'd passed. No TVs, no radios, no conversation. But I'd heard each and every step I made, creaking and squeaking as the old wooden floors beneath the floral runner announced to any and all that someone was coming. "Private. Great."

This place was old school, and everything about it said it'd been here a long time. The ceilings were at least ten feet high, and above each door was a transom, harkening back to the days before air-conditioning. Each window was dark, no lights on inside. There was literally *no one else* staying on this floor. The walls were covered in damask pink floral wallpaper with about two feet of dark cherry wainscoting, details that were lovely if a bit dated. And hung in a perfectly straight line down the hallway were photographs of the hotel's heyday, black and white and filled with pictures of unsmiling people holding tennis rackets and croquet mallets.

It wasn't that they weren't happy, it was that in old-timey photographs people had to hold these poses sometimes for ten minutes or more, and who the hell wanted to smile that long? Logically, I knew this. But in the back of my mind as I walked down the hallway all I could see staring back at me were long-dead, angry-looking people.

Now. Let me just say. For the record. I don't spook easy. I don't scream at scary movies, I don't hide when things go bump in the night. But this hallway . . .

Remember in *The Shining* when Danny goes riding his Big Wheel around and around the hallways at the Overlook Hotel? Yeah. That.

Why Are the Hallways so Effing Creepy was going straight to the top of my to-do list when I had my first sit-down with the Bryant family.

"Come on." He laughed, noticing my reticence. "It's not too much farther."

Finally we arrived at my room, number 668.

"Oh, you're joking, right?" I chuckled in disbelief. The spooky hallway, the twists and turns, the dead guys in the pictures. "Why not just put me in six-six-six and be done with it?"

"Oh no, no one stays in room six-six-six," he said gravely, shaking his head as he reached for my key. Clicking the door open, he looked back over his shoulder at me. "Except for a certain bestselling writer who specializes in horror novels, typically based in Maine . . . you might've heard of him?"

He was enjoying this too much. I cast one more look down the long hallway, at the darkened room across the hall, then hurried past him into my room.

Flipping on the light, not at all in a panicky way, I looked around. The same Victorian theme was running strong throughout this entire hotel. The room was large, though, a nice surprise for a building as old as this one was. But even given the size, there wasn't the expected king bed, the size I'd requested when I booked my reservation, but instead twin beds, each made up with bedspreads—actual bedspreads!—the fabric of which consisted of pink cabbage roses set against deeper pink stripes. At the top of each bed was a single pillow, the bedspread pulled tightly up and over and tucked underneath in a manner and style I had never actually seen in real life but had glimpsed in many pictures from the 1950s. An antique dresser with an actual ironstone pitcher and bowl—wow!—sat against the far wall, and though the edges of a beautiful wide-planked wooden floor were visible, the rest was concealed beneath a mauve-and-turquoise nightmare of a rug.

It was *The Golden Girls* meets *Titanic* by way of 1970s motor lodge. But hello, what's this?

"A fireplace?" I said, staring down at a small but beautifully ornate hearth. "That's impressive. Where's the switch?"

"Switch?" he asked, stacking my bags in the closet.

"To turn it on?" I asked, looking around. "Wait, it can't be—"

"Wood burning? It is," he replied, pointing at the card on the mantel. "Just call guest services and someone will be right up to start a fire for you."

"No way," I breathed, momentarily stunned. A fireplace in a hotel room was already a luxury, but wood burning? "That's pretty unusual."

"Bryant Mountain House is an unusual place, Ms. Bixby. You'll find we're full of surprises."

"I'm getting that," I murmured, running my hand along the intricately carved wood along the mantelpiece.

"Now, just through there is the bathroom, and your private balcony is through there. With this rain there won't be too much of a view this evening, but if it's clear in the morning you should be able to see all the way to Hyde Park. Will you be dining in your room tonight, or in the main dining hall?"

"Hmm? Oh, dining hall," I said, still looking around the room. Something was missing.

"Very good, will there be anything else, Ms. Bixby?"

"Yeah, actually," I said, confused. "Where's the TV?"

"No TV."

"Wait, what?"

He smiled. "The Bryant family has always felt very strongly that nature should come first and foremost up here on the mountain."

I crossed my arms across my chest. "What the hell does that have to do with my TV?"

"The Bryant family feels that television can be a distraction, and detract from the natural world that is literally right outside your door."

"I don't necessarily disagree with that concept in the abstract, but in the practical shouldn't guests be allowed to decide whether or not they want their nature with a side of prime time?"

"The Bryant family would argue that guests do make that very decision when they decide to vacation here. That by choosing a hotel such as this they are making a clear and distinct choice to leave the outside world behind and commune with nature without distraction."

"Your website says this hotel is the proud host of the annual Hudson Valley Polka Festival and Accordion Race. How the hell is that not a distraction?"

His eyes widened, his expression heating. "The Bryant family feels that—"

I held up my hand. "You know what, enough with the Bryant family feels. Which frankly sounds like it could be a soap opera, playing out on the exact contraband I'm talking about. So come on, out with it. There's got to be a television here somewhere, right?"

"Of course." He nodded, adjusting his glasses. "You're welcome to visit the Sunset Lounge on the first floor anytime you like, there's a communal television there."

"The Sunset Lounge? You can't be serious."

He blinked. "Of course I'm serious."

"That's absurd."

"What's absurd is a person's inability to be fully inside nature."

I shook my head, eyes widening. *Was this guy for real?* "'Fully inside nature'? How in the world can you make the leap between 'hey I'd like to watch the *Today* show in the morning while I get ready' to my inability to be *fully inside nature?*"

"Bryant Mountain House has always maintained the strictest of ties to the natural world."

"Bullshit, Trish had a package of Twinkies behind the check-in desk. I'd hardly think your version of nature includes cream filling, particularly not when said cream filling is *fully inside* a fluorescent-yellow fake sponge cake."

He frowned. "That's not within protocol, I assure you."

"Protocol schmotocol, how do I get a TV brought up to my room?"

"Impossible."

"Nothing's impossible," I quipped, crossing my arms in front of my chest.

"Extra pillows? Possible. Plush comfortable robe?" He walked over to open the closet with a flourish. "So possible it's already here. Ice cream sundae at three in the morning?" He walked toward the phone and picked it up. "Nothing would make us happier than to accommodate this request."

"So no one in the history of this place, since the invention of the talking picture box, has been allowed a television in their room?"

He paused for the smallest of seconds before answering smoothly, "Not to my knowledge."

"Not an elderly sick woman who was unable to visit the Sunset Lounge but still wanted to watch her afternoon stories?" I pressed. "Or perhaps this *horror writer from Maine* who might've requested a television to watch one of his many novels that made it to the small screen? You're telling me that not a single one of your many VIP guests who have visited, including, as your website proclaims, every sitting president, ever once was allowed a television in his room?"

He frowned. "There may have been a small exception made, in a very extreme circumstance, but—"

"Aha!" I cried. "And that's what we have here, an extreme circumstance. So you just scurry on down to your extreme circumstance closet and bring me up a nice flat screen." I plopped down in the stuffed chair in the corner, disrupting several layers of lace doily with one giant poof.

The doilies may have softened not only the effect of the chair plop but the effect of my statements as well, as the bellman's expression turned from barely contained frustration to one of *aaand we're done here*. "Ms. Bixby, I'll be more than happy to communicate your unusual request to the management team, now is that it?" He smiled, showing his even teeth.

A television is an unusual request. Unbelievable.

"That's fine, I'll be fine." I sighed, now tired of this conversation. I wanted to unpack, settle in, and see what the hell else was weird about this place.

"I'll leave you to it, then," he replied, and as he stepped out into the hallway, he said, "Hope you have a great stay while you're with us, Ms. Morgan."

"Thank you, I— Wait a minute, what did you call me? Who are you?"

"Archie Bryant," he replied, his grin now changing to something more like pure calculation. "Welcome to Bryant Mountain House."

The door swung shut and I was left standing there. Glaring. Archie Bryant, the son of the man who hired me. Who knew exactly who I was, that I was very much *not* Melanie Bixby, and that I'd checked in under false pretenses.

Sonofa . . .

Chapter 3

$\mathcal{I}$ breathed in the cold air, exhaling in a puff as I contemplated how to deal with this wrinkle.

Once the fair Mr. Bryant had left, I headed out onto the balcony. Every room, no matter the size, came with a balcony complete with two beautiful antique rocking chairs. And you'd want the rocking chair, provided the weather was a bit nicer, because this view . . .

High up in the Catskills, the view was breathtaking. Even with the gray storm clouds it was stunning. The deep valley just below the resort gave way to the mountains marching off into the distance, the remains of the last snowfall still present on the tippy tops. Cold air swirled around my ankles, but I stayed a moment longer, lost in the quiet stillness. I rocked back and forth from the heel to the ball of my foot, my legs cramped from sitting in the car all day. I longed to get outside, stretch, run, my body screaming for a workout. But the rain had indeed turned to a wintry mix of slush and sleet, and I knew better than to take on a new trail in inclement weather.

But I couldn't get my mind off the fact that the bellman was the owner's son. I should've suspected. He was dressed awfully nice for a bellman—take away the fleece, which was covering up a white button-down and a tie, now that I thought about it, and those preppy chinos and shiny wingtips should've been a dead giveaway.

Ugh, and that ridiculous conversation about the TV, something he'd surely remember when I was introduced to him in two days, after "Clara Morgan" officially checked in.

Ah well. I'd had more controversial conversations with a hotel team than "get TVs, please." I just would've preferred to begin that conversation on my own terms.

Seriously. No TV. What year was this? And a TV room down in the Sunset Lounge was quaint to be sure, but that didn't exactly help me when I needed some background noise.

As long as I could remember I've preferred to have a TV on, even if I wasn't watching it. When I ate, when I read, when I slept for sure, I needed the noise. I even left it on sometimes when I wasn't home so it wasn't so unearthly quiet, needing to hear something other than echoing silence when I came back at night. I'd scroll through until I found something that I could leave on in the background, interesting but not so interesting it would keep me awake. My favorite was when I could find an infomercial for one of those Time Life collections, maybe songs of the '70s or my personal favorite, Classic Country. Nothing like a little Tammy Wynette or Marty Robbins to sing you to sleep, right?

The fact was, I hadn't gone to sleep without a TV on in . . . Jesus, how long had it been? My mind was racing already at the thought of sleeping tonight, trying to sleep tonight, in all that empty quiet. I wasn't even sure I could sleep without that noise to break things up.

When there was no noise, my mind began to take over. The nonanalytical part, where things were best kept packed up and sealed tight and stored away.

I shook my head to clear it, took another deep breath of the chilly air, and decided to head back inside to unpack.

"Oh, for the love . . . ow!" I shouted, as the bed banged down on my head for the third time. Unpacking proved difficult when the only closet in the room was in fact not a closet but a hiding place for another ancient contraption, the Murphy bed. Habit had me turning for the closet door as I unpacked each piece of clothing, and I kept forgetting that up on this mountain, with all the nature and the principled living, while there may not be a TV in every room there was most certainly a Murphy bed.

I rubbed my head as I pushed the stupid thing back into the "closet," then headed over to the armoire with another stack of clothes. Then marched straight to my bag, grabbed a Post-it and a marker and stuck a note on the closet that read, "Don't fucking open this again!"

I made another note, this one in my planner, adding something else to my list of things I'd need to address in this hotel.

And with that, I was unpacked with the ease and economy of someone who literally spends the better part of her adult life living out of a suitcase.

Not just her adult life.

I cued up a travel podcast on my phone and cranked the volume, knowing I certainly wouldn't disturb anyone on this floor. I closed my planner, once more running my fingers across my name on the front. It was obvious to me now that Archie had seen it, read it, realized I wasn't who I said I was . . . but decided to play along? Was that the reason I was stuck over here in no-man's-land, in the one occupied room on an otherwise entirely unoccupied floor? And if he *did* know who I was, which he did, why was he such . . . hmm . . . well . . . an ass?

⁓

Deciding I'd better lay low until I figured out exactly what was going on, I canceled my dinner reservation and ordered room service instead. I contemplated calling back and asking them to send someone up to start a fire, but then realized they may very well send up Bellman Archie, so I put the kibosh on that real quick.

I took a long soak in the deep tub, an antique claw-foot, of course. I read back over my notes on the property, caught up on email, did some research on the town of Bailey Falls . . . and was bored out of my gourd.

I didn't tell my girls I was coming to town—nothing betrays a pseudonym faster than two crazy people running pell-mell into the lobby and shouting, "Get your ass over here, Clara!" To be clear, while it would likely be Natalie doing the shouting, it'd be Roxie doing the pell-melling—no one would be safe.

But now, as it got later and later and I was running out of things to do, and no television in the near future, my mind was beginning to spread out a bit. Always dangerous.

Restless, I got up and headed over to the window. The icy slush slapped against the pane, making me regret not biting the bullet and ordering up a toasty fire. I peered through the frost that crept along the edges of the frame, seeing just a glimpse of a single lantern below and then a vast open shadow where the mountains lingered just out of sight. Another person might feel lonely. Another person might look out into all that inky blackness and see the one tiny light from just the one lantern and wonder if there was anyone else out there at all.

Another person might. But I didn't get lonely. You couldn't be lonely unless you allowed yourself to feel it, and I'd learned at an early age to steel myself against that. To stiff upper lip it, to spine straighten and stand tall and turn what possibly could have been lonely feelings into a deep and certain resolve. A resolve that had protected and shielded me through seven different foster homes, keeping me focused on school and work rather than friends and family.

Now, as an adult, I had the friends. As far as the family . . .

I sighed, shook my head, and turned back to my room. Seeing that it was late enough now to justify going to sleep, I pulled on my pajamas and crawled between the sheets. Hmm, a bit thin and crackly. I grabbed another Post-it, wrote the words *thread count* quickly, and slapped it on the front of my planner. The to-do list was growing already and Clara Morgan hadn't even officially arrived.

I flipped off the lights, slipped farther down into the bed, and listened to the squeaks and creaks of an old building turning in for the night. A slight whistle from the radiator in the corner, icy slush still hitting the window—all noises a blessed television would tune out.

Turning on another travel podcast, this one about the central market in Istanbul, I willed my body to shut down and rest. My last thought before slipping into sleep was that if Archie Bryant knew who I really was all along, then he really was an ass for not saying so.

Archie Bryant. Pffft.

The next morning was clear and cold. When my alarm went off at my usual five thirty, I woke up groggy and foggy. I hadn't slept well, which was unusual. I was on the road so much, I actually slept better in hotels than at home. Occupational hazard I guess. It wasn't just that the bed wasn't comfortable—it was a bit soft and sagged in the middle slightly—but it wasn't anything I could put my finger on. I'd just spent the better part of the night flipping and flopping.

I thought about indulging in a rare occurrence, an extra nine-minute snooze, but now that the Bryant family knew I was on the property, I needed to be ready for whatever might come at me today. The first thing I'd do, however, was get in a run.

I'd always been a runner, it was something I'd picked up early on, around seventh grade. I was fast as a kid, but I quickly realized that what I really had was endurance. I was energetic almost to a fault when I was small, something I'd been reminded of frequently. But put me on a cross-country course and I could run for days. Hot, cold, rainy, it didn't matter as long as I could feel the ground beneath me and hear that steady drum of my feet passing mile four, mile five, mile six, and on and on and on.

All runners know when you hit a certain point, your body just takes over and you sink into your rhythm. I did my best planning when I was running. The ideas took shape, solutions to problems were presented in a coherent way, and a plan came together as I moved over whatever terrain I was running on.

I was nineteen when I completed my first marathon. It was the year I was in Santa Barbara with Roxie and Natalie, and I'd gotten it into my head that I could do it. My friends hated running, exercise of any kind wasn't something to enjoy, it was merely something to be suffered through occasionally when they were trying to work off that entire batch of churros we'd all consumed in our pastry class. Mine were inedible. Natalie's may have been toxic. But Roxie's were epic.

So yeah, I ran alone mostly. After that first marathon it was like a light went on, and I realized there was an entire community of road warriors just like me who loved to run through that perfect pain that comes when you push your body to do something, especially when it's pretty sure it can't but does it anyway. The mind over matter, conquering that little voice in your head that tells you to stop, it's too much, it's too hard, you can't do it.

I could do it. And I ran my ass off up and down the California coast that year, addicted to the thrill of crossing that finish line. A fair swimmer and a pretty good bike rider, I was twenty-one when I completed my first triathlon. I had to train harder for that than anything, the water and cycle portions not coming to me as naturally as running, but as I became more and more efficient in these sports, I began to enjoy triathlons almost as much as marathons.

I was always training. I was always conditioning. And I was always either recovering from a race or getting ready for one.

My line of work lent itself perfectly to this lifestyle, and a lifestyle is exactly what it was. I could never call what I did a hobby, because it really was a key part of everything and anything I did.

I was in great shape, so I could indulge in food and wine as I pleased, but I still exercised moderation in all things because while an extra slice of chocolate cake might not stick around long as unburned calories in my body, it could throw my sugar off, make me sluggish, and make a five-mile run—my usual three to four days per week—pure hell.

I slipped into leggings and a T-shirt, laced up my running shoes, and headed down to the gym.

Oh boy.

The "gym" at Bryant Mountain House was . . . oh man, it just *was*. Added onto the main house sometime in the 1920s as a "gymnasium," it'd been overhauled in the 1980s when Jane

Fonda fever swept the country and then put into dry dock ever since. It was huge, but that was all it had going for it. There were a few ancient exercise bikes, some free weights and benches, an honest to God NordicTrack next to a row of honest to wow ThighMasters. All along the walls were ballet studio mirrors interspersed with inspirational posters, including a cat that was still desperately Hangin' In There. But underneath the high-gloss mauve and turquoise I was now becoming accustomed to as the Bryant palette, there were beautiful wide-planked floors of pumpkin-colored pine. Faint outlines of the original "gymnasium" were still evident here and there along the floor, and each end of the gym was, of course, anchored by fireplaces.

And tucked into a corner, one new piece of equipment—a state-of-the-art treadmill.

Wondering which wealthy donor had passed away and willed this to the cause, I shrugged and stepped up. And *into* some of that fully inside nature. Stretched out before me through an enormous picture window was the entire property, including an unobstructed view of the Catskills. I spent my time on the treadmill gazing out at the bare trees and sparkling blue sky above.

What I already loved about Bryant Mountain House was that up here, it was like time had literally stood still. This forest and the hills surrounding it were as gorgeous as they were when the Bryant brothers came here that very first time, looked at it and knew this was where they'd build what would become their legacy. This place was purposefully pristine and a guest could so easily imagine a Jennifer Grey scampering up a woodland path in her jean shorts and Keds ready to cha-cha with the Bailey Falls version of Patrick Swayze. Sigh.

But what I already loved about this place was also what I was going to work very hard to tweak. I'm all for traditions, maybe even more than your average girl, but there were definitely some things that needed to be brought into this century. The rooms, the palette, the furniture, most certainly the gym. And it was going to be fun finding that balance between new and old, traditions but with a twist.

I increased the incline slightly, raising the speed by one. My brain was beginning to puzzle out a plan for Bryant Mountain House and I needed to clear the mental decks.

By six forty-five, I'd finished my run, wrapped a towel around my neck, and was leaving the gym when I ran smack into one very tall, very polished, very surprised Archie Bryant.

Not seeing who it was initially, I pulled out my earbuds and tried to apologize. "Sorry! I'm so sorry, I—"

"Careful, watch where you're—"

Speaking over each other, we both stopped short, our words hanging in the air as I tried again. "Mr. Bryant, I'm sorry about that, I didn't think anyone else would be up this early."

"Early bird gets the worm, Ms. Bixby," he replied, untangling his paperwork from my gym bag. Dressed impeccably in a dark gray suit, pale green tie, and paisley pocket square, he looked every inch to the manor born. He looked down at his suit now with distaste, as though I'd left a sweaty-girl imprint for him to wear on his chest all day. I gave it a quick once-over just to make sure that had in fact not happened, which of course it hadn't. I was sweaty, but I wasn't dripping wet for goodness' sake. But it was time to bite this particular bullet.

"Don't you think we can drop the whole Ms. Bixby stuff?"

"Oh, until you're able to explain to my father and the rest of our team why the fancy expert he brought in from Boston is running around crashing into people while using a pseudonym, I'll refer to you as any other guest who's checked in to our beautiful hotel." He leaned down a bit closer, and once more I could see the spray of freckles across his nose, this time against a significantly redder background. Angry, he was angry with me. And this clearly went beyond just an untimely bump in the hall. "I'm sure he'll be most happy to make your acquaintance this morning."

"This morning?" I asked, crinkling my nose in confusion. I wasn't scheduled to meet with the team for another two days.

"Yes, there's a meeting this morning for the entire senior staff at seven thirty. Camellia Conference Room on the third floor. I slipped a note under your door with the particulars."

Who says *particulars*?

He began to walk away, but shot back over his shoulder, "Everyone, including my father, is looking forward to meeting the mysterious Ms. Bixby."

"Oh good, maybe he's the guy I can talk to about getting a TV!"

"No TV!" he called back without turning around.

"Ridiculous," I muttered to myself, then looked at my watch. *Dammit, less than an hour to shower and change and make it to the meeting.*

I spun quickly on my heel and headed in the opposite direction Archie had gone, skipping the elevator and running up the six flights of stairs.

He thinks he's got one over on you, I thought, as I hurried to my room. *He thinks he's got the upper hand.*

Well, Mr. Archie Bryant, let's show you just exactly how wrong you are.

Chapter 4

At seven twenty-five I stood outside the Camellia Conference Room on the third floor as requested, five minutes early and ready to meet the man who had hired me, Archie Bryant's father, Jonathan Bryant. Dressed to kill in a cherry-red bandeau top underneath a tailored, slim-cut black leather jacket, black pants, and three-inch red Choos, I had on my armor—necessary when meeting the team a few days ahead of schedule.

I wasn't nervous—I never get nervous—but I had no idea what Archie had already told his father. I could be getting my pink slip before I'd even officially started, which would kiss my partnership bye-bye. Mr. Bryant Sr. could've called this meeting with the express intent of firing me on the spot, while his son with the freckles looked on with a delighted smile.

Which is why I was so surprised when the delighted smile that greeted me in the conference room belonged to Jonathan Bryant, who not only stood when I came in the room, but came over to shake my hand and welcome me officially to Bryant Mountain House.

"Ms. Morgan, lovely to meet you, just lovely. Thank you so much for meeting with us this morning. I hope we haven't intruded into your stay with us too much?"

"My stay?" I asked.

"Yes, my son told me you were here under a fake name and—"

"Mr. Bryant, I can assure you the only reason I was here under the name Bixby is because I—"

"—wanted to get the lay of the land without us knowing you were here? Wanted to experience Bryant Mountain House as a regular guest? Interested in seeing how we really tick without all the extra bells and whistles we'd certainly be sure to throw at a well-known hotel branding expert?"

I grinned at Archie, who was standing directly behind his father, as his expression went from anticipatory, to confused, to frustrated, to now positively livid. "Yes, yes, and yes, Mr. Bryant, all of the above." I shook his hand heartily, now focusing all my attention on the father and not on the son. "And it's lovely to meet you as well, please call me Clara."

"Clara." He nodded. "It's a genius idea, of course, when you think about it, wanting to understand a property as a guest before trying to understand it as a professional." He gestured toward a long table filled with an array of pastries and fruit, bagels and cream cheese. At the end, coffee urns beckoned. "Please make yourself at home. Have something to eat. And then I'd love to introduce you to our team."

Jonathan Bryant was a great-looking man; it was easy to see where Archie got his good looks. But where Archie seemed quite cool and distant, not to mention like a real jackass, his father was the epitome of warm and welcoming. He stepped away, giving me the green light to grab something to eat and a cup of coffee. Not wanting to seem ungrateful for the hospitality, I did just that.

I scooped a few berries and some melon into a bowl, dropped a wheat bagel into the toaster, and as I was pouring myself some coffee I took a moment to appreciate the beauty of the room. Wood paneled like everything else on this mountaintop, it was elegant and refined. An enormous table anchored the room, with comfortable swivel chairs all around. I noticed that there were place cards for the staff in front of each seat so I knew exactly whom I'd be meeting.

"Let me help you with that," a familiar voice said over my shoulder.

"Help me right off a cliff, I'm sure," I said just under my breath, arching my eyebrow as Archie stepped in front of me to pick up my bowl.

"Well, we are on a mountain . . ." he muttered.

"Do you speak to all of your guests this way or is it just me who gets this very special treatment?" I asked as we headed to the table.

He placed my bowl in front of a chair on the left side of the table. "Are you a guest, Ms. Morgan?"

I placed my coffee, and myself, in front of a chair on the right side of the table. "At your father's request, yes." I looked pointedly at the bowl of fruit that was now across the table from my chosen seat. His left eyebrow arched, he tilted his head at me, once more examining me with those searching eyes.

"My father," he said, picking up the bowl and depositing it in front of me, "would do anything to save this hotel. Including bringing someone in from the outside."

"Oh, so *that's* what this is about, I'm *from the outside*." I whispered the last part like I was saying *I have the leprosy*.

"Ms. Morgan, before yesterday how much time had you spent at Bryant Mountain House?"

"Before yesterday, Mr. Bryant? None."

"Interesting, and before yesterday how much time had you spent in the Hudson Valley?"

"None," I answered promptly, to his instant smug smile. "Unless you count four years in Ithaca. Which you undoubtedly won't, since Ithaca technically belongs to the Finger Lakes region of New York State." I offered my own smug smile. "I received my degree in hotel management from Cornell."

Realization dawned. "Ah yes, you did attend Cornell, I must've forgotten that detail."

I looked at him, brow crinkled in confusion. "You forgot a detail that I never mentioned?"

"I forgot a detail I read in your file. Won't happen again."

"My file?"

"You don't think I'd let my father hire someone to turn our entire world upside down and not do my due diligence to make sure she's qualified, do you?"

My eyes boggled. "A file. You've got a file on me. Wow."

"Wow?"

"Wow as in, dude, that's weird."

Now his eyes boggled. "Dude? Did you just call me dude?"

"Dude, I also called you weird. How did you miss that part?"

I suddenly became aware of a great silence, the kind that presses in on you, a tangible Saran wrap clinging thing. Archie and I were just inches from each other, his hands on his hips and my finger pointing at his chest through the hole in my bagel while everyone else waited to see what would happen next. I looked at his father, who was watching us with crossed arms and a delighted grin.

Archie and I each took a step back, then another, like two high school drama kids given their first set of stage directions. I resisted the sudden and wild urge to curtsy and instead calmly, and with what I hoped was incredible grace, sank into my chair.

I met Jonathan Bryant's eye, nodded and said, "So, let's get started."

The meeting went surprisingly well considering how it began. I met the entire senior team of Bryant Mountain House. Heads of housekeeping, catering, dining, groundskeeping, recreation, historical, guest services, and accounting. If a team wasn't led directly by a member of the extended Bryant family, then it was led by someone who'd been here long enough to be an honorary member. Early favorites included Mrs. Banning, dining, and Mrs. Toomey, housekeeping. They'd insisted right from the beginning that any help I needed, any at all, I was to come find them right away and they'd make sure I had what I needed.

Although to be fair, this sense of generosity, a willingness to listen and learn seemed to extend to the entire team.

Except to Archie Bryant. He sat back during the meeting, staying quiet during the introductions, listening intently as his team shared some of their concerns. His father was clearly leading the meeting, but it became just as clear that Archie was the real eyes and ears of this resort. But when asked a direct question by me, he answered quickly and efficiently, offering no other information other than what was specifically asked for.

This wasn't uncommon. Several of the hotels I'd worked for over the years had those among them who didn't enjoy having someone come in "from the outside" and tell them how to turn their resort around. But never like this, never had I had someone so vocal about voicing their displeasure over my mere existence.

"So one of the things I'll be doing, before we even start talking about implementing changes, is simply observing. Watching. Getting a feel for how things run."

Archie snorted.

I didn't react, ignoring his nasal outburst and continuing on anyway. "Mrs. Toomey, how long have you been working at Bryant Mountain House?"

The older woman smiled, tucked a pen behind her ear, and answered proudly. "I started here as a swimming instructor when I was eighteen years old."

"She and I both started the same summer," Mrs. Banning interjected, arching an eyebrow. "She played in the lake all summer while I was making beds inside. Before we installed the air-conditioning."

"Be that as it may, we've both been here more years than we care to count," Mrs. Toomey said, and both women laughed.

"Forty-nine," Archie said from the other end of the table, and ten heads swiveled at the same time. "You've both been here forty-nine years," he repeated, smiling at the ladies. "Dad's already planning your fiftieth anniversary party."

"That's incredible," I crowed, as the ladies blushed a bit. "Other than the fact that Mr. Bryant here just told us all how old you are, that's incredible." Laughter rang out around the staff, but Archie merely raised an eyebrow. "So Mrs. Toomey, you started out in recreation, when was it you moved into the kitchen side of things?"

"Oh goodness, I've done so many things here it's hard to remember exactly. I suppose I started working in the kitchens more and more after I moved inside in the late eighties? I'd moved around quite a bit, working in reservations, at the front desk, even housekeeping for a minute—although luckily by the time I was making beds it was after we installed air-conditioning. But then there was an opening in management in the restaurant—they needed someone to run the dinner service and I've been there ever since."

"And your head chef, he recently retired, correct?"

"Retired?" she asked, leaning forward in her chair. "He's not here anymore, but I'm not sure he really retired."

"Do we need to hash this out again?" Archie sighed.

"It's not hashing it out if she asks," Mrs. Toomey quipped back, smiling broadly at me as though encouraging me to please yes, dig a little deeper here. But I'd already stepped in it with Archie enough as it was, so I decided to hedge my bet a bit.

"You know what, let's table that for now and move on to over-all bookings. Mr. Bryant was kind enough to send me figures for the last two seasons, as well as projected bookings for this summer," I said, turning toward the senior Mr. Bryant.

He smiled warmly at me. "You'll have to start calling me Jonathan, everyone does."

"Oh, I don't know, I—"

"You should call him Jonathan, really. He'll insist," Archie interrupted, a resigned expression on his face.

"What can I say, I love Walt Disney." Jonathan laughed.

I shook my head. "I don't follow."

"Walt Disney had his first name, and first name only, put on his name tag, no one was ever allowed to call him Mr. Disney. He felt it separated himself from his team too much, he wanted everyone to feel like they had an equal stake in the outcome."

"I love this idea," I said, agreeing instantly with where he was coming from. A few of the others were chuckling, including Archie. "You don't feel the same?"

"It's not that I don't want everyone to feel like they're on the same team, but—"

"Archie takes a more formal approach than I do when we're at work, always has. Much more like my father in that respect, I suppose," Jonathan said, not without some pride.

"Grandfather took a formal approach to everything, Dad. He'd have hemorrhaged if he saw men in shorts at the breakfast service."

"Shorts?" I asked.

"We relaxed the dress code several years ago," Archie explained.

"Twenty, it was twenty years ago." His father laughed. "I'll never forget because you walked into your graduation brunch in the main dining hall in Bermuda shorts and your grandmother whispered to me that it was a good thing he'd died the year before because the sight of bare knees in the dining hall would've put your grandfather in an early grave."

Someone at the end of the table remarked that he certainly didn't have a problem when miniskirts were all the rage in the '60s and the conversation was lost at that point. Stories about days gone by, tall tales and laughter and memories and traditions. As I sat back and watched this family, by blood or by proxy, I was reminded once more that the stories this family had in their back pockets alone could stack a library ten feet high. This is what I needed them to remember when the changes began. I decided not to circle back and bring up the projected bookings for this summer. Why bring the room down when they seemed to be having so much fun reminiscing? They could go back to worrying later on, and worry they would. If the metrics were correct, they were due for their worst summer ever.

As talk wound down, I waded back in. "Thank you, everyone, for this impromptu meeting this morning. I know some of you may question my methods, up to and including the reason I checked in yesterday under a different name." I lifted my bagel in Archie's direction, and he lifted his coffee cup in return. "But I really am here to help. And I want to hear these stories, all of your stories, to get a better idea of who you all are, and what the inherent DNA is of this place. So please, hold nothing back, share whatever you feel comfortable sharing, and I promise you, I'll work my tail off in return. Agreed?"

Voices echoed back from around the table. "Agreed."

I was about to stand up when Jonathan spoke.

"You were checked in under Melanie Bixby for two nights, correct?"

"I was," I replied, a you-got-me look on my face.

"Well then, you're still Melanie Bixby as far as I'm concerned. Which means you're still on vacation. So no shop talk for the rest of today, I want you to relax and enjoy yourself. Make yourself at home. We'll start, what did you say, *working our tail off tomorrow*, got it?"

Surprised, and pleased, I nodded.

"And as a special treat, Archie will be your personal tour guide today."

"Wait, what?" we both said, making Jonathan smile bigger than I'd seen him smile all day. He sat back in his chair, hands steepled together and looking back and forth between us.

"Yes, I think a tour is definitely in order."

The meeting now over, everyone filed out, chatting companionably, giving me their own *welcome* and *thank you* and *excited to get started* as they passed by. Jonathan was the last to leave, giving me a broad smile and a strong handshake on his way out.

And then it was just me and Archie. Staring each other down.

I nodded, resigned to it. "Um, okay, well, I'll just go put my bag in my room and—"

"If you want a tour, you might want to consider changing into more comfortable shoes," Archie interrupted, looking down at my heels. A habit I'd picked up from Natalie, I was obsessed with stilettos, the taller the better. I noticed he looked at my shoes, but then his eyes lingered on my legs. My eyes narrowed.

"Oh, I think I can keep up."

And that's how I got my own personal tour of Bryant Mountain House.

"So, where should we start?" I asked, as we left the conference room.

He regarded me coolly. "There's a tour every morning of the resort, led by a different member of the staff. Mr. Phelps is leading it today, and he's a great guide, very informative. It'll get started in a few minutes, leaving from the Lakeside Lounge. Should give you a good idea of what it is you're working with." He started to walk away, but I called out after him.

"I thought *you* were going to give me my tour?"

"Ms. Morgan, I have many things to do this morning, many things. The last thing I have time for is a walk around the grounds."

I gritted my teeth. "And the last thing I want to do is to spend my morning with a cranky owner's son disguised as a bellman who says he can move mountains for his guests except manage to get a television into a hotel room, but I took this job, and your father hired me, so I'm going to do whatever it is your father wants. And *he* wanted *you* to give me the tour, not pawn it off on poor Mr. Phelps." Like it or not, he was going to be my tour guide. "So, where do *we* start?"

He turned back toward me, looking more irritated than he had all morning. "Are you this much of a wrecking ball on all your projects?"

"Funny you should mention wrecking balls, Mr. Bryant, as that's exactly what I make sure doesn't happen on any of my projects."

He flinched. "That'll never happen here. I won't allow that to happen here."

"And that's exactly why you need my help," I reminded him.

"My father hired you, not—"

"You?" I interrupted. I could play that game too. "I know your father is the one who hired me. And I'm going to go out on a limb and say my gut tells me he's retiring next year, right?"

"End of this year, your point?"

I knew it. "And you'll be taking over after him, right?"

"January first."

"January first, huh? New Year's Day? Will that transfer be taking place before or after the Lake Plunge?"

"After, we— How do you know about the Lake Plunge?"

I steeled my gaze. "The Lake Plunge, one of the oldest holiday traditions here at Bryant Mountain House, I believe? After midnight on New Year's Eve, staff and guests alike—the brave ones at least—march down to the south end of the lake and polar bear plunge through a patch of ice that's been cleared specifically for this. Sounds crazy to me, but I think you all have been doing it since the twenties, yes?"

He studied me carefully, searching with those indigo eyes. "Since 1919, actually."

"Great, then we're coming up on a hundred years, we'll have to make a big deal out of that. Break a record for the most fools freezing their noonies off at the same time."

"Their noonies?"

I shrugged. "I assume most of the fools are men. Tell me I'm wrong."

He laughed then, an honest to goodness laugh. And it changed his face entirely. For the first time, there was no suspicion, no irritation, no trying to figure out what I was going to say so he could beat me to it. I realized with a start he wasn't that much older than I was. Laughter, plain old laughter, took years off his face. "Are you ready for that tour?"

I breathed a sigh of relief. "Yes, yes I am. Where should we start?"

"Lakeside Lounge, that's where the tours always start," he replied, turning smartly and starting for the staircase. "You coming?"

"You're still gonna pawn me off on someone else?" I asked, falling into step beside him.

"Nope, I'm taking over for Mr. Phelps. Sure you don't want to change into more comfortable shoes?"

I ignored the blatant challenge, although this one was delivered with less spite. Progress. I'd take it.

"Noonies," I heard him mutter under his breath.

Yep. Progress.

Chapter 5

Every morning, since the dawn of time apparently, a house tour was conducted by a member of the staff. Could be someone who worked the front desk, could be someone who worked in catering, could be Jonathan Bryant himself. Didn't matter, the point was that each staff member told essentially the same story, with a few personal anecdotes to personalize the history of this grand old hotel.

It always left from the Lakeside Lounge promptly at 9:30 a.m., and it always covered, weather permitting, the main house, the gardens, and the dock. When Archie and I had arrived at the Lakeside Lounge, he was stunned to realize I hadn't seen that side of the resort yet.

"What do you mean you haven't seen the lake yet?" he asked, incredulous.

"Weather was terrible last night, and after finding out that my bellman was the owner, and not at all happy about me checking in early, it seemed like a good idea to stay in my room and not get in your way." He had the decency to look the tiniest bit chagrined, perhaps feeling as though he'd jumped the gun yesterday. "Plus I didn't want to go wandering around the halls late at night, all those creepy people staring back at me from the walls."

At that Archie rolled his eyes, any fleeting glimpse of apology gone the moment I mentioned the creepy pictures. It occurred to me that I didn't need to mention those creepy pictures, not yet at least, but I couldn't resist. Was I poking the bear a bit? Perhaps.

"Nevertheless, you should take a moment and see the lake. It's like going to the Grand Canyon and just trying to see it from the parking lot."

"You're comparing a lake in the Catskills to the Grand Canyon?" I asked, arching an eyebrow.

"We've got five minutes before the tour starts, Ms. Morgan, see for yourself," he replied, gesturing for me to head into the lounge as he turned to speak to someone from the front desk.

I did really want to see the lake, so I headed inside. But not because he told me to.

The Lakeside Lounge was aptly named. Relaxing and comfortable, it boasted several long trestle tables stacked with games like Monopoly, Trivial Pursuit, and for the kiddos, Chutes and Ladders. Thick, double-wide planks of pine covered the floor, smooth but pleasantly scarred with years of use. Armchairs and love seats, clad in more cabbage roses and toile, were clustered into conversation areas, the walls were covered by gorgeous inlaid-wood paneling, and there was another one of those gargantuan fireplaces.

This one was flanked by emerald-green glass tiles, blackened here and there from years of smoke and ash. The mantelpiece was a single length of carved wood, and the andirons alone could support a sequoia. As I explored, someone from the resort hurried in with a basket of kindling, and set about lighting a small bonfire inside the cavernous hearth. Opposite the fireplace was a long and cozy-looking leather couch and several rocking chairs, and it wasn't hard to imagine curling up here on a chilly afternoon with a good book and a hot chocolate. I looked around, expecting to see just that, but the place was almost entirely deserted, except for two older gentlemen playing cards in the corner and three little old blue hairs and their knitting needles, the silver flashing as they worked and chatted.

Hmm. We'd need to work on bringing in a younger clientele for sure. But right now it was all about the hint of blue to my right that begged for my attention. Wide windows spanned the width of the room, opening up to a long porch where at least fifty rocking chairs beckoned. And just beyond? The lake.

I'd seen pictures and read up beforehand, but nothing could have prepared me for the sheer beauty of this water.

Carved into the mountainside millions of years ago, almost like mirrored glass reflecting the puffy clouds above, the lake was wide and long and filled with the bluest water, deep blue, almost indigo.

Almost as blue as Archie's eyes.

The thought bubbled up quickly, unbidden. I just as quickly batted it away.

Stay focused, Clara, there's a job to do. And a lake to admire.

Ringed around it were enormous craggy boulders, spilling down into the water like a giant had been tossing pebbles. They were visible under the clear water, stretching down into the depths. A forest of pine circled the lake on all sides, protecting it from much of the wind that whipped down this very mountain, resulting in the smoothest glassy surface on the water.

A pine dock reached out from the edge, dotted with beautiful old canoes and rowboats, but I could see several kayaks and paddleboards stacked up as well.

Twisting off from the main porch off the lounge were

walking paths and hiking trails, some leading around the lake and some heading up the mountain. And high above, almost at the farthest reach of the lake, was a stone observation tower at the top of the nearest cliff.

In a word, it was stunning. The sense of peace I got just standing on the porch for a few minutes was restorative, soothing. It was so easy to imagine carriages full of wealthy families from New York and Philadelphia, just off the sooty train into Poughkeepsie station, traveling those last few miles up to Bryant Mountain House to spend their summers out of the hustle and bustle of the big city, and the sense of wonder they must have shared at this glorious landscape.

No wonder the Bryant family settled here, determined to share their love of nature with their guests.

A summer up here could be exactly what world-weary families could still benefit from.

Rejuvenated, I headed back inside, ready for my tour.

Two other guests had joined us. Two. Both at least in their eighties, if I was being generous. Very generous. Both ladies were gazing adoringly at Archie as he chatted with them—clearly they knew him well and had been coming here for years.

"Thank you for joining us, Ms. Morgan."

"Wouldn't have missed it. You were right about the lake, by the way, it's beautiful."

He looked pleased. "Well then, let's begin. Ladies, I know you've accompanied me on this tour numerous times, but we've got a new guest today, first time up on our mountain."

"Oh my, welcome, welcome!" one of the ladies squealed, clutching her handbag to her chest as though it were a teddy bear. "Isn't it just the most?"

"Yes." I smothered a laugh. "It is the most."

"You've been a guest with us since, oh, since you were a little girl, isn't that right?" Archie asked Handbag, and she squealed in delight.

"Since Archie's father was just a young boy, I used to look forward to coming here all year. My parents brought me, and then I brought my children, and that's how it goes!"

"I used to spend every single Fourth of July here, my family would rent out a few rooms for the entire summer," the other woman chimed in, eager to add her story to the mix. And perhaps to bask in the glow of Archie's grin as well. "Back then, the wives and children would stay the entire time and the husbands would drive up on the weekends." It was like this at many of the old hotels I worked with, generation after generation full of similar memories. Fourth of July and Handbag smiled at each other, then at Archie, and I coughed to hide my chuckle.

"Well then, I should let you ladies give the tour, I bet you know it as well as I do," Archie said, giving them a grand smile that made them giggle once more. I was struck suddenly with an image of Cary Grant, smooth and suave and a real old-school charmer. That's who Archie reminded me of, complete with an upper crust East Coast accent.

Once the giggling subsided, the tour finally began. And almost instantly, I was immersed in the history of this place. It all started in 1872 when the Bryant brothers—Theophilus and Ebenezer—purchased the small eight-room Sky Inn on Sky Lake, just outside Bailey Falls proper. Construction began the following spring on a larger hotel, specifically aimed at bringing in wealthy families from around the Northeast to take in the mountain air and rejoice in the church of nature. The Bryant brothers were strong proponents of being stewards of the earth and protecting nature, buying up much of the surrounding countryside and farmland and setting it aside as a protected nature reserve for generations.

"That's when they began hosting what they called the Greater Good Society. The brothers felt, from early on, that if they could bring world leaders, heads of state and heads of industry together in a place as beautiful as Sky Lake, they could influence one another to work together for the greater good."

"Well, that's genius," I said.

He whipped his head toward me, looking skeptical. "Are you speaking sarcastically, Ms. Morgan?"

"Not at all, Mr. Bryant," I replied, wondering if we'd ever move beyond the Mr./Ms. stage. "I actually think that's genius."

"Well, yes. And very much ahead of its time."

"How's that going these days?"

"Oh, the Greater Good Society was officially disbanded back in the thirties, just before the US got involved in the war. There was talk about reviving it afterward, but by then Ebenezer had passed away and Theophilus had ceded control to his son, who was running the day-to-day operations of the resort. Remember, after the war was when things really picked up around here, every single day there were people coming and going, the lines at check-in sometimes spilled back outside!"

I was about to ask him how he knew—his own father was only a baby in those days—but he answered my unasked question. "I've seen the pictures," he explained, and I nodded. "I had a feeling more sarcasm was on the way."

"It was," I admitted, but then asked, "Given the times we're living in now, Mr. Bryant, getting that society back up on its feet might be a great way to increase community involvement. And if we can market this strategy through Facebook, Twitter, Snapchat, etc., we could introduce an entirely new set of visitors to the resort. Hopefully ones with an enormous social-media presence."

"Are you suggesting if I get Taylor Swift up to my mountain she can solve world peace?"

"Now who's speaking sarcastically?" I asked, giving him a pointed look.

He grumbled something unintelligible under his breath, then hurried us along. "Now you'll see here, ladies, as we head into the music parlor, when they designed this room they had the utmost concern about acoustics . . ."

The tour lasted a little more than an hour, and it was the best crash course in all things Bryant I could've gotten. We peeked into the dining room as they were setting up for lunch, went to the fourth-floor balcony to see the view of the lake from there, and made a stop at the spa, which I was pleasantly surprised to see had been renovated recently. I'd be taking advantage of the spa as soon as humanly possible.

And my favorite part? The old-fashioned soda fountain. Located inside the gift shop, it boasted a long counter with twisty barstools, a mirrored backsplash, penny candy, and rows and rows of barrels of homemade ice cream. In addition to all the sweet treats, they served a very limited selection of lunchtime snacks for those who didn't want the more formal and full-service lunch buffet in the main dining room. Several signs hung behind the counter depicting some of the menu highlights, and I noticed one along the bottom called—

"The Archie Special? Hold up, you've got a sandwich named after you?" I asked as Archie tried to hurry us away.

"You betcha," the woman behind the counter piped up. Easily in her sixties, she wore her gray hair in long twin braids down her back and her eyes danced with fun. "Wanna know what's in it?"

Archie looked mortified.

"Oh, I'd literally love nothing more," I replied, keeping my eyes on him.

"Well, you start out with some plain white bread," she began, and Archie shook his head.

"Judith . . ."

"—top piece gets ketchup, the other Miracle Whip, right, Archie? Never mayo for this kid!" Judith jerked her thumb in his direction and he shrugged sheepishly.

"—and you add three slices of pickle—"

"Love that pickle!" Handbag squealed and Fourth of July giggled.

"—and you finish her off with one big glob of braunschweiger spread stem to stern."

"Ew, that should be illegal." I laughed.

"Thank you, Judith," Archie said from the far end of the counter.

"Does anyone actually ever order that?" I asked.

"Sure, Archie gets the Archie Special at least three times a week, although every so often he gets the Jonathan."

"What's the Jonathan?" I asked.

"Same thing, but with onion."

"Good God, no," I said, with a horrified face.

"Thank you, Judith," Archie repeated, ushering us all back out into the lobby.

"When do we get to try some of that Archie Special?" Handbag whispered, prompting Fourth of July to giggle all over again while Archie blushed to the tips of his ears.

"Let's continue the tour, shall we?" he said, leading us away from the soda fountain where Judith was waving proudly.

"Oh, I can't *wait* to see what's next," I chimed in brightly.

Handbag and Fourth peeled off with a waved good-bye and a final giggle in Archie's direction, and the two of us ended up in the TV lounge.

"You see, Ms. Morgan, you have access to a television any-time you want one," he smiled, saccharine-like.

I rolled my eyes, looking around the room. Like everything else up here, it was bedecked with beautiful dark carved wood, lined with comfortable-looking easy chairs and love seats, all clustered around an ancient console television that had begun its life sometime in the early '80s.

"If I didn't know better, I'd think this was a joke."

"No joke."

"You have an actual VHS player, Mr. Bryant, and you're going to stand there with a straight face and tell me 'no joke'?"

"Look closer, it's a dual VHS/DVD player."

"Wow. Just . . . wow."

"My grandfather did consider installing televisions in the rooms back in the '60s, my father as well a few years later. But they saw, as I continue to see, the benefit of truly being able to come up here and escape. These days it's even more important to be able to disconnect and unplug."

"You've mentioned this before."

"However," he continued, "of course we've always seen the need to remain somewhat connnected to what's going on in the world, so we've always made sure there was a television available when necessary. Guests love being able to watch the ball drop on New Year's Eve together, crowded into the same room where guests watched Neil Armstrong walk on the moon. Super Bowls, the Olympics, election nights, all events when our guests have remained in touch with the world but somehow connected to-gether in such a unique way."

"Okay, I get it. I do, especially this shared community space you've got going here. It's quaint, it's homey, it harkens back to another time and place and blah blah blah. But for God's sake, people like TVs in their rooms! Especially for how much you're charging per night!"

"Price per night, are we back to that? Ms. Morgan, what you fail to realize is that everything is included in the price. Meals, activities, afternoon tea, entertainment . . ."

". . . but no TV. Come on, you gotta work with me on this, at least a little bit."

"Why is it so necessary that you have a TV in your room?" he asked, in a challenging tone. A fair question, even if he was a nosy fucker.

But how do you explain to a stranger why silence and quiet were simply unacceptable?

"My reasons are my own," I hedged, not wanting to explain why a grown woman preferred the cool twangy stylings of Classic Country brought to you by Time Life rather than let the voices of the past swoop in and drag her down.

Conway Twitty versus your mother went to jail and left you in foster care?

Actually, that could be a country-western song . . .

"The point, Mr. Bryant, is that while I can appreciate your family's devotion to nature and the preservation of a quiet respite, for God's sake you gotta loosen up a little bit!"

He held up his hand.

"Are you shooshing me?" I asked, crossing my arms.

He cocked his head to the side. "Can you hear that?" He leaned down to the large radiator in the corner, listening closely.

"Can I hear . . . hey! Hey, come back here," I yelled as he took off through the lobby at a brisk pace, grumbling under his breath. "I was talking to you!"

"Well then, keep up, Ms. Morgan."

"Oh you little . . ." I took off after him, chasing him through the lobby, through a double set of doors behind the reception desk, and down two flights of stairs.

"Literally, I was in the middle of something with you, and you just take off like a bat out of hell!"

"Not everything can revolve around you and your incessant need for a television."

We went around a corner, past some old lockers, and down another steep staircase.

"That's exactly my point, Mr. Bryant, that I'm not in the minority here. Practically everyone has a television in their room, certainly when they're on vacation. Quit trying to make me feel like I'm totally off base here!"

At the bottom of the staircase he paused, grabbed a flashlight off a shelf, and made a sharp right turn.

"If you're feeling off base that's your own doing. I am merely trying to point out that when you're up here, away from the big city and the noise and the hubbub, you should be able to unplug."

"Did you really just say *hubbub*?"

We hurried through old brick archways, past stone-lined cold rooms, and when we ran past an old barrel-vaulted wine cellar he interrupted his critique of my television addiction to go back to playing tour guide.

"That's where they used to store the hooch during Prohibition."

"Really? I figured this place would have been as dry as the Sahara back then."

"It was officially, of course."

"Of course." I grinned, thinking about all those buttoned-up Bryants down here swilling gin with the help. "Still got some down here?"

"It's not even noon, Ms. Morgan."

"Will we be wherever we're going by cocktail hour? Where is it we're going exactly?" I asked, as I followed him down another twisty tunnel, this one the darkest yet.

"Boiler room" came the answer, floating down the long, dark hallway in front of me.

"As in Freddy Krueger?"

"The red-and-green sweater guy?"

"The razor blades for fingers guy, yeah." I brushed cobwebs away from my face, peering into the darkness. At the end of the hallway, a heavy metal door swung back on its creaky hinges and he stood in the doorway.

"Then yes, that kind of boiler room."

"Great." I swallowed, and then was swallowed up by clouds of steam. "Good lord, it's like pea soup down here!" I exclaimed, narrowing my eyes to see better through the clouds. An entire city of pipes and pumps lived down here, incredible roaring metal and steam . . . everywhere steam.

"No wonder you've got fireplaces in every room," I said, looking over the equipment. Stone Age, these boilers were from the Stone Age! "Where are the guys in overalls shoveling in the coal?"

"Aren't you being a little bit dramatic?" he asked as he consulted a hand-drawn map on the wall. "Lakeside Lounge, Lakeside Lounge, aha!" He started fiddling with gauges and levers.

"I don't think so, Mr. Bryant," I said, looking around with a more critical eye. "Do you have any idea how much money you'd be saving in heating costs, let alone the tax credits you'd receive, if you switched over to greener technology?"

"Wait, just wait a second, you just got here and already you have me installing an entirely new heating system? We've been using this system for years and it's never failed us before." The steam was getting really thick, the room was hot and sticky and good lord was it getting hotter by the second.

I tugged at my leather jacket, trying to flap a little breeze in. "Then why exactly are we down here? Why exactly did you run away in the middle of a conversation?" He looked at me incredulously just as a loud knocking began ringing out from the furnace on my right. And the furnace on my left started to spew an enormous jet of steam, filling the already hazy air with an even bigger cloud.

"You were saying?" I asked, smirking more than a little bit.

He stepped closer, ducking underneath a pipe, tugging at his tie as he came. "Oh, you're an expert in heating systems now? When did hotel management school cover that?"

I could feel a trickle of sweat running down my chest and I gave up trying to flap a breeze and just tore off my jacket. "I literally know nothing about heating and cooling, other than when I turn on my AC in the summertime I don't want to hear a groaning unit. What I do know is your bottom line, and I know the amount annually spent on utilities is staggering."

"I have a huge hotel," he countered, taking off his own jacket and grabbing a giant wrench.

"That I'm sure is sealed up nice and tight for the winter," I replied, ducking under a pipe and stepping right in front of him. "You want me to tell you about the draft in my room last night? My bed was freezing! First I thought it was from the balcony, then I thought it was coming under the door from the hallway outside. Turns out it was from both. It was like a freaking wind tunnel."

"I am sorry, Ms. Morgan, that your bed was so cold last night."

"Says the guy bragging about his huge hotel."

We stared at each other, locked in a silent battle of wills. Archie's glasses were beginning to fog over, yet there we stood, toe-to-toe. We breathed in at the same time, and I could see his pulse beat just below his jawline beneath the barest hint of five-o'clock shadow. We were both worked up, angry, annoyed. Then he licked his lips. Just the tip of his tongue flickered out, catching the tiniest bead of sweat. "Has anyone ever told you that you're incredibly rude?"

"Everyone who's ever hired me."

"And you're *proud* of this track record?"

"Every one of them is now a sterling reference. I can give you their contact info whenever you like."

He shook his head, turned away, and set to work with the wrench, turning down the thingamabob, throwing his entire body into it. He grunted at one point, and because of the steam I could see the muscles in his back straining through his white shirt. I took a step closer, just the one, to watch as he struggled with the whatsamahoozit.

"Almost . . . got it . . . there!" he cried, turning around trium-phantly in a final burst of steam and whistle to find me standing much closer than I had been only a moment before.

Surprised it was over so fast, and totally caught staring, I mustered up a "Bravo, Mr. Bryant," and then internally slapped myself for sounding so *Happy Birthday, Mr. President* when I said it.

He smirked. I scowled.

Asshole.

We emerged from the basement sweaty and sticky, messy and a little bit sooty. Back in the Lakeside Lounge where we'd started the tour, I clapped my hands together, eager to get us back on track and away from whatever it was that just . . . whatever.

"Well, thanks for the tour, particularly that very eventful end-ing. Do all the guests get that extra-special ending or . . . ?"

"Just you, Ms. Morgan," he said, making a show of putting his hand to his ear and listening to the radiator. "Listen to that, purring like a kitten."

"A kitten who's carrying around a kettlebell maybe." I snorted. "It's still clanking."

"Patience, some of these systems need a little extra stoking from time to time, but in the end, it's worth the extra-special attention."

"Stoke this, I'm going to go get cleaned up. And then, per your father's request that I enjoy my day up here on your mountain, I'm off to do a little sightseeing."

"Yes, yes, of course," he answered, cleaning the last of the steam and soot from his glasses.

"Where do you think I should start?"

"Massage?"

"Maybe."

"Too chilly for a swim in the lake."

"Agreed, I was thinking of going for a hike, any thoughts on which trail I should take?"

"You're going to hike? In this?" He looked out the picture window at the drizzle that had started up again. It was a bit warmer than yesterday so this time it was rain only, no icy slush. No slippery slopes.

"I won't melt. Besides, anything more than a day indoors and I start climbing the walls."

"You could hike around the lake. It's flat, covered in gravel so it shouldn't be too muddy. It's a nice way to see the property, and you get a great view of the hotel."

"Done," I said, turning to go.

"Do you have dinner plans?" he asked, so quickly I wondered if he was asking me to— "I mean, do you need me to make a reservation for you in the dining room or will you be dining in your room again?"

"How did you know I dined in my room last night?" I blinked innocently.

He shook his head dismissively. "This is my hotel, Ms. Morgan, do you really think I don't know everything that's going on?"

I chose not to answer. "I'll be in the dining room tonight, I've got a date. Two, in fact."

"Oh. Really." Statement, not a question.

"Mm-hmm, my friends Roxie and Natalie are coming up for dinner. Any recommendations?"

"Everything is excellent," he replied, once more that sense of pride creeping over his face.

"Really? So all those TripAdvisor and Yelp reviews I've been reading were wrong? I guess we'll find out since one of my dinner dates is a professional chef, and I'm sure she'll have lots to say about how excellent everything is."

The pride was gone, irritation was back, and I decided it was time for me to head out on that hike.

Chapter 6

When I'd booked my original reservation, they'd informed me that while breakfast and lunch were casual, guests dressed for dinner. Men were required to wear a jacket and tie, women were expected to appear in business casual or "resort wear." Knowing this, I'd packed my suitcase full of fun swingy dresses and kicky heels. For my first official Bryant Mountain House dinner I'd chosen a deep-pink wrap dress that was sprinkled with darling little cherries. Pairing it with red pumps, a liberal application of cherry-red lipstick and a sleeked-back 'do for my blond bob, I looked every inch the retro dynamo. If I did say so myself.

And I did say so myself.

Dressing for dinner, what a lovely and, at times forgotten, concept. Too often my meals consisted of takeout on the couch in front of the TV, which was not going to happen here if Archie had anything to do with it, so I relished the opportunity to dress up a bit. I was excited to see my friends; it'd been a while since all my girls were together, and I was happy to finally be seeing the famous Bryant Mountain House dining room.

I was downstairs promptly at six fifteen and could hear my girls before I could see them. Per usual.

"This is *it*, I swear, Rox, this is where you and Leo should tie the knot."

"I don't know, it's so formal. I always saw us getting married somewhere a little less showy, something a little more home-grown."

"A little less showy? You mean than Maxwell Farms, with its enormous mansion and barn made out of marble?"

"The barn is not made out of marble, don't be ridiculous."

"Is there or is there not a marble cornerstone that was laid down by the former governor of New York?"

"The president."

"The president of New York?"

"No, the actual president, like of the country. Apparently he was a friend of Leo's great-great-great-grandfather."

"I literally can't even talk to you anymore, I'm not fancy enough for this conversation. And this is coming from a woman wearing next season's Louboutins."

I shook my head in amazement and peeked around the staircase to see both of my friends shrugging out of their coats and scarves and drawing looks from every male over fourteen and under eighty in the vicinity. Roxie was all girl-next-door, with curly brown hair and sparkling eyes that just radiated good health and happiness. Most of the happiness these days came from her smoking-hot boyfriend, Leo Maxwell, the local farmer with the old blue-blood New York family name, whom she'd wrapped around her finger, and then wrapped around his torso, to his absolute delight.

If Roxie was the girl next door then Natalie was the devil across the street, the one you hope your husband never sees when she comes out in her T-shirt in the morning to pick up her newspaper.

Stunningly beautiful, with ivory skin and strawberry-blond

hair, she had a head full of Manhattan and a mouth full of Bronx. She was all curves, all the time, and woe to any man who thought he stood a chance before the force of nature that was Natalie. So it made sense that the man who did stand a chance was an equal force of nature—an incredible-looking, football-playing, cow-milking, butter-churning ridiculous hunk, and I mean hunk of man, Oscar Mendoza, the dairy farmer she'd been plowing for months now.

My girls shared the details whenever we were all together, and over the phone when we weren't, and it seemed obvious that they were convinced that the next plowing that'd be taking place would be in my field.

But wait, speaking of field . . .

"Did I miss something? Are you getting married?" I asked, coming down the last few stairs and interrupting their bicker.

"Girl, get your ass over here," Natalie shouted, surprising more than a few guests and delighting at least one. "Good goddamn, you look fantastic."

"Watch your mouth, Grayson," I shot back, launching myself at them both and letting them hug me tight. Where they were tall, I was tiny, and it was nice to be in our sandwich again. "Seriously, what's with the wedding talk?"

"She's engaged," Natalie said, and I turned to squeal.

"She is not engaged," Roxie corrected, holding up the still-naked third finger on her left hand, but then switching it out for another finger. "Quit saying that."

"Why is she saying that?" I asked, confused.

"Ask her where she went last weekend. Go on, ask her," Natalie instructed. Before I opened my mouth, however, she answered her own question. "She went into the city, *my* city, without telling me, and looked at motherfucking engagement rings at motherfucking VC&A."

"VC&A?" I whispered to Roxie.

"Van Cleef & Arpels." She blushed.

"Who calls it that?" I whispered back.

Natalie finally realized she'd lost her audience and brought us back by pinching us both on our cheeks. "Anyone who has a house account calls it that, which the Maxwell family does, for fuck's sake."

"But wait, wait, hold on, let me see your hand," I said, rolling my eyes at Natalie's chatter. "I don't see a ring."

"That's because for all this nitwit is going on about, I'm not actually engaged. We merely . . . looked."

"At giant diamonds," Natalie interjected.

"Yes, at giant diamonds," Roxie answered, a bashful smile creeping in. "Which I made him stop looking at, honestly, how does he expect me to cook with an ice cube sitting on top of my finger?"

"Call Leo right now, tell him I'll take the ice cube. I will take the ice cube!" Natalie made to get out her phone, but I placed a calming hand on her shoulder.

"How about we wait for Oscar to do that, huh? And in the meantime, we'll eat dinner, sound like a plan?" I asked.

"Yes. Done. Let's eat," Natalie said, nodding her head. "But while we eat I'm going to make her draw you a picture on her napkin of what this ring looks like."

"You really think they have paper napkins at Bryant Mountain House? This place is all linen, all the time, right, Clara?" Roxie asked, and I smiled.

"Whatever, I'll find some scratch paper so you can draw that ring. Huge. Huge! And I'm with Oscar, so you know I know huge."

"Oh, for God's sake, come on," I said, tugging the two of them to the dining room.

As we traipsed down the hallway, Roxie was marveling at everything she saw. "I haven't been up here in ages, not since I was a kid! Mom used to bring me here every year for Easter—they've got the most incredible Sunday brunch, after the egg hunt on the front lawn, of course. But what I remember best were the hot cross buns."

"Hot cross buns, as in, one a penny, two a penny?" Natalie asked.

"Oh, I'm sure these cost more than a penny. These were the best, all puffy and flaky and cinnamony on the inside with the tiniest little currants you've ever seen, glossy golden brown on the outside, and this perfect white cross made out of glaze on the top. I used to take them apart piece by piece, bite by bite, to try and figure out which spices other than cinnamon they put in, whether they stirred or folded in the currants, oh, they were the best."

Natalie and I were used to Roxie waxing poetic about her food; it was clear it'd always been her calling. Once she spent twenty minutes—and I know this because I looked at my watch when the story was over—telling us the history of the carrot and how orange carrots edged all the other colored carrots out of the marketplace and into our hearts forever. And I'd like to tell you I was paraphrasing, but she used that exact wording.

"I like hot cross buns. I like to eat them with my mouth. I don't really care how they got made." Natalie never could resist.

"Okay, weirdos, be on your best behavior tonight, please and thank you," I instructed as we made our way toward the entrance to the dining room. We'd passed by it earlier on the guided tour, but I hadn't actually been inside yet.

It was gorgeous! As we followed the hostess to our table, my head swiveled like an owl as I took in the soaring ceilings, the artistry that went into the carvings on the walls, the sheer amount of wood that went into the construction of this room.

And once more, a fireplace big enough and wide enough to roast a pig.

Once we were seated, I took a look at the rest of the dinner guests. Making mental notes all the while, I realized that not only was the dining room barely half full, I only counted two couples even close to my age, and only one family with small children. Nearly everyone else was retirement age at least, older in many cases. Great for client loyalty, but realistically they'd need to be replaced with new clients, new families and couples who viewed Bryant Mountain House as their special place in the mountains.

"You're working, aren't you?" I heard Roxie ask, and I turned to find her looking at me expectantly.

"Hmm?" I shook out my napkin and placed it in my lap. A napkin that had been folded together and placed inside a ring, an honest to God napkin ring. And finger bowls, good night, there were finger bowls on the table. I hadn't seen a setting like this since I toured the *Queen Mary.*

"You're working. I can see those wheels turning."

"Oh, sorry, I guess."

"She's always working, this one, always with the working. You can't turn it off, can you?" Natalie pointed a finger at me.

"Excuse me, that is why I'm here," I said, pointing a finger right back at her. "And I'm not technically working, I'm here with you fools." They were right, though. It was hard to turn off. Even the rare vacation I took, I couldn't help but look critically at whatever hotel I was staying in.

Usually I was alone, so no one had to watch me jump through my mental hoops.

These two, however. They knew me too well.

A waiter with a tray of glasses appeared out of nowhere. "Ladies, your cocktails."

"We didn't order any cocktails," I started to say, as a glass of bubbly was set down before me.

"Every meal at Bryant Mountain House begins with a champagne cocktail," he said, setting down the final glass with a flourish.

I inspected the flute, filled to the brim with bubbles and with a tiny sugar cube nestled at the bottom and topped off with a twist of lemon. "Every meal?"

"Or another cocktail if you prefer, maybe a Grasshopper? Pink Squirrel?"

"A Pink Squirrel? What the hell year is this?" Natalie asked through the side of her mouth.

"I'm no longer sure," I answered, raising the glass to my lips. "Well, shall we?"

We each sipped at the same time, grimaced at the same time like we'd planned it, and quickly set them aside.

"A champagne cocktail, I can't wait to tell my mom about this, I had no idea they were still doing this up here!" Roxie laughed, reaching into her purse and firing off a quick text to Trudy.

"I take it this is another one of those long-standing mountain house traditions?" I asked. "I'll add that to my list of *wow, seriously?*"

"How's it going, by the way? Too soon to tell?" Roxie asked.

"I'm just barely scratching the surface, but I've got some thoughts," I mused.

"It's amazing up here, isn't it? I mean, we could never afford to stay here when I was growing up, but we still made it up here for some of the bigger events. Christmas, sometimes Halloween, and they always had the most beautiful Easter Sunday celebration."

"With the buns," I reminded her, and she smiled.

"Totally with the buns."

"Speaking of buns . . ." Natalie said, and I followed her gaze. There was my tour guide, moving smoothly from table to table, chatting up the guests and charming the blue hair right off those little old ladies. Dressed in a charcoal-gray suit, powder-blue tie, and yet another coordinated pocket square, Archie filled out his attire quite nicely, I had to admit. If Leo was the rugby player and Oscar was the football player, Archie looked like he'd play water polo. Long and lean, his shoulders were broad, his waist slim. And the buns?

Yeah. Even I had to admit they were pretty great.

But I worked for those buns. So . . .

"Let us not discuss Archie's buns, okay?" I said, picking up my menu card and examining my choices.

"How'd you know I was talking about Archie?" Natalie said, casting a quick glance at Roxie.

"You weren't?" I asked.

"Oh, I totally was, but it's just interesting that you knew immediately who I was talking about when I mentioned that someone in this room, other than me, had a great ass."

I looked to Roxie for help. "Tell her to stuff it, please and thank you."

She nodded. "I'll tell her to stuff it right after you tell us how you knew exactly who she was talking about."

"We're not having this discussion, he's my boss. And an asshole."

"She's blushing, she's totally blushing. Clara never blushes." Natalie laughed, and I held my head in my hands. "You've got a crush. You got here yesterday and you've got a crush."

"I'm not blushing. I'm not crushing. I'm trying to eat dinner with my two lunatic friends who came up here to visit me in my new place of work, mind you, and instead all we're talking about is Archie Bryant's buns!"

"Samuel," I heard a deep voice say over my shoulder, "it seems the ladies at table fourteen haven't gotten their bread basket yet, can you bring that right over?"

"Sure thing, Mr. Bryant!"

Because fate is a funny fucker, standing there with an amused look on his face, knowing full well when I prattled on about his buns they were not of the bread basket variety, was Archie Bryant.

Now I blushed.

Luckily, I didn't have to say anything. Smoothly taking control of the situation, the situation being Natalie and Roxie looking like this was the funniest thing ever and me looking like I'd rather be swallowed by the floorboards than still be sitting here, Archie extended his hand to Roxie.

"Roxie, good to see you, how's Zombie Cakes coming along?"

"Good. Really good, actually." Roxie had started Zombie Cakes last fall, a food truck out of a very cool retro Airstream trailer. Specializing in old-fashioned cakes with an updated twist, Zombie Cakes was making quite a name for itself not only in the Hudson Valley but in Manhattan as well.

"I still need to get you up here sometime for an official chat. We'd love to start featuring some of your cakes on our menu."

"Oh my God, seriously?" she asked, beaming. "Any time!"

"And speaking of any time," Natalie interjected, and I held my breath, not knowing what was coming next, "we gotta talk soon about getting you into my Bailey Falls campaign. Why in the world did we not photograph you when I was up here last fall? You're way too cute not to be in those commercials—you've seen them, right?"

Archie nodded. "I've seen them, Ms. Grayson."

"Call me Natalie."

"Very well, Natalie. I've seen them, although I'm not sure

the overall tone of your advertisements sends the right message to the kind of clientele we've tried to cultivate here at Bryant Mountain House."

"You don't want young hip twenty- and thirty-somethings with disposable incomes taking pictures of everything they love about this place and posting it to all of their friends, who also have disposable incomes?" Natalie asked, arching an eyebrow at him.

"Yes, in fact, that's exactly the kind of clientele we're looking to bring in," I interjected, before it could go any further.

"And another thing," Natalie went on, and I dropped my head back into my hands. So much for not going further. "When I said you're too cute to not be featured, I meant it. You're smoking hot so take it as a compliment, okay, Arch?"

I saw him do a double take at Natalie, undoubtedly taken aback by her say-it-when-she-thinks-it delivery, but he rallied as any good host will do. "Natalie, although I'm not sure what me being cute has to do with my resort, I do thank you for the compliment." He turned to me. "It was a compliment, wasn't it?"

"Yes, it was," I said quickly, wanting to avoid another argument. "Sorry about the buns thing, I—"

"Buns thing, Ms. Morgan? What *buns thing* is that exactly?"

I stammered. "Um . . . I . . . uh . . ."

"Well put, Ms. Morgan. Ah yes, thank you, Samuel, very good. Ladies, enjoy your meal." And as Archie reached down with silver tongs to place an actual bun on my plate, he turned toward me, away from my girls, with those gorgeous indigo eyes dancing, and gave me a very purposeful wink. "And your buns."

This guy.

He knew.

He knew about the buns.

He brought me the buns.

And still . . . he winked.

Maybe there was more to him than meets the eye. Especially when what was meeting the eye was extremely good-looking.

"Flirt. Flirt. Flirt," Natalie chanted as soon as Archie was out of earshot.

"Oh please," I replied, picking up my warm roll and noticing instantly how perfectly it fit in my hand. Oh lordy.

"Bailey Falls strikes again," Roxie murmured, and Natalie threw her head back and squealed.

"Okay, everyone settle down. Pick your entrée. Bailey Falls didn't strike anything, can we all just please be adults for like a minute? Honestly, you two are children and . . . Natalie, what the hell are you doing?"

"Trying to see if he's looking at you." She was perched precariously on the side of her chair with her compact mirror open and angled nowhere near her face.

"Not encouraging this right now. So, Roxie, what are you going to get, the steak medallions or the salmon en papillote— that means it's baked in parchment paper, right?"

Roxie herself could've been baked in parchment paper for all the attention she was paying me. "Dude, he's not looking, he's not looking . . ."

"Not you too. I have zero, and let me repeat, zero interest in Archie Bry—"

Roxie interrupted me. "—he looked! He totally just looked back at you, Clara!"

"He did?" I squeaked, and just then Natalie was no longer perched on her chair. The precarious became nefarious and down she tumbled to the floor, her skirt flaring up and exposing a ruby-red garter belt. Three busboys and an eighty-year-old man tumbled after her to try to be the one to help her up.

"I'll have the steak medallions, medium rare, please," I told Samuel, who was still standing there holding buns.

Dinner was a bit calmer after that. The service was impeccable, the food was . . . eh. Not bad, not great, but eh. I asked Roxie what she thought.

"It's okay, tastes a bit like catering food you'd get at a midline wedding," she replied after I noticed she mainly pushed around but didn't finish her meal.

"I mean, it's a bit old-fashioned, nothing new to see here. But you can't beat this setting." The broad expanse of windows that in daytime would be showcasing the view of the mountains mirrored back the candlelight and twinkling lights overhead. It was a cavernous room, but somehow felt cozy and intimate.

"What's with the menu cards, why so few things to choose from?" Natalie asked as we dug into our desserts.

"They call it rotational dining, a somewhat outdated concept but fairly typical at these old resorts. The menu changes nightly, usually three to four appetizers, three to four entrées, and then a bunch of different desserts. It might repeat once during the week but only once," I replied.

"So if you're here for a week with your family, you could eat here every night and never get the same thing for dinner," Roxie added.

"Exactly. But I'd be willing to bet this is the same menu they've been serving for a long time," I said, thinking out loud.

"Gee, you think? I mean, Baked Alaska is always killer, but seriously, when's the last time you saw it on a menu?" Roxie said.

"I love Baked Alaska," Natalie replied, curving her arm around her dessert. "Don't you dare take away my Baked Alaska."

"No no, that's not what Clara is saying."

"Not at all, but maybe we could change things up a bit. Keep some classics, clearly the ones that have been here forever, but maybe update others a bit." I pulled out my notebook and jotted a few ideas down while I was thinking about them. "Rox, you should come back up here again. Meet with Archie about Zombie Cakes, but maybe we could also get into the kitchen a bit more, see what's actually going on back there. I'll pull some menu cards and see how often they get changed."

"I can do that."

"I want to come too," Natalie said.

"You stay in town with Oscar, churning butter or whatever the hell it is you two get up to down there."

"We get up to plenty. Just last night he had me on top of the kitchen counter, dress over my head, his mouth full of—"

"So anyway, with you involved I'm hoping that Archie will be a little more receptive to the changes I want to make around here." I looked pointedly at Roxie, knowing better than to let Natalie continue.

"Is he not playing nice?"

"He's playing kind of jerky, which believe me when I say is honestly the best word for it. But it feels different this time, more . . . I don't know. When it's happened before at other hotels I've worked at, it's because they think I show up with a giant red pen and start changing anything and everything I can get my hands on, and they see it as me throwing out everything they've ever worked for when in fact it's the opposite. This place is incredible, I just need to make it profitable again. Bring it into this century, dust it off a bit."

"It's pretty pricey. I mean, there's plenty of money in the Hudson Valley, but what they charge per night is pretty tough to swing for most people," Roxie agreed.

"Yeah, I'm going to have to talk to them about their pricing. I'm sure Archie will go through the roof. Any tips on how to get through to him?"

"Me? I barely know him."

"Come on, you grew up in this town."

"True, but there are two sides to Bailey Falls. I'm on the diner side, families like the Bryants and the Maxwells are on the country club side. Plus, he's older than I am, I only know the little bits my mom has told me over the years. She's good friends with Hilda Banning who works up here, and she said he changed a lot after Ashley."

"Ashley?" I asked.

"Ashley?" Natalie asked, through a mouthful of Baked Alaska.

Roxie nodded. "His wife."

"Oh," I said, feeling my spine deflate and sinking back into my chair. Of course he was married, what guy looked like that and wasn't married. I looked across the room to where he was talking to a group of waiters and noticed for the first time the wedding band he wore on his left hand. Of course.

Wait, why of course? Why do you care? Whether or not Archie Bryant is married has absolutely nothing to do with the job you were hired to do. So eat your Alaska and go back to work.

I picked up my fork while Roxie continued. "Yeah, according to Mrs. Banning he was a mess when she passed away."

My head snapped back.

"Whoa, wait, what?" Natalie asked.

"Oh," I breathed. Oh.

I looked at Archie again, watching him move around the dining room, greeting and meeting, all the while knowing now that something terrible had happened to him.

"How did she—"

Roxie interrupted Natalie. "I don't know, I didn't live here at the time so I never got the details."

"Jesus, does it matter?" I asked as his eyes met mine across the dining room. For just one instant, I saw something flash across his face. Interest? Intrigue? And for just an instant, I felt that flash run wild across my body. But before I could finish flashing, the look was gone and that cool, reserved expression was back.

Chapter 7

"No . . . no . . . please . . . no . . . NO!"

I awoke suddenly, soaked through with sweat, tangled in the sheets, clutching my pillow with tears streaming down my face. My breathing, my panting were so loud in this room, this entirely too-silent room. "Dammit," I snarled, still clutching the pillow with one hand and dragging the other through my damp hair. "Dammit," I repeated, a little softer this time as my heartbeat began to slow, the stored-up tension beginning to leave, relaxing my frozen-in-fear joints.

This fucking nightmare. I'd been having it for as long as I could remember but not nearly as often anymore. And usually not after a night spent with my girls. Always the same dream, always the same beginning.

I'd picked up my suitcase and started out walking through the front door of a pretty brick colonial house, just your average house on your average street in average town USA. But on the other side of that door was another door, on another street in another town. I kept pushing through the doors, one after the other, never getting anywhere, never able to stop and settle and breathe. Each time I looked down, I had another suitcase in my hand, stacking up one by one until a mountain of trunks and boxes was dragging behind me.

I finally pushed open the last door, and there they were. A mom, a dad, a dog, a cat. My family. They were waiting for me. Set your bags down, *they said.* Stay awhile, *they said.* You have a beautiful room waiting for you, *they said,* it's just up that staircase.

But as I started for that staircase, my heart beating fast and a nervous smile beginning to creep across my face, I heard another voice. Loud, authoritative, unflinching.

"A mistake has been made."

I turned to see a woman, severe in her high-buttoned collar and tight suit, too tight for her to wear comfortably. How does she sit down in that, I'd always wonder, without popping every single button off?

"A mistake has been made," she repeated, quickly crossing the floor to me.

My hands were slick with sweat as I struggled to hang on to my suitcase. "A mistake?" I heard my own voice ask, tiny and tinny and small and yet, still so hopeful.

"You don't belong here."

The family turned away, even the cat, turned away from me and my suitcases. The dog growled, low and slow and in that grumbly way that almost doesn't register at first in your ears. "Go away," he seemed to say, "you don't belong here."

Now I heard them all saying it, chanting it, singing it. Loud voices, nasty and cruel, razor sharp and thin. You don't belong here. You don't belong here.

I ran, suitcases banging against my little-girl shins, which were covered in bruises, not from falling down on the playground but from those never-ending doors, those never-ending suitcases, bruised inside and out and crying, crying so hard as every single door slammed shut behind me and I was alone. In the world. Alone.

Until I woke quick, thrashing in my bed, tears streaming down my face as I whispered the words I always did . . .

"Let me come home."

Fucking hell I missed that television.

I got out of bed and headed for the bathroom for a cool cloth to wipe my face and neck, the sweat now feeling cold and clammy. I looked at myself in the mirror, knowing sleep was now a goner for the rest of the night.

That nightmare was singularly capable of taking me down, knocking me out, and getting me completely off track. For years it'd been my Achilles' heel, my soft spot. If I let it in, if I let those damn demons back into my head and my heart, it was bye-bye, Clara. Frustrated at the thought of endless hours lying awake thinking thoughts I truly didn't want to think, I realized there was only one thing to do.

I hit the gym hard, running on the treadmill until my lungs burned. I needed the sweat. I also needed the focus.

The running had always helped. It shut out the dreams and the memories, my feet slapping the pavement or the grass or the packed sand or the rubber of the treadmill. Right then left. Right then left. A rhythm, a pattern, something that was always there, always constant, always waiting for me when I needed it. Right then left. Right then left. Eventually, if I ran fast and hard enough, it was all I heard.

And then the magic happened. The world fell away, the nightmare itself fell away, and my brain took over. The good part of my brain, the part that helped me plan and create, solve and fix. I thought not about my past and the pain that existed there, always in the past, no pain in the present, never pain in the present, and I focused on my job, my work, my literal salvation.

By the time dawn broke over the Catskills, I had an entirely new approach to the Bryant Mountain House problem.

∽

"So I've been going over the bookings for this summer. And the last few years. How do you think you've been doing?" I asked.

I was in a meeting with Jonathan, Archie, and a few other members of the senior team, including the heads of guest services and reservations. I'd been somewhat surprised at how cordial Archie had been when I arrived this morning, pleasant even. Maybe we were over the hump, and he'd realized I was here to help, not hurt, his family's legacy.

Don't trust it . . . he's up to something.

"Summer is always our busiest time, with a burst around each holiday," he answered a bit haughtily. Wearing another perfectly pressed gray suit, it was accented with an orange tie and pocket square today. "We even have a waiting list in case any of the regular families cancel over Memorial Day weekend."

"That's great, that's really great. But what concerns me are the other weekends, the non-holiday weekends, when bookings seem to be down across the board almost seven percent."

"Seven percent over last year?" Archie asked.

"Yes."

"That's not too bad, I'm sure we'll make it up by summer's end. We always have a huge party Labor Day weekend, everyone looks forward to it, almost every room is booked," Jonathan interjected, but his son looked concerned.

"Seven percent," Archie repeated.

"Over last year." I nodded, then pursed my lips together. "On top of a five percent decrease the year before, and a whopping eleven percent the year before that."

"Well, we're still recovering from the hit everyone took in '08, no one was taking vacations that year."

"Or the year after that," I added, watching as Archie did some scribbling on his notepad. "Bottom line, even taking '08 into account, your summertime bookings are down almost twenty-five percent when you compare them with a decade ago. And yet you've raised your rates every other year."

"Well, that's just in line with our normal rate increase. We've always done that, our guests know and expect that even an institution like Bryant Mountain House has to keep our pricing current with the market," Jonathan answered.

"That's just it, Jonathan," I said, passing out some printouts, "you're now overpriced. At a time when people are still struggling to get back the money they lost in their retirement plans and value is at a premium."

"But we provide a premium product," Archie said, two spots of red appearing high in his cheeks. "We can't possibly offer our rooms at bargain-basement pricing. You mentioned value? The value of a vacation at this resort is incalculable."

"Actually, it *is* calculable. Very much so. And while a rate increase is standard when costs are commensurate, you've implemented those same increases while your growth has slowed, effectively pricing out the most valuable commodity in the hotel industry—butts in beds." I looked around the room at eyes that weren't wide with shock but focused. They were listening. "Those old families are the life's blood of your resort, no one is disputing that. The fact that you have a waiting list is incredible, bravo. But what happens when those old families are no longer? What happens when those last few dozen matriarchs pass away, and the old family stories and traditions of summers up at Bryant Mountain House are just memories that the younger generation can't afford?"

"Those rate increases reflect things like the cost-of-living wage adjustments we provide to our staff every single year." Archie spit these words out in a chillingly quiet way. But now his voice was rising, as well as his body, right up out of his chair. "Maintenance alone on a resort of this size is astounding. If we reduce our rates, how do you expect us to stay in business?" Archie snapped, throwing his notepad to the table.

I stood as well, leaning across the table, challenging him. "By getting your town involved. By getting local merchants involved. By bringing in the people of Bailey Falls and including them in this dynasty, instead of just sitting high up on your mountain and catering only to the wealthy."

I heard gasps from either side of me, but I kept my eyes solely on Archie's. He was the key here, the linchpin this entire operation rested on. Jonathan Bryant may have been the CEO and he may have been the one to hire me, but he was retiring. Archie was who I needed. If I didn't have his buy-in, the rest of the staff would follow his lead and this place, and their entire way of life, would pass into the faded pages of history of what was once great.

I took a deep breath, and continued. "Now, I'm sorry if you think my words are harsh, but based on the numbers, we need to do something significant in order to save this hotel. It starts with what I like to call my Five R Plan. Number one, Refresh. We identify costs that we can offset over the years by upgrading to more cost-effective technology, like the HVAC systems. Two, Refurbish—we look into ways we can update the guest rooms and use some of what's already there. Three, Rejuvenate and breathe some new life into stagnant areas, specifically with our menus. Revive is number four, not all that is old is boring.

Let's bring back some of the traditions that may have gone by the wayside and couple them with new customs. Let's revive the partnership this hotel used to have with Bailey Falls in a much more specific and targeted way. And finally, Renovate. The specifics on this are TBD until I can drill down some very specific cost projections, but expect this last point to be a whopper."

I looked around and saw wide eyes. It was time to make sure they knew they were still very much a part of this. "Believe me, I'm open to any and all suggestions, however outside the box they may be. In fact, the zanier the better, the more outlandish the better, the furthest away from 'but this is how it's always been done,' the better."

The room was quiet but not a good quiet. I knew it, I'd pushed too far too fast, and now I'd find out I was fired and byebye, partnership.

So when it was Archie who spoke first, I was the most surprised. But it made sense, since it was Archie and only Archie who could turn this around. "While I may not care for the method of delivery," he said through gritted teeth, "Ms. Morgan is correct. We do need to do things differently, and boldly, if we're to keep this hotel afloat. And as long as your plan does not call for filming an episode of *Keeping Up with the Kardashians* on our mountain . . . then I think we . . . I . . . need to give you the benefit of the doubt and hear your plan in its entirety."

His eyes pierced mine, the challenge clear in those indigo depths.

"To be fair, the Kardashians would bring a tremendous amount of coverage to the resort, one tweet from Kim alone could—"

"Ms. Morgan, I think I speak for everyone when I say *not on your life*." But he said it with nasty smile, like he'd just tasted something terrible.

"Okay then, let's get to work."

We broke for lunch around noon, and an enormous amount of work had been accomplished. I could feel plans beginning to take shape. Everyone had a scratch pad full of notes, dry-erase boards covered the walls with parking lot questions and to-do lists, chairs had been pushed back and rearranged, and by the end even Archie had taken off his jacket, loosened his tie, and rolled up his sleeves.

Which just made my eyes flicker back and forth almost nonstop to his forearms. I was a sucker for a nice forearm.

Forget the forearm.

No, you forget the forearm.

Wonderful, now I was literally, and most adult-like, fighting with myself.

When we broke for lunch, I headed over to the picture window at the far end of the conference room overlooking the lake. Stretching my arms over my head, I could feel my back crackle and pop. Hard work wasn't always good for the spine, but luckily my current job site included a world-class spa. Occupational hazard and all.

"Ms. Morgan?"

"What's up, Mrs. Banning?" She'd had some of the most interesting ideas so far this morning. It was nice having someone on my side.

"I just wanted to tell you, I'm really glad you're here."

"Well, that's nice of you to say, Mrs. Banning, I'm glad to be here."

"Oh please, call me Hilda."

"Only if you'll call me Clara. This Ms. Morgan stuff is for the birds."

She shot me a mischievous look. "Jonathan likes things a bit more relaxed, although once he retires I have a feeling Archie will want us to return to a more formal working environment."

I laughed. "Well, we'll just have to show him how much fun it can be to loosen up a bit, right?"

"If you don't mind my saying so, you already have," she said, lifting her chin in the direction of a laughing and smiling Archie, who was worlds away from the buttoned-up aristocrat I'd met yesterday.

"He has to loosen up, at least in the way he's thinking about this place, or he'll lose it."

She looked stunned. "Oh, is it really all that bad?"

I looked at her sadly. "I'm afraid so. Not this year, maybe not the next, but if we don't get things turned around . . ." My voice trailed off. They needed to know, they needed to see what was coming. And as I spoke, my gaze was pulled back to Archie, who had pulled away from the rest of the group and was now pacing in front of all the notes I'd left on the dry-erase boards lining the walls. "I'm sure it's not easy for him to hear that, he seems like he lives for this hotel."

"Yes, I think you're right. You know, he's just never been quite the same since his wife passed away." Her face clouded in sadness. "I've known him since he was a baby, he literally grew up here with his parents, coming and going from this huge hotel like it was one giant backyard. I feel, we all feel, actually, that he needs this hotel to succeed almost more than anything. Ashley would've wanted that for him."

"Ashley, his wife, right? Had they been married long?" I asked, my cheeks heating. Much as I had no business knowing the details, I couldn't help digging to try to find out what made this guy tick.

"Married only a few years, but they'd been together forever. Known each other since grammar school, high school sweethearts those two, why, he even proposed here down on the croquet field at the end of a game one evening. Their lives were fully wrapped up in each other, and wrapped tightly with this hotel too." She sighed then, remembering. I pushed my luck.

"How'd she die?"

Her face blanched. "Cancer. Ovarian, which then spread to her liver. Came out of nowhere, by the time they knew what it was, it was almost too late." She blinked. "She never stood a chance."

"How old was she?"

"Thirty-two."

I gasped. "Jesus Christ, she was only thirty-two when she passed away?"

Mrs. Banning nodded, but then suddenly her eyes widened and a look of shame crossed her face, before she looked down toward her feet.

I knew he was there before he spoke.

"I realize you think you have access to anything and everything that has to do with the Bryant family, Ms. Morgan, but let me be the first to tell you that my wife"—I felt a hand on my shoulder, turning me around. His face was pale, his eyes absolutely blazing—"my wife is off-limits."

"Of course, I was only—"

He cut me off, waving a hand in the air. Without taking his eyes off me, he said, "A word, please, Mrs. Banning." Not a question.

And with that, he turned on his heel and exited the room, Mrs. Banning hot on his heels.

I'd not only gotten her in trouble, I'd literally lost every nanometer of ground I'd finally gained with Archie.

Fuuuuuck.

Chapter 8

The weather had finally broken. The ice had been melting for a few days, the sun had been shining, and a warm wind was blowing from the south, bringing with it the first real taste of spring. It hadn't rained again in almost a week, the mud had finally dried . . . and it was time to run again. Outside.

Spring had sprung.

I'd been dying, *dying* to run outside, sick to death of the treadmill and the inside air. And this morning was finally my chance to get out there and tear it up a bit. I'd been poring over the trail maps, plotting out a course, and chatting with a few of the recreation guys to see what paths would be best this time of year.

I scrambled out of bed, the sun not even yawning yet, and pulled on a pair of leggings, a Dri-FIT shirt, and a thin Gore-Tex pullover. Spring had sprung, but it was still chilly. I filled my water bottle, laced up my shoes, and literally bounced down the stairs.

I'd been here long enough now to have established a routine. There weren't many people up this early, but the few that were let me do my thing. I said hello to Howard, the nighttime guy at the front desk. I nodded a quick hey to Paul and Shawn, the modern-day scullery maids who were tasked with running around each morning and starting fires in the million and one fireplaces that covered this joint. The first urns of coffee were being put out in the Lakeside Lounge by Nancy, who helped out in the kitchen overnight and managed any late-night room service requests. I sniffed longingly at the scent of those heavenly roasted beans, but only after my run would I have any.

Slipping out onto the long porch, I raised one leg and then the other, stretching and feeling the good burn along the back of my quads. By now the sun had begun peeking over the tree line, the sky lightening to a soft gray rather than the charcoal it'd been when I left my room. I consulted the map I'd tucked in my jacket pocket once more, and trotted off in the direction of the trailhead.

I warmed up slowly, gradually picking up speed as my muscles relaxed and fell into their natural rhythm. The birds were chittering away by now, talking to each other and reporting their feathery news. I moved deeper into the forest, the trail twisting this way and that with a steadily increasing incline that a treadmill could mimic but never fully replicate.

My lungs filled with air, good clean mountain air that was chilly but invigorating. *Chilly.* That was the word to describe Archie at this point. Soooo chilly. The weather may have been thawing, but good lord, that man had icicles in his blood. Well, icicles when it came to me. When it came to the rest of the world, his beloved staff on his beloved mountain, he was all smiles. But for me? For me he reserved the iciest of everything, even when he managed to address me directly.

On at least three separate occasions he'd left the room when I'd entered. Literally left the room before I even had a chance to say a good morning or a howdy-do or a hey that bagel looks good are there more?

During the morning meetings when the entire team was required to be together he avoided asking me questions directly and when he did deign to address me personally, he did so in such a dismissive way that even his father had raised an eyebrow. And when he did argue with me about something, which was often, it wasn't friendly fire.

"Wrong."

"Excuse me?"

"Wrong."

"I'm sorry?"

"I'm sorry too, Ms. Morgan, that I had to sit here through an entire presentation on whether or not we need to change how we make our hot chocolate. We have always had homemade hot chocolate here at Bryant Mountain House, since the original lodge was here we—"

"You had hot chocolate waiting in a kettle over a roaring fire for guests to enjoy when they came in from their horse-drawn sleigh ride, complete with jingle bells and mashed potatoes tucked into their pockets to keep their gentle little East Coast hands warm and toasty," I interrupted, having been painted this particular picture numerous times since I'd been here. Currier and Ives might actually be buried on this property for all the nostalgia I was being fed on the daily. "And I get it, I do. But for God's sake, Mr. Bryant, you use three different types of imported chocolate to make the stuff! It's ridiculously expensive! Do you have any idea how much money you could be saving in just one year in imported chocolate alone? Guests barely even drink it anymore, but that damn kettle is filled to the brim with hot freaking imported chocolate every day at teatime like there are still gaggles of horse-drawn sleighs zinging all over this mountain!"

"Baked potatoes."

"What the hell is baked potatoes?" I sputtered, looking at him like he'd had a stroke.

"They didn't carry mashed potatoes in their pockets, Ms. Morgan, they carried baked potatoes, heated in the very ashes beneath the kettle of hot chocolate." He took off his glasses, cleaning them on the edge of his red paisley tie. "Mashed potatoes," he scoffed. "Where are you going?"

"I'm off to the kitchen to slam my head in the oven a few dozen times, maybe toss in a few potatoes while I'm at it," I shouted over my shoulder as I flung the door open and walked out of the meeting.

"Make sure you prick them first or they'll explode" was what wafted out before the door shut, his tone telling me he thought he'd won this round.

"You know what," I started, going right back into the meeting like I'd been using a swinging door, "I'll give you something to prick—"

"Let's take five, everyone, shall we?" Jonathan interrupted, as eleven department heads scattered from the conference room like buckshot, Archie being the last to saunter out casually with a satisfied grin.

"Fourteen thousand, seven hundred and thirty-three," I seethed as he walked past.

"What's that?" he asked, looking down over the bridge of his glasses at me.

"Fourteen thousand, seven hundred and thirty-three dollars is what you spent last year on hot chocolate supplies."

He blanched.

I stuffed my notebook in my bag and headed for the door, passing just under his nose. "I haven't even started adding up how much this place spends on freaking lemons for your special old-timey lemonade you serve in the summer. This is the shit, Mr. Bryant, and I'm sorry for the choice of words, but this is the shit that *tanks old resorts. When you're ready to discuss the very real and practical ideas I have to keep this place afloat, and keep your hot chocolate flowing, you let me know."*

Ooh, but he made me mad! I had no idea how to break through to the guy. I'd tried to apologize, several times in fact, but he either changed the subject, talked over me, or flat out walked away.

In another world, I'd give up. I'd chalk it up to a missed opportunity, get the job done, and walk away knowing I'd been able to do my job and do it well in spite of the fact that the boss's son hated my ever-loving guts. Sometimes people just didn't like me, and I could deal with that.

Two things made this other world not possible. One, I was up for partner. And while Barbara technically was in charge, she did have other partners who needed to weigh in, and I didn't think Archie would be too kind on my final report card. And two, I still really wanted to apologize. I overstepped my bounds; I'd literally pried into his personal life like a gossip and worse, was caught while I was doing the prying! But now I was being denied my chance to correct that.

My feet pounded the gravel, the terrain getting wilder as I moved higher up the mountain. I adjusted my gait, adjusted my breathing, and continued on. What could I do, how could I get the chance to talk to him, and make him listen to me? Really listen to me. No more potato fights.

Speaking of listening, over the crunch of my own feet I could hear other feet crunching. Someone else was on the trail, and not too far ahead. I saw a whisper of movement around a corner, the switchbacks up here getting shorter. Speeding up a bit, I saw a bright yellow windbreaker moving steadily along the trail, attached to long, strong legs, and a shock of auburn hair.

Archie. Up on his mountain. Alone.

And he wouldn't be able to get away from me.

I put my head down, took a deep breath, and began to give chase.

Now, I realize the optics of this, a perfect grade school scenario. Girl chases boy, literally chases boy, as he runs away.

I ran faster. As he rounded another corner, he glanced over his shoulder and saw me barreling up the mountainside toward him, hell-bent for leather. I was close enough that I could see his expression. He was surprised, but then he scowled and proceeded to run faster.

For fuck's sake.

So I ran faster too, because see . . . right before he scowled, there was the briefest flash of something else.

Challenge.

Come on, Bryant. Show me what you've got.

We both increased our pace. I gained five feet, then lost three when he put on a burst of speed around a boulder. He lost his footing on a loose patch of gravel and I pulled to within slapping distance, but then I lost my own footing on the same patch and slipped behind once more.

I was breathing hard, but I was close enough now that I could hear him too. The switchbacks were almost a ninety-degree incline by now, and the landscape was blurring by. I scrambled over a downed tree he'd touched just seconds before; he whirred around a puddle. The trees thinned for a moment and I caught the briefest glimpse of the lake, now far, far below us.

I saw the end of the trail—we were nearly at the top. I dug deep, and willed my feet to move faster, all out sprinting to the top. Our legs moved together now, pumping fast, mud and gravel splashing and spitting up between us. I was groaning, panting; he was grunting with every step. My chest burned, my feet ached, my legs trembled, and there was no way this motherfucker was going to beat me to the top.

I pushed harder than I'd ever done before. I willed my legs to become pistons, my muscles cramping but pushing me higher and higher and higher. We were even now, both of us flying, perpetual motion, limbs a muddy blur of mixing color.

With one last grunt and groan, and a triumphant grin on my face, we rounded the last corner and raced onto an open field, tied at the top. No winner. No loser.

But kind of me, winner.

I ran a few more paces, slowing down now, gulping air, my lungs grateful. I could feel the sweat pouring down my back, my hair plastered to my face as I turned it skyward, feeling the morning sun. Here, on top of a mountain, with nothing around but trees and sky and dirt and grass, I could feel that high creeping in, dulling the cramps and the pain that would most assuredly creep back later on. But for right now, bliss was settling in.

I ran another twenty feet or so, toward a stacked stone tower at the edge, the observatory. I could hear him behind me, just a few feet away, his feet as heavy as mine. As I neared the tower, the world stretched out before me, farms and streams and beautiful red barns marching away into an almost endless horizon. On a clear day you really could see forever.

I peered back at him to offer a congratulatory grin and, when I could speak again, thank him for such a great race, but when I saw his face, I froze.

"You," he grunted, reaching me quickly since I had frozen solid. "What the hell is wrong with you?"

"Me?"

"Who chases someone up a mountain?"

"Who runs away from someone chasing them up a mountain?" I fired back. "I just wanted to talk to you."

"Talk to me? You want to talk to me, you ask me. You request a meeting, you send me an email, hell, you pass me a note while

I'm sitting next to you at a meeting for Pete's sake, you don't chase me up a mountain!"

"I request a meeting?" I shouted back, incredulous. "What the hell is wrong with you, that's the most ridiculous thing I've ever heard! I want to talk to you, I'll talk to you."

He got close, really close, in my face. I took a step back, then another, backing up until I was against the tower.

"Don't you get it? Whatever it is you want to say, whatever it is you seem to need to tell me, I don't want to hear it."

"But if I could just—"

I couldn't say anything else. Because his mouth was on mine, fire and heat and burning searing against my lips.

Shocked, my eyes stared into his, which were swirling with anger.

I bit down on his lip, then pushed him away. "The fuck?" I said, frowning, brow crinkling as he panted in front of me.

And then my hands were filled with his jacket as I yanked him back against me, fingernails digging into his chest, pulling his face to mine and kissing him again, hard and insistent.

I slapped at his shoulder as he groaned against my lips, slanting, as my tongue pushed inside his mouth. I moaned, growling as he nipped at my skin, his hands now rough, slipping around to the small of my back, pushing everything together. I could feel the stone digging into my back, my hips bumping into his as I scrambled to get my legs under me, but after that run they were jelly.

"You're a fucking lunatic, you know that?" he asked, tugging me into him hard, everything hard, everywhere hard.

"I'm the lunatic?" I asked, biting down on his lower lip again, this time hard enough I tasted blood.

He dipped his head down, his eyes level with mine. "Don't do that again," he warned.

"Don't tell me what to do," I warned back, digging my hands

into his hair and pulling it back, tilting his neck and allowing me to nip at his skin there. It was warm, and sweaty, and sticky, and I could taste salt on my tongue.

One hand shot up and slapped at the stone behind me, while the other tugged me closer, circling his hips against mine and pressing himself farther between my thighs.

"You're infuriating," he said, his voice heated steel. "And you're too short." And with that, he picked me up against him, my legs wrapping clumsily around his hips as he held me against the tower.

Now eye level with him, I glared. "I'm exactly the right height." And as he pressed his lips against my neck, his tongue darting out to lick and suck at my skin, I let my head fall back against the stone with a thud. "And you're an asshole."

His hips surged forward, my legs spread wider, and as he ground into me I held his head, his mouth trailing down, pushing under the edge of my jacket, his lips dropping hot wet kisses along my collarbone. I kissed the very tip of his ear softly, then whispered, "And I'm sorry."

He froze. Then his head snapped up, his eyes, which had been filled with lust, began to be crowded by confusion and sadness and . . . fear.

The moment was over and he set me down, gently unwrapping my legs from his waist and, as I tried to tilt his face back up to mine to tell him again that I was sorry, he shook his head.

"I'm . . . Jesus, I can't do this."

He backed away, turned, and headed down the mountain.

I didn't chase him this time.

I stayed up there for a good thirty minutes, watching the morning take over the valley. My mind was racing, running through possibilities, calculating the risk and benefit and realizing that I needed to step down, step away. With Archie, I'd scratched at something I had no business scratching at. This was bad on so many levels, and I needed to shut this down, tie it off, and forget it ever happened.

But did I *want* to forget this happened?

My fingers fluttered up to my lips, feeling the heat that was still there. I could still taste him, could still feel him as he pressed his mouth against mine again and again. It'd sparked something deep within me, an instant heat, an instant lust, a carnal reaction so quick and fiery, I had to admit I was surprised by the intensity. I'd never felt something like this before.

But it's for your boss, so . . .

Right. Right! I shook my head to clear it, taking in big gulps of cold, clean mountain air. He was my boss, and I needed to straighten this out. A couple of great kisses couldn't derail everything good I wanted to do up here, no sir.

I loved it up here, would have loved to stay up here and do everything I knew how to do to make this right. But I'd stuck my foot in it, and now my tongue, and I knew better than to get in deeper.

I wandered toward the top of the trail and saw the resort from this angle. It had been photographed from this place many times, and was really the million-dollar view. The lake, the grounds, the dock, everything was beautiful from up here, as the website, postcards, and prints in the gift shop boasted.

I took one last look, then headed down, ready to search him out, find him, and explain to him exactly why this could never ever happen again.

Waiting for me at the bottom of the trail was Archie, looking way hotter than I needed him to be.

Chapter 9

"We need to talk."

Good goddamn he was attractive.

"We need to talk," he repeated.

Like not just attractive, insanely handsome. Classic good looks, strong jaw, broad shoulders but a nice tapered waist, maybe he—

"Ms. Morgan?"

"Hmm?" I asked, my eyeballs not able to move up from the white T-shirt peeking out above his fleece.

"I'm asking you to listen to me," he interrupted. His lower lip was puffy from my teeth, and I could see at least one scratch on his neck from my fingernails. His hair was tousled, his jacket was almost completely unzipped, and I smiled in spite of myself when I saw the muddy prints my shoes had left on the sides of his running pants.

I shouldn't talk. I shouldn't get in any deeper than I already was. But I'll admit I was curious. And dammit, I was still 100 percent turned on by this gorgeous but infuriating ass.

See, dangerous.

Get in your head!

"Mr. Bryant, yes, got it, right here with you," I said, dazed.

But regaining control. "No need to talk, we're good. Won't happen again, this isn't a thing, doesn't need to be a thing, let's just move on, shall we?"

"Oh, I think we better talk before we move on," he replied.

Against every part of my brain screaming at me to push past him, to go directly to my room, I nodded and let him lead me toward a small summerhouse a little ways off the main trail.

Settling onto one of the wooden benches, I waited to hear him out. Like he said, I'd chased him up the side of a mountain, so I wasn't about to be the one to go first this time.

He paced a few times, walking the length of the gazebo back and forth, his gait smooth and even. I should've known he was a runner, his frame practically ensured it. Long and lean, every step measured. Conserving energy.

But when he let that energy run wild and free? Damn. I shifted a bit on the seat, the feeling of his fingertips digging into my skin still burning. I'd be willing to bet that by tonight I'd have ten little bruises on my hips.

Why the hell was that so thrilling?

"What's the longest relationship you've ever been in?"

Whoa. "Um, what?" While I'd been ruminating on my hips, he'd stopped pacing and asked me a question. He repeated it.

"I don't know that it's any of your business."

He looked skyward, dragging his hands over his face. His hair really was still messed up.

"I'm asking because I'm trying to explain why I had such a reaction to you asking about Ashl"—a look of pain crossed his face—"about my wife."

Oh boy. "Listen, I'm really sorry about that, I never meant for you to hear me and it wasn't like I was trying to gossip or anything, I just . . ."

"Because the longest relationship I've ever been in was the

one with my wife, and it started when we were in high school. To be fair, it started long before that. I knew her almost my entire life. I assumed I'd spend the rest of my life with her. Turns out, it was only the rest of her life." He blinked, and his eyes were so very blue. "So even though she's gone, and I know she is, sometimes it rears up to surprise me in the strangest ways. You can't . . . know someone that long and suddenly know how to handle it when they just disappear from your life. You can't be with someone that long and not still feel the need to step in, to fight for them, to protect them."

I couldn't believe he was talking to me, like really talking to me. This was such a one-eighty from everything that had happened up until now. He'd been so closed off and angry up to this point, and now he was opening up? And about something so tragic. "I can't even begin to imagine." And that was the truth. I'd never felt the need to protect anyone other than myself. There was certainly no one to watch out for me. Ever.

"I meet new people every single day in this business. They come into what I feel like for all intents and purposes is my home, and I welcome them and make them comfortable. No one knows the story, no one knows what happened, because these are all new people you see, and they're just here for the lake and canoes and the hiking."

"And the fireplaces, you have some really great fireplaces," I added, and he grinned. He really should grin more, it does incredible things to his face. There's a sense of heavy that I sometimes feel around Archie, a sense that he's seen too much for a young man. When he smiles, that goes away. The lines soften, smooth out, lines that I now know were put there by tragedy.

"And the fireplaces," he agreed. "The people who work here, they're my family. They know the story, they know everything, so they never mention it. Why would they? So you see, it's a very safe place for me. And then someone comes in, someone I never wanted here in the first place."

I raised my hand. "That would be me."

"That would be you." Another smile. "You're a real pain in the ass, you know that?"

"Am I supposed to answer that?"

"You asked about my wife."

I took a deep breath. "I did."

"Why?"

I wanted to walk to him. I wanted to go over to him and lean up on my tippiest toes and press a soft kiss on his cheek, but oh boy, there were ninety-nine reasons why I shouldn't and no real reason why I should.

Other than every single fiber of my being wanted to do so, and not stop there.

So I did the only thing I could do. I sat on my hands. And tried to explain. "You're also a huge pain in the ass, and I don't mind telling you that. In fact, someone should tell you that, repeatedly and often. But when I found out about your wife"—his eyes sprang open, searching—"you became more than just an ass. It's not pity, but I did feel sad for you. I asked the wrong person. I should've asked you."

He sighed. "When someone dies, the people left behind, no one quite knows what to do with them. They don't want to talk about it, but sometimes you need to talk about it. But I never liked knowing that other people were talking, does that make sense?"

"It makes perfect sense." I nodded. "So you tell me about her."

"You sure we shouldn't talk about what just happened? Up there?" His eyes flickered up to the observation tower, observing us right at this very moment.

"Oh, we're gonna talk about that, Mr. Bryant," I said, arching my eyebrow, "especially how you took matters into your own hands up there. And by matters, I'm speaking specifically of my ass."

"I did nothing of the kind," he murmured, the indigo flashing fire once more. "Your hips, on the other hand . . ."

"Remind me to chase you up a mountain more often."

He laughed then, and it was magic. And it was into this magic that I did walk over to him, reach up toward him, not with my lips but with my hand, and gently brush back the shock of auburn hair that had fallen down over his forehead. He closed his eyes, then instantly leaned into my touch, almost like a cat. Jesus, when was the last time someone had touched this guy?

The truth was, however, it'd be the last time I'd be touching him, at least in this way. "And since people seem to go a little crazy up on these mountains, I recommend we stay a bit closer to the ground."

His eyes remained closed, and he nodded, agreeing with my words. But he didn't pull away just yet, and neither did I.

In the end, it was people coming up the trail, other early birds anxious to get out in the nice weather this morning that blew apart our little world inside the summerhouse. We backed away from each other, finally putting a respectable and appropriate distance between us.

But even at that respectable distance, his eyes blazed with heat.

The next day I arrived at the morning meeting and was surprised to see Archie there. Surprised because he hadn't attended all week, only coming to meetings that he was specifically requested to attend and then to either sit and listen and not volunteer any information, or if asked a direct question respond in such a way as to prompt an argument with me as soon as he could.

Today when I walked in he immediately rose, brought me a cup of coffee, two sugars and a splash of cream, exactly the way I take it, and before I could stammer out anything he turned me toward the rest of the group and announced, "Starting today I will be embracing Ms. Morgan."

I didn't quite spit-take my coffee, but only because I'd swallowed it almost entirely, burning my esophagus in the meantime and blistering my tongue. The rest of the team simply stared at him in anticipation, wondering what in the hell kind of meeting this was about to become.

My reaction and their staring prompted him to immediately reevaluate his words, and he offered a nervous laugh. "Embracing her ideas, of course, her ideas. I've been, well, I think we can all agree, a real pain in the ass up until this point."

I raised my hand. Although, to be fair, I might've been signaling someone to bring me ice cubes for my throat.

"Some of her ideas may be a bit unconventional, but I'm willing to try and see things her way. Within reason, of course."

"Of course," I croaked out, managing a smile while wondering what in the world he was up to.

Famous last words. The truce lasted barely an hour. By ten thirty he was frustrated, I was irritated beyond belief, and I wanted nothing more than to pick up my now empty coffee cup and whap him squarely in the middle of the forehead with it.

"You can't keep dragging your feet on this, Mr. Bryant, it's got to happen this way or we will literally never get anywhere."

"Nothing has *got to happen* until I say it's *got to happen*, Ms. Morgan, and I'll thank you to remember that. I'm willing, more than willing, I think, to look into upgrading some of the rooms, but—"

"Not upgrading. Overhauling. New mattresses. New bedding. New pillows. Speaking from my own experience here, my bed, in a word? Sucks."

"The beds don't suck, Ms. Morgan," he sputtered. "And I'll thank you to remember that each of those beds has been a part of this hotel for over a century—"

"New wallpaper," I continued, feeling on a roll and running with it, "and an entirely new concept for that carpet, if indeed there will be carpet. There's money in the budget for this, if we can—"

He exploded. All over the Camellia Conference Room and all over the department heads who'd been passing the economy-sized bottle of Tums back and forth between them. "The budget? How in the world do you expect us to pay for this overhaul, and reduce the room rates, and bring in additional entertainment for the summer season, and—"

"May I see you for a moment?" I asked, interrupting his tirade. "*Privately?*"

He looked as though he was about to say something else, but bit it back. Exhaling heavily, he pushed back from the table. "Everyone take fifteen."

Stoically he followed me out onto the porch overlooking the lake. I usually took my breaks out here, getting a little hit of nature when I needed it.

I needed it right now. I needed to pitch him something pretty drastic and I needed to have him on board.

"Ms. Morgan, I realize I got a little heated back there, but you have to realize all these changes are going to be expensive and—"

I cut him off. "You're going to have to close for a few months every year, for probably the next five to eight years, in order to keep this place going."

He tilted his head like he didn't actually hear me. "Come again?"

"Look, I've been over and over the books and it's the only way I can see making the changes we need to make and keep within the budget. You're literally bleeding money in your off-season, you're barely at thirty percent full, it no longer makes financial sense to be a true winter resort. At least for a while. It's drastic, but it's what needs to be done."

His lips pressed together hard enough that they turned white. "We have *never* closed, not one day since we opened our doors. Not for blizzards, not for wars, not for major repairs, not for anything."

I sighed, knowing this was a lot to take in. "I realize that, and I know I'm asking for a lot."

"You are literally asking for the impossible."

I shook my head. "It's not impossible. We did it at the Manor Crest in Colorado and at the Seaspray in Rhode Island. Granted, they're still doing it, but Manor Crest is on track to reopen full-time in two years . . . a year ahead of schedule."

He shook his head slowly. "You want to close Bryant Mountain House."

I nodded just as slowly. "For ten weeks, starting in mid-January. Get through the holidays, have a helluva New Year's party, and then close up shop. We can discuss reopening for Valentine's Day, although I don't recommend it, at least for the first year."

"And we reopen?"

"Right before Easter. I'd say Easter weekend, but since that date is fluid each year, I'd aim for the third week of March."

"The third week of March," he whispered, the idea as foreign a concept to him as if I'd suggested we iron each other's feet. "We'd miss the entire winter season, all the outdoor activities. We get snow before Christmas, sure, but the big stuff doesn't really come down until January, and the lake doesn't freeze until then anyway. No ice-skating on the lake, no snowshoeing through the woods, none of it."

"I'm sorry, Mr. Bryant, I truly am." I had to make my hand into a fist behind my back, it wanted so much to reach out to him, touch him, soothe him and make this better. I resisted. "But we can make this work, and you'd be surprised how much we can do when the hotel is empty of guests and with only minimal staff."

"The staff, what will we do with them? They depend on their salaries, many of them, they've worked here for years. We can't just, I can't just . . ." He trailed off, shaking his head again. "This'll never work."

"It can work. But you're going to have to trust me," I said, stepping a little closer. We were within sight of anyone who might be walking around the lake or down on the dock, not to mention the rest of the team inside. But I still took that step, that very small step. He needed to know I was on his side. "I realize I'm asking for a lot here, but you have to trust that if you don't come on board, if you don't guide your team and your hotel through this, in a few years you won't just be closed for ten weeks in winter." I watched as his face went through a range of emotions: hopelessness, frustration, and finally, resignation.

"I'm going to need details, and details about those details. And I'll ask a lot of questions. And it'd be helpful if you didn't act like every time I ask you something you're expecting World War Three."

I bit down on a chuckle. "Agreed, but it'd also be helpful if you didn't look at me every time I open my mouth like I'm trying to ruin you."

He shot me a sideways look, then nodded. "But before we bring this to the group, to my father even, you're going to have to lay out your plans in their entirety, tell me everything you want to do. No more surprises."

"Agreed."

"Tonight."

"Tonight?"

"Tonight. You'll tell me everything."

I exhaled. Why did that statement make me uneasy?

We went back into the meeting a united front, with plans made to have dinner, in town this time, to go over *my* plans. Neutral ground? Maybe. But for the first time with this guy, I felt hopeful.

Chapter 10

At five minutes to seven I descended the stairs to meet Archie in the lobby. It was funny how in the relatively short time I'd been here, I'd come to know certain parts of this hotel like the back of my hand. I knew the potted ferns on the fifth floor were a bit on the droopy side and looked like they weren't being watered regularly. I knew that the last room on the right on the fourth floor always had afternoon tea in their room, the service still usually sitting outside by the time I went down to dinner. I knew that on the third step between the third and fourth floors there was an extremely loud squeak if you stepped on it just right.

The main staircase really was a thing of beauty, all carved wood and twisty columns. Between the second and first floors it became even grander, the showpiece of the center lobby. As I turned the last corner and saw Archie waiting at the bottom for me, a slow grin crept over his face as I moved down the steps.

"This feels very *Titanic*." I chuckled. Though Jack Dawson in his borrowed finest had nothing on Archie Bryant in a sweater and jeans. The sweater being a soft-looking beige cashmere V-neck with just the edge of his white collared shirt poking out, so he was still neat and tidy but a bit more approachable than in his customary finely tailored suits. "You know, Jack and Rose, center staircase, all that?"

"That's terrible, I don't plan on hitting any icebergs tonight."

"You shouldn't plan on hitting anything tonight," I said, raising one eyebrow and coming to a stop a few steps before the bottom. Eye level.

His blue eyes twinkled. "Let's just try to get through dinner without yelling, that'd be a start, Ms. Morgan."

"Wait a minute," I said. "We're going into town for dinner, right?"

"That was the plan."

"Then I'm Clara. You're Archie. Once we come down from the mountaintop and all."

He mulled this over a moment. "Agreed." He nodded. "Clara."

An involuntary shiver ran through my body at the sound of my name on his lips. Mercy.

Work dinner. It's a work dinner. Stop shivering.

But my name. On his lips? Divine.

Work. It's work. Focus!

I took the last two steps down, coming to rest next to him. He'd been right, I am short, I barely came up to his shoulders. He held my coat open for me, and as he slipped it onto my shoulders he asked, "Are you ready?"

"Hell yes" was out of my mouth before I could stop myself, and he chuckled in my ear, low and a bit growly. Goddammit, I shivered again.

Archie + growly = *mercy*.

We sailed out the front door under the watchful eye of literally every single employee, half of whom I'm pretty sure weren't even on the clock but had somehow materialized at this very moment.

Yeah, it was a very good thing we were heading into town.

∽

"So this is . . . pretty nice." I'd been tucked into the front seat of a very nice, very luxurious BMW. The heater on, my toes stretched out against the warmth, grateful after the chilly run to the car.

"Are you interested in German engineering, Ms. Morg— Clara?"

Oh yeah, I could get used to this guy saying my name over and over again. "Not necessarily."

"What are you interested in?"

"Is this what we're doing now? Asking questions?"

He waved a good-bye to the guard at the security shack, shifted smoothly, and then shot me a pointed look. "You had your tongue in my mouth yesterday, don't you think a few questions are the natural progression?"

"My tongue in your mouth was after *you* put your tongue in my mouth, Archie. Let's not forget that."

"I don't think I'll be forgetting that anytime soon."

The car was silent. Full. We were heading down the mountain, dark pressing in on all sides. His words hung in the air, I could still hear them in my ears. Did I want that tongue in my mouth again? To quote myself, hell yes. But it didn't matter, because I was here to do a job and I wasn't going to put my entire career in jeopardy because some supercute nerd kissed me. And, technically, I kissed him back.

Take control, Clara!

"Running."

"What?"

"You asked what I was interested in. Running. Sometimes swimming."

"If you swim as fast as you run you must be part fish."

"And cycling, although between all three I prefer running."

"You should do a triathlon."

"You should come see me do one. My next one is in June."

"You're kidding."

"I'm not."

"Seriously?"

"Seriously. Ironman. Technically, Ironwoman. But I'm thinking about doing a Tough Mudder before that."

"You mean those races where you splash through mud and run up walls?"

"Yep."

"Isn't that filthy?"

"God yes, the filthier the better." I laughed, turning so I could see him. "You want to come with me?"

"To a mud race?"

"Sure."

"You want me to come watch you get muddy."

"Hell no, I want you to come get muddy with me."

"And why would I do this exactly?"

"Are you kidding? It's a blast!" I punched his shoulder excitedly. "It's such a rush, you push yourself, you think you can't do it, but then you do, you bang your elbows, you scrape your knees, you probably cry at least once, you may even vomit . . . it's the best time."

"I wonder if my father knows he hired an actual insane person to help turn his hotel around."

"Oh shush," I huffed. "You'd do great. It's not a big deal to get a little dirty sometimes."

"I'll take your word for it." He laughed, swinging the car right and just like that, we were in Bailey Falls.

I'd seen pictures. I'd heard Natalie wax poetic about the cuteness, and even Roxie now admitted that her hometown was

nicer than she remembered. I'd grown up in an urban environment, and still chose to live in a city. But when I got to go out on
jobs, they tended to be either set in or just outside lovely small
towns. And I admit, I did love me some quaint.

For the same reason I loved old family-run hotels, I really
enjoyed the sense of pride I felt whenever I was in a small town.
There was the "everybody knows your name" aspect, sure, but
there was also just such a sense of belonging, of togetherness
that was totally foreign to me. It never made sense for me to become "one of them" when I was on a job in a place like this, but
I sure as shit could enjoy what it looked like from the outside.
And Bailey Falls was obviously no exception.

The graceful homes, the tree-lined streets, some still sport-
ing their original cobblestones for goodness' sake, the mom-
and-pop stores on Main Street and a good old-fashioned town
square. Good God, was this place adorable or what?

And the most adorable of all, the one place I'd been dying to
see but hadn't yet visited, was Callahan's. The diner owned by
Roxie's mom, Trudy. And to my surprise, we pulled up right in
front.

"Wait, we're going to Callahan's?"

"Is that okay?"

"Sure, sure, I just figured, I don't know."

He turned off the car and looked at me carefully. "You just
figured what?"

"I pegged you for a more formal guy. I guess I thought you'd
want to have dinner at a fancy pants Frenchie or whatever."

"Is that a real place?"

I rolled my eyes. "You just seem like a guy who likes to eat in
a place that has finger bowls."

"You should probably get to know a guy better, then, before
you chase him up a mountain."

Okay, that's it. "For the last time, I may have chased you, but it was only to talk to you and then you—" But I was cut off by his door closing, and a wink and a grin through the windshield. I hadn't lost any steam by the time he opened my door. "—pushed me up against that damn tower and made out with me like you just got out of prison and—"

It wasn't just towers that he got off on. Because the next thing I knew I was pressed into the cold brick wall in between the diner and a taxidermist with Archie and his impossibly strong hands all over my hips.

"You really are a pain in the ass," he said, his breath fogging up the space—the very little space—between us.

"You're the only person who's ever told me that."

"I find that incredibly hard to believe."

I sank my hands into his hair, twisting the auburn locks in my fingertips. His blue eyes went wild.

My heart went wild too, beating almost out of my chest. This was wrong, this was so fucking wrong. I knew better than this. "I find it hard to believe you're not kissing me yet." I knew better, but in that moment I didn't care.

His lips were on mine in an instant, all traces of the calm and collected Mr. Bryant gone as he ravaged my mouth with his own. He kissed like he'd never get enough, like I was going to disappear.

"Oh God," I murmured as he tugged my hips into his, ferocious and hungry.

"You taste incredible," he whispered back, sweeping kisses along my cheekbone, nuzzling against my neck. "How can you taste this sweet?"

I pulled his face back to mine, staring deep into his eyes, wrapping one leg around his hip, pulling him into my heat.

Stars. I saw stars. In his eyes, in my eyes, in the actual night sky, I don't know. I just know that when he thrust up against me, wild and crazy, the world changed somehow, and suddenly everything was all bright colors and his face was stunning.

"Oh my God," I moaned, my voice muffled against his neck. "Oh my God, I can't believe we're doing this."

"We're officially not doing this," he groaned, his hand traveling up my leg, palming my thigh.

"It's bad, this is so bad," I gasped.

"It's the worst," he agreed, then silenced us both with a searing kiss.

I heard footsteps. Footsteps close by, on the street. The footsteps slowed down.

"Dude, someone is going to town in the alley over there."

"No they're not, where? Oh. Ohhhh."

"Should we stop watching?"

"I want to say . . . yes?"

The footsteps never started up again. Jesus, we had an audience.

I lowered my leg, peeking over Archie's shoulder and saw two men unabashedly staring, unabashedly delighted. And then somewhat embarrassed when they realized they'd been caught peeping, they hurried on down the street.

My heart pounded in my ears, that was too close. They'd seen my face, but no one knew me, not in this town. And Archie's back was to them, they couldn't have seen his face.

"Jesus, who gets caught making out in an alley." I sighed as he leaned his forehead to mine, both of us out of breath.

"I'm so sorry," he said, his cheeks flooding red. "I'd normally never . . . I mean, what kind of guy . . ."

I kissed him quickly, firmly. "I feel it too, whatever this is. We just need to stop doing this."

He looked into my eyes, the right corner of his mouth lifting.

But also realizing what was at stake. He backed away, both of us straightening ourselves up a bit.

We took the few steps back to the street and headed inside the diner. Where we were instantly greeted by familiar faces sitting around a large table in the middle of the restaurant.

Roxie.

Leo.

Natalie.

A hulk who I assumed was Oscar.

And two more faces that, upon seeing my face, sported Cheshire cat grins.

The two guys from the alley. Shit.

"Clara, what the hell, why didn't you tell us you were coming in for dinner," Natalie said, standing up as soon as we came through the front door. "We would have . . . oh, why hello, Archie," she finished, her voice going all sing-songy.

"Hello, Natalie," Archie replied, giving her a confused smile.

She slipped her arm through his and immediately began leading him toward their table. "Now, you two must come and sit with us, right, Clara?" She looked at me over her shoulder and gave me a thumbs-up. Oh, for the love . . .

"Actually, Nat, we were planning on working through dinner, you know, boring shoptalk, wouldn't really interest anybody and—"

"Hey, Arch, how's it going! I haven't seen you in a while, it's been ages," Leo said, jumping out of his seat and coming over to throw an arm around Archie's shoulder. The one Natalie wasn't currently curled into. "What's been going on?"

Leo I'd met before, when he and Roxie had spent a weekend in New England and stopped in Boston to take me to dinner. Sandy-blond hair, crazy green eyes, and all farmer-boy hot. It was a wonder Roxie spent any time vertical. Born into one of the wealthiest families in America, he'd left the family banking

business behind to start up Maxwell Farms, an organic organiza-
tion here in town that was one of the nation's leading examples
of sustainably grown farming. Brains, money, good looks, he had
it all. But the best part was, he was a nice guy. Plus, he adored
Roxie, which gave him an A+ in my book.

"Not much, keeping busy, you know how it goes. How're
things on the farm?"

"About to blow up, it's our last little bit of quiet before the
crazy begins in a few weeks. We've already got things kicking in
the greenhouse."

"I'll bet. Roxie, good to see you again," Archie said, then nodded at the giant. "Oscar, I trust things are well at the creamery?"

I stared, honest to goodness stared, at the amount of incredible that unfolded in front of me. He stood up, but just seemed
to get taller and taller and taller. An ex–professional football
player, Oscar Mendoza was six feet six inches of fucking Poly-
nesian love god. Golden skin, chocolate-brown eyes, dark hair
pulled back in a ponytail that should technically straddle the
line between pretentious and cheesy but somehow worked, he
was known in these parts for three things. His incredible dairy,
his love for his woman, and his gift for gab.

"Archie. Hey" was his conversational offering, and a fist bump
that Archie took in stride. His next move was to pull Natalie over
to him, wrapping one hand firmly around her ass, a slow grin
spreading over his face as soon as she was back at his side.

"Clara, you haven't met Oscar yet." Natalie preened, leaning
against him.

"I've been hearing about you for forever it seems, I can't believe we've never met!" I extended my hand and it was engulfed
in what seemed like a grizzly bear paw.

"Nice to meet you, Clara," he replied. His words were short,
but his eyes were kind.

"Seriously, we'll bring over two more chairs, unless you'd rather sit alone? All that shoptalk?" Roxie offered, halfway toward the stack of chairs in the corner but giving me the chance to bug out.

I nodded. "Thanks, but we've got work to do and—"

"Nonsense, Ms. Morg—Clara." He stopped himself, then shrugged his shoulders. "Sounds like fun." Two chairs appeared instantly and I was ushered into one of them.

"Great," I said through clenched teeth as I was now perched across the table from the other two guys, neither of whom had said anything yet, but gave me another matching set of mischievous grins.

"Clara, this is Chad Bowman."

"Oh sure, *the* Chad Bowman, I've heard all about you," I said, grinning as I shook Chad's hand. "Roxie had a crush on this one in high school, right?"

"I did," Roxie confirmed. "And this is his husband, Logan, who I now have a crush on instead of Chad."

"It makes sense in a weird way." Logan laughed, also shaking my hand. They both looked back and forth between me and Archie several times, wondering what exactly might be going on here. While I'd also love an answer to that very question, I silently asked them, with my eyebrows only, to shut it about the alley porn they'd just witnessed.

Chad's eyebrows asked if it was a secret.

My eyebrows said yes, yes it was.

Logan's eyebrows waggled several times, telling me that while it was hot, and it was, my secret was safe with them.

Archie was oblivious to all of this, already engrossed in a conversation with Leo and Oscar about the Yankees' spring training and blah blah lips moving.

Settled now, Roxie leaned over. "Chad here is a town

councilman, he was the one who brought Natalie's firm in to help work on the Bailey Falls promotion."

"Yes, it's Chad I have to thank every time I have no cell reception or find myself whistling 'The Farmer in the Dell' under my breath like some crazy country person," Nat said, smacking her menu on the table. "What the hell am I ordering?"

"I hear the Zombie Cakes are really good," Roxie said out of the corner of her mouth.

"I hear the girl who makes Zombie Cakes is a little bit full of herself," I heard a familiar voice say as a tray full of water glasses was thunked down on the table in front of me. "And how in the world did I get stuck waiting on this table, huh?" I turned to see Trudy, a perpetual love-struck hippie who also happened to be Roxie's mother. "Why, Clara Morgan, I didn't know you were in town! Get up here and give me a hug and kiss."

I stood and was instantly enveloped in her arms, the familiar scent of patchouli mixed with french fries comforting. "Hi, Trudy."

"How are you? You visiting the girls?"

"Kind of."

Roxie piped up. "She's working her magic up at Bryant Mountain House, Ma. She's helping Archie out."

"Archie Bryant, I haven't seen you in forever." She patted him affectionately on the shoulder, then squeezed the length of his arm. "You need to come in here more often, you're too thin. You're getting the pot roast tonight, extra mashed potatoes." She looked down at me, still pinned under her other arm. "How about you, you got a race coming up that needs carb loading?"

"I don't, actually, not for a while."

"Then you get pot roast too." She peered deep into my eyes, searching. "You look like you need the iron. I'll put an extra slice on there for you. The rest of you knuckleheads figure out what you want, I'll be right back. Great to see you, Clara." She pushed me back into my chair, then suddenly looked at Archie and me like she just realized we were sitting next to each other. "Mm-hmm."

And with a wave of her pad and pen, she was off, muttering to herself about ginkgo biloba and vitamin D.

"So much for getting our work done," I murmured to Archie, and he leaned down closer.

"We can always take a drive afterward."

"Oh really?" I asked. He merely smiled, and bumped me with his elbow. Then we both realized we were very much in public and pulled away from each other, looking up, down, across the room, anywhere but at each other.

Butterflies from an elbow. This was dangerous.

✑

"What was Trudy saying about a race?" Leo asked.

"Clara's a runner. And a swimmer. Hell, Clara's an every-thinger," Natalie chirped.

Oscar dropped a kiss on her forehead. "Not a word, Pinup."

"Bite me, you knew what I meant, though."

"What kind of races do you do?" Leo asked.

"Endurance races, that kind of thing. I try and do several marathons a year, depending on where I'm working. If I can slip in a triathlon, I make it happen."

"You're a badass, aren't you?" Logan asked, and I shrugged.

"She's tough," Roxie replied, and her eyes met mine across the table. She was right. I was. I had to be.

"You ever do one of those mud courses?" Chad asked.

I nodded. "We were just talking about that on the way over here. There's one coming up soon in Syracuse, looks like a great course."

"That's the one I was telling you about!" Logan exclaimed, pounding Chad on the shoulder. "We gotta do it."

"Oh man, one of those Tough Mudders?" Leo asked, looking at Oscar. "What do you think, Mendoza, can you handle it?"

"Mud?" he asked. "Sure. It's just wet dirt."

"Excellent, you in, babe?" Leo asked, swinging an arm around his girl.

"How did I get involved in this? You boys go do that, Natalie and I will watch from the stands."

"Yeah, I'll go for hot dogs," Natalie replied, winking at Oscar.

"We're in, we're so in," Leo said, looking at Archie. "You're doing it, right?"

I started to speak up, wanting to get him off the hook, but once again he surprised me.

"Sure," he said with all the confidence of someone who'd just decided something a split second ago, but seemed pretty sure about it. "What the hell."

Excitement erupted around the table as everyone began congratulating themselves on their general awesomeness or in the case of Roxie and Natalie, an overall feeling of supportive disgust.

I listened to all of this, wondering how a simple night out to talk to Archie about his hotel had become this big friendship ball. Everyone talking over each other, laughing, joking, it was a bit chaotic and almost a little . . . overwhelming? In a good way, but there was a moment when I had to sit back a bit and just breathe, feeling all those personalities banging into each other and rushing over me.

I wasn't used to all the chatter. I'd seen Hollywood's glorified version of what a big family dinner was, but I'd never been smack-dab in the middle of it. I listened to the conversations as they zinged around, I laughed along with everyone, but there was a part of me that felt just a bit . . . on the outside. My usual default, but this time I was on the inside, I was the inside. Why did it feel overwhelming, then?

I didn't feel lonely, never let myself go there. So why, when I was surrounded by my friends and their friends and having a grand time, did I feel somehow a bit hollow on the inside? Can you feel lonely when you're surrounded by people?

I rubbed at my chest, feeling an ache begin to set in behind my ribs. I was there, I was involved, but only partway. Part of me was hovering outside this, on the edge, unnoticed.

But then Archie did notice me. His eyes caught mine, and the warmth there burned right through me, into exactly those carved-out hollow places.

And when Leo started asking me about different races I'd done before, and Logan was telling me about the time he fell off a ropes course and how it was the coolest thing that had ever happened to him, I couldn't help but get pulled in, letting myself enjoy the evening for what it was. A night out with friends. And pot roast. And repeatedly accidental-but-very-much-on-purpose elbow bumping.

A few hours later we were headed back up the mountain. It had been a fun night, lots of laughing and storytelling and name-calling. Trudy made me promise to come over for dinner, and soon. I'd enjoyed meeting Oscar, and while Archie seemed to have literally not a thing in common with him, they got along quite well.

Chad and Logan seemed to get it—once it came out that I was working up at the mountain house, they'd exchanged a quick look and then a subtle nod in my direction. I'm sure I'd have to explain at some point, but for now it was contained.

Even contained, this was a risk and I couldn't have that. This only had one possible outcome from where I was sitting, and there was no way it could end well. I chanced a glance over at Archie's profile as he drove. Those long fingers wrapped around the steering wheel, gracefully tapered. Strong nose, chiseled jawline, full lips, now turned up in a small, secretive smile. He'd enjoyed himself tonight. Had it been a while? I kind of got the feeling it might have been.

"Do you get out much?" I asked.

"Explain."

"Out," I repeated, tucking my legs underneath me and facing him across the console. "Out and about. With friends. With . . . whoever."

"Not really, no," he answered, turning smoothly into the driveway toward the resort.

"Which part?"

"I tend to be pretty buried up at the hotel, if that's what you're asking, not a ton of time for a social life."

"I see."

"And if you're also asking whether or not I'm dating anyone, which I think you are, the answer to that is the same."

"I wasn't asking."

"Okay."

"Because we work together."

"You work *for* me, technically," he replied, with more than a hint of humor.

"I work for your father, technically. And anyway, it doesn't matter, because what happened back there, the whole make-out by the trash cans, it can't happen again."

"Agreed." He nodded.

I looked at him carefully. He'd agreed awfully quickly. "I'm serious, Archie, it's a bad idea."

He pulled the car over suddenly, off to the side of the road. Killing the lights, he turned to me. "I know what a bad idea it is, Ms. Morgan. I know every single reason why this cannot and will not happen again."

"Good," I said uneasily. "Then we're in agreement."

"We're in agreement." He nodded. "We're also in agreement that what we both want me to do right now is pull you across this console and see how fast I can get you naked on my lap, but that's not going to happen." His jaw clenched. "Because we're in agreement."

"Oh Jesus, yes, I am so agreeing," I said, aware that I was panting as I said it.

Carefully, and with great effort, he put the car in Drive and we headed back to the hotel.

Chapter 11

"If you close the east wing for renovations, and fill the west wing to capacity with your existing bookings, you'll be able to save some money on housekeeping by not bringing on the extra help for the summer season so early. Plus, then guests won't feel so spread out."

"Spread out?"

"Dude, I've practically got my own floor, do you know how spooky it is down there?"

"Fun fact: did you know that at the turn of the century, the twentieth not the twenty-first, something happened in a room just a few down from yours when—"

"If you finish that story I will walk out of this meeting so fast, Mr. Bryant, your head will spin. Have you ever read some of your online reviews? This place is known for its, and I quote, 'abundance of spooky hallways.'"

"Duly noted, Ms. Morgan. Spooky hallways. Got it. Continue."

Archie and I were meeting over breakfast in a quiet corner of the dining room. I'd insisted we be in public, in a brightly lit area to boot, to make sure no making out occurred. And we were back to Mr. Bryant and Ms. Morgan. But I couldn't deny the innate thrill I felt when he called me by my name.

Clara.

He said it like he enjoyed saying it, like he was happy to string those letters together in the hopes of getting me to turn my head.

And inside my own head was the only place I'd be indulging this thought; I couldn't let it manifest again and run wild. Again.

So I took steps to make sure. When he came in this morning, I'd already commandeered a large round table against the window and had my plans spread out everywhere. We needed to hash some things out once and for all before we brought it to everyone else this afternoon. And having a few feet of table in between was incredibly important, especially when he got that hungry gaze and started looking around for something to push me up against.

"Why did you stick me in that room anyway?" I asked, tucking into a bowl of steel-cut oats. It was raining again today, so while I couldn't run outside I'd managed five miles on the treadmill, and I was starving. The breakfast buffet here was pretty good, hard to mess up breakfast, and was full of anything and everything you could think of. Unfortunately they set out a spread like there was a full house when there were fewer than fifty guests here right now. The amount of food was insane.

"You think I had anything to do with that?" he asked all serious. But it was his eyes that gave him away, dancing behind those tortoiseshell rims.

"Is it common practice to stick a guest two miles away from the next one?"

"You seemed like a girl who'd enjoy some . . . privacy."

"Do I also seem like a girl who keeps bread crumbs in her pocket? Because I practically have to drop them to find my way back each night."

He rolled his eyes. "I didn't put you at the end of the hall, I put Melanie Bixby at the end of the hall." He gave me a pointed look. "Clara Morgan wasn't due to check in that night."

"Point taken. Now that we've established I'm a sneaky fucker, I'll be switching rooms. Suite, please and thank you."

"You want a suite now?" He laughed.

"I checked with Becky in reservations, the Tower Lakeside suite isn't booked until mid-April. Gimme."

"That's the most luxurious suite we have."

"I'm aware."

"We normally keep that suite empty in case of last-minute royalty."

"Last-minute royalty? I sometimes wonder if you even hear yourself."

He had the decency to look sheepish. "I admit, it doesn't happen that often anymore, but it has in the past."

"Right, in the past. And the woman who's here in the present to save your future would like to move in by noon."

He studied me for a moment, seeming to weigh my words. "Done," he finally pronounced. "Pack your bags, Ms. Morgan, you're moving on up."

"Story of my life." I grinned.

"I'd like to hear that sometime," he replied, and my grin froze. "Have you always lived in Boston?"

"Mm-hmm." I nodded through my frozen smile. "I'd like to go over some thoughts about the room renovations, particularly what you call the Victorian rooms."

"It's the oldest part of the hotel," he answered, looking at me carefully. "What part of Boston, where's your family from?"

"Oh. All over. Here and there." I pointed to the Victorian wing on the map in front of me. "If it's the oldest part of the hotel, that explains why it's also the stuffiest."

"I beg your pardon?" Archie said, positively offended. But offended meant he was off the scent.

"Beg me all you want, it's stuffy and needs a freshening up." I sighed in relief when I saw the little vein pop out on his left temple. That meant he was ready to argue and would forget asking me questions about where I grew up. I never knew how to answer those questions—you start telling someone you lived in foster care most of your life, and the pity parade started immediately. I hated parades.

But lucky for me that temple was throbbing. "Do you have any idea how much the antiques in those rooms are worth? And you want to bring something new, something cookie-cutter, in there?"

"I'd love for you to tell me when exactly I mentioned the words 'cookie' or 'cutter,' because that's the last thing I want to do."

"You say words like 'freshen up' and I hear modern and streamlined and boring and suddenly we're an airport Marriott."

I slammed my spoon down, oatmeal flying. "Yes, that's exactly why you hired me, so I could turn this place into an airport Marriott. Would you give me just the slightest amount of credit here?"

"How can I possibly when you are literally turning my entire world upside down?"

He flung his own spoon down in response, and a grapefruit wedge plopped into my coffee cup. We stared at each other as if in a standoff, both of us breathing heavily, faces flushed, fists clenched. Our waiter circled nervously, no doubt waffling back and forth between quickly cleaning up the mess his boss had made and not intruding into a heated conversation.

Archie's glare made up the waiter's mind, and he scurried away with a muffled "I'll just give you two a moment."

I folded my cloth napkin gracefully, stood up, and threw it onto my empty seat.

"There's no one staying on the third floor in the Victorian wing right now."

He looked back at me, his expression saying, *Am I supposed to know what that means?* "Go get a key for one of the rooms and meet me up there in twenty minutes," I instructed. "I'm going to show you exactly what I mean."

There it was. The fire. Hidden behind the tailored suit and the preppy glasses. "Make it fifteen," he shot back.

I walked quickly back to my room to grab my camera. I wanted some pictures of these tired old rooms to show them to a few designers for some feedback, get some fresh ideas for how to renovate these rooms, bring them into the now instead of keeping them in the creaky old past that this guy seemed to want to live in!

Damn this guy! There was no way I'd be able to do my job with him fighting me at every turn, not to mention get any work done when the same fighting made not only my blood boil, but other parts of me also get warm in the storm.

Did he know when he was irritated he chewed his lower lip?

Did he know when he was angry his skin paled and his freckles jumped out?

Did he know when he was frustrated his voice lowered and got all kinds of gravelly?

Did he know it was all I could do to stop myself from launching over the breakfast table and wrestling him to the ground amid oatmeal flakes and plopping grapefruit?

I ran out of my room, down the main stairs, and across the lobby, getting more worked up as I went. Never had I ever encountered such a roadblock as this fucking guy. This breakfast meeting was supposed to be the beginning of a collaborative effort to save this place, and it was already beginning to unravel because I wanted to make necessary changes and he wanted to just keep on arguing. How can I work like this? How can I function?

I hit the main staircase on the opposite side and ran up two flights, arriving on the landing just in time to see Archie come around the corner at the other end.

He held a gold key on a ring, which he spun around his finger. We walked toward each other.

"Room three-seventeen good enough for you?"

"Perfect, nice and stuffy," I replied. I dipped my head toward the door, indicating he should open it.

"What you think is stuffy, Ms. Morgan, is what we like to call classic," he said, slipping the key into the lock smoothly and turning the knob.

"Whatever, just get me inside and out of this spooky hallway."

He shot me a look over his shoulder, then pushed the door, holding it open for me to go first.

The rooms were smaller in this part of the hotel, lacking actual closets but having large armoires to house clothes. No Murphy beds either. But given that this was the Victorian wing, every single surface was covered in a lace doily. The cabbage roses that were in my room were here, times eleventy. Damask rose–printed wallpaper, portraits on the walls depicting fruit bowls and water pitchers framed by flowery gilt edging, and small uncomfortable-looking ladder-back chairs were flanking the window.

"Ladies and gentlemen, Grandma Esther's room." I walked the length of the room, pausing to admire the view of the mountains in the distance. No matter the stuffy, each room still had a helluva view. It had just started to rain, just barely a pitter-patter, but the mountains were still there.

"Every piece in this room is an antique," he said, standing in the doorway.

"Every piece in this room is an antique," I agreed, playing with the fringe on an old lamp, "but it also looks like Nellie Oleson might go running through here at any second on her way into the mercantile."

"Who is Nellie Oleson?"

"Forget it," I said, crossing over to the bed, "my point is, look at this bed. It's an antique, but, for God's sake, it's a full size. Not a king, not even a queen, but a full. Who the hell sleeps in a full-sized bed anymore?"

"People. People do it all the time."

"No, they really don't. Unless you're grad students in your first apartment, couples want at least a queen. And speaking of doing it, you need to be courting the weekend-away guest, the married couples who want to get away from their kids and spend a romantic weekend up in the mountains. Believe me, when they get here, they'll want to do it in a big bed. A king, ideally. Doing it in a full-sized bed just feels like you're still making out at your parents' house."

"I can't believe I'm having this conversation," he said, shaking his head.

"Believe it, hotel boy, people fuck when they go on vacation."

"Ms. Morgan, I don't think there's any need for language like that, please keep your voice down."

"And they don't want to fuck at Grandma Esther's!" I said just as Mrs. Banning from housekeeping walked by.

"Well hello, what's going on here?" she said, her eyes lighting up like a cat who just saw Tweety Bird.

Archie's jaw clenched. "Nothing, Mrs. Banning. Just discussing some ideas Ms. Morgan has for breathing new life into our stuffy old hotel rooms."

"Oh, that's wonderful!" she exclaimed, clapping her hands together. "I've always thought some nice new lace curtains would work wonders to—"

"Thank you, Mrs. Banning," Archie said, quickly patting her on the shoulder and closing the door. He turned back to me just as quickly. "Are you always this crass when you speak to a boss?"

"My boss is your father, and he hasn't made me nearly as irritated as you have."

"Ms. Morgan, let me tell you—"

I held up my hand. "Stop. Literally, stop. I'd love to go another ten rounds with you on who's got the bigger dick, but honestly—"

"If that's actually in question, then perhaps you have something to tell me that's not visually apparent?"

"—it's time to get some work done. Since we seem to be unable to get through a conversation without actually deciding something before the fighting begins, I'm going to tell you everything I think we need to be doing to turn this place around. Since we seem to be unable to stay on topic when we're both allowed to speak, here's what I propose. You will listen, you will not speak, and when I am done you may ask questions, but not before. Agreed?"

He fumed. He nodded.

"First, we revise. The hotel closes for ten weeks each winter, which we've already discussed. I've got a formal proposal I'll email to you for review—it has all the details on how to handle staffing changes, existing reservations, all that fun stuff that we could argue over for hours or you can just read it, digest it, and then tell me what a genius I am."

He opened his mouth, and I pointed at him. "Nope, not done."

He closed his mouth. He fumed. He nodded.

"Second, the room renovations. When I said stuffy, I probably could've used another word. How about 'dated'? I don't want to get rid of any of the antiques, I agree they're beautiful and perfect and the workmanship is exquisite and all the other platitudes that begin and end with 'they don't make 'em like that anymore.' So they stay. Some of them. Some of them could maybe be repurposed. Did you know you can take antique bedsteads and convert them into modern sizes to fit a mattress made today? And for some, maybe it's time to say bye-bye. Can you imagine how much fun selling off some of this stuff would be? Own a piece of Bryant Mountain House history, or something like that. The point is, even the antiques that stay don't have to necessarily live in the land of flower and doily. I have a designer in mind who I think would be perfect for the job. She worked on a hotel redesign in California that is stunning and could be very much in line with the DNA of Bryant Mountain House."

He opened his mouth, thought about it, then closed it again.

"If you were going to say anything about how in the world could I possibly know the DNA of this place in the short time I've been here, save it. It's my job to know the DNA, okay? I've got this."

Onward he fumed. Onward he nodded.

"Third, we revive. I want to bring Natalie in, make a bigger pitch for this place to be featured more prominently in the Bailey Falls campaign. While you were mentioned briefly in the initial rollout, I want us front and center in the second phase. Fourth, I want to bring in the community, get them more involved in this place. Chad mentioned to me the other night that he thought the town council would be really receptive to any promotions we wanted to do, and I'd like to talk to him again about it, feel him out. Holidays are a huge deal up here for your loyal guests, I'd like to make it part of the greater Bailey Falls experience as well. Halloween, Thanksgiving, Christmas, all of it. Easter is right around the corner, let's really go to town. You've talked to Roxie about bringing her Zombie Cakes in—do it. And while you're at it, bring up Leo to help overhaul your summer garden, you could even sponsor a farmers' market up here in the summer, get people up here to see what it's like. Hell, let Oscar move some cows onto . . . well . . . no . . . cows can stink up the joint . . . but at least keep his butter in stock. The whole country is going gangbusters for locally grown, sustainably grown food, and you literally have producers in your backyard. Make it happen. You've priced this town right out of the mix for the most part, no one who lives around here can actually afford to stay up here, and that's no good. You could be filling up this place in the off-season with local residents, and that's exactly what we're going to do."

I stopped to breathe. He wasn't fuming or nodding anymore, just listening.

"Finally, the last thing I want to mention today. Rejuvenate. Price reductions. Yes, this is a luxury hotel catering to a luxury clientele, and I don't want to lose that experience. But I think we can work on the pricing at slower times of the year, implement a resident pricing system where we offer deep discounts for local residents, and start building up and going after the corporate retreat business. It used to be something this hotel was heavily involved with, and then after '08 it slowed down to the point where now it's almost nonexistent. We can get it back, I know we can. But we need to be competitive on pricing. After a few years, when things are on the upswing, you can revisit it. But for now, we need to dig deep." I stopped, knowing I'd just thrown a lot of information at him all at once.

The only sound was the rain, which had changed from a pitter-patter to a full-on gusher. It was coming down so hard it was eclipsing every other sound. Outside the mountains were gone, everything was gone, the rain like a wall, literally a sheet of water pouring down, blurring the outside world and trapping us inside.

He walked over to the window, looking out at that wall of water, then back at me, and then scrubbed his hands over his face like he was trying to scrape it all away. It was a lot to take in. Everything would change.

"Are you done?" he asked, his voice muffled by his hands and by the rain.

"For now," I replied, rocking on my heels a bit.

He took a step, then another, then another, until he was standing just in front of me, looking down. His eyes were serious, searching, poring over every inch of my face. I waited, giving him time to let this all sink in. He'd need to think about this, weigh some options, look at everything I'd presented. Which is why what he said next surprised the hell out of me.

"I'm in. Let's do it."

My breath let out in a whoosh. "What? Which part?"

"All of it," he said, shaking his head even so. "Except the part about the staffing. We'll need to work something out. Cash out some vacation, extend some vacation, hell, I'll even stop taking a salary for a while, but I'm not letting anyone go."

"That's generous."

He offered me a rueful smile. "What can I say, they're family. You know how it is with family."

I felt an unexpected lump rising in my throat, and I willed it to go back down. "Okay, well, um, we can go over the details now, if you like, why don't we go back to—"

"Oh no, Ms. Morgan. I think we may have just agreed on something, don't you think?" he said, reaching out and looping a finger through my belt buckle, pulling me forward.

I swallowed hard, harder than normal because that damn lump was still there.

"We shouldn't," I said, as I 100 percent let him pull me even closer. "Really, this is a terrible idea."

Should I?

You're alone with him in a hotel room. Kiss him.

Hmm, we were safe in here, no one could see. Plus, I'd just won an argument, so I should treat myself a little, right?

Maybe just a peck?

Just the one. I leaned in and quickly brushed my lips lightly over his, instantly feeling that spark of flame beginning to fan something that was getting harder and harder to ignore. I kissed him just the one time, and then looked down as his hands slipped from my buckle to my waist. I caught a flash of metal and realized, again, that this man was still wearing his wedding ring.

Dear God, he was still wearing his wedding ring. His wife was dead, several years now, and he was still wearing her ring. It was sweet, really. When you think about it in the abstract. And kind. And good. But as the person he was currently holding, it was also unnerving. And a little strange. And exactly what I needed to see to remind me of yet another reason why this just couldn't happen.

He nuzzled my neck and with a strength I didn't know I had, I pushed him away. "I'll send you that email, put all those ideas together. Then how about we meet in the conference room this afternoon? Start making some real plans?" I scooped up his hands and gave them a squeeze, but moved them safely away from me. It was harder to think clearly when there was actual touching involved.

He looked puzzled. "You're leaving . . . now?"

I didn't want to. Jesus Christ, I didn't want to, which is why I knew I should. I also didn't trust myself to actually answer, so I nodded instead. He looked like he wanted to argue with me, to try to get me to stay . . . but in the end nodded back. This wasn't going to happen. It couldn't.

"Why don't you go out first, I'll wait here a bit," he suggested, straightening his tie.

"Sneaky," I chided. "But a good idea. Don't forget about switching my room, though."

"Your room?" he asked, confused.

"My new suite, remember? I expect a TV in there, by the way."

"No TV."

"Goddammit," I muttered.

I heard him laugh as I peeked into the hallway and made sure it was all clear. By the time I made it to the staircase, the lump in my throat was long gone. I was an expert at squashing it all down. I'd been doing it my entire life.

"You never call, you never write, it's like you've forgotten all about me."

"When have I ever written you?"

"An actual letter? Never. But an email every now and again might be nice, just so I know you haven't fallen off the mountaintop."

"I haven't fallen off the mountaintop."

"Well, that's a start," Barbara said, and we both laughed. "I know when you first dig in at a new property you tend to go radio silent."

"You know me, you know me very well," I replied, feeling my grin spread across my face. No one on the planet, not even Roxie and Natalie sometimes, knew me like my boss did. Friends got some of you, most of you, but when you spend forty hours a week with someone, they see everything. And she could read me like a book. I don't rely on much in this world, but knowing I had someone like Barbara in my corner was a constant that I needed in my life.

And knowing me like she did, she knew I could handle things on my own and gave me a very long leash. I just had to check in from time to time which, when buried in my work, I had a tendency to forget to do.

"Sorry I've been MIA, I meant to throw up a flare so you knew I was still breathing."

"No big, but now that I've got you, how are things going, kiddo?"

"I should have an actual status report ready to email to you tomorrow, but so far, so good. Really good, actually. Full swing, all systems firing, green across the board."

"What's wrong." A statement, not a question, from my boss was never a good thing.

"What do you mean?"

"When you start in with your mission control lingo I know something's up. Spill."

I bit my lip. Whatever could be up? I'm only making out with the man who hired me whenever we can steal a few minutes away, the man who will ultimately decide whether I'd done a good job or not, the man who holds the fate of my partnership in his hands while I'm dying to hold something else in my hands, whatever could be up?

"It's all good, Barbara, I just get carried away sometimes. They were showing *SpaceCamp* in the TV room the other night."

"Mm-hmm," she said, not buying it for a second. "How's the Bryant family doing?"

"Pretty good, I think. Some resistance at first, especially from the son, but he's on board now."

I heard her shuffling some papers. "Archibald, right?"

I stifled a laugh. I'd have to ask him about that later. "He goes by Archie, but yes. He's playing ball now."

"That's good. How fast do you think you can wrap this up?"

I frowned. "Um, we're just at the very beginning stages, but I'm on track. Why, what's up?"

"Nothing, nothing's wrong. Just some stuff going on here at the home office. I'd love to have this locked down sooner rather than later, that's all."

Now I wondered what was up. "Is there something I need to know?"

"Oh goodness, no, nothing like that." She laughed, and I instantly felt better. If Barbara said everything was good, then everything was good. "Just thinking ahead to the fall, trying to line things up. You know me, always planning ahead."

"Did you ever find out if the Waterside Hotel in Virginia was bringing someone in to consult?"

"I did, and let me tell you that story, it's a doozy," she said, and launched into the tale. We chatted for a while and I brought her up to speed on everything going on at the hotel. She made some notes, made some suggestions that were astute as always, and by the end of the conversation I thought she'd forgotten about the beginning of the conversation.

"You take care of yourself up there, and if you ever need to talk, you know you can always talk to me. You know that, right, kiddo?"

"Of course I do," I assured her, crossing my fingers behind my back. I could, just not about this.

Maybe after I was partner. Then I could tell her. Only after. Until then, I was determined to squash this down.

What I would have an even harder time squashing down was the goose-down featherbed that came standard in my new

Tower Lakeside suite! A king bed, four-poster no less, stretched out before a grand fireplace, resplendent in rose marble with ebony inlaid trim. If I stacked my pillows three high I found I could see both the crackling fire and the lake, the very definition of Hudson Valley luxury. Two bedrooms, two bathrooms, two balconies, and one glorious sitting room—this suite had a waiting list a mile long in the summer season. But good luck to anyone on that list. The same three families reserved it all summer long, June through August. They'd been coming here for years, multiple generations vacationed here together, occasionally renting out entire floors of the main tower. I'd seen how much it cost per night; I didn't need a calculator to know that if they could afford four weeks of that, they deserved to see both fireplace and lake at the same time.

I used one of the bedrooms as my base of operations, asking housekeeping to help me clear out the furniture and move in my heavy artillery. Dry-erase boards, vision boards, a cheese board courtesy of Bailey Falls Creamery, and an entire wall dedicated to parking lot questions . . . the land of questions that hadn't yet been answered but would be, and soon.

Things were beginning to move up on this mountain. We were still a couple of weeks away from Easter, plenty of time to roll out a few new ideas before the first wave of loyal guests returned.

The team was mostly on board with all the new changes, and Jonathan was ecstatic. He, like Archie, had initial concerns about the price reduction, but I'd eventually won him over, although we were still working out the details. He loved the idea about bringing the town back into the picture, and wondered why they hadn't done it sooner. "Sometimes when it's right in front of you, you can't see it," he quipped one day while we previewed some of Natalie's TV spots that would run in the big East Coast markets next week.

Roxie was a big help as well. When she came up to chat with Archie about featuring Zombie Cakes on the dessert menu, the existing pastry chef took one look at her 7 Layer Blueberry Dream Cake and threatened to quit on the spot. The head chef was only too happy to take her resignation—apparently that'd been brewing for quite some time.

"He's not leaving because of all the changes, is he?" I asked Mrs. Toomey when I heard the news. I'd hurried down to the kitchen before the dinner service staff started to find out.

"Mostly no, he's been thinking of retiring for a while now, but I think he feels this place needs some new blood to take over, someone new in the kitchen who is a little more up-to-date."

"Oh no, I feel terrible," I moaned, leaning on the counter with my head in my hands. "I never wanted anyone to feel like they were being pushed out."

"That's not what's happening here, dear, not at all. These changes are good. They needed to be made. The staff is excited, that I can promise you. And I'll tell you something else," she said, looking over her shoulder to make sure no one could hear her.

"What?" I asked warily, also looking over my shoulder.

"I haven't seen Archie this happy since . . . well . . . since . . ."

"Since before his wife died?" I asked, wincing.

She thought a moment, her eyes going soft. "You know, I have to admit, I don't think I've actually ever seen him this happy. And that's the truth."

And with that, she turned on her heel and headed back into the dining room.

Huh.

Speaking of Archie, the man was a machine. No no, not like that.

He worked sixteen hours a day. He never stopped. Once I got his buy-in on the changes, he was all in. Something I'd noticed in that very first meeting was proving true. He really valued other people's opinions, and he listened. That was hard to find sometimes in a boss, but he really went out of his way to make sure the entire team was involved and felt they were being heard.

Had he always worked this hard? Or had work taken over his life since his wife passed away? When there was pain or hurt, or bad memories crowded in, work could be a literal lifeline, taking your mind away from what you couldn't deal with and channeling it into something good, something tangible.

Was work how he coped too?

One night after dinner, I took a wrong turn and found myself in a part of the hotel I hadn't been before. Having nowhere to go and not at all tired, I wandered a bit before heading back to my room.

Tucked away at the far end of the east wing, on the first floor down by some of the offices, there was a portrait gallery. Every generation of the Bryant family, starting with paintings of Ebenezer and Theophilus—the brothers who had started it all—hung on the walls. As I walked along the hallway, the same expression reflected back to me in many of the faces. Strong, fearless, patrician, and yet somehow all carefully guarded. No chink in the armor here, no insight into what made any of these folks tick beyond a sense of duty to their family and the life they'd created here on their mountain.

I could see suggestions of Archie here and there, Jonathan too—they all shared some similar features. The elegant jawline, the strong straight nose, the indigo eyes, all clearly noteworthy throughout the family history.

But at the end of the line there was a portrait I hadn't expected to see, but was unable to tear my eyes away from.

Ashley Bryant. Archie's wife. She was beautiful.

Icy blond hair, tumbling in soft curls. Gorgeous green eyes, captured by the artist in a tone resembling freshly grown summer grass. She had a warm smile, high cheekbones, and the same easy going "isn't life grand?" expression that everyone in this family seemed to have.

An image jumped to mind of a picture I had in my apartment, one of the few photographs I'd actually taken the time to frame. Me with Natalie and Roxie after just crossing the finish line in my first-ever Tough Mudder race. Literally covered head to toe in dirt and mud, hay and somehow sunflower petals, I'd finished strong and immediately hugged my friends who'd come to cheer me on, and got them just as dirty as I was. It was one of my favorite pictures of the three of us. I told them I'd framed it because it was a great picture of all of us smiling, and that was true, but I also selfishly loved that picture because it reminded me of how strong I was. Covered in earth and sweat was when I felt the most alive, the most able to conquer anything and everything that got in my way, and whenever I looked at that picture I felt a flickering of pride, an emotion that wasn't one I experienced often.

Ashley didn't seem like a woman who'd ever had a hair out of place, a dress that was wrinkled, or forgotten a birthday. She had engraved stationery. She drove an immaculate car. This was a woman who'd lived for a finger sandwich.

None of this I knew for certain, mind you, but I'd been around enough of these types my entire adult life. But she wasn't snobby. She was likely a genuinely good person, the kind you think you'll hate immediately, but she's so darn charming it's impossible to do so.

I didn't know her. I barely knew Archie for that matter. But staring at this gorgeous woman, cut down in her prime, I could see she was a perfect match for her husband.

A husband who was still wearing his wedding ring.

I allowed myself another moment to study this seemingly perfect woman, and when I was done tallying up all the many ways I was her total opposite, I went back to my room.

Chapter 12

"Is it weird that there's this internationally known, highly rated resort twenty minutes from where I grew up and still live, and to this day I've never spent a night there?"

I was sitting across from Chad Bowman, town councilman and perpetual high school crush, listening as he told me his impressions of Bryant Mountain House. After meeting him at Callahan's, we'd made plans to get together to talk about ways Bailey Falls and the resort could help each other out. I'd also wanted to pick his brain on how the town saw the Bryant family, and what they could do to win them back around, as it were.

"It does seem strange," I agreed, scooping up another bite of my blue-plate special. It made sense that we'd meet at the diner since I'd promised Trudy I'd stop by the next time I was in town. And once I found out the special of the day was chicken and dumplings? Heaven. "But surely you've been up there before."

"My family *always* made a point of going to their Easter brunch, we never missed that, and then when Logan and I moved back here we've gone hiking up there a few times, bought the day pass."

"Easter brunch. Roxie talked about that too."

"Oh yeah, everyone brought their kids up there when I was growing up. We always did Easter, sometimes we'd go for the Christmas dinner if my mom didn't feel like cooking, but we never missed Easter. Egg hunt on the lawn, then brunch with those fucking killer hot cross buns."

I scribbled in my notebook. "Roxie mentioned those too, they must be really good."

"If I could figure out how, I'd have those buns in my mouth every single day."

"Watch your mouth, Chad, this is a family establishment," Trudy said as she sailed by with a tray of drinks. Ten seconds later she sailed by again, this time whacking him on the head with a stack of menus.

"Trudy, get your mind out of the gutter, you're as bad as your daughter." He grimaced, rubbing his head. He looked at me. "You knew what I meant, right?"

I blinked innocently. "All I heard was how much you loved those buns."

"I'd kill to sink my teeth into a pair of those buns right now . . . ow!"

"What did I just tell you?" Trudy asked, leaning over the back of the booth and leaving a bright pink lipstick–stained kiss on his cheek. She winked at me. "How're those dumplings?"

"They're amazing, like light and fluffy balls."

Chad raised his eyebrows, waiting.

Trudy said nothing.

"You're not gonna smack her for talking about balls?" he asked.

"Now who's got their mind in the gutter?" Trudy sang out, exiting stage left but not before landing one more good whack on Chad's head.

"Honestly, I don't even know why I come in here anymore,"

he grumbled, leaning over the back of the booth and making sure everyone heard him say, "the service is terrible!"

"Says you!" came the reply from the kitchen, where Trudy had just disappeared through the swinging door.

"Anyway," he said, pushing away his now-empty plate, "where were we?"

"Buns."

"Right!" He rubbed his head absently, no doubt still feeling Trudy's thwap. "The thing is, other than those holidays, it never really felt like the resort was a part of the town. I mean, don't get me wrong, almost everyone I know has had at least a summer job at one time or another, but it always felt . . . detached from the town itself. It was always filled with rich families who came up to get away and sometimes they'd come down into town and marvel over how adorable our little country hamlet was, but then they'd go back up there and relax in their rocking chairs and play their croquet and have their fancy afternoon tea. Not that there aren't rich people here in Bailey Falls. And not that we don't have fancy afternoon tea, because Hattie Mae's tea shop over on Elm Street serves traditional English cream tea every day at three on the dot. But I don't know . . ." He sighed, his eyes going a bit dreamy. "Bryant Mountain House always just felt a little too highbrow for me. I can afford to stay there now, but do I really want to? Eh."

"Eh?"

"Eh. I'll get around to it. I must admit, I've always wondered how it is at nighttime. All those long hallways. Is it creepy?"

I snorted, thinking back to my first few nights there. "A bit. But we're working on that. And I'm working on a plan to make it more accessible to townsfolk, as I'm calling you all in my head."

"Makes us sound like characters in a Dickens classic."

"There's something very classic about everything up here,

the hotel, the town, the people." I scooped up the last bite of chicken. "The dumplings."

"Don't let Roxie hear you, she and Trudy fought for a week when she tried to change that recipe."

"Change it, why would she change it?"

"She wanted to add kale."

"No."

"Yes. Trudy put her foot down."

"Listen, Roxie is my girl. But kale does not belong in chicken and dumplings."

"I hear that." He laughed. "But I know what you mean about this place, there's nowhere else quite like the Hudson Valley. Logan and I were both living in the city, that's where we met. But we knew once we were ready to settle down, we wanted a small town. He came home with me one weekend to meet my family, took one look at the town square and started looking at Realtor sites that very night."

I looked out the large picture window in the front of the diner, the late-afternoon sun shining down brightly through the trees. Green was busting out all over, from the tips of the trees to the onion grass beginning to tuft up the front lawns. Crocuses peeked out from behind tree trunks and around a few listless leftover snow piles; daffodils and tulips had begun pushing up through the earth. From the window I could see the four streets that made up the town square, and people were out and about for their afternoon shopping. There was a mom-and-pop grocery just across the square, a dance studio, a jewelry store, and what looked like an incredible dive bar. As I watched couples walking hand in hand, families with small kids, and older couples hurrying home from their shopping, everyone seemed happy. Everyone smiled at each other, and more often than not, they seemed to actually know the people they were passing.

"Roxie calls this place Mayberry," I mused.

"Correction, she calls it fucking Mayberry."

I folded my napkin in half. "I don't know why people always say that like it's a bad thing, there's definitely something to be said for fucking Mayberry."

"It has its moments," he agreed.

"I watched a lot of Nick at Nite when I was a kid, and I loved reruns of *The Andy Griffith Show*."

Chad smiled, and began to whistle the theme song.

"It's funny that Roxie had to move away to realize what she had here growing up." What I didn't say was that what she had here was something I would've killed for. Everything about this town screamed happiness, comfort, community.

Safety.

"Sometimes you need a different perspective to see it, though, you know? I never thought I'd come back, but seeing it through Logan's eyes? It fit. He came from a small town, and he always knew he wanted to end up there. Me, I figured I'd stay in the city."

"Manhattan?"

"Up here if you say the city it's just assumed you mean Manhattan. Basketball means the Knicks, baseball means the Yankees."

I laughed. "I know a bunch of Red Sox fans back home who'd say otherwise."

He groaned. "Oh man, I've been trying to place that accent. You're from Boston?"

"Born and raised."

"What part?"

I hesitated for just the tiniest of seconds. "All over, mostly South Boston."

"There was a guy I went to business school with from Boston, Back Bay, I think?"

I snorted. "Yeah, that was not my neighborhood."

"Is your family still there?"

My ears burned. "No. Are we getting cake? Let's get some cake." I waved at Trudy and mouthed the word *dessert* at her.

"You are full of mysteries, aren't you?"

"Who, me? I'm the most boring." I folded my napkin again.

"Okay, little miss make out in the alley."

"What alley?" Trudy asked, setting down the dessert menu.

"No alley, no nothing," I chirped, flashing a "keep quiet" glance at Chad. "How's the black walnut cake?"

"Roxie says it's awesome." Trudy laughed. "Don't tell my daughter, but I also think it's awesome."

"I'll take the awesome, then," I replied.

"Make it two awesomes," Chad agreed.

Trudy headed back to the kitchen, and I shook my head at Chad. "You, shut up with your alley talk."

"I will if you spill."

"Oh God, you're rhyming now?" I held my head in my hands. "Seriously, you can't tell anyone. No one knows."

"I am great with a secret. Just ask Homer over at the hardware store—no one but me knows about those magazines he keeps under the counter."

"And now me."

He looked crestfallen. "Oh shit. Oops. The point is, though, I can keep a secret. Logan and I haven't told anyone you're schtupping the hot hotel guy—"

"I am not schtupping the hot hotel guy!"

"—but believe me, we've been talking about it nonstop ever since we saw you in the alley"—Trudy showed up with two pieces of cake and a curious look on her face just then—"alley, alley cat. We want to adopt an alley cat. We're thinking about a pet, so it just makes sense to pick up one of those alley cats, right?" He nodded at me enthusiastically, which I mimicked vigorously.

"Well, you're in luck, I heard quite the racket the other night in the alley, almost like a moaning . . . must've been one of those alley cats in heat," Trudy said.

Chad and I both shoved enormous bites of cake in our mouths. She looked at us like we were crazy, and headed back to the kitchen, shaking her head.

"This is fucking great," I said over the mouthful.

"It is," he said, "and what else would be great is if you'd tell me the goddamn story before I actually have to get a goddamn cat."

"Ah jeez, how did we get onto this?"

"We got onto this because you got onto that," he said, pointing with his fork. "So how long has that been going on?"

"Okay look, there's nothing going on. Not officially. Or unofficially for that matter." I licked a bit of walnut off the tines of my fork, thinking back to that night. The way he'd pushed me up against the wall, the way his eyes seemed to glow when he looked at me, when he pressed into me and his fingers dug into my skin. "I will say, however, when you caught us in the alley, thank God you did because holy fuck can that man kiss like it's going out of style, and if you hadn't come along . . ."

Chad practically wiggled out of his seat he was so jubilant. "I knew it! I always knew that guy had it in him, he's always so together and serious and buttoned-up, but secretly you just know guys like that are wild in the sack. Tell me he is, even if he isn't, lie to me. But just make it a good lie, lots of details."

"Okay, slow down there, Councilman. I barely know you."

"By proxy," he said, although it was muffled by more cake.

"Pardon me?"

"By proxy, you know me by proxy through Roxie. Hey look, I am rhyming."

"I can't believe this conversation."

"The point is, I've known Roxie practically my entire life. And Natalie, I've got that girl wrapped around my little finger. They're your best friends, right?"

"Right?" I frowned, trying to follow the logic.

"So there, you and me, by proxy, are besties too. So gimme the dirt."

"Oh my God," I said, dropping my fork with a clatter. "If I had one wish, one wish in the world, it'd be to go back to that night and make sure you never saw us."

"And if I had one wish it'd be to go back five minutes earlier so I could see more of that super-hot make-out session." He grinned, waggling his eyebrows. "So give it up, girlie."

I folded my napkin, making it into a tight little origami-style ball. "Okay, you got me. I was making out with my boss, or boss's son, I don't honestly know which is worse. And it was hot. Crazy hot. And crazy stupid, which is why you can't tell anyone. Like, this is really bad, I've never done this before, I'm breaking literally every rule in the book. So please, you can't talk about this outside this table, right here, right now."

"Are we really back to that? I promise you, mum's the word." He patted my hand. "But come on, gimme something."

I sighed, then looked him dead in the eye. "He's got the softest lips."

His eyes widened. "I love it."

My eyes narrowed. "And very large hands."

"Stop it."

"And he's still wearing his wedding ring."

"Hmm."

"But that's not weird, right? I mean, they were together a long time."

"They were, they really were," Chad said, nodding. "He's

older than I am, we weren't at school together, but even I knew about them. They were prom king and queen, they were literally high school royalty. And then when she died, Jesus. Everyone felt so bad for the guy, I mean, can you imagine? Losing someone like that?"

I winced. I could. Maybe not in the same way, but I knew what it felt like to be the one left behind.

"Anyway, if this is happening with you two, whatever it is, I think it's great. You both clearly are into it, can't you figure out a way to make this work? He needs it, in so many ways. And if you don't mind my saying so, you need it too."

"You don't even know me," I said, raising an eyebrow.

He raised one right back. "Honey, a stranger could see you need to get some."

Chad's words stuck in my head on repeat the entire way back up to the resort. I mean, it had been a while, but long enough that you could see it on my face?

I started ticking off months on my fingers, and when the number of months exceeded the number of fingers . . .

"Holy shit, I do need to get laid," I mumbled to myself. And just like that, I came around that last bend and lookie lookie who was in the road.

Archie. Trench coat. Standing next to his car, the last bit of golden afternoon light shining down directly on him like some kind of divinely handsome intervention, an answered sexual prayer, as it were.

I pulled up alongside him, rolling down my window. "What the hell are you doing in the middle of the road?"

"A branch came down, I was moving it so those guys didn't

have to come down and do it," he said, nodding over his shoulder at the entrance shack. "What're you up to, heading in for the night?"

I looked up the mountain to where the warm, cozy hotel was waiting for me. Short ribs were on the menu tonight, my favorite. And they were showing *Deliverance* in the movie room as entertainment, which was tempting. And I did have about a hundred emails to answer, a stack of paperwork to proofread, and a book I'd checked out from the local library, *Hudson Valley: A History*.

Then I looked at Archie.

"You feel like doing something?" I asked. "Maybe get a drink?"

A slow smile spread across his face, and he nodded. "I'm just heading home."

"Great, pick a bar in town and I'll follow you and—"

"Or," he said, and everything on my body that could stand up straight did so immediately. "We could just have drinks at my place, Clara."

"Oh."

Oh.

Reflexively my right foot stepped down hard, revving the engine, and if it wasn't for already putting the car in Park, I'd have driven right off the cliff.

Shaking my head a little, I said a little bit dazed, "That'd be nice."

"Excellent." He chuckled, and jumped behind the wheel of his BMW. He waited for me to turn around, and with me following closely behind, he drove us to his home.

Every bump in the road, every stop sign, I kept hearing Chad's words echoing back to me . . . *Honey, a stranger could see you need to get some.*

Good God and *how*.

∽

He didn't live far from the resort. A few turns here and there, down a quiet country lane, and the house appeared out of nowhere. I wasn't really sure what Archie's house would look like. You could usually get a better idea of someone by seeing their house, it told the story people didn't. Was it messy? Clean? Modern? Traditional?

Huh. I wonder what mine said about me.

Single girl who is never home.

True. But Archie's, on the other hand . . .

Set back from the road in a thicket of trees was a cottage. Two story, gray cedar shake, bright red shutters and door. Long porch, complete with swing. Flower boxes under each window, naked now but easy to imagine spilling over with summer blooms. Gravel driveway, flanked by old-growth elm trees.

Beautiful. Charming. Archie's. And once upon a time . . . Ashley's.

I sat in the car a moment, staring up at this fairy-tale home, drumming my fingers on the wheel and wondering if I should turn around and head back to the hotel. But then he got out of his car, all slow grin and freckle and I couldn't resist smiling back.

He came to my door, opening it for me like a gentleman, and extended his hand to help me out.

Get out of the car, Clara.

I got out of the car. Slipping my hand into his and feeling that little butterfly jolt I felt each and every time I touched him, I let him lead me toward the house.

"It's lovely," I said, and I meant it. You couldn't look at this house and not think *wow*.

"It's old, turn of the century. It was part of a farm that the brothers bought when they created the preserve. Not technically part of the hotel but part of the original grounds. It was used as the groundskeeper's cottage for a long time—my parents lived here when they were first married, grandparents too."

"Keep it in the family," I said quietly, heading up the driveway.

"Hmm?"

"Nothing, just, your family, it's just . . . is it ever . . . what's the word . . . overwhelming?"

"How so?"

"Just, Bryant family this, Bryant family that, does anyone ever go off the reservation and do something else? Did you ever want to do anything else?"

"I don't know," he said, tilting his head as he considered. "Maybe? It's just all I've ever known." He unlocked the front door and held it open for me. "As far as anyone doing anything else, there've been a few who have gone and done their own thing."

"Traitors," I teased, and he chuckled.

"We stick them on the sixth floor when they come to stay." He winked. "West wing. *Your* wing. Some of them are still rattling around up there."

"I knew it!" I laughed, setting my purse down next to his briefcase in the entryway. He helped me with my jacket, hanging it on the tree next to his trench coat. "Oh. Wow."

The entryway opened up to an enormous living room, soaring high to the loft above. Fireplace, comfy-looking couches and chairs, and what I could already tell was a gourmet kitchen peeking around the corner.

"This is incredible."

"We did a major renovation about eight years ago, ripped out walls, added space on the second floor, made it our own, you know? My wife used to say that . . ." He trailed off, looking uncomfortable. He stared at the mantel, which I could now see was covered with pictures of Ashley.

He looked so confused, so clearly at war with what he wanted to say but felt like he shouldn't. I walked up to him, and slipped my hand into the crook of his arm. "What did she used to say?"

He smiled down at me, relieved. "That this place smelled like mothballs and it was about time some young people lived here."

"Ha!" I said, and more of that relief washed over his face. Relief that he'd been given permission to talk about her? To acknowledge that this was weird for him too? We were here, together, in the house he'd shared with his wife. Maybe coming back here wasn't such a good idea, maybe this place was too full of memories, too full of the past.

"Is this weird?" he suddenly asked, and I immediately began nodding vigorously.

"Glad it's not just me," he said, chuckling. "I'm kind of in untested waters here."

"Oh, I think we both are," I replied, looking around. "I've never gone home with the boss before." I chewed on my thumb-nail. "What the hell are we doing? I mean, this can't possibly go anywhere, there's literally a laundry list of reasons I shouldn't be doing this." I counted them off on my hand. "One, I work for you. Technically your father, but still, bad idea. Two, I'm leaving as soon as this job is done, off to the next hotel, off to the next project, likely never to return. Three, I don't get the sense that you've dated anyone since your wife so, holy shit, do I want to be the girl who gets to break you back in? No pressure there. Four, I don't even like you that much, you're kind of an asshole who just happens to be ridiculously good-looking, but that shouldn't outweigh the whole aforementioned asshole thing."

Five, reasons one through four pale in comparison to the real reason I can't do this, because you are exactly the kind of man I've dreamed of spending the rest of my life with and if this didn't work out it would break me.

"So you see," I whispered shakily, every part of me dying to touch more than just his blessed elbow, "what the hell are we doing?"

"I don't know," he answered, looking down at me. "You're incredibly rude, a know-it-all wrecking-ball girl who is more than a little bossy."

I laughed in spite of myself. "What lovely things to say, coming from a pretentious, snobby, incredibly rude himself hotel boy who'd rather rattle around spooky hallways and spend time with antiques than listen to reason."

"Spend time with antiques?"

"Yeah well, you like them so much," I huffed. Great comeback.

"I like *you* so much," he replied, "more than I ought to." My head and my heart heard those words at the same time and everything inside me liquefied. He reached down and traced a path along my jawline, pausing to gently brush against my bottom lip. "And you *are* bossy."

"So kiss me, Hotel Boy," I breathed, not caring about any of those perfectly thought out and completely true reasons.

He put his hands on me. He put his lips on me. And it was all I could do to still feel the earth underneath my feet. Because when this man kissed me, I forgot everything. And reasons one through five waved bye to the fucking bye.

"This is, and I hate to admit this, the best damn martini I've ever had."

"Is the fact that I made it the reason you hate to admit it?"

"It really is." I sipped. "But very nice."

We'd kissed for longer than I can say, and when we finally pulled apart, lips swollen and hungry for more, we both decided it was time to come up for air and have that drink.

It was precisely because we *were* hungry for more that we stopped—somehow knowing that taking it beyond the exploration we'd already indulged in would be going too far. And I think we both knew we weren't quite ready for that.

A stiff drink, however, *that* we were ready for. And Archie could mix a mean drink. Set into a cabinet in the living room was a fully stocked bar, complete with shakers and tongs and monogrammed glasses.

"Wedding gift?" I'd asked, as he tumbled ice into the shaker along with vodka and a kiss of vermouth.

"Why do you ask?"

"Just wondered," I said, watching as he expertly carved a lemon into two twists. "That's usually where people get this kind of stuff."

"Actually, it's a set I liberated from the hotel." He laughed, pouring the martinis into the tall-stemmed glasses etched with the letter *B*. "An old set from the forties, but Ashley was the one who had the monogram put on. Monograms are very important in my family, you might have noticed."

"Yeah, it's been hard to miss the giant *B* on the towels in my room, or on the coasters, or on the sheets."

"Family name, family business, gotta keep up appearances." He smiled, handing me my glass.

We'd moved onto the couch, getting comfortable.

"Did you ever want to do anything other than this? I mean, inherit the family dynasty?"

He raised an eyebrow, but then grew thoughtful. "I don't think so, not really anyway. The last generation of my family has been a bit slacking in the heir department."

"Literally, and I mean this literally, I have never heard anyone use that phrase in my entire life."

He shook his head as though trying to convince me. "It's true, my father only had one brother who died before he was eighteen, and I'm an only child. There are a few second cousins here and there, a few who still work for the hotel, you've probably met them, but when you look at our family tree, which used to be expansive, there's really only me left."

"So you're pretty much locked in," I said.

He nodded with a faraway look in his eye. "I suppose so, but I never really thought of it that way."

"So even when you were a kid, or in high school, or in college, even, you never thought about, I don't know, running away to join the circus?" I turned toward him on the couch, curling my feet underneath me.

"Oh sure, there were a few circus moments here and there. I thought, for about five minutes, about going to medical school. I thought, for about seven minutes, about becoming a teacher, I've always loved history."

"That actually makes perfect sense," I said. "I could totally see you on a college campus, rattling around with your pipe and your busted briefcase." And I could too. "I bet all the young coeds would be fighting to take your class."

He let out a laugh. "I hardly think I'd be the type that anyone would fight over."

I looked at him, warm auburn hair glowing in the firelight, those freckles peeking out from beneath his twinkling eyes. "I'd probably throw an elbow or two."

"This elbow?" he asked, reaching out and gently brushing against my arm.

"Mm-hmm," I breathed, once more the touch of his fingertips sending shivers out all over my body.

We both sipped our martinis, eyes meeting over the rims. Jesus, this guy.

"But," he said, breaking the spell as well as the eye contact, "once those seven minutes were over I remembered how much I loved this place and I wasn't about to let someone else take it over."

"Until I got here." I laughed.

"Yes, until this tiny bossy person showed up and started acting like she owned the place."

I sat up on my knees, fist-pumping. "Worst day ever for you, Hotel Boy."

He smiled, but it didn't quite reach his eyes. "Not the worst day," he said softly.

My gaze flashed down to the ring on his left hand. We sat in silence for a moment, other than the crackling of the fire, and when the clock in the hall began to chime, I sighed. "I should go."

Part of me wanted him to say no. Stay. And I think part of him wanted to say it too. But instead, he just reached for my hand, squeezed it, and said, "I'll walk you to your car."

He kissed me before I drove away, this time crazy soft and sweet. When I crawled into bed later that night, I could still feel the whisper of his lips on mine.

Chapter 13

A Night of Stars. That was how tonight's entertainment at Bryant Mountain House was advertised. Internally, hotel guests only. I'll explain.

Every night at Bryant Mountain House there was in-house entertainment for the hotel guests. It could range from supremely entertaining to entertaining in only the most very literal sense of the word. Every morning each guest received a "newspaper" under their door with the day's activities. *The Bryant Bugler* listed exercise and yoga classes, what was on the lunch menu, the weather report, you get the picture. There was also a section for nighttime, such as what movie would be shown, what times were available for dinner, and what was on tap for the nightly entertainment, typically held in the Lakeside Lounge. Since I'd been working here, I'd attended lectures on soap making, witnessed three magicians and their disappearing rabbits, attempted to learn to square dance, and watched a group billed as the Schmanders Sisters, not kidding, boogie-woogie until the boys came home.

And these evenings were always well attended. I'm telling you, take people's televisions away and pow, let's all learn how to macramé becomes oh so special. I'd asked Archie about the nighttime entertainment once, if he felt it needed to be punched up at all, and he honest to God asked me, "Why, what's wrong with the entertainment?"

So when a Night of Stars popped up on the *Bugler,* I'd assumed it'd be some kind of variety act where jugglers and ventriloquists would vie for top billing only to come up short to a dancing poodle.

No no, it was actually something very cool. An astronomer was coming up to lead us on a nighttime hike up to Skytop to watch a meteor shower. Thinking I'd finally found the one event I was ready to invite everyone to, I put the call out.

"You gotta come up, it'll be so cool."

"Wait, hike? At night? In the dark? To see stars?" Natalie had a firm grip on the obvious.

"Ow, Pinup, not so hard," I heard in the background. Apparently the obvious wasn't the only thing she had a firm grip on.

"Jesus, morning boning? Are you guys animals?" I asked, rolling my eyes.

"Listen, just because you're not getting it doesn't mean I'm not getting it."

"Touché," I replied. "So you're coming?"

"Gimme five minutes and yeah, I'll be coming." She laughed, and I sighed heavily.

"Tonight? Up to the resort? Are you in?"

"Let me ask Oscar," she said, covering the phone. I heard things that, even though they were muffled, I had no business hearing, but eventually she came back on the phone. Albeit breathless. "We're in. What time?"

"Seven thirty, we'll meet in the lobby, and I'll tell the guard shack you're coming up and to let you through. Make sure you wear boots and . . . Jesus, I'm hanging up now."

My next call went somewhat smoother.

"A nighttime hike? That sounds . . . interesting. Won't it be cold?"

"Yep. The way to combat that would be to wear a coat and mittens."

Roxie laughed. "I'll double-check with Leo, but that should be fine. Polly is spending the night with Trudy."

"Oh, I hate to take you away when you guys have the night to yourselves, I know that doesn't happen too often." Roxie adored Leo's daughter, Polly, but dating a man with an eight-year-old did have some limitations.

"No no, it's good. Besides, it's nice having you in town. Leo was just saying how much fun it was hanging out with you and Archie."

"Me and Archie?" I scoffed. "There's no me and Archie. I mean, there's me, and then there's Archie, and we work together, and I suppose he's pretty cool when he's not being an asshole, but there's definitely not a me and Archie per se, like in the traditional way. Why would he say that? Me and Archie? That's crazy."

Silence on the other end of the phone.

"Um, okay," she said, her tone measured.

I nearly smacked myself in the forehead when I played it back, how crazy had I just sounded?

"So, um, yeah, anyway. Seven thirty?"

"Sure. Got it." She paused for a moment. "Everything okay up there?"

Shit. "Fine!" I practically shouted. I made myself take a breath. "Fine," I repeated in a much calmer tone. "Everything is fine. Working hard. Doing my thing. You know me."

"I do know you."

"Mm-hmm."

"So, if there was something going on, something you wanted to talk about, you know you could talk to me, right?"

"Mm-hmm." Sooo much trouble.

"Because you know, I'd hate to think that one of my very best friends had something going on that she was excited about, but didn't feel like she could tell me because who knows why . . . but I know that's not happening because of course you'd tell me, right?"

"Mm-hmm." I was humming because my lips refused to unseal.

"Okay then," she said, with the sweetest-sounding voice ever. "We'll see you at seven thirty."

You already know my response.

Okay, so. Roxie was onto me. She knew something was up. But if I could play it cool tonight, she might just let it lie. If Natalie sniffed something, however, I was screwed.

Sigh. I really couldn't talk about this with those two. They'd already been planting seeds left and right about the magical gravitational force that was Bailey Falls and how hard it could suck me in. If they got a whiff that there was actually something going on between us? They'd never let it go. And it wasn't that I didn't confide in my girlfriends, these two were my family. But when I talked to Roxie and Natalie about something, it was something. And if I didn't even know what this was, whether it even was something or not, I didn't want to make it more than it was.

If I told the girls, then this shit was real. And when shit was real, it could hurt. So I needed to minimize their interest in this.

I called Chad and invited him and Logan. They could run interference if needed. Plus, they were fun. And we needed fun young people up at the resort, if for no other reason than to tell other fun young people to book a weekend trip. In fact . . .

I headed down to Archie's office, poking my head around the corner to find him behind his desk, working.

"Hey."

"Hey," he said, looking up with a smile.

"I invited some people up tonight for the meteor hike, Roxie and Natalie and company, seven thirty?"

"Of course."

"I was also thinking, maybe we could invite some of the locals to come up for a free weekend. People like Chad on the town council, the mayor, et cetera. Let them see what they're missing and then roll out the new Bailey Falls resident pricing program. They could really help spread the word about how much fun they had."

He sat back in his chair, thinking. "I like it. Invite them all up. We've still got some rooms free Easter weekend. Do they have plans?"

"Easter?" I gulped.

"Sure, we can ask them tonight. What time did you say everyone was coming?"

I gulped again. "Seven thirty."

"Great," he said, looking pleased as punch.

I started to head out when he called me back in. "Where do you think you're going?"

"Um, back to work? I've got a meeting with the front desk crew in a few minutes."

That night I headed down to the lobby a few minutes before everyone was due to arrive. My stomach all flip-floppy, a bundle of nerves. I wasn't sure why, we'd all had dinner together at the diner and I hadn't been nervous.

That was a happy accident. You invited them here this time. To spend time with you . . . and Archie.

Not officially.

Keep telling yourself that.

It was true. My worlds were always kept apart, such as they were. My professional world was for me and me alone. *Alone* being the key word. I spent time with my friends when I could, of course, but I led a fairly isolated life. My work took me wherever it took me, I never said no to a job far away. It wasn't that I didn't like spending time with my friends, I loved my girls. But suddenly my work life and life life were mixing, through my own invitation, and it just felt . . . strange. Flip-floppy was honestly the best way to describe it.

"Think you'll be warm enough?" I heard behind me, and I turned to see Archie standing there, admiring my faux-fur hat. "You look like you'll be invading Poland in that thing."

"Laugh all you want, but you lose most of your body heat through your head, and it's cold tonight."

"There'll be a campfire."

"Won't that make it hard to see the stars?"

He leaned down closer to my ear, inside my faux fur. "The campfire is for after."

"After?"

"After." He nodded, and I could feel his breath on my neck. I shivered. He noticed. "Guess it's a good thing you've got that hat on after all."

I pulled away, laughing, and gave him a playful swat on the chest just as the front door burst open.

"We heard there were stars up here," Natalie said, pulling Oscar along. "Let's see 'em."

"Hold your horses there, woman, we gotta get up to the top first. How in the world are you planning on hiking in those?" I asked, pointing at her high-heeled boots.

"You said wear boots. I wore boots." She stuck up her foot,

clad in three-inch heels. "Besides, if I get tired I'll jump on his back."

"She'll get tired," Oscar replied. "She thinks I'm her pack mule."

"Jackass, babe, I called you jackass."

"Quit calling my friend a jackass," Leo scoffed, popping his head up over Oscar's shoulders where he was standing with Roxie.

"Everyone's a jackass, just get in here," I instructed, waving them all in, including Chad and Logan, who were bringing up the rear. "Hey guys, glad you could make it."

"Are you kidding, I've been dying to get up here and see this place, it's incredible!" Logan said, looking everywhere all at once. "Show me everything, I want to see everything. Right now."

"Okay, well, we don't have too much time before we need to meet the astronomer, we should probably—"

"Oh, I think we've got some time," Archie said, patting me on the shoulder. Something eagle-eyed Natalie and Roxie noticed immediately. "And Clara here can give the tour."

"I can?" I asked, as he moved me in front of him like a teacher in front of her students. "Wait, I can?"

"Sure, you've seen the house tour a number of times now, you should know it by heart. We won't have time to see every-thing, but at least give them a tour of the first floor. Unless you don't think you remember the details?"

I looked back over my shoulder at him, his eyes twinkling. "Was that your version of triple dog daring me?"

"Depends, are you going to give the tour?"

I narrowed my eyes, and while still staring at him, I started in my best tour guide voice. "Bryant Mountain House was started by two brothers, Ebenezer and Theophilus Bryant, in 1872. The original inn on the lake was named . . ."

I gave the tour. I kicked ass. I took them through the lobby, pointing out the important artwork there. I took them down the hallway to the gift shop and soda fountain, correctly identifying the main ingredient in a Green River and telling them how to make a cherry phosphate, an egg cream, and the Archie Special, the latter of which they all agreed sounded horrific and wrong. I took them into the main dining room and discussed the importance of dressing for dinner and why it'd always be a tradition up on this mountain. Finally, we ended the tour in the Lakeside Lounge, where I not only explained the significance behind the fossil embedded in the keystone over the main fireplace, but also asked if anyone in the group knew what kind of wood made up the bulk of the paneling in the room, a question every employee who led the tour would ask and almost no one ever answered correctly.

"Mahogany?" Leo offered.

"Nope."

"Rosewood?" Chad asked.

"No, but that's a great guess. There's rosewood in the reading room on the second floor."

"It's chestnut," piped up Natalie.

"It is chestnut." I beamed, looking at my friend.

"How did you know?" Archie asked, looking surprised.

"My family's in construction. I know this place couldn't have been built this way even thirty years later because of the chestnut blight that went through the Northeast, eventually the country. Chestnut is almost impossible to find as a building material after 1910 or so, it just became too valuable. It was all gone by the 1940s, which is what makes a room like this so incredible. You've got yourself something pretty fucking special here, Mr. Bryant, if you don't mind me saying so."

"My girl," Oscar said, crushing Natalie into his side with an arm like a grizzly bear's. "She knows wood."

"Okay, let's meet up with that astronomer before this gets out of hand," I said quickly, knowing by the shit-eating grin on Natalie's face that this topic would quickly devolve into idiocy if I didn't head it off at the pass. I looked over to Archie, ready to apologize for my friends and their crude language when I saw he was grinning with delight, and not just because someone recognized chestnut in all its impossible-to-find glory, but because he was genuinely enjoying himself.

I looked around at this group, some old friends, some new. Everyone was laughing and talking, bundling up for the hike. I watched as Archie showed Leo and Oscar on the big map where Skytop was, and what hike we'd be taking tonight. Chad and Roxie had their heads together, while Logan helped Natalie relace her inappropriate boots. All the while the fire crackled merrily, enclosing us all in a cozy little vignette.

I stood off to the side, taking it all in. This was what it was like. Friends. Family. Together.

I felt a strange pull in my stomach, like my very center of gravity was being tugged and rearranged. I shook my head to clear it, just as one of the guys from recreation came in to introduce our evening's guide to a Night of Stars.

"You ready?" Archie asked, coming over and tugging lightly on the end of my furry cap.

I pulled it down tightly. "Mm-hmm. Let's get out of here."

"So have you ever given any thought to lecturing about what you've done with Maxwell Farms?" Archie asked Leo as we hiked up to Skytop.

"I do it all the time, actually," Leo answered. "Not as much during the summer when we're at our busiest, but during the winter I go around New York, New Jersey, Pennsylvania, talking about what we do. Sometimes I go to high schools, but a lot of time a learning annex or community college, garden clubs, pretty much anyone who's interested in how to grow and eat sustainably."

"I'd love to have you maybe do a series here, we've got a great lecture space up on the second floor. Would you be interested in that? I'm sure our guests would be."

"Of course, sure! That'd be great," Leo agreed, clapping Archie on the back.

"Maybe Roxie could teach a Zombie class sometime, pickling or canning?" I offered, winking at my friend.

"Oh my gosh, yes! I'd love to!" she squealed. "There was a super-popular class when I lived in Los Angeles on exactly that, you'd be surprised how many people would love to know more about how to do things like that."

"Well, why stop there," Archie said, rubbing his chin as he thought. "What if we made a kind of learning annex up here at the resort, not just for guests but for people in town and all over the Hudson Valley? We could include things like home gardening, I'm sure our landscaping team would love the chance to get out of their greenhouses a bit. And Oscar, what do you think, feel like teaching a cheese-making class?"

Oscar looked at Archie with a raised eyebrow. "I'm not so great in front of a classroom."

"Of course, sure, whatever," Archie acquiesced.

"Of course he will," Natalie replied from her perch on Oscar's back, her boots giving out ten minutes into the hike. "I can be the gorgeous mouthpiece in the front of the classroom, you just grunt and point and I'll interpret."

"You know who you should get," Chad interjected, piping up from the back of our group. "Remember Hazel, who runs the flower shop on Elm?"

"I've known Hazel since I was three." Archie laughed. "She used to always pin a carnation on my lapel when I was in town."

"Me too! She'd be great, I bet she'd love to teach a floral arrangement class. Oh man, one Sunday at church she pinned a chrysanthemum that was so heavy on my jacket I almost fell over."

"That's Hazel." Archie laughed again, and so did everyone else.

I didn't know Hazel. In fact, I'd never heard of Hazel. I listened to the group laugh and tell stories about this woman who half of them had grown up with, and the other half now knew from living in town, and I began to feel that pang again, that hollowness just under my breastbone.

There'd be a learning annex at Bryant Mountain House. A freaking genius idea. Spearheaded by Archie, taught by Roxie and Leo and Oscar and Natalie, attended and contributed to by Chad and Logan. This is a plan that'd come together over countless lunches and dinners, cocktails and porch swings, and would premiere to the town and the resort with a great chance for success and would likely continue on as one of the centerpieces of the new Bryant Mountain House.

After I left Bryant Mountain House.

After I left this group of friends, this group whose lives would go on without me, undoubtedly missing me in the case of Roxie and Natalie, and maybe Archie, but still, I was the one piece that could be dropped in and pulled back out without disturbing the group as a whole, as a thing, as a unit.

There was an entire ecosystem of Bailey Falls that had existed before I arrived and would remain long after I left. I'd be off on another job, another project, another hotel room with empty suitcases in the corner and a rental car in the parking lot and room service eaten at a coffee table while I scratched out another master plan on a stack of legal pads while an info-mercial for Time Life's Classic Soft Rock filled my ears with the sounds of Jim Croce and Linda Ronstadt and made sure that while that TV was on and giving my brain the static it needed to function, I wouldn't be thinking about this group, this thing, this unit, this family in Bailey Falls.

I rubbed my chest. A few paces ahead I heard the astrono-mer talking about the meteor shower and where to look to make sure we didn't miss it. I surged ahead, leaving my group and joining him to listen. I needed the static.

"You tired?"

"A little, you?" I asked, leaning against the main banister in the lobby. We'd packed up the crazy people and sent them back into town. It had been a fun night, and the great news was everyone was ready to book their resident weekend. And come back for Easter.

Archie'd invited everyone so easily, like they were his friends. Which I suppose they were. But tonight, everyone had blended together nicely. It all seemed very natural, like we'd been friends for years. All happy, all coupled up. Except that wasn't the case. Not with Archie and me. Right?

"Not too tired?"

"Why?"

He smiled. "Come with me, I want to show you something."

"Do I still need my mittens?" I asked, raising an eyebrow.

"Definitely," he replied, and started going up the staircase.

"We're not going back outside?" I asked, confused.

"Stop asking questions," he said over his shoulder, and I had no choice but to follow him. Up six flights of stairs. And down three hallways. Around several corners. All the way to the end of the line, the very edge of the east wing.

Past a broom closet and almost hidden behind an armoire, a heavy six-paneled door stood with a thick-looking lock.

"Is this where you keep the guests who couldn't pay?" I whispered, peeking under his shoulder.

"They check in, but they never check out," he replied, in his best Vincent Price voice.

"For the record, that's creepy as fuck."

"So is this," he said, twisting the old metal key so the door swung open.

Darkness beckoned, and through the gloom I could just make out a narrow, steep staircase. "I mean, come on."

"Scared?"

"I'm not stupid. Staircases like that are never meant to be climbed unless there's a guy running behind you with an ax."

"I can see if Walter from maintenance is available."

"I can see if Walter from maintenance is available to kick your ass for saying shit like that while standing at the bottom of the staircase from *Psycho*."

A door opened and closed at the other end of the hallway and we both jumped.

"Okay, buddy, you've got thirty seconds to tell me what this is about or I'm heading back to my room to a bubble bath."

"Hmm, a bubble bath."

I punched him in the arm. "Twenty-five seconds."

He laughed, then yanked on a string. A single bulb shone down, illuminating the staircase and making it a few degrees less creepy. I peered up; the stairs went on at least two stories, maybe more. "Okay, I'll bite. Where does it lead?"

"Nothing ventured . . ." he said, and started up the stairs. Creepy stairs, or the newly planted mental picture of an ax-wielding Walter?

I followed him. The walls were down to the studs, plaster over wire over brick. The stairs were paneled about halfway up the wall, then open.

All along the paneling were signatures carved into the wood.

Jeremiah, 1897
Bartholomew, 1912
James. Mickey, 1933
George, 1941
Jonathan, 1952

"Who carved all these?" I asked, running my fingers over some of the names. There were other words too, mostly of the limerick variety. There once was a girl from Nantucket . . .

"People who worked here. People who lived here. Did you know back in the thirties they used this part of the hotel to house a boys' boarding school? It only lasted a decade or so, there are pictures in the library of the bunk beds they installed. In the summer, the boys would sleep out on the balcony, before air-conditioning, of course."

"A boys' boarding school," I mused, reading a poem about a rather busty girl from Tallahassee. "Did you know there are boobs carved into the wood?"

"Boys will be boys," he muttered, and I rolled my eyes. "That was my favorite panel to look at when I used to come up here."

"And where is here exactly?" I asked, as we finally reached a landing. The bulb was far below us now.

"Just a few more steps," he said, turning a corner and disappearing into the darkness.

I stood there, rolling on my ankles when I heard a thunk then a squeak then his voice floating back to me.

"Don't be chicken."

"Oh, please," I said, and marched around the corner into that same darkness.

Cool air swirled around my legs. Silhouetted by moonlight, Archie stood in a doorway that opened up into an inky black sky punctured by twinkling stars. He was on the roof.

"Careful, give me your hand," he said, helping me over the knee-high ledge that separated the staircase from the roofline.

"Whoa, whoa, whoa, wait a minute, I—"

"Trust me," he said softly, his hand strong in mine, "I've got you."

I stepped. Out into a different world. Up this high, we could see everything. The entire hotel spread out below us, the golf course, the parking lots, the gardens, everything. The lake was calm tonight, reflecting back a perfect mirror image of the moon and stars, ebony and alabaster and pure magic.

"This is incredible," I breathed.

"There's supposed to be another round of meteor showers soon, thought we might catch that show from up here."

"How cool is this!" I squealed, looking in every direction at once, not wanting to miss a thing. "How close to the edge can we go?"

In response he tugged my hand toward the rock railing that ran along the roofline. I peeked over the edge. On the lakeside, I could see the porches below, all the different levels, and the lanterns that lit the way to the dock. It looked far away but peaceful and somehow comforting.

"Watch where you step, this roof hasn't been patched in a few years."

"What?" I yelped, stepping closer to him.

"Kidding, I'm kidding," he soothed.

I glared up at him. "You're a bit twisted."

He gazed down at me, an expression I couldn't quite identify on his face. "You're a bit wonderful."

And in a scene right out of central casting, as I stared up into those warm indigo eyes, a sparkling trail blazed across the sky, arching right over his head with perfect Disney timing.

"The shower is starting up again."

"Is it?" he said, still gazing down at me.

I gulped. "You're going to miss it."

He leaned down, pressing his forehead to mine. "I guess I'll miss it."

"But I thought you wanted to—"

"Stop. Arguing. With me."

I stopped arguing. He started kissing. And it was on.

I slipped my hands up around his neck, and suddenly realized I wanted to be able to feel him, touch him, get a sense of his skin that I just couldn't with my stupid mittens on. I tore them off, flinging them over my shoulder as I sank my fingers into that ridiculously soft hair of his, never once taking my lips from his, not wanting to break this contact once it had begun.

His hands, meanwhile, had slid around my waist, tugging me closer to him, his fingertips splayed wide around my hips, dipping down lower to my bottom. I sighed into his mouth as one hand slipped up and underneath my shirt, his cold fingers feeling white hot against the small of my back.

"God, you feel amazing," he groaned, breaking our kiss as he swept kisses along my jawline straight back to my ear. "Your skin . . . I want to . . ."

His mouth was back on mine again, swallowing whatever it was he was going to say and instead tangling his tongue with mine over and over again. His hands pressed me into him farther, and I could feel him, Jesus, I could feel him, thick and hard and *oh he was hard and thick,* and my eyes rolled back in my head just imagining what it would feel like to fuck this man.

My hands roamed restlessly now, down along his shoulders, along his arms, and back up again. I wanted more. I needed more. Meteors were fucking screaming across the sky and *I needed more.*

The hand that was under my shirt now slipped higher, moving around front and spanning my rib cage, long and strong fingers playing my skin. His mouth was on the move again as well, back at my ear, whispering, "I want . . . I need . . ."

"What," I asked, "what do you want?"

He didn't answer with words. But he did answer. He spun me, pushing me up against one of the chimneys, wrapping one hand around the back of my knee and hitching it around his hip, opening me up to him.

And he thrust against me. *Yes.* He thrust against me again, his eyes now burning down into mine. *Yes, yes.*

Wonderful, brilliant friction was building as he pressed into me again and again. Cold brick and stone scratched my back, incredible. Bits of papery soot rained down from above, collecting in our hair, fantastic. My right foot scrambled to find purchase on the gravelly surface, twisting this way and that and even rolling painfully enough once that I knew I'd feel it the next time I tried to run. Fucking awesome. Because while my right foot was rolling, my left foot and all its toes were pointing skyward as oh my God I can't believe Archie Bryant was dry humping me straight into an insane orgasm.

"Oh my God," I heard myself say, heat blooming everywhere. "Oh my God, oh my God."

He cinched me tighter around his hip, rocking into me, using his body to bring me higher and higher.

"Clara," he said, and my name on his lips caused me to shatter. Broke me wide open. Waves coursed through me as starry streaks crossed the sky above. As I clung to him, panting, boneless, witless, all I could think was that I never wanted to come down from this roof again, if it meant I could stay wrapped around this guy.

And once the meteor shower had finished, this thought spurred me into action faster than anything else could have, and as soon as politely possible, I kissed him and ran back downstairs.

Danger. Danger. Danger.

Chapter 14

After feeling empty and cavernous for weeks now, the hotel was suddenly alive and buzzing with excitement with the arrival of Easter weekend. The floral arrangements were more elaborate, the bellmen were moving with a little more pep in their step, and for the first time since I'd been there I couldn't get a dinner reservation that entire holiday weekend because they were—and these are the words every hotelier lives for—all booked up.

"I love when a hotel feels like it's bursting at the seams, don't you?" I sighed, standing at the bottom of the stairs in the lobby with Mrs. Toomey late Friday afternoon, watching car after car pull into the porte cochere. "Families coming from all over the place, deciding to spend their weekend away from home, somewhere they'll be treated a bit like royalty. Someone makes their bed, someone brings them their paper, someone folds their towels, and who doesn't love coming home after a long day to find a chocolate on their pillow?"

"I know what you mean," she said, "especially on these holiday weekends. It's like having one big extended family all under one roof.

"Whoa, can we help you with that?" Mrs. Toomey said as

Archie came around the corner, carrying an enormous egg tree. Wintry branches were crammed into a large vase and littered with eggs painted in springtime colors. It had been a crafting project that some of the evening activity guests had been working on all week, making tiny pinpricks in eggs and blowing out the insides to make the shells empty. They were then decorated with tiny beads, glitter, ribbons, all delicate and beautiful. One more Bryant family tradition carried on for another year.

"This looks great." I admired the tree, wanting to bat at the eggshells like a cat but knowing that'd be frowned upon. "Where is this ending up?"

"Right . . . here," Archie said, balancing left and right and finally setting the tree down delicately in the center of the lobby table. "That way the guests can see it when they check in."

"It looks great, really, better than I expected."

"You doubted our egg tree?"

"I walked into the lounge one night to find seven old ladies blowing eggs . . . what the hell was I supposed to think?"

Mrs. Toomey smothered a laugh. "I'm just going to go find something to do."

"We'll be at full capacity by tonight, I'm sure there's something to do," Archie joked, and she swatted at him as she toddled off to terrorize the girls at the front desk. Once she was out of earshot, he looked carefully at me. "Have you been avoiding me the past few days?"

Yes. "Yes."

"Care to tell me why?"

Because I can't stop thinking about you. Because you've got me all tied up in knots. Because I don't know how much longer I can go without seeing you naked and underneath me. Because now I'm feeling some feels beyond what I know how to deal with. "I've been super busy."

"Hmm," he said, not buying it. I looked away, not wanting to meet his gaze. "You don't look super busy now."

"I'm slammed, actually. I've got a meeting with the guys in room service to make sure they have everything set for the new menu we're rolling out, I've got to talk with Lucy in the greenhouse about bringing up some fresh-cut tulips for the elevator lobby, and I still need to stop by the spa and make sure they have everything they need to roll out the new Spring Awakening package this weekend, and I wanted to check the bookings."

"Dye some eggs."

"Excuse me?"

"Dye some eggs. Room service menu is good to go, the tulips are being set out as we speak, and the spa is booked all weekend, they've even got a waiting list, I just checked. So come dye eggs with me for the egg hunt."

"I have a degree in hotel management, work for the best rebranding firm in New England, have turned countless hotels around, and you want me to dye eggs?"

"Based on what you just said, you need some humility. You've also come into my hotel, thrown everything up into the air and out on its ear, not to mention driven me half mad with not only that bossy mouth but the incredible sounds you make when I'm kissing that bossy mouth, and now, by God, it's my turn to make you part of one of the oldest traditions here at Bryant Mountain House. Dye some eggs."

I thought for a moment. "Okay."

Twenty minutes later I was sitting at an enormous table in the back corner of the kitchen, surrounded by crates of hard-boiled eggs. "I don't get it, couldn't you order these already dyed? Surely there's a specialty food service that could've delivered these. "

"Well sure, but what's the fun in that?" Archie asked, rolling up his sleeves as he prepared to dip an entire tray into a deep-purple wash.

"Where indeed," I wondered. I tried to mimic what he was doing with a similar tray and the green color. "Why does this smell like salad dressing?"

"It's the vinegar."

"There's vinegar in egg dye?"

He shook his head. "Are you a communist? Haven't you ever dyed eggs before?"

My hands shook a little, but I managed to keep my eggs in line. "Yes, I'm a communist. How long do they need to sit in here?"

"Wait a minute, let me get this straight, communism aside. Have you really never dyed eggs before?"

"It's not really a character flaw, is it?" I asked, arching my brow at him.

"No no, I just can't . . . well, what the hell did you do before Easter? Or did your parents just surprise you with eggs on Easter morning? I always used to wonder why we dyed them for the bunny to hide, if he was the Easter bunny he could've just brought his own eggs."

"The bunny brought them, yes," I replied, rolling my shoulders. "Not everyone did the same thing growing up, though, you know?"

"I suppose—every family's different, right?"

"Mm-hmm." I looked at his eggs. "So how long do they need to stay in the dye?"

"Depends."

"Depends on what?"

He looked up at me over the rims of his glasses. "On how deep you want it."

Ungh. I breathed. Then blushed.

"How deep you want the color, that is."

I considered. "Pretty deep."

"I had a feeling." He looked proud of himself. Hmm.

"Shallow has its benefits, though," I said innocently. Not taking my eyes off my tray, I tilted my head to the side. "Sometimes just a little bit, just barely inside, like really slow? It can drive a person positively crazy, you know?"

His tray shook slightly.

"I mean, anyone can just thrust it right in there, but when someone can do it really slow? And shallow? Making sure that everything gets covered, not missing a single spot? That's almost as good as when it's really deep."

His tray shook again, this time more than slightly.

I lifted my tray out of the green dye, then bobbed it lightly back under, leaning over as I did, making sure to give him a peek down my shirt. "But that's just me."

"Not just you," he grunted, and I chanced a look at him. His hands were gripping the tray, white knuckles standing out stark against the purple dye. Forearms bunched, shoulders tight, jaw clenched.

His eyes met mine, and I drew in a breath. "I had a feeling," I whispered, plunging my tray back under the green.

Egg dyeing was fun.

"Okay, so explain this to me like I'm an idiot," Natalie said as we sipped Bloody Marys from the Sunset Porch.

"Gladly," I answered.

"You hide the eggs on the side of a mountain."

"Yes."

"And then you tell toddlers to go find them."

"Basically."

"Won't they just tumble off into the Catskills?"

I snorted into my cocktail. "They're not hidden on rock ledges and on top of trees, for God's sake."

"I'm just saying, it's weird."

"They've been doing the egg hunt on this lawn for a hundred years—I think they've got this."

She plucked her celery stick from her drink and gave it a chomp. "It's not how I planned on spending my Easter, that's for sure."

"And how exactly have we ruined your Easter? What else would you have been doing?"

"First of all, it's a holiday. I like to spend my holidays under the covers and under Oscar. Or over Oscar, depends on how tired he is. Secondly, my mother is livid that I'm not in the city right now, she threatened to call highway patrol and have me bodily brought back home. There's only one reason I was allowed to leave my island."

"And what, pray tell, is that reason?"

"You."

"Me?"

"Yup. When she found out you were up here, actually venturing out of your cave on a holiday, she said mazel and made me promise that if your self-imposed ban on holidays was over I'll bring you for Thanksgiving this year."

I chomped on my own celery in answer.

"Oh no, Trudy already called dibs on Thanksgiving," I heard from over my shoulder, and I turned to see Roxie slipping into a rocking chair next to us. "She said, and I quote, 'Tell that little shit if she's going to be spending all this time in Bailey Falls, then she's required to come to my house for Thanksgiving for the best gravy she's ever tasted.'"

"Well, that's sweet, but—"

"She also told me to tell you she still thinks you're low on iron and she wants you to start taking these." She plunked a bottle of vitamins down on the railing. "You need the color, she says."

"Oh my God, it's April! How about we not talk about November yet?" I said, waving at the bartender and ordering a cocktail for Roxie as well. "Please thank your mother, and your mother, for the invites and the pills, but I'm good."

Both Roxie and Natalie had told me over the years that there was always a standing invitation to their homes on each and every holiday. And each and every holiday I'd thanked them politely, and declined. They knew why, and wisely chose not to press me on it. Frankly, it was all I could do to not fly out of this rocking chair and head for the hills, as it was. Holidays made me nervous at best and a wreck at worst. Holidays were empty for me when I was a child, and as an adult they always felt like just a reminder of those special days I'd missed out on. Can you imagine what it's like to have to sit through a Christmas party in elementary school, surrounded by kids who were getting everything they wanted under their Christmas tree, when the closest I'd get to any kind of celebration were the stale snickerdoodles I was eating at that very party?

One foster mom had tried her best to do something fun each year. Her drunk husband tried his best to ruin it. Honestly, it just always felt like a waste of a day to me, and I'd made it my practice to avoid holidays whenever I could.

But this year was different. This year I was working over the holiday, at a hotel that was famous for its Easter brunch. And the egg hunt. And those blessed hot cross buns everyone kept going on about. And I had friends in this town, friends who wanted to be with me. So here I sat, on a grand porch in a grand hotel overlooking a grand egg hunt on a lawn set into the grand Catskill Mountains.

The Bloody Mary was excellent. The company was first-rate. And I wondered if any of the kids picking up the purple and green dyed eggs hidden in the grass knew just how verbally stimulating that egg dyeing had been.

I grinned into my drink.

"So where's Archie? I figured he'd be right here with you, watching the festivities?" Roxie asked.

"With me?" I asked, choking a bit on tomato juice. "No no, he's down there, supervising the eggs and the toddlers. Natalie is convinced they're all going to fall off the side."

"Nonsense, I came up here when I was a kid to look for eggs," Roxie scoffed.

"You say that now, but what happens when—"

"No one is tumbling off the side of a cliff today, for God's sake." I sighed, rolling my eyes.

"Stranger things have happened," Natalie said, and I stuck my tongue out at her.

"See, he's right there with— Oh boy." The three of us looked out onto the lawn and saw Archie and Leo, covered in egg yolk and each holding about thirteen baskets, with Oscar bringing up the rear, wearing the most lopsided bunny ears I'd ever seen. "Jesus, I don't think I've ever seen your guy smile that big." I laughed, nudging Natalie.

"I have, but usually when I'm about to sit on his—"

"No no." Roxie shook her head. "I'm literally begging you to not finish that sentence."

"I'm in full agreement," I added, fist-bumping Roxie. Natalie let out a huff and went back to her Bloody Mary. The three of us sat there a moment, watching the guys playing with the kids, Archie and Leo still trying to wipe off the egg yolk. Archie looked happy, relaxed, caught up in the moment and fully at ease. I smiled just watching him.

"So how is Archie anyway?"

"Fine. He's fine," I replied, my gaze still fixed on him. And as though he could feel me watching him, he turned just then and gave me a small wave. I waved back, my grin growing toothier by the second, just as I could feel Roxie and Natalie's eyeballs boring holes in the sides of my skull. "I mean, I assume."

"Yeah, that's not what I meant," Natalie said.

"Oh?"

"I meant how is Archie, in the biblical sense?"

I sputtered. "What? Why? What?"

"Smooth, real smooth, Nat," Roxie muttered.

Natalie sat up in her chair. "Hey, I would've said what's it like to fuck that guy, but it's Easter, so I made it about the Bible."

"Now, just wait a minute," I snapped. "What are you two up to?"

"That's funny, I was going to ask you the exact same question." Natalie cackled, leaning back in her chair and almost upending herself.

"We just, that is, me and Natalie, we just wondered . . ." Roxie said, trailing off and waggling her eyebrows.

I let her keep doing it for a moment simply because she looked like she was having some kind of fit. "I'd love for you to just ask your question," I finally said, putting her out of her misery.

"Are you and Archie up here fluffing the pillows every night or what?" Natalie asked.

"No."

"No?" they both asked.

"No, we are not fluffing anything."

"Bullshit," Roxie said, and I looked at her in surprise. It was usually Natalie I could count on for the bullshit in a china shop attitude. "Bull. Shit."

"What is it you want me to say, huh?" I asked, staring down into my cocktail. I could feel both of them staring at me, so it made me very interested in my olive.

"That you've been making sweet, sweet hotel love since you showed up on his mountaintop," Roxie said.

"That you've been riding him but good since you showed up on his mountaintop," Natalie added.

"Neither. And that's the truth."

Roxie started, "But—"

I cut her off. "There is something going on, yes." Natalie clapped and almost lost her balance again. "But before anyone starts tap dancing, may I remind you of a few things? One, I'm leaving. Not now, but eventually. Two, I'm leaving because this is my job, and he's my boss, and I'll thank you both to stop clapping and rocking back and forth in your chairs, going on and on about sweet love and riding his mountaintop because I work here. Three, his wife died. It's been a few years, sure, but they were together since time was invented and that's not something he's going to get over anytime soon. He still wears his wedding ring, in case you didn't notice, and how can I compete with that? Four, I positively adore him and he's the best kisser ever and I want to fuck the ever-loving mountain out of him, and if either of you say anything else I'll kick you in the colon." I drained my glass. "And I am positively and one hundred percent fucked."

"Whoa, just, hang on a second. So something is going on, but you haven't . . ." Natalie made a very specific motion with her finger.

"No, that hasn't happened." I sighed, reaching over and taking Roxie's Bloody Mary since mine was now empty. "But you guys . . . shit. He's just . . . shit."

"Clara, sweetie, I know you don't like to open up and talk about this stuff, but we're gonna need some actual words other than *shit*," Roxie said.

"Okay, how about these. Awesome. Incredible. Mind-blowing. Frustrating. Pretentious. Obnoxious." I paused and took a breath. "Freckles."

"Freckles?" Natalie asked.

I nodded. "Fucking hell, the freckles drive me crazy. I want to count them and then kiss him that many times."

"Oh my God," Roxie said, putting her hand over her mouth.

"Don't," I warned quietly.

"But Clara, oh my God," she continued to say through muffling fingers.

"Don't say it," I repeated.

"You fucking love this guy," Natalie said, taking another bite out of her celery.

"Goddammit." I sighed, leaning back in my rocking chair. "This conversation is over."

"Like hell it is, because, news flash? That guy fucking loves you back," Natalie said.

"It doesn't matter because, wait, what?"

"He totally does."

I shook my head. "How could you possibly know that?"

"Did you just meet me? Do you have any idea how many men have fallen in love with me over the years? You don't think I know what a man in love looks like?" She leaned back in her own rocking chair, tugging at a piece of celery stuck in her teeth. "That guy right there loves you. And if you love him, I just don't get it."

My mind was reeling. What she said, what both of them said, could I? Could he? Could . . . shit. No. NO! My palms sweaty and my heart beating in my ears, I turned to my friends. "You don't get it, okay. It can't happen, it just, don't you see, it can't happen."

Roxie leaned forward, concern in her eyes. "Why can't this happen, why can't you have this?"

My throat suddenly felt like it was squeezing shut. "You can't understand because until Leo came along, you didn't give a damn about falling in love. You thought it was bullshit, that it was a waste of time, that it was for suckers. And you, Nat, you literally left a trail of men behind you, wasted in love with you as you moved on to the next guy. Now, am I pleased as fucking punch that you've found the loves of your lives? Of course, because you deserve it, both of you, I'm so happy for you, but neither one of you ever got fucking left in your life, and you don't know what that feels like. You don't, Roxie, because you never took a chance before Leo and you don't, Natalie, because you made sure you never got in too deep with anyone. So neither of you were ever left behind, thrown out like trash, all alone. I have a job, a job that I love and is my life, my entire life. I won't ever put myself in a position to be left again, which is why I can't afford to fall in love, goddammit, so please, don't push this on me, okay?"

Tears had sprung into my eyes somewhere between *pleased* and *as fucking punch* and I brushed them angrily away. "I love you guys, I do, but it doesn't matter what I feel or might feel or could feel for Archie because I just can't let myself do it." Out of the corner of my eye, I saw Mrs. Toomey and one of the pastry chefs waving at me frantically. I sighed, pushed my way out of the rocking chair, and looked at the two of them, silent for once. "Now, if you'll excuse me, I've gotta see a man about some buns."

"Wait a minute," Roxie said, grabbing my arm just before I could run off.

"I have to go," I whispered, balancing right on the edge of a knife here.

"You're right, you know, I did everything I could to make sure I never fell in love, I put up walls and hid behind them, only letting a guy over that wall for a night or two, and only then if I knew it was someone I could never get serious about. And yeah, Natalie broke a couple of hearts over the years—"

"A couple?" Natalie chimed in, but Roxie shook her head.

"—but that's because she had her own walls, we all have fucking walls, Clara. Yours are thicker and higher than those of anyone I've ever met, with good reason. But when he comes along, and it's scary as hell when he does, but when that guy, your guy, comes along and busts down those walls? Leo was literally the last thing I was looking for, and I did everything I could to mess it up, but we figured it out. It's messy sometimes, and it's scary sometimes, but it's so goddamn worth it."

"Oscar tunneled under my walls, sneak attack. I didn't even know I was in love with him until I was," Natalie said, her voice soft. "And it scared me to death. I let one guy into my heart before Oscar, just one, and it nearly broke me in two. And I wasn't ever going to let anyone do that again. And it wasn't easy with Oscar at the beginning, and it still isn't sometimes, but there's nowhere else on the planet I'd rather be than right here, right now." She reached out for my hand and squeezed it. "Except sitting on Oscar's face."

"Jesus Christ," I muttered, looking up at the sky and then down at my two friends, my family, and wondered what in the world I'd done to deserve crazy people like this in my life. And wondered maybe, just maybe, if there was a splash of truth in what these two were saying . . . or if it was just the Bloody Marys talking.

Twenty minutes later I was in the main dining room, watching the staff scurry around to get the last of the tables set and make sure that everything was exactly in its place. I watched them scurry while I tried my damnedest to get myself under control. Any second now the doors would open and families would pour in dressed in their Easter best to break bread and celebrate the return of spring, giddy and glad and bursting with love and happiness.

I was freaking out.

Everyone seemed pumped today, even the staff. This was their family. They had to work on the holiday, sure, but they were always together and there was still a festive feeling in the air. The candles were lit, the flowers were beautiful, the last of the winter fires were burning merrily in the fireplaces, and the beautiful brunch was laid out for everyone. Gorgeous hams, studded with cloves and shimmering with honey glaze. A thousand kinds of potatoes, each one more decadent than the last. The first asparagus. The first peas. Every kind of casserole you'd ever wanted, and every kind of "salad" ever prepared by your aunt Judy or grandma Ruth.

"Jell-O molds, can you believe it?" Mrs. Banning said as she zoomed by with a tray of quivery red towers. "They still make Jell-O molds!"

"Oh, they tried to get rid of them a few years ago, but the guests demanded they be brought back, they practically stormed the kitchen with pitchforks," chimed in Mrs. Toomey as she also trotted out a tray full of the molds. "Well, forks, but you get the idea."

"I think it's that everyone still wants it the way their mom did it, you know?" said Mrs. Banning, pausing beside me and surveying the table. "Everyone just wants to re-create how it was in their childhood. Even if we're in a hotel, we still want our mom's home cooking."

I nodded and smiled through gritted teeth, feeling a swirling ball of panic begin to rise.

"But there's nothing like this family's hot cross buns," Mrs. Toomey said, flanking me on the other side and wrapping an arm around my waist. The three of us stood there as they brought out tray after tray of the most beautiful, perfect fluffy buns I'd ever seen. Just the smell of them was incredible. Buttery, cinnamony, flecked with currants and dripping with gorgeous white frosting. "You know, those buns have been in Archie's family for over a century."

So many things I could say right now . . .

"Tradition," she went on, not knowing what a land mine she'd just laid out there. "This entire hotel is built on tradition. And family. It's everything, don't you think?"

The panic ball moved out of my stomach, pushing through to my spinal column and was now climbing each vertebra, leaving an icy trail behind. My throat bunched up a bit, and I wondered how it all got so damn thick in here.

"Oh, listen to me going on, holidays just make me all squishy inside."

"Squishy?" a deep voice said from just behind us.

"There you are, we were just talking about you," Mrs. Toomey said as Archie stepped next to us, looking around the room. Tall and proud, cleaned up after the egg hunt and back in his tailored charcoal-gray suit. Today the tie was a sunny, springtimey yellow, with a pocket square covered in—

"Bunnies, Mr. Bryant?" I managed, looking at the little white cottontail butt sticking up out of his suit. My voice sounded shrill, forced.

"Don't mock the bunnies, Ms. Morgan. It's Easter." He turned to Mrs. Toomey. "Everything is perfect, as always. The guests will love it."

She glowed under his praise. Everyone did. He worked hard, he asked everyone else to do the same, and when a compliment came, it was well earned.

The women excused themselves and headed back into the kitchen, and I willed the panic now blooming upward of my rib cage to stand down.

"I think we're ready to let the stampede in, don't you?" he asked, looking toward the double doors that were still closed.

"Yeah, everything looks ready, and—"

"You look beautiful," he murmured, his eyes darting around the room so as not to draw attention to us, but the warmest smile tugging at his lips was just for me.

"Thank you," I whispered, not trusting my voice anymore.

Run. Get out of here. This is too much.

"You'll be dining with us, all of your friends will be. This year we had to stretch out the family table."

"Oh?"

Jesus, it's too much.

"It's always nice when families grow, isn't it?"

This hurts. This actually hurts.

"So listen, I've got a bit of a headache and was thinking that—"

"There you are!" I winced when I heard Natalie behind me. "I'm starving. Let's get this show on the road."

"Well said, Natalie. Is everyone here?" Archie asked. I opened my eyes to see the entire gang, plus a child I assumed was Polly, spread out like a picture in a family newsletter. Behind them, a horde of well-dressed guests were streaming in, taking their usual tables and beginning to line up for the buffet.

"We're all here. Hey, thanks for inviting us, Arch, I haven't been up here for Easter brunch since I was a kid. My mother loves it," Leo said.

"Of course she does," Roxie muttered, earning a giggle from Polly.

"It's our pleasure," Jonathan Bryant said, swooping in out of nowhere and shaking hands all around, exchanging names and pleasantries and nice to see yous/nice to finally meet yous/we love your butters (that one was for Oscar) and everything else. Archie took the moment to lean down and whisper, "You were saying something about a headache?"

I knew this was my out, my chance to slip away and feign a migraine and spend the afternoon either in my room or hiking in the hills. Or running. It was literally my chance to run. I took a deep breath, prepared to duck and dodge, but as I looked around at the assembled group, I really looked. My best friends in the whole world, with their one and onlys. And in Roxie's case, her one and only's plus one. My new friends Chad and Logan. The man who hired me, a lovely fatherly figure who loved a Jell-O mold as much as the old biddies and was already pointing out to Polly which one was his favorite. And Archie.

A man who wore tortoiseshell glasses and a bunny pocket square like no one else on the planet. A man who was currently looking down at me with the nicest and sweetest eyes ever, full of concern but also tinged with hope that I'd be okay and stay. For the buns.

I could do this, right? It was just a meal, it was just food. Just time spent with friends, what was I worrying about so much? I could do this. I needed to do this. And if there was ever a time to just get over myself and deal, it was right now. "I'm good," I said, and boy, did I ever want those words to be true. Then I saw how happy my words made him, the smile coming over his face so quickly. "I'm good," I repeated. Saying the words actually pushed that panic ball down a bit, slipping backward down my spine, the tendrils that had been spreading out and wrapping around me seemed to be recoiling back down to where it was manageable. "I'm good," I said once more.

Ohhh, I was so very not good. Brunch was coordinated chaos. Not in the overall dining room but at our actual table. I couldn't get a word in edgewise, everyone was talking over one another, I couldn't think, I couldn't focus, I didn't even know who was talking half the time.

"Cadbury Creme Eggs."

"Gross."

"Gross? Leave this table right now for such blasphemy."

"Creme Eggs fall under the category of blasphemy now?"

"If you're talking smack about them, they do."

"Forget the Creme Eggs, you can't have Easter without Reese's Peanut Butter Eggs."

"YES! Oh my God, this, this a thousand percent. Reese's Peanut Butter Eggs are the best!"

"My mom always made sure I had tons of those in my basket."

"A basket covered in ribbons, right?"

"Totally! And full of that plastic green grass."

"Plastic green grass! Oh my God, I haven't seen that stuff in ages! You'd go to grab a piece of candy—"

"—and half of the grass would come with it!"

"My mom used to make a kind of nest out of that green plastic grass in the middle of our dining room table and put a huge chocolate bunny in the middle, then scatter jelly beans all around. And Peeps."

"PEEPS!"

"YES, PEEPS!"

"How in the world have we not talked about Peeps yet?"

"Did your mom ever let you put them in the microwave?"

"No way, she knew I'd burn the house down."

"My mom would never let me do it, but at some point when she wasn't around my Dad and I would sneak over to the micro-wave and blow up the Peeps."

"My mom would've killed me. Besides, we were too busy shoving Cadbury Creme Eggs in our mouths to worry about bullshit candy like Peeps."

"I told my mom I was having Easter brunch at Bryant Mountain House, and she made me promise to smuggle out some of the hot cross buns inside a napkin. Think anyone will notice if I do?"

"I could always get you a pan right out of the kitchen, would that be enough?"

"Maybe? Two, two pans would be enough."

"New tradition: we have Easter brunch together up here every year."

"I second that."

"I third that. More buns, please."

"Deal. Every year. All of us together. Now, someone please pass me more of that Jell-O mold before we all turn into a pile of mush."

"I have to go."

"What?"

"What?"

"What'd she say?"

"Yeah, I gotta go. I'm not . . . feeling well."

"No no, don't go."

"She's not feeling well?"

"Clara."

"I gotta go."

Chapter 15

I thought about what Roxie and Natalie had said all day. That it wasn't perfect for them, that it was sticky and messy and crazy, but at a certain point they just gave up and gave in. There was a part of me that wanted to give in.

So give in.

Brunch just proved I couldn't. Full of talk of family and tradition and shared memories and common ground. People take for granted the primer that runs like a baseline throughout much of your modern American family. Half the people at the table didn't know one another a year ago, and yet they all had a similar background, a shorthand when thinking back on their collective childhood and how it just was. I didn't have that. I didn't have half of that.

So they were planning on brunch again together next year. Same time, same place. The idea of this, just the casualness of people making plans without a care in the world. If someone couldn't make it, eh. No biggie. If Natalie and Oscar decided to spend their holiday in Manhattan with her family instead, no biggie. Plans change, one sweet family vignette can easily be swapped out with another because most people have

Norman Fucking Rockwell on tap, ready to serve up at a moment's notice.

Plans get changed. And sometimes people get left out and left behind and forgotten without a second thought. But if you didn't make those plans, see, and you kept it all loose and free and no commitments, no ties, no binds . . . well then. You were the only person who had the power to break your heart.

I was the only one who could break my heart.

I sat on my balcony for hours, ignoring the texts I knew were pouring in from Roxie and Natalie, just rocking in my chair, watching the lake, relishing the outside. The air was cool, gentle, soft. Outside. I could hear owls calling to each other, the soft lap of the waves rocking the dock below, the wind in trees wearing their new spring green. Outside. The night sky was clear, a thousand stars twinkling down on this Easter Sunday. Outside.

It was easier on the outside.

I heard the knocking on my door, but I ignored it. It came once, twice, then three times, each time a little harder and more insistent. I ignored them all. Things were cracking open wide, and I needed the space outside to handle it.

But when I heard my front door open, and I heard footsteps walking across the floor inside, I knew who it was.

"Not a good time right now," I said, my voice sounding gruff and scratchy even to me.

"You don't have a headache, do you?" he asked. From inside.

"No," I answered. From outside.

"I'd love to know what's going on in that beautiful head of yours," he said. Inside.

I let out a watery sigh, squeezing my eyelids shut tight. "No, you really don't." Outside. "How was the rest of the day?"

Footsteps across the floor. When he spoke, he was just inside the balcony door. "Fine. Good. Smooth. Terrible."

"Terrible?"

"It wasn't the same," he said softly. "Without you."

I wanted to be inside. Oh God, I wanted it more than anything. I wanted my own piece of it, my piece of this American pie that everyone else had. To be included, in step, in touch, cared for and caring, inside. But could I do it?

I heard him take one more step, his footsteps changing from soft muffled carpet to sharp scraping slate. He was outside now, with me.

I stood, turned, and saw him standing there. Tall and strong, freckled and bespectacled, his warm eyes connected with mine and there he was.

"Hi," he said, his voice low and raspy. He'd worked hard all day, making this day special for everyone he encountered.

"Hi," I said, my own voice sounding breathless. I hovered just out of reach, on the balls of my feet, teetering right on the edge. I wanted to turn around, to sink back into my rocking chair and tell him to go away, stay inside, stay safe. But then he smiled, you see. And I ran. What had been cracking open wide all day now completely disintegrated and I gave in and fucking ran. Toward him.

I threw myself into his arms, and he caught me, half inside, half outside. I was overwhelmed, but this time instead of panic, I felt butterflies and moonbeams and no small amount of straight-up lust.

I ran to him because I had to. Under a night sky literally on top of the world, where no one could see and no one could hear, and then my mouth was on his and it was everything.

I hit him with such force he groaned, but he groaned into my mouth, which was a little piece of sexy heaven. In an instant his arms went around me. In that same instant, I wrapped around him, my hands wild and my fingers searching, seeking, finding heat and warmth and smooth skin and a tie goes flying. And then his hands were all over me, pushing at my dress straps, his lips pulling at my skin there, on my shoulders and on my collarbone, finding willing and wanting and wanton flesh there, and my breath goes sighing. Walls are crumbling down and feet are stumbling around and the stars are above and my fingers are below and a belt goes zinging while my skin is singing.

His fingers plunged into my hair, anchoring me rough and tender as I sank to my knees, cracking my kneecap on the cold slate, but I didn't even care because his breath is uneven and choppy and his back thuds up against the stacked chimney and tiny bits of sooty brick rain down on me and everything smells like forgotten bits of burn and char and what once was, but under that there is the hint, the promise of underground green growing things and renewal and spring.

New. Fresh. Clean. Untarnished. Simple.

And, oh my God, I need to have this man now.

"Clara. Clara." He said my name with urgency, scraping the sky with heat and need. I scrambled at his zipper and he's there, he *is* heat and need, and as I open my mouth and bring him inside, his entire body stiffens and his hands freeze in my hair and my name becomes the only word he knows because right now, under these stars, I'm the only woman he knows and needs and wants and . . .

He's fucking incredible. And he's fucking my mouth. This man with the pocket square is fucking my mouth. I chanced a look up and good lord he's silhouetted against blazing stars, his head thrown back and the world is his jawline and it's the single most erotic thing that I've ever experienced.

Guttural. Frenzied. I released him only to take him back into my mouth again, licking and thrusting with my tongue as he thrust against it, barely in control, and that was more than okay because I love when this man loses control and puts his hands on me.

And he did. Holy fuck, he did. His fingers dug deep into my hair, tugging and pulling, and *why does that feel so empowering when it shouldn't*, but holy fuck, it did. His hands were large, his fingers long, wrapped around my head, lost, then found again as he moved me on him.

I grasped him firmly at the base, fingertips trailing up and down as I released him from my mouth slowly, only to take him in again once more, slow and sure.

"That's. Incredible," he murmured, and his fingertips moved, untwisting from my hair, sliding across my face, slow and sure. Sweetly, he traced down over my cheekbones, along my jaw, so gently. "Incredible."

And then he moves, pulling me off him and kneeling in front of me, kissing me again, licking at my lips, and once more I opened for him, tasting salt and sweet and Archie everywhere.

"I need to see you," he whispered, and both of us scrambled for the buttons on my dress. In a tumble of hands and fingers, my elbow goes one way and his face goes another and his glasses went flying off into the darkness.

"Sorry." I chuckled, but marveled at how open he seemed like this, nothing between me and those beautiful indigo eyes.

He hung his head, laughing himself. "The terrible part is I can't see a thing without those, everything is literally a blur."

His hair tickled pleasantly at my collarbone. "That's something a girl loves to hear."

"Won't be a moment," he said, patting around on the balcony next to him. "Now, this is sexy, isn't it?"

"Are you kidding?" I asked, leaning up on my elbows to watch him, trousers askew, tie hanging sideways, hair every which way. "It's ridiculous how sexy you are."

"Hmm," he said, still looking for his glasses.

"Go right." I guided him. "They're right there by the—"

"Shit."

I gulped. "—railing."

They were long gone, pushed over the side by Archie's roving hands. "Unbelievable," he muttered. "Of course this would happen."

I sat up, then crawled toward where he was. "Come on, you don't need to see me," I said, running one hand down his back. "To see me." I picked up his left hand and brought it to my breast. His breath caught. "Tell me."

"Tell you?" His voice was thick and strangled.

"What you feel. How I feel." I brought his other hand to my face, turning into it and pressing a kiss in the center of his palm. "What you're thinking."

"Eventually, Clara, you're going to have to tell me what you're thinking."

Oh. I nodded, unable to speak, unable to answer, but knowing if I was giving over to this, I was giving everything over. I nodded again into his hand, and that was what he needed.

The hand on my breast brushed lightly across, the cotton of my dress thin enough that I could feel his fingers curving as the heat of my skin guided him. I shivered, my skin reacting to his touch instantly. Reaching up, I thumbed one button open, then another, pulling at the bodice of my dress to grant him access. I wanted, no I needed, to feel his hands on my bare skin.

"Tell me," I murmured again, needing his words as much as his touch.

"You're . . . soft," he said, a faint smile ghosting across his lips. "So soft."

"Mm-hmm." I sighed as his fingers found the opening of my dress and slipped inside.

"Lace?" he asked. His thumb brushed across my nipple and my back arched.

"Mm-hmm." I sighed again.

"It's rough, a little, I can feel the tiny threads catching against the grooves on my fingertips," he said. "But then your skin, so smooth."

I slipped down onto my elbows, my head dropping back as he moved over me. His mouth trailed kisses down the column of my neck, licking at the base of my throat, nipping at my collarbone. He held himself above me, his hand still exploring. He circled my nipple, feeling it rise under his touch.

He smiled. "You're excited."

I could feel him against my thigh, hard and thick. "You're not?"

His response was to nip harder, his teeth nibbling along the top of my breast, which was now rising and falling with my every breath, growing faster and more heated with every kiss. He slipped my bra strap from my shoulder, dipped his head, and put his mouth on me.

Every nerve ending twisted, every neuron fired, and every toe pointed as his rough tongue dragged across my nipple.

"Mmm . . . Archie . . ." I sighed, my back arching off the ground as his lips surrounded me. But where I was a wriggly squiggly mess beneath him, he suddenly stilled. His back stiffened, his hands froze, his entire demeanor changed.

"Archie?" I asked, reaching up to smooth his hair back from his brow.

"I need to tell you something," he whispered, still frozen.

"Okay . . ." I replied, wondering what in the world? The tension beneath us had changed, shifted somehow. He was worried, anxious, and still frozen. "You want to tell me, or my boob?"

He snorted, his breath warm on the very boob in question. But the tension broke once again, and I could see him relax, if only a little. I curled my arm beneath my head, propping myself up so I could see him. He leaned on one arm over me, his other hand reflexively pushing the missing eyeglasses up his nose.

He was still nervous.

"I've only slept with one woman my entire life."

Oh. *Oh* . . .

"I've only ever had one first time. Ashley and I were sixteen, we'd snuck away to her parents' beach house. We had candles, and wine, and soft music, and it was all very planned out, very perfect."

I mentally flashed on the backseat of a 1972 Chevelle with Chuckie Sullivan, Nickelback on the CD player. I shuddered.

He took my shudder as laughter. "I know, it sounds silly, right?"

"Not silly, it actually sounds really nice," I replied, smoothing his hair back again.

He leaned into it, closing his eyes, turning his head to kiss the center of my palm. "I was just thinking how funny it is, losing your virginity. It's something that happens to everyone, but in such different ways.

"The point is, I was with Ashley, and only Ashley. I've never done this with anyone else. I wasn't sure I'd even want to do this, after she was gone."

"Listen, Archie, we don't have to—"

"Until you, Clara," he interrupted, his eyes flashing open and searing into mine. "I want you, I fucking want you more than I ever thought possible, but I'm . . . well . . . a little out of my depth here."

"Archie?"

"Yes?"

I moved swiftly, rising up and rolling to the side, bringing him with me, rolling us both so that now I was on top, moving his hand down to my leg and hitching it around his hip. "Believe me when I say, you've *so* got this. But if you want to stop then you just say the word."

His eyes, good lord those eyes. Deeply blue, deeply troubled, at war with his past and his present. They searched my own for answers. I couldn't tell him what to do, but I could give him a hint, couldn't I?

Breathless, I slid his hand farther along my thigh. Breathless, I hooked his thumb through the band of my panties. And then, still breathless, I placed both of my hands on his chest, waiting to see what he would do.

He did nothing. His chest rose and fell, and I rose and fell right along with him. My head was telling me to smile, to reassure him, to tell him it was okay and we could take this slow and at whatever pace he needed.

My heart was telling me to be patient, because any second now Archie's internal war would be over and he'd be ready for fast filthy fucking, the kind without candles and soft music.

Any second now.

Any second now.

Any second n—

His thumb moved. The thumb, the thumb that controlled the fate of my panties. And of the world. It was one and the same as that perfect thumb dragged against my skin, hooked to the flimsiest scrap of silk you ever did see, even if Archie couldn't without his glasses, and God bless America if he didn't drag those panties right off.

And then I took over. Because I knew he needed me to. And because I wanted to. I rose up over him, my dress hiked up around my hips, and breasts spilling out of the top, and grasped him firmly, positioning him just so that when I slipped down down down he

Oh
He
Was
There
And
Oh
He
Was
So
Hard

and something very much like wonder crossed his face as I took him inside of me.

And then something exactly like lust crowded in as *he* crowded in, *Christ he crowded in*, filling me up and raising me up and he thrust into me from below.

Uncertainty was gone. *Should have*s and *what if*s were gone. And in their place was pure carnal heat. Archie's hands gripped my hips, pushing and pulling as he filled me up and I moved on him, rocking, feeling every ridiculous inch of him inside, he was inside while we were outside and it was frightening and maddening and *Jesus was I coming* and *how could I be coming already* and I shuddered and shook as all the colors ran and the world narrowed down before it exploded.

He sat up beneath me, lips on my breast and hands on my backside as I rode him hard, rode him to another orgasm and another, anchored by those searching eyes, swirling ink and beautiful as his own powerful orgasm shook through his body.

When his hips finally stilled, when his fingers released my skin, when the cords in his neck finally receded and the flush in his cheeks flooded in, we collapsed onto the balcony, his lips alternating between dropping tired kisses onto my neck and whispering my name.

Clara, he said, over and over again. God, I loved hearing this man say my name.

Chapter 16

"Are you sure you want to go?"

"I don't want to, but I really can't see a thing. I'll be back in just a few minutes. If you want me to come back, that is."

"I want you. To come. Back." I grinned, tucking my arm through his as I led him to the door. "See what I did there?"

"I didn't, which is why I'm running down to my office to get my spare glasses. But yes, I see what you did there."

We'd come inside from the balcony, messy and tumbled looking, blissful and happy looking, still kissing and touching, but when Archie tripped over an ottoman and careened off a lamp, he'd insisted on retrieving his extra set of glasses from downstairs.

I didn't want him to leave. I could still feel him, where he'd been, inside me. But . . .

I peeked out into the hallway. "The coast is clear."

"Are you sure?"

"There's no one in the hall," I said as I guided him out the door. Whether or not we'd been moaning and groaning on the balcony only moments before was beside the point, he was still in charge here, and I'd rather not anyone see him ducking out of my room with messy hair and swollen lips. And lipstick on his collar. And, oh dear, lipstick on his . . . pants. I swooped in quickly, licking my thumb and rubbing at his collar.

"What's this?" he asked, taking the opportunity to slip his arms around my waist and hold me close.

"Trying to cover up the evidence," I whispered, scrubbing at the stain. "Eh, you're gonna need to send this out to the cleaners. And not your regular cleaners, unless you want them to know you've been fooling around with someone who's been wearing fuck-me-red lipstick."

"That's not really the name, is it?" he murmured, kissing my neck.

"Might as well be. Send those pants out too," I said, laughing when he missed my neck and nearly kissed the door instead. "Honestly, you're like Mr. Magoo."

"Mr. Magoo wouldn't have made you come three times, Ms. Morgan."

"You just called a coatrack Ms. Morgan, but you're right about the other thing."

"Three times," he said once more, unable to keep the pride out of his voice.

"Three times, Mr. Bryant," I agreed.

"So far," he whispered deliciously in my ear, pulling me tightly against him.

"Someone could see," I warned, as his hands dipped below my waist, grabbing a handful of my backside and giving it a squeeze.

He looked left, then right, decided he could see well enough to know that no one was there, and leaned in to kiss me slowly. And thoroughly. "Give me ten minutes. Just let me get my glasses."

"You don't need your glasses, Mr. Bryant," I answered, breathless.

He bit his lower lip. Then he bit my lower lip. Then he said, "When I get back, I'm going to fuck you again." I gasped. "And this time, I want to watch."

He took the key from my hand, then gave me a little push back. Pocketing my key, he winked. "Ten minutes."

And then he was gone. Hot damn. I loved a well-dressed man who had a filthy mouth.

Exactly ten minutes later I smiled as I heard the key in the lock turning. I heard the door open, then close, and then his footsteps as he crossed through the living room.

"Clara?"

"In here," I replied, turning the water on. A moment later I saw his reflection in the mirror as he entered the bathroom. I turned from the faucet just in time to see his eyes widen behind his glasses. And then his jaw clench.

Standing in the middle of the bathroom, I slipped the robe from my shoulders and let it fall to the floor. I heard his intake of breath as he saw me for the first time, naked and waiting for his return.

"I was a little cold from being outside. Spring is here, but it's still a bit chilly, don't you think?" I spoke as though it was perfectly natural for me to be naked, walking toward him. I made sure my hips swayed a little more than normal, made sure there was a little extra bounce there, and in my breasts as well. I reached across him to grab two towels, and in doing so brushed up against him. "I thought I'd warm up in the bathtub, maybe you'd like to join me? It's big enough for two."

"Big." He nodded, his eyes round as he watched me move across the room. I watched his gaze slip across my body, his lust evident, his body taut like a live wire.

I stepped into the tub, slipping under the water. "I'll just be in here, when you're ready." I grinned, feeling the warmth swirl all around. He unbuttoned the rest of his shirt, kicked off his shoes, and pulled his suit jacket off.

I knew what he meant when he said he wanted to watch. I wanted to see him, see his body, take in every angle and plane that I'd missed on the balcony in the darkness. With each article of clothing that hit the floor, I saw more of this man, and more of what I'd been missing.

"You're kind of gorgeous, you know that?" I called out to him as he stepped out of his pants. He was gorgeous. Broad shoulders, long strong arms, narrow tapered waist. A little bit of auburn-colored hair covered his chest. That same hair blazed a trail south, disappearing below the band of his boxers.

"Gorgeous?" He ran his hands through his hair, making it stand even farther on end. He walked over to the bathtub, kneeling down just beside it. He watched me, the tips of my breasts just breaking the water's surface. He gazed down at me, watching me, taking everything in. "Jesus, look at you."

I bit my lower lip, looking up at him through heavy lids. Keeping his eyes on mine the entire time, he slipped off his boxers, and stepped into the tub.

I could feel the water change as he moved behind me, the water rising to the very edge of the tub but stopping just shy. I watched as his hands slipped around my waist, tugging me back against him. Christ, he was hard, I could feel him sliding across my bottom.

"You're very tall," I remarked, as his legs snaked around mine, at least a foot longer.

"Am I tall or are you short?" he asked, nipping at the exact spot where my shoulder became my neck.

"Both, I suppose." I leaned back against him. "If we flood this bathroom how much trouble are we going to be in?"

"Who's going to flood the bathroom?"

I turned to look back at him, the movement disrupting the

water and making it nearly overflow. "See, I gotta let some of this water out."

"Clara, don't worry about it," he started to say, as I leaned forward toward the drain, unplugging it to let some of the water out. "On second thought," he groaned, running his hands down my back toward my hips, which were now poised in the air as I sat forward on all fours, "what a wonderful idea, feel free to let out as much water as you feel is necessary." And then he kissed me. On my backside. One cheek, then the other, his teeth nipping my skin and then . . .

"Oh!" I exclaimed, tipping forward against the front of the tub, slapping at the tile.

"Hold still," he growled, as he tilted my hips forward, angling them upward as his tongue licked at my clit. We both moaned as he touched me this way for the first time, his mouth surrounding me, working me, sucking and fucking. The cold tile pressed against my breasts as his hot mouth devoured me as I rocked my hips against his face. His groans were as guttural as mine as I came in his mouth, on his tongue, seeing stars and splashing water everywhere as I came apart for him once more.

He splashed plenty of water of his own as he rose up behind me, put me on all fours properly and drove into me hard from behind.

"The water," I panted, his hand slipping across my back and sliding under me, tweaking a nipple on his way to my shoulder to hang on tight, moving me back against him. "The water is . . . fuck off that's good . . . the water is going everywhere!"

With his left hand he swept a pile of towels off the shelf and onto the floor exactly where it had started to puddle, then slipped his hand down along my back, ending with a resounding wet smack on my ass.

"Let me worry about the water, Bossy, you just concentrate on how this feels."

And I did. I gave over and threw back my head, arching my back, arching into him, letting everything I was feeling run wild across my body as his groans became deeper and more animal by the second, using my body, hot and wet and slippery and right exactly . . . there.

∞

"I'm spoiled now, you realize this?"

"Spoiled?"

"Mm-hmm," I murmured as his hand traced a path down my shoulder, along my elbow, slipping down to my hip, smoothing across my bottom and back up again. His hand made this trip over and over again, while the other one held my breast. Curled around me almost entirely, we lay like spoons in a drawer. A very cozy, warm, contented drawer. After refilling the tub and enjoying an actual bath we'd retreated to my bed, exhausted and waterlogged but still unable to stop touching each other. Before retreating, however, Archie took a few moments to build a fire and the result was spectacular. With the room lit solely by firelight, everything seemed softer somehow. Corners were rounded, edges were blurred, even the very air seemed gentle. It was quiet and comfortable, and just feeling his hands on my body felt soothing, grounding somehow.

"All of this. The fire, the bed, the gorgeous." I kissed his forearm, nuzzling against it. "My bed won't feel quite the same now without you in it. I've been spoiled."

"Well, I'll do my best to stay in it as long as possible," he replied, kissing me just behind my ear and bumping his hips into mine. Everywhere we could be touching, we were. Skin to skin, contoured and full snuggle.

As much as I was loving the full snuggle, the reality of what had happened, what had been happening for weeks now, was unavoidable.

"What's wrong?"

"Hmm?" I asked.

He kissed behind my ear again. "You sighed. Almost like you were deflating."

I shrugged. "Just thinking about what happens next. How do we handle this? What do we do?"

"I'd like to think we'd have another go, but you've exhausted me. I'm not complaining, just exhausted."

"Not about that." I laughed, flipping over so I could see him. The sheet nudged down, uncovering my bare bottom. I was thrilled to see his eyes wander, his pupils dilate, his breathing change. He might be exhausted, but there was no doubt he'd be having another go before the night was through. But for now . . . "I mean, about us. This was amazing, you're amazing, but what the hell are we doing? Like, seriously, what are we doing?"

"I don't really think it's up to me," he said, keeping his eyes on my body and not meeting my gaze, "is it?" And now his eyes were on mine, searching, wondering.

"I'm leaving." My body went cold even saying the words out loud, to say nothing of the light that dimmed in his gaze. "I mean, not right now, not tomorrow, not even next week. But I am leaving. Eventually."

"I know." I ran my hand through his hair, and just like that very first time he leaned into it, hungry for my touch. "I could lock you up in the attic like a little stowaway, tie you up, latch you to the bedpost."

"I feel like this conversation has taken a turn."

"Best possible turn. Lonely hotelier can't stand the thought of his tiny sex goddess leaving him, so he hides her away from the world. Makes her dress up like Princess Leia or the woman from *Flashdance*."

"What's happening here?"

"Hey, you're leaving, I might as well get all my fetishes out on the table now, right?" His tone was teasing. Mostly.

I kissed him. "I wish I could promise you more, but I just can't right now. My life, my world, is swooping in and fixing things and then swooping out to help someone else. I'm like a luxury-brand Mary Poppins."

"First of all, thanks for putting the idea in my head of you dressed up like a Victorian governess, that'll be impossible for me to ignore the next time you call me Mr. Bryant. Second of all, why did this happen? Tonight. What changed?"

I bit my lip, thinking. Then spoke from the heart. "Today was hard for me. I don't do holidays. Or family gatherings." I shook my head. "They aren't really my thing. I tend to avoid. But today, being with everyone, and being with you, it was . . . what's the word . . ."

"Incredible? Awesome? Super-terrific?"

"I didn't vomit."

He frowned. "That's three words. And not what I was expecting."

"If you knew me, really knew me, then you'd know today was a victory. I mean, I did panic and I did run away, but I didn't tell you to go and to tell you the truth, before, when we were all together, when I wasn't freaking out, and I wasn't focusing so hard on getting through it, I actually enjoyed myself. And when you showed up, looking ridiculously cute, it just hit me like a ton of bricks. I realized if I only have this little bit of time with you, then I want you. It's unprofessional, it's scandalous, it's literally the worst thing I could possibly do, sleep with the guy I'm here to work with."

"Just to be clear, I'm the guy, right?"

I grinned, but went on. "But in the end, there were a hundred reasons to run like hell today, and only one reason to stay. And you're the reason, Archie." He closed his eyes, and smiled. "I'll have to go away one day. And I don't know what will happen then, which makes me so fucking selfish for saying this, but I'm going to say it anyway. I want you. For as long as I can have you."

He stared into my eyes, and I felt like he wanted to know more. To ask more, to dig deeper and find out what was really going on under the surface. But maybe he also saw in my eyes that I'd said all I could tonight, and it was more than I'd shared in a very long time. Maybe he thought I was selfish, but wanted to be selfish too. God knows if there was ever a man who deserved a moment or two of pure carnal bliss free of obligation it was Archie. In the end he said nothing. He rolled me over, slowly, until he was on top of me once more. My legs slipped around his hips as naturally as can be, no thought needed.

I needed to say one more thing. "We have to keep it quiet, though, okay? No one can know."

He nodded.

"I'm sure that'd be better for you too, right? Not having to explain what we might be up to?"

He paused a beat, then kissed me softly. "If I thought you'd let me, I'd walk you down the center staircase tomorrow morning, with my hands all over you for all the world to see."

I kissed him back, just as softly. "Impossible."

He nodded. Pulled his hips back. And entered me with one slow, smooth thrust.

I dropped my head back onto the pillow, a small smile toying at my lips. "I thought you were exhausted?"

"Impossible," he murmured, drawing back out almost all the way. "What was it you were saying the other day?"

"When?"

"About liking it shallow."

I felt him move inside me, slow and barely there, drawing it out and making me shiver. "Yeah. Shallow is good."

Chapter 17

$\mathcal{I}$ spent the day working. Working in only the very most literal sense of the word. Because in actuality while I was doing this "work," I was having a devil of a time getting my mind away from where it wanted to spend its time . . . with Archie. While I was revisiting the finer points of up-selling with the staff in the reservations office, I was really considering the finer points of his ass, and what a fine one it was. Especially when I thought about my hands on it, gripping it as he drove in and out of me, impossibly shallow, impossibly maddening . . . as promised. So when he looked at me across the table during the meeting and asked if I was ready for another round, I spit my coffee, and it was only after he concluded his sentence with the words *of cost projections* that I managed to recover and get Mrs. Toomey some napkins to clean up the blouse of hers I'd just ruined.

As I went over the books from the spa's weekend business and saw that not only was my new special a hit, but that the team wanted to keep it going all spring and possibly into the summer, what my mind was actually remembering was Archie's voice as he spoke low and deep to me in bed the night before, telling me to keep it going, just like that, and don't you stop and you're incredible to see when you come. So when he popped in to check on how spa bookings were coming along for the next month and told the ladies who had just finished their mineral bath plunge to make sure they come again soon, I coughed into my hand so hard that one of the attendants actually brought me a bottle of water.

And when the lunch menu featured a sausage bar . . . I turned tail and literally ran, covering my reddened face and struggling to keep the giggles in check. Archie saw me running from the dining room and laughed so loud I could hear him over the din of a hundred guests.

I was giddy. And giddy girls giggle. But they also try very, very hard to get through their working day. Especially when at the end of the day there was something (someone!) waiting for them.

Are you busy tonight?

Depends.

On?

What you've got
planned for me.

Ice skating.

Oh.

Not a fan?

I was hoping for some-
thing a little more . . .
horizontal.

That'll come later.

As long as I do.

Three times, Ms. Morgan . . .
three times.

Indeed. So, skating? Isn't
it a bit warm for that?

Indeed. Technically we closed
the rink last weekend, but
we usually leave it open for a
few extra days for the staff.

I smiled in spite of myself. This shouldn't be so complicated, but it just was.

Not sure it's such a good
idea for us to go skating.
Isn't that a little "public"?

Already thought of that. Last
night was the last night for
the staff.

And you're not techni-
cally staff, so . . .

So, ice skating? 8 p.m.?

Sure. Then what?

Then the horizontal.

You've never seen
me skate. It'll happen
sooner than you think.

8 p.m.?

Done. Meet you there,
Mr. Bryant.

I'd jogged by the skating rink several times during my stint at Bryant Mountain House, but since it was set back from one of the main lake trails, I'd only gotten a little peek from time to time. With the guest count so low this spring they hadn't really been keeping it staffed, and I'd yet to hear a single person actually mention that they wanted to go skating. It really was too bad. This place was literally made for winter sports, but with the snowfall less and less every year they just weren't able to offer the kind of snowshoeing and cross-country skiing they'd been famous for in the good old days.

The good old days. Personally, I'd always known my best days were ahead of me, but not so for most. I'd found many people lost more time revisiting the past than they spent planning their future, whereas I'd always been planning. To get away, to be on my own, to succeed and create the kind of life for myself where I could come to a place like this, stay in the biggest suite they had, order an ice cream sundae at ten thirty in the morning on a Tuesday just because I could and not expect anyone but me to pay for it.

I could too, by the way. I had no life to speak of, but I made a great living. I lived on the road most of the time, free room and board typically, and I'd logged enough frequent-flier miles to fly first class around the world several times over . . . enough for me and a guest, should I so choose.

But I never so choose. I never even got close to so choose. I banked mileage and hotel points like they were going out of style, and I was one of the only people my age I knew who had two years' worth of salary just sitting in an emergency fund. Like I said, I had no life.

But tonight, I was ice-skating. So I chased away those blue thoughts and filled them instead with auburn, freckly thoughts.

While still chilly enough for an oversized sweater, the air was warmer tonight, which made it nice to leave the coat and scarf behind. I wore my mittens, though, knowing I'd be spending the better part of the evening on the ice rather than gliding effortlessly across it.

There was a dip in the tree line, a narrow muddy trail with a sign marking the left turn to head up to Bryant Rink. They sure liked to put their name on things.

As I got closer, I could hear music. Just before I went around the last bend, there was a rope going across the pathway with a sign that said Closed for the Season.

"Archie?" I called, wondering if I should just head on in.

You should have called him Mr. Bryant, anyone could be in there with him.

Dammit. "Mr. Bryant?" I corrected, trying to see through the trees. And why did that music sound so familiar?

"Come on up," I heard him call down, and I slipped underneath the rope. Coming around the last bend, I could see the rink as the trees thinned. Framed by an arched timber roof but open on the sides, the rink wasn't big, it wasn't small, it was just right. A small window opened to what I guessed would be a kitchen, serving hot chocolate on cold wintry days; there were a few chairs scattered around, an equipment counter for checking out ice skates, and because it was Bryant Mountain House, an enormous fieldstone fireplace, complete with rocking chairs in front of the roaring fire.

"You built a fire? For just the two of us?" I called out, still not seeing Archie. Walking around toward the fire, I saw a mug of the expected hot chocolate, still hot enough to be steaming, then heard a whoosh from behind.

I turned to see Archie skating across the white ice. He was fast, his feet laced into thick black hockey skates, and as he neared the edge he did that weird thing boys always do to girls at skating rinks.

He stopped short and sprayed me with ice.

"Is this because I don't have a pigtail for you to pull?" I sputtered, wiping the slush from my face.

He muttered something that sounded an awful lot like 'I'll give you something to pull' as he leaned over the railing. "Ready to lace up?"

"We're just going to go right to it? No warming up, no easing in, just boom, we're doing it?"

"I had no idea ice-skating could be so riddled with innuendo."

"I live in the world of innuendo."

His eyes twinkled. "I can take another pass around, shoot you with some more ice if you want, but . . ."

I shook my head. "Point me toward the skates, Hotel Boy, and you'll see just how fast I can go down."

He coughed, not quite smothering a laugh. "I picked out a few sizes for you, one of them should fit. I had to dip into the kids' skates, your feet are really tiny."

"Good thing my boobs aren't."

"A very good thing," he said, and this time made no effort to contain his laughter. I chanced a look back at him, and he was skating backward away from me, holding his hands out like he was squeezing melons.

I looked on the counter and there were indeed several pairs of skates lined up. He was right, the only ones that actually fit me were kids' skates. I knew they were for kids because they were pink and covered with kittens.

"What's taking you so long, Ms. Morgan?" he yelled across the ice.

"The laces, they're all double knotted," I yelled back, struggling to get them untied. A few quick swooshes later and he was by my side, then at my feet.

"Gimme."

"Ask nicely."

"Bossy, please gimme."

"That's better," I said, handing him the tangled mess.

He worried at the knot for a moment. While he did, I took that same moment to admire him. It wasn't often that I got to see Archie dressed more casually, and while there will never be anything as gorgeous as this man in a tailored suit, there was something very appealing about seeing him dressed down and comfortable. Wearing well-worn jeans and a wheat-colored cable-knit sweater with just a hint of a blue T-shirt sticking out of the top, he looked relaxed and happy. Well, he was happy until he started working on the knot I'd given him.

"It's terrible," he murmured.

"I tried to tell you," I protested as he set the skates down and looked up at me. His eyelashes were the exact color of his hair, maybe even a little more deeply red. Set against the deep blue of his eyes, they were mesmerizing.

"It's terrible," he repeated, placing his hands on either side of the wooden bench I was sitting on and rising up on his knees, "that this is the first chance I've had to kiss you all damn day."

"That is terrible," I agreed, as he brought his face to within inches of mine. I could feel his warm breath puffing against my lips.

He kissed me once, then again. Soft, gentle, warm.

He pulled back to look at me. "I thought about you."

"You did?"

He nodded. "I thought about that little body of yours, naked in the tub, all wet and waiting."

I licked my lips. "Not just wet from the water."

"Jesus," he exhaled, hanging his head on my shoulder. I took the opportunity to drop a kiss on the top of his head.

"Let's get this skating over with so we can go be naked somewhere," I said. His shoulders shook. "Are you laughing or crying?" I asked.

"Both," he answered, lifting his head and kissing me soundly. "Come on, Bossy, let's hit the ice."

Knots untangled, he helped me slip the skates on, not without taking the time to run his hands from my ankle to my hip and back again, and then took my hand to help me up.

I waddled to the railing. "What I said earlier, about being shitty at skating?"

"Yes?" he asked, stepping out onto the ice, still holding my hand.

I took my first step out onto the ice. He looked back, then down.

"Yeah, I wasn't kidding," I replied, my butt hitting the ice within a nanosecond of my trying to actually stand on it.

"Oh man," he murmured as I floundered below.

"You should definitely not help me up." I scowled, trying like hell to get my feet underneath me but failing miserably.

"You run marathons," he said.

"Yep." My left foot shot out in front of me.

"You compete in triathlons."

"Also. Dammit." My right foot shot out behind me. "True."

"You chased me up a mountain, for God's sake, and almost beat me."

"I did. Beat you." I hung in midair, the only thing keeping me from plunging back onto the ice with my legs crossed was his hand, which I clung to like a chin-up bar.

"But you can't skate?" He was incredulous.

"You're lucky you're so pretty." I huffed, puffed, struggled, and strained to regain my balance, and the tiniest bit of dignity. I scrambled back up, climbing Archie like a ladder, until I stood before him once more. Teetering violently but standing.

"I can't believe I found something you're not good at," he said, his voice full of wonder.

"Now, look," I started, poking him in the chest and in doing so, losing my balance once more. This time he caught me tightly against his chest to prevent me from going down again. "Don't you make fun of me," I said directly to his belly button.

"Oh, if I only had a camera," he mused.

"Oh, if I only had a hammer, I'd hammer you in—"

"Let's try something different," he hastily proclaimed. Pulling me back up to my full height once more, he stepped carefully around, expertly dodging my flailing blade-laden feet, to stand just behind me. Grasping me around the waist firmly, he tucked me back against him. "Give me your hands."

"What's happening, what are you doing?" My hands were what kept me from eating ice; the idea that he was taking that away from me was scary at best, world ending at worst.

"Shhh," he soothed, his mouth at my ear. "Just relax. Literally relax, your muscles are like knots." Slowly, he pushed off with his own skates and moved us both across the ice.

"This is a terrible idea," I moaned, feeling the ice passing under us. "I'll end up taking you down with me."

"Not possible," he said, his own skates moving sure and steady across the slippery surface. "Get your balance, just trust it."

"But I'll fall. There's no way I won't fall, there's no way this won't end badly."

"Shhh," he said once more, squeezing my hands. "I won't let you fall."

"But you can't know that, we could hit a bump in the ice or a really slippery patch or—"

"—or we could skate around this motherfucking rink as many times as we want." He wrapped his strong hands once more around my mittens. "Now breathe. And enjoy this."

I started to protest again, to tell him how this was a terrible idea and when I did eventually crash and burn that I'd take him with me, but just as I opened my mouth I saw the most amazing thing. Coming up on my right was the equipment counter. And then . . . the fireplace. We'd gone around the rink, all the way around, back to where we'd started.

And I hadn't fallen. And hey look, there was my hot chocolate. The whole world had literally gone by, and was going by again, while I was in my head worrying about what might happen.

Point taken. I let out the breath I'd indeed been holding, and gave over.

"There she is," he whispered, feeling my body relax and ease into this. "You've totally got this."

"Well, I don't know if I got this, but . . ."

"Give yourself some credit," he replied. "Want to go a little faster?"

I didn't. So I said yes. Because I knew myself well enough to know that sometimes the very best thing I could do was do the exact opposite of what I wanted.

He pushed off just as the music changed, and I realized why it sounded familiar.

"Is this the *Dirty Dancing* soundtrack?" I asked as the world began to whiz by.

"Mm-hmm." He brought our hands down farther, letting go

for just the very splittiest of seconds before he firmly grasped my hips. "You said this place reminded you of the movie."

"It does." I chanced a look down the mountain toward the hotel that stood across the dark lake, the lanterns winking along the water's edge. "I thought you hated this movie."

"Everyone who lives up in the Catskills has been asked about this movie more times than I can count," he replied, guiding me around the turn with a speed that, if I'd been alone, could have taken out the fireplace. "But it did have great music."

"We should have a *Dirty Dancing*–themed weekend up here, how is that not a thing?"

"Because we don't want to turn our hotel into a theme park?"

"That won't happen, unless there's a Johnny Castle roller coaster, in which case I'm riding it."

"You see, this is how it starts."

"Are you going to show me your pachanga?"

He dropped a kiss on my neck, swooshed us even faster, and whispered, "You have no idea."

We skated for a minute or an hour, I have no idea. But it was fast and brilliant and breathless.

"You should take a turn on your own."

"But I did so well with you, shouldn't we just chalk it up as a success and not press our luck?"

"Once around the rink, Ms. Morgan, and then you can press anything you want."

"See, you think that's going to work on me, but it won't."

"You make it around the rink once on your own and I'll lick your pussy until you black out."

Next Winter Olympics you'll see me representing the good old US of A. The event? Speed skating.

Chapter 18

I'd been sleeping with Archie, and very much not sleeping, for three weeks, six days, fourteen hours, and thirty-two minutes. Forty-three minutes if you count the quickie in the broom closet . . . but who counts quickies, really?

Actually, technically, we should count quickies because even with limited time and elbow room, that man can lay it the fuck down. And pick it the fuck up. And lay it back the fuck down again.

We'd been discreet—at least I think we had. According to the rules in my head no one was the wiser that the man who stood at the bottom of the grand staircase each day welcoming guests with a kind word and hearty handshake was the same man who stood at the bottom of my bed, my legs thrown over his shoulders, AND spread me wide with his tongue until I was shaking then flipped me over like a top and thrust into me like a man possessed.

And as someone who has been possessed by this man countless times, trust me when I say it is something to witness.

His focus, his attention to detail, married with his absolute animal strength and wild passion, had laid me bare more times than I could count.

But he counted. Oh, he counted. He was like the accountant of orgasms, tallying them up and filing the total away, always chasing another, always pushing me until I was shivering and wrecked, a ball of sexual energy incapable of surviving another . . . but he always got one more. He knew my body, knew what I could do even when I thought it impossible, knew exactly what I needed.

And let me tell you a little something about Archie Bryant, the man with the buns. He loved it sideways, backways, frontways, and all ways, but what he loved most of all was when I sat astride him in one of those antique rocking chairs, taking him deep and then deeper with every thrust, every rock of that damn chair, my feet scrambling for purchase on the old Victorian carpet while he watched me fuck him wild in the grand gilded mirror that hung in the living room.

I'm telling you, it's always the guys with the freckles and the glasses. They're the ones you want to set your sights on. They're the ones who'll make you forget your name, but get you to say the filthiest things imaginable.

But today, I had to focus. Today, we had a visitor coming to the hotel.

Caroline Reynolds-Parker was an interior designer from the West Coast. I'd seen some of her work in a small boutique hotel in Sausalito, and later on in a spa just outside Philadelphia. She worked for a small firm in San Francisco, but had been focusing more and more on commercial design rather than residential. Based on her portfolio and reputation, I thought she'd be the perfect candidate to take a crack at shaking things up a bit here in the Catskills.

I waited for her in the lobby, watching as bellmen ran to and fro with luggage. We were getting close to summer now, and things were beginning to get busier. It was still pretty slow during the week, which is why I'd scheduled Caroline's visit on a Wednesday, but weekends were creeping up to about half full. Compared with how it was when I arrived in mid-March, business was booming.

The doors opened and a tall, slim woman with gorgeous blond hair walked in. Styled to a T with perfect California business casual, she sailed through the lobby with confidence borne by someone who was good at their job, and knew it.

"You must be Caroline," I said, greeting her with a smile.

"I must be," she said, answering my smile with one of her own. "If you're not Clara, then color me creeped out."

"Don't be creeped out," I answered, looking over my shoulder toward the front desk. "Beverly, we don't have Ms. Parker slated for room six-six-six, do we?"

"No ma'am, we've got her in . . . let me see . . ." Beverly, caught off guard, scrambled to find the booking.

"Never mind, Beverly, just kidding."

"Oh, this place is gonna be fun." Caroline laughed, setting down her bag and taking in the three-hundred-sixty-degree view of the lobby. "And gorgeous." She wandered over to the wallpaper, running her finger down the seam. "Linen. Expensive. A solid choice."

"Really?" I asked, my heart sinking. Maybe I didn't know as much as I thought I did, maybe the look of the hotel was exactly right and on point.

"A solid choice," she repeated, then looked me straight in the eye, "if it were still 1982."

I let out my breath. "Which it is not."

"Nope," she agreed, taking a few steps farther in. Looking down at the carpet, she rocked back and forth a few times, thunking her heel down. "There's hardwood under here, you just know there is." Her eyes danced.

I decided at that exact moment that no matter what she wanted to do, I was going to do my damnedest to make sure she got hired. As long as I could get Archie to cough up the money.

"I literally can't wait to see this place, I've been reading up ever since you contacted my office last month," Caroline said as I picked up her bag and led her to check-in. "I've already got some great ideas, although I'm sure you've got some of your own since you said we needed an overhaul of epic proportions."

"She said what?"

Dammit. I set the bag down, looked sideways at Caroline, and we both turned with the sweetest possible grins plastered across our pretty faces.

"Epic proportions only in the sense of the scale of the rooms, Mr. Bryant. Of course, when I emailed Jillian Designs and requested the world-renowned interior designer Caroline Reynolds—"

"Hyphen Parker," she chimed in.

"—of course, hyphen Parker, she was delighted when I told her how big and grand the rooms were, how truly luxurious and exceptional this property was," I continued, nodding at Archie.

"Oh yes, and can you imagine how thrilled I was that I'll be able to say that I worked in the famous Bryant Mountain House? Why, it'll practically ensure I can work at any hotel, I can't thank you enough, Mr. Bryant. Archie, I presume?" Caroline smiled, batting her lashes just enough that I knew he was done for.

Archie stood there, looking back and forth between the two of us, slightly befuddled but too gracious to show it. Bless his heart. He'd never be able to go up against the two of us.

But we'd let him think he won a few rounds.

I spent the morning giving Caroline the grand tour and reassuring Archie repeatedly that we wouldn't go overboard and that yes, this was necessary.

"I just can't get over the fact that these are all antiques, real antiques, not reproductions," Caroline gushed. We were standing in one of the Victorian rooms in the east wing, the wing I'd suggested we close down next winter to begin the renovations. "And the fireplaces, my God! Who would ever build a hotel these days and put fireplaces in every single room? Wood burning, no less."

"No one, is the easy answer," I replied, moving to the window and looking at the mountains. "No one would ever build a place like this again. It's too big, too fancy, the raw materials alone would price any builder right out of the market, to say nothing of the liability from an insurance perspective of having wood-burning fireplaces in every single room." I sighed. "A place like this will never be built again."

"I hate to say it, but you're right," Caroline said. She ran her fingers over the wall, tapping at the wallpaper. "There's plaster under this, actual plaster. Laid over chicken wire, and likely three layers of lath. That plaster is held together by lime, sand, possibly seashells, and almost definitely mixed with horsehair to bind it together. Can you imagine?" She pointed up at the ceiling where pictures hung by wire from the molding. "That's why there's almost always a picture rail in everything constructed before the turn of the last century, sometimes even through the twenties. That plaster is strong, almost like cement, but you drive a nail through it, something that was never supposed to be done, and it'll crumble like sand. But taken care of? You almost never need to repair it." She smoothed her hand over the wall. "Not even a ripple. They literally built this place to last."

I smiled. She got it.

"The interior design, however," she said briskly, grabbing her camera and beginning to work. "That was not meant to last. This we can change."

"Change?" Archie asked, standing just inside the door. He'd

excused himself for a bit to finish up some work before rejoining us for the room inspection.

"Easy, Mr. Bryant," I cautioned. "Nothing crazy, just a face-lift, right, Caroline?"

"Exactly," she answered, moving around the room as she took several pictures. "Here's the thing, Archie, do you know why so many houses from the 1920s have white-painted woodwork? Wood paneling, floor to ceiling in some cases, like in a dining room, but it's been painted over, do you know why?"

Archie looked at me, then back at Caroline, his face draining of color by the second. "You're not planning on painting over any wood paneling, are you? Because when I mention the words 'heart attack' and 'myself' in the same sentence, I can assure you it is not an exaggeration."

Caroline ignored the question. I couldn't ignore the way his freckles stood out against his imaginary heart attack face in the cutest way.

"The wood paneling got painted over, Archie, usually in the forties, because housewives then didn't want a house that looked like their mother's. When those homes were built, everything was beautiful wood paneling. Now we look at it as gorgeous, beautiful, exquisite craftsmanship and timeless detail. Right?"

"Right." Archie stood firm.

"But those new wives looked at it and saw dark, dark, dark. And, they saw their mother's house. No one wants to live in their mother's house, they wanted light and bright and new. They wanted something different. And it didn't stop there. Those same women who painted over their woodwork had families, raised them, and those daughters moved to the suburbs and wanted new and different. The ranch was born. Wall-to-wall shag carpet. Rec rooms, oddly enough with wall paneling, although this time it was thin veneer designed to be glued to the existing wall.

Then those women had kids and their kids ushered in the age of mauve and my personal favorite, the wallpaper border. I can't tell you how many homes I've redone covered in wallpaper border. You should've seen my kitchen in Sausalito when we first bought that house, good God. My point is, Archie, that every generation changes things. Right now, you're in luck, because everything old is new again and there's such an honoring of history right now. It's hip to have old things, repurposed and reimagined, but old. So we're going to make some changes, but they're changes you'll be able to live with. Changes that'll be so seamless with the original design of this hotel, changes that will honor the integrity and inherent beauty of a place like this, changes that, when I'm done, you'll swear you couldn't have imagined it any other way."

Damn. She was good.

"Damn. You're good," Archie breathed. He looked back and forth between the two of us. "Good God, if you two ever got together you could take over the world."

"Oooh," Caroline and I both breathed at the same time, and Archie threw up his hands in defeat.

"Forget I mentioned it." He laughed, but then looked serious again. "Everything you've said up until now has been very impressive, but I'll need to see examples of what you've done, and what you're planning to do, before I approve anything. I'm sure that's something we can all agree on, yes?"

"Of course," Caroline said, and walked over to shake on it.

He looked at her a moment, assessing, then at me, then shook her hand. "I look forward to it." Shifting his gaze from Caroline to me, he said, "Ms. Morgan, a word?"

"Of course, Mr. Bryant." I nodded, walking over. "Caroline, don't start the taking over the world plan before I get back."

"Of course! I'll need a dirty martini before I can start planning that."

I grinned and followed Archie out into the hall. He waited until I closed the door before rolling his eyes. "Where the hell did you find her?"

"San Francisco," I replied.

"She's going to be able to bring this in under budget?" he asked, looking over my shoulder.

"She says she can," I answered, looking over my shoulder as well. No one there.

"And she isn't allowed anywhere near my wood paneling."

"You got that right," I breathed, taking a step closer to him. Instead of stepping closer to me, though, he looked over his shoulder. "Is Walter stalking you or something, what the hell?"

"Don't mention Walter to me right now," he muttered, pulling a key from his pocket and slipping it into the lock of the room next door.

"What are you doing?" I asked, as he whisked me inside quickly. "Where did you get that key?"

"Skeleton key, I can get into anything in this hotel anytime I want," he said, shutting the door behind me. In an instant, I was up against the wall just inside the door. "And right now the only thing I want to get into is you."

"You've got to be kidding, we can't—fucking hell, Archie," I moaned, as he flipped up my skirt with one hand and covered my mouth with the other.

"You've got to keep your voice down," he warned, his voice muffled, his head being under my skirt and all. "You don't want your new friend to hear you."

I stepped out of the room, smoothed down my skirt and my hair, and headed back into the room where I'd left Caroline. She was measuring the inside of the windows, and stacks of blinds were strewn across the bed.

"Sorry about that, little crisis that blew up out of the blue."

"Oh, no trouble at all," Caroline said, calmly handing me the measuring tape, then walking over to the opposite wall. "You get everything worked out?"

"Hmm? Oh yes, yes, crisis solved, everyone was satisfied."

She smiled. "That's good. You know, I was thinking, even though I'm pretty sure that the plaster is fairly thick, you might want to have some insulation blown in, you know, just to pad the walls a bit? They've done wonders with insulation these days, we can have it added through a small hole down in the base, wouldn't cost nearly as much as it would've even ten years ago, and you'd be amazed what it can do not only for helping to regulate the temperature, but also how it can cut down on the noise." She looked me dead in the eye on that last part.

"Noise?" I asked, my voice higher than normal.

"Mm-hmm," she said, making a fist and thumping on the wall. The wall I'd just been on the other side of. "Thin walls, you know."

Mortified. I was. Mortified. Trying hard to keep my voice level, I stammered. "Oh. Y-Yes, I can see how that could be . . ."

"Clara?" she said, snapping her tape measure back open.

"Yes?" My voice had climbed three octaves. Mariah would be so proud.

"Don't worry about it." She extended the measuring tape about ten inches or so. "I've got one just like him back at home."

"I don't understand, what are you telling me?"

"Look, right now, you know what I know. No one's talking, at least the ones who actually know something. The rest of us are left wondering what the hell is going on. I wish I had more to tell you."

"But there's a possibility that this merger isn't actually going to happen?" I asked Barbara, my mind reeling as I tried to process everything she'd just told me. She'd been suspicious for a while—senior management hadn't been as forthcoming as usual, forecasting had been skewed, and there'd been mid-level human resources types sniffing around the last week or so, allegedly brought in by the board to ascertain the efficiency of each department, but our own internal HR department wasn't aware of it beforehand. Add to that the rumor that The Empire Group, New York City's top marketing firm, which had an entire department dedicated to brand awareness with a strong hotel division, had recently been entertaining the idea of scooping up some of the smaller boutique firms on the East Coast— exactly like the one I worked for—and there you go. Corporate merger as a possibility suddenly became an idea that was firmly rooted in reality.

"But what will that mean? I mean, no, actually, that is what I mean, how will this affect us? Projects already underway, future start dates, you know I wanted to bid for the Oakmont job when this one is wrapped up, will that even be possible now?"

Barbara sighed the heavy sigh of a woman whose own world might be turned inside out and upside down. She'd worked for the firm for as long as anyone could remember, she was this firm, surely if anyone was safe it'd be her, right? "I don't know, kiddo, I'll tell you everything as soon as I hear it. For now, just keep your head down and do the best you can. Your work speaks for itself, but right now it needs to scream, got it?"

I did, actually. My work needed to be outstanding, above reproach, and my references when I left this hotel had better be pitch-perfect. It's amazing, when faced with the possibility of an outside audit, how quickly you begin poking holes in your own balloon. My work was good, had always been good, and this job was no exception. Except, of course, for Archie.

"Barbara, what a mess," I groaned, leaning my head on my hand.

"Hey, don't get down about this, nothing's been confirmed yet. For now, we just do our jobs and keep the lights on. It'll be fine. Now, tell me all about the summer bookings at the Mountain House, how're they looking?"

Barbara and I talked for a few more minutes. The conversation was strained, stilted, and unlike any we'd had before. Normally, I could count on Barbara for three things. To kick my ass, to praise me while she was kicking my ass, and to make sure I always had my true north. She was my professional compass, and she always made sure I was pointed forward and thinking ahead, making sure I made the choices in my career to keep me that way. For the first time, she seemed unsure, and that made my true-north needle bobble.

A merger? What would that mean? Would I still be able to pick which jobs I wanted? Go where I felt I was most needed? I'd worked my ass off for years to get to a certain place within this company, was that going to be undone? And what if what had happened up here in Bailey Falls came out right as a new management team was taking over? Hey, here's our star employee, Clara Morgan, she schtupped the client, but bookings are way up so we're overlooking that part.

I could hear Barbara in my ear, telling me not to worry until there was something to worry about.

I tried to point my compass north.

❧❦❧

I shivered, wrapping my arms around myself.

"Are you cold?"

"A little."

"You should've worn a coat."

"I wasn't thinking, someone was kissing on my neck when I was trying to get ready and it slipped my mind."

Archie grinned. "To be clear, I was that someone, right?"

"Right." I laughed. We were in town, a rare thing these days as we were busier than ever at the hotel. Roxie had been after me since I arrived to come to Zombie Pickle Class, and in a weaker moment I agreed not only to come but to bring Archie.

Roxie and Natalie knew what was going on at Easter. But they'd been dying to see it in person. So down the mountain we came. And it was cold.

"I mean, it's really cold," I said again, swinging my arms back and forth to warm up. Roxie's class had gotten more and more popular over the past few months, and they were nearly outgrowing their space at the diner. Parking spots close to the diner were all taken, and we'd had to walk nearly five blocks to get there on time.

"Here, take this," he said, shrugging out of his coat and slipping it onto my shoulders.

"No. Please. I couldn't possibly." I said all of this deadpan while eagerly snuggling into the warmth. "You smell good, by the way."

His laugh rang out across the tiny town square. "I smell good?"

I shrugged. "You do." I inhaled deeply. "Yeah, you smell good."

"What do I smell like?" he asked, sliding his arm around my shoulders and pulling me closer. I glanced around nervously, wondering how many people could see us and how quickly word could spread that the owner of Bryant Mountain House and the outsider they'd brought in to fix things were hanging all over each other downtown. But the weight of his arm, the way he tucked me into his side so easily, so casual yet so caring, made it impossible for me to concentrate on anything other than trying, in vain, to capture the scent of Archie.

"Wood."

"Pardon me?"

"Wood. I took a woodworking class once, extra credit in high school, kind of the last hurrah of shop class before the teacher retired. We made birdhouses out of walnut. The days we cut the wood it always smelled really fresh, almost astringent-like. But the days we sanded the wood, really spent time with our hands working on it, there was a different scent, kind of . . . I don't know. Fresh and green but a little bit warm too. Cozy. Which made sense at the time, as I was making a cozy little house for some future bird family to enjoy. You kind of smell like that."

"I smell cozy," he echoed.

"Plus a little mapley."

"Walnut and maple?"

"Syrup this time, maple syrup."

"I do love pancakes." He wrapped his arm more firmly around my shoulders. "So you took shop in high school? Interesting."

"I don't want to build you a birdhouse, if that's what you're hoping for."

"No, I was just thinking that it's one of the first things you've ever mentioned when it comes to your childhood. You know, where you grew up, what kinds of things you liked to do."

"Oh. Really?" I said, pulling the jacket tighter.

"Where are you going?"

"Hmm?"

"Get back over here." He laughed, pulling me back into his side. I'd pulled away and hadn't even noticed I'd done it.

"Wow, looks like quite a crowd," I said, pointing at the diner, glad we were almost there. I didn't want to talk about birdhouses, or shop class, or childhood anymore. I wanted to get inside, and learn to can or pickle or whatever the hell we were learning tonight.

"All these people are here for a cooking class?" Archie asked, as we watched another horde go inside.

"Roxie said it's gotten really popular, but I had no idea." When Roxie had first moved back to Bailey Falls, it'd started out as a bit of a joke, Chad and Logan wanting to learn how to make jam and pickles. Something about the zombie apocalypse and all the old people dying and no young, healthy people knowing how to make jam anymore. Jam being important in the aftermath and all. So she taught them. And they mentioned it to a few friends, and the next week a few more people showed up. And so on and so on, bam. Most popular cooking class in town, and more to the point, one of the most popular social activities for your local Hudson Valley hipster.

We paused just outside the door, watching the festivities inside already in full swing. It struck me suddenly that in all the time we'd spent together, I'd never once heard Archie mention spending time with friends, or even mention a friend in general. What a lonely life he must've had up on his mountain after his wife died.

He's not some crazy hermit in a fantasy novel . . .

Right.

Before I could ruminate on it for too long, Natalie's cleavage was pressed against the front window and by the way her mouth was running I could approximate she was saying "Get your ass inside now."

"Your friends are . . ." Archie trailed off, unable to take his eyes off what she was presenting.

"Weird?" I finished.

"So weird," he agreed, dragging his eyes away with a laugh and a shake of his head.

"Come on, the sooner we get in there the sooner we can leave. And do naked things."

He froze with his hand on the door, hanging his head dramatically. "Why in the world are you just telling me this now? We could've been doing naked things this whole time?"

"Who knows, if I have enough wine tonight," I said, ducking under his arm and sailing inside, "I might do naked stuff in the car."

If I didn't know better, I'd say the guy with the pocket square growled.

✧

Zombie Pickle Class was a success. We'd come on a banner night, something the class had been asking for all winter long. It was piecrust night. After we said hello to everyone and Roxie got us sorted at stations, I listened as my friend took charge of a class that was literally bursting at the seams. They spilled out across the restaurant, into the kitchen, along the counter, each table was taken and there were even makeshift stations set up in the entryway.

"She needs a bigger place," Archie whispered, while we listened to Roxie explain what was required to make the perfect piecrust.

"She's been looking, but in a small town like this, it's not like there's tons of space for a professional chef. Leo offered some space over at Maxwell Farms, but I think she wants to do it on her own, you know? I think that's why she was so excited when you brought up the idea of bringing it up to the resort and—"

"Is there something you'd like to say to the rest of the class?" Roxie asked, as she made her rounds.

"Yes, I'd like to say that I'm excited to be here, and the teacher is awfully pretty." I batted my lashes at her as she rolled her eyes.

"I am awfully pretty, so I'm not going to argue with you," she replied, inspecting our table. "I see you've got your flour all measured, your butter is cut into perfect squares, ice water is at the ready, pastry cutter in hand."

"Yup," I said proudly. My station was neater than anyone else's. "I'm ready to go."

"One question," she asked. "What are you going to let Archie do?"

"What?" I asked, looking up in surprise.

"This is a team effort, Clara, you've got to let him do something. One can't learn to make perfect piecrust without actually getting to do some of the making. Now back away and give him the pastry cutter."

Archie chuckled under his breath as I pushed the pastry cutter in his direction.

"Of course he gets to do some of the making, I was just getting things set up for him," I muttered, rolling my eyes in her direction.

"I saw that," she said as she sailed away.

"I meant you to," I shot back.

When class was finally over, most everyone left except for a few of us who gravitated to the kitchen to help Roxie clean up.

"I can't believe I made a piecrust," Archie was still saying, shaking his head as he kept an eye on his perfect pie on the counter as though it might disappear.

"You did really good, Arch, you guys should definitely come back next week," Roxie said, leaning against Leo as he stacked clean dishes on the shelves.

"What's on the menu next week?"

"Homemade chicken stock. I taught it last fall, but that was before the class got so big, and everyone's been asking for it again."

"Oh, we'll be here, we will definitely be here," Archie said enthusiastically, nodding and wiping his sudsy hands on his apron. He was washing up the last of the plates, and Oscar was drying them. Natalie and I sat together on top of the stainless-steel prep table in the corner. "Won't we?"

"Hmm?" I asked, looking up from my nails to see Archie looking at me expectantly. "Oh yeah, sure, we'll be here. Next week."

Archie went back to the sink, laughing as Oscar glared at a slippery glass that he couldn't seem to get ahold of. I felt some-one else's eyes on me, and I turned to see Natalie looking at me expectantly.

"What's up?" I asked, crinkling my brow.

"You tell me," she said, crinkling her own brow like she was trying to see inside my brain.

"You know I don't like when you try to mind-read, just ask your question." I sighed, suddenly exhausted. It was warm in the kitchen with all the people and the hot water.

"Someone's making plans for you," she said, lifting her chin in Archie's direction. "Someone is making plans to make stock with you, next week."

"Yeah? So? It was fun tonight, didn't you have fun?"

"Sure, it's fun every week. Oscar and I never miss a class when I'm in town."

"How very homemaker of you," I replied, hearing the snap in my voice and regretting it almost immediately. "Sorry, that was bitchy."

"A little," she agreed, bumping my shoulder, "but I won't hold it against you. Why are you being bitchy?"

"I don't know, I'm just . . . I guess feeling a bit overwhelmed with all this." I sighed again.

"With all this . . . what?" Natalie asked, looking at me with a secretive grin. "You finally ready to admit that you and Archie are dirty dancing up there on your mountaintop?"

I buried my face in a dish towel. "Yes, yes, I give up."

"I knew it!" She laughed, slapping at my shoulders. "Tell Natalie everything, starting with how much he loves it when you ride him like a cowgirl."

"Oh, for God's sake," I snapped, now covering my entire head with the towel. But then I peeked out a little. "Actually, that's one hundred percent correct, how the hell did you know that?"

"It's a talent." She sighed. "Seriously, though, good for you. It's about time."

"It is about time, in fact it's all about time, and that time will eventually come to an end," I said, watching the boys finish up the dishes. Archie was laughing, snapping towels and ducking as Leo threw a soapy sponge his way. His eyes were crazy blue, catching the light and twinkling merrily. His hair was messed up, his shirtsleeves were soaked even though they'd been rolled up, and he looked completely relaxed and at home.

They all did, in fact. The boys were playing, Roxie had wandered over and was going on and on to Chad and Logan about the play that Polly was involved in at school and whether they'd be able to attend next month. It was like an episode of some sitcom where everyone was good-looking and happy and having all the sex they could ever want before heading down to the local coffee shop or diner to one-up each other with jokes and one-line zingers.

And I was the girl sitting on the prep table under the dish towel trying to figure out exactly where she fit in. I was the girl who came in for a four-to-five episode arc, the one whom one of the main characters fell for, and he became part of a stronger, more defined story line as he weathered whatever this outsider had to offer. Even though, technically, I'd been around just as long as anyone, I was still on the outside. Because I'd be leaving at the end of my story line, packing my bags and heading out into the gray wasteland of sitcom characters, blowing out of scenes just as quickly as I blew in.

Archie would remain. I'd be the Girl Who Brought Him Back to Life. Or the Girl Who Made Archie Great Again. Or worse, the Girl Who Broke His Heart.

I winced, rubbing at the sudden hollow feeling in my chest. I needed to get back to the hotel, I needed to lie down and get some sleep and not think about this right now. But that wasn't in the cards.

"I can see you working yourself over there, kiddo," Natalie said, "but I think you're overthinking this a bit."

"How can I not overthink this? I overthink everything, and you're telling me this is the time to just trust the universe to not cock it up?"

"Yes. I literally think that exactly," she said. "Get out of your head, Clara. You got this, trust it."

I didn't answer, just kept rubbing at that space in my chest as things wound down for the evening.

"So, since everyone is here," Roxie said, jumping up on the table next to Natalie so we were sitting in a row, "I have some news." Leo came to stand in front of her, grinning big. "Well, we have some news."

"You're pregnant. I knew it! I fucking knew it, didn't I tell you Roxie was going to be the first?" Natalie crowed, waving at Oscar and trying to pull him over to her with her own version of a laser tractor beam. "Didn't I tell you?"

"Hush, Pinup, let her talk," he groaned, but submitted to the tractor beam.

"Yes, Pinup, let her talk," Roxie said. "But no, I'm not pregnant."

"Not yet," Leo said, running his hand possessively along her leg.

"Everyone hush," I instructed, leaning forward so I could see Roxie's face. She was beaming. "Except Roxie."

"Well, it's not a huge surprise, I suppose, but Leo asked me to marry him. And—"

"She said yes!" Leo yelled, swooping her up into his arms and swinging her around the kitchen, nearly taking Archie's head off in the process.

Squeals of congratulations and mazel tovs rained down on the happy couple, Natalie bowling everyone over to hug Roxie tight. Archie shook Leo's hand and slapped him on the back, Oscar did the exact same thing and nearly bowled Leo over in the process. Roxie's hand was forcibly removed from her back pocket by Natalie and there it was, the ice cube.

Sparkling and shiny, a diamond the size of a skating rink sat on the third finger of her left hand. And just as sparkling and shiny, her eyes and his face. Thrilled. Proud. The two of them gleamed like they were lit from within.

I was thrilled. I was proud. So why did it feel like my own grin was plastered on, that my congratulations and that's incredible and of course I'll be a bridesmaid were heart-spoken but not heartfelt?

A question I continued to ask myself the entire car ride home. Archie, however, prattled on enough for the both of us.

"I'm thinking if we use the smaller dining room on the first floor for Zombie Pickle Class, the one we only open up when we're booked to capacity, then we shouldn't run too much into the regular dinner service. We'd have to figure something else out in the summer, but maybe if we change the time or switch it to weekends in June and July . . . I don't know, what do you think?"

I barely had time to take a breath to answer before he was off on another tangent.

"Another thing, I'm wondering if we should offer a discount on overnight stays to anyone who takes the class. Might be another way to introduce some new faces around here from town, I know how much you want to bring in locals more and more, this might be a good way to do it. Not during the high season of course, but if we offered a discounted rate in the fall, maybe thirty percent off and throw in a room upgrade? Not everyone could take advantage of the offer, but maybe more than we think, any thoughts?"

This time he didn't even wait for me to answer, he just launched into another monologue.

"Oh, before I forget, I talked to Oscar about bringing up a few of the cows, just a couple, and maybe one of the calves. Bryant Mountain House has a barn, it just hasn't been used for years, but maybe this summer we could partner with him to introduce a new farm-to-table concept to our guests, get Leo involved too. Did I ever tell you there used to be cows up here, just for milk and cheese and butter? It's true, I came across an old menu card last year from the thirties, and it said 'featuring milk from our own Bryant Family cows.' Can you believe that? I bet Leo could help us get some chickens going, our guests would love knowing they're eating eggs fresh from the farm. And if Oscar brings a calf up too, what a great learning opportunity for the kids when they come to stay up here, especially for those city kids who never see where their food comes from. Leo was telling me all about the program he started a few years ago where the Maxwell family sponsors schools in the city to bring kids up for field trips, and did you know most of them have never even seen a chicken? Bears and lions, yes, because they've been to the zoo, but can you imagine kids who've never seen a chicken?"

"Not every kid gets to visit a farm, Archie. Not every kid even gets to go to the zoo." I sighed, looking out the window and into the night. It might be spring on the calendar, but tonight upstate New York was frosty cold.

"Most kids get to at least go to one or the other, though, even if it's just a field trip. I remember my entire class took the train into the city when I was in fourth grade just to go to the Bronx Zoo."

"When I was in fourth grade my foster mother refused to sign my permission slip so I could go on a field trip because it was my punishment for spilling paint in the kitchen. When I was in fifth grade my next foster mother couldn't afford the twenty dollars for me to ride the bus into downtown Boston with the other kids in my class for a field trip, so I spent the entire day doing an extra-credit project on Paul Revere and his magical midnight ride in the cafeteria with the elementary school counselor who was concerned I was suppressing my emotions. Which I undoubtedly was, considering in first grade my real mother came on my field trip to Gloucester to see the fishermen, but she got wasted in a bar at lunch instead of spending time with the kids like she was supposed to, and then ended up getting caught doing one of the fishermen we were supposed to be meeting later on. So yeah, field trips seem to be a bit dicey for me."

The car was silent. But for me, in my head, all I could hear were those words pouring out and exploding over our heads and painting the interior of this sleek German driving machine with other terrible words, unsaid but surely thought—

Baggage.
Issues.
Scars.
Worthless.

Don't scratch this surface because, sweet Christ, what would you find underneath?

No Ashley here. No picture-perfect childhood surrounded by a loving, caring family, there to shelter and guide and hide the monsters away and prepare you for a life of love and laughter and perfection when you finally meet that perfect man, the man you've known since you were a child and you grew into adulthood with, grown-ups living in your perfect castle on your very own mountain, where there are no harsh words or uncaring arms, just love, love, love.

I'd never been more painfully aware of just how different I was from Archie than in those silent moments in the car.

I was shaking.

He pulled the car over.

He pulled me out of my seat and across the console and onto his lap after he unbuckled my seat belt.

I was shaking.

He pulled back the edges of his coat, the one I was still wearing, wrapped his arms around my waist and leaned forward, holding me against his chest like a baby, resting his chin on top of my head.

I was still shaking. But I was breathing. And I was breathing in that good Archie air, the wood and the mapley pancake scent and underneath it all was just that warmth, below that strict tailored East Coast suit was just the warmest of men.

We didn't go back to the hotel that night. We drove straight to his house, walked straight to the fireplace, took everything off that was between us, and when he entered me by the firelight, I gasped and he groaned and he filled my body, my mind, and my heart.

He didn't ask me to explain that night. But as I lay in the comfort of his arms, wrapped up in him in every way possible, I knew it was coming.

And I didn't know what I was going to say.

Chapter 19

We slept on the living-room floor all night long. Neither of us mentioned the fact that we both seemed to be avoiding his bedroom, the bedroom he'd once shared with his wife, and maybe that was a good thing. Naked, Archie had gathered up pillows and blankets and quilts, and naked, I'd helped him arrange everything into a wonderful little nest before the fire. He didn't ask anything and I didn't offer anything, but I opened my eyes the next morning to find him watching me.

"I kind of blew up last night," I said.

He reached out to brush a piece of hair away from my face, tracing his fingertips along my cheekbone tenderly. "You kind of did."

I stretched, wondering if I could bide my time long enough to get a cup of coffee. Reading my thoughts, he smiled. "How about I make some coffee, you make some toast, and then we talk a bit?"

"What time is it?"

"Doesn't matter."

I frowned. I knew we needed to talk, but I still had a job to do. "How late is it?" I asked, scrambling up, taking one of the blankets with me.

White. Everything was white. "Oh my." I sighed, staring out the big picture window. The world was covered in snow. Puffy and fluffy, it clung to every treetop and limb, edging the water and blanketing the lawn. At least a foot of snow had come down while we'd been sleeping. "Was this in the forecast?"

"Nope, surprise snowstorm," he said, coming to stand next to me by the window, wrapped in his own blanket. "We usually get at least one late snow each year, but it's been a while since it was this much with almost no notice."

"And the roads won't be plowed, I'm guessing?"

"They will. We have our own plows at the hotel, and I imagine they've started to clear the main road already. But they won't come down to this part until all the guest roads are clear. So for a while . . ."

"We're stuck here," I finished for him, looking out again at the snow cover. Snowed in. And we were both still naked. Which would normally be the stuff dreams are made of, but I'd picked the wrong night to unload my stupid baggage. So now a snow day would be turned into a feelings day.

Fuck me. If this was going to happen, I was going to need protein. "You have any eggs to go with that toast and coffee?"

Ten minutes later we were sitting at his breakfast bar with scrambled eggs, toast and jam, and blessed coffee. Archie had given me an ancient Bailey Falls High School sweatshirt to wear, bearing the water polo championship logo. The sleeves were rolled up about five times, so I wasn't completely swimming in it. See what I did there?

"These are good," he said as he forked up a mouthful of eggs.

"Thanks, I added a little of the cheese I found in your fridge."

"I have cheese in my fridge?"

"Like three different kinds, who put it there?"

He smiled. "My housekeeper, Greta. She's worked for the

family for years, she insists on doing my grocery shopping each week even though I rarely cook. A full fridge equals a full life in her mind."

"Did your wife cook?"

He paused, the fork halfway to his mouth. After a second or two, he lifted the bite to his mouth, chewed, swallowed, and looked at me carefully. "Are you trying to talk about anything other than what happened in the car last night?"

I chewed. I swallowed. "Yes."

"And why is that?"

I chewed. I swallowed. "I'm not really comfortable talking about my past. Any of it."

"Everyone has a past, Clara."

"But not everyone needs to revisit it. It's the past, as in, its time has literally passed. Why drag it up?"

He covered my hand with his own. "Whether it's dragged up or talked about on a daily basis, the past seems to always have a way of showing up, getting in your face until you let it have its say. Then, yeah, sometimes you can move on. But it's never really passed."

I slipped my hand out from under his, picked up my now-empty plate and carried it over to the sink. "How long do you think it'll take until the road is plowed?"

"Wow, not even thirty seconds. Impressive."

"What?"

He carried his plate over to the sink as well. "And here I thought we were going to get somewhere today."

I pushed back from the sink, face burning, hands on hips. "And what exactly did you think we'd get to? We're snowed in, nowhere to run, nowhere to hide, let's push Clara until she caves? That's not really fair, is it?"

"My wife died at thirty-two. Life isn't fucking fair. The sooner you realize that, the better off you'll be."

"No!" I snapped, pointing my finger. "Not better off, the exact opposite. Look what's happening, literally right now, you bring up the past and immediately we're fighting about something so stupid! It's my past, Archie, and if I want it to stay buried then it stays fucking buried. I'm sorry I said all those things in the car last night, it was a mistake, a momentary slip, and believe me when I say it won't happen again. And yes, I know your wife died at thirty-two, and that's a really shitty deal, but I'm not her and I'm the furthest thing from perfect and if you think I'm ever going to be anything like her, then—" I stopped cold, mid-yell. "You know what, this is exactly why I never should've started this in the first place, I knew this was a bad idea." I stomped off in search of my clothes. Once again, I was shaking. In the span of twelve hours I'd let that smooth surface crack and I was already paying the price. I was saying things I should never say, and I was hurting Archie, I could tell.

This is the very reason I don't get involved. Because when two people share something, anything, someone gets hurt. And I promised myself a long, long time ago that I'd never be the one to hurt someone else. I needed to get out before anything else was said.

"Where the hell do you think you're going?"

"Home. Back to the hotel."

"In the snow? You're going to walk a mile, uphill, in the snow?"

I stabbed my legs into my pants. "You don't think I can do it?"

"It's not about that, for God's sake." He ran his hands through his hair in frustration. "Is everything a competition with you?"

I grabbed one of his winter hats out of the coat closet, along with a coat as well, and shoved it down on my head so hard it covered half my face. I pushed it up angrily in a huff. "Yes. No. I don't know. Just shut up."

He bit his bottom lip, trying not to laugh.

"What?" I asked. He didn't answer. "What?" I shouted, stamping my foot.

"Your pants are on backward and when you pushed your hat up your nose got caught and, I shouldn't say this, but I'm gonna, you looked like a piglet."

My jaw dropped.

He grinned. "And I think you're an idiot for running out in the snow just to prove a point. Because this is horseshit."

"Horseshit?" I sputtered.

"Horseshit," he agreed, grinning wildly. "Horseshit that you would let something like your past keep you from spending the morning with me. Maybe put on some snowshoes and go out for a hike in the woods. Or I could fuck you senseless in the bathtub. Whichever. They're both great options. Up to you. But don't leave just because you don't want to talk about your past, that's silly. We're grown-ups." He turned to head back into the kitchen, but then stopped and looked back over his shoulder. "And believe me, I know you're not anything like my wife. But you're crazy if you think she was perfect. She was impatient, had no attention for detail, was famous for leaving messes and not cleaning them up and most of all, she could be a real pain in the ass sometimes." He tilted his head to the side. "Huh, you two do have something in common."

He headed over to the sink to do the dishes, whistling while he worked. He didn't look back, he didn't say anything else, he just did his thing.

Which infuriated me. "Listen, Mister Pry Into Everything, just because you're ready to talk about my past doesn't mean I am, okay? And that doesn't make me horseshit."

"I didn't say you were horseshit," he corrected, pointing at me with a scrub brush, then gesturing broadly. "I said *this* was horseshit." He turned back to his dishes. "You can't let the past define you, Clara."

"Says the man still wearing his wedding ring," I muttered. His back stiffened, his head snapping up on his neck. I stood my ground. If he could push me I could push right back.

But as I watched and waited for him to explode, to yell at me, to tell me I was wrong, to tell me that this was his sacred cow and I had no business even bringing this up to him . . . the opposite happened. His back relaxed, he shook his head, and he went back to his dishes. A moment later, he spoke.

"Fair point. I won't push." But then he looked over his shoulder at me. "Today. But I will again, and soon." He went back to his dishes, calm and cool and collected. "But you really don't have to leave."

I considered. It did look cold out there. And the snow was really deep. And being a late snow, it was wet and heavy—it'd be really hard to wade through all of it. Uphill, like he said.

I looked back toward the kitchen. He was making another pot of coffee, it smelled heavenly. He was whistling "Stay" from *Dirty Dancing,* that sonofabitch. A snowshoe hike did sound nice. The bathtub fucking sounded nicer. The question was, could we go all day without talking about shit I just really wasn't ready to verbalize? He said he wouldn't push, but would he?

Uphill versus fucking.

I pulled off my hat. I pulled off my pants. I walked soundlessly back into the kitchen, picked up a towel and a plate from the rack, and started drying.

I chanced a look at him, next to me, still whistling. His grin was enormous.

I kept my eyes on the plate. "So, to be clear, the fucking is happening before the hike."

He set down his plate, set down my plate, picked me up

by slipping his beautiful hands around my naked bottom, and started heading upstairs. "And after the hike."

⁘

Archie was as good as his word and didn't push me. But there was something hanging over us now, something palpable, a tension that wasn't there before. Or rather, it'd changed shape. Before I'd been trying to avoid getting involved. Now I was involved and trying desperately to avoid talking about anything of substance. I was leaving, that we both knew, so why muddy the waters with more details that can't change anything? And speaking of muddy . . .

The snowstorm that blew in and out over the course of just two days left the ground wet, muddy, sloshy, and gross. Exactly the kinds of conditions that make for a great Tough Mudder race.

Natalie was hoping that we'd all forgotten about the race, and more important, that she'd said she'd participate.

"Pretty sure I said I'd be cheerleading, as in from the bleachers," she said as we all arrived at the Mountain House before six on the morning of the race.

"You're doing it, Pinup," Oscar growled, picking up the enormous cooler filled with drinks and snacks and loading it onto the back of the bus. Everyone agreed to leave their cars in the hotel lot for the day and ride up together, camp-style. To complete the camp theme, Archie was driving us in an old school bus, painted green and white and bearing the name of the hotel across the side. Used by the staff for years on campouts, it added to the ambience of the day, big kids playing in the mud.

Oscar brushed his hands off on his pants, then pulled her close. "Besides, you like it dirty."

"I'm wondering how many innuendos can be crammed into just one day," Leo mused, calling out to us through the window as he tugged Roxie toward the back of the bus.

"Speaking of getting crammed in," Roxie said, laughing over his shoulder as he made like he was going to bend her over the seat.

"It all comes down to in-you-end-oh!" Logan laughed as Chad shuffled by with sleep still in his eyes. He gave Logan the finger, then came to stand by me.

"I'm glad you're here, really, I am. You're a great addition to this gang of fools, but will all the adventures you're going to be planning start at five a.m.?"

"Probably." I grinned, watching as Logan and Archie hauled bags of towels onto the bus. Sleeping with the manager of a hotel was pretty great when it came to supplies. He'd had the kitchen make up a bunch of sandwiches and salads for the day trip, and then raided housekeeping to get stuff to clean up with after the race. "Mornings are the best time for stuff like this, although it makes for a chilly start."

Chad shivered on cue, and I pushed him toward the bus, laughing. Archie swung down from the steps, eyes dancing. "You ready to go roll around in the mud?"

I heard Natalie's voice float across the air, still complaining about how filthy she'd be getting. I waggled my eyebrows. "One hundred percent ready."

It was a little over a three-hour drive through some beautiful country up to Syracuse. Once we were on the road and everyone had had their coffee, the natural road-trip rules took over and everyone got into it. Beef jerky was consumed, Def Leppard songs were sung—loud and bad as nature intended—and the jokes just got raunchier as the day went by.

Archie drove, I sat shotgun up near him, and everyone else spread out. The gang was chatting, talking, laughing, it was a little like what I imagined traveling with the Partridge Family must be like. About an hour away from Syracuse, Roxie made her way up front, sitting down across from me.

"So how hard will this race be? Be honest," she asked, looking a little nervous.

"It's tough," I admitted, thinking back on some of the courses I'd done over the years. "Not everyone makes it, and not because they're pussies and just give up, it's just a really hard race to complete."

"Great, that's just great. Leo will finish and I'll be drowning in the mud with Nat."

"Not necessarily, there's tons of guys who don't finish. Fit guys, super-in-shape guys. Women finish all the time, and there are men just strewn across the course behind them. I'm not saying that's what's going to happen today, but you shouldn't go into it assuming you won't finish. Go in assuming you will, otherwise you might as well just sit on the sidelines and eat hot dogs."

"I like hot dogs," she mused.

"They'll taste better when you're eating them afterward, covered in mud," I said, "and victory."

"You don't quit, do you?"

"No," I answered truthfully. I caught Archie's eyes on me in the rearview mirror.

"Somehow just the thought that there'll be a wiener waiting for me at the finish line makes me want it all the more," Roxie said, and Archie choked back a laugh.

"Wieners are good," I agreed.

"I wonder if I could get away with having them at the wedding," she mused, and I tore my eyes away from Archie's.

"At the wedding? Why in the world?"

"For exactly that reason. It's the last thing you'd expect at the wedding, which is why it's kind of terrific."

"Your mother-in-law's head will literally blow off her body if you serve hot dogs at your wedding," I warned. As down to earth and cool as Leo was, his mom was the exact opposite. Blue-blooded, and a little bit cold-blooded from what I'd been told, she was hardly the picture of hippie-style warmth that was Trudy. Roxie had made inroads with Leo's mom, true enough, but there was still a distance there. A distance that hot dogs would hardly breach.

"Maybe that's part of the reason I'm thinking about it. I mean, I'd make sure they were really good hot dogs for goodness' sake, there's a butcher over in Hyde Park who makes incredible homemade sausage, but I kind of like the idea of having food like that served in that fancy house."

"So you're definitely having it on the farm?" I asked. Leo's farm was located within the grounds of what I liked to call a compound. An enormous old Hudson River estate, the farm fit easily into the hundreds of acres owned by his family, and included a huge and high-up-on-the-bluff stone mansion. Which Leo pointedly didn't live in, instead opting for a house he'd built himself on the other side of the property.

"I think so, I mean it makes sense. We both love Maxwell Farms, the barn is incredible, and hey, guess what, it's free."

"It is beautiful up there," I agreed.

"But?"

"No buts. It's beautiful. It'll be a beautiful day for a beautiful bride and groom and we'll all eat beautiful wieners." I felt a strange tug on my heart. I'd of course be back for the wedding, I was in it for goodness' sake, but I wouldn't be here anymore. Depending on when they decided to tie the knot, I'd have packed my bags and headed down the mountain by then, off to another hotel, another property, another town, possibly even another country.

I'd be involved in the wedding, as involved as I could be through texting and FaceTime and emails and doing anything and everything I could do to be the best bridesmaid possible. Except for the day-to-day squealing and stressing and laughing and crying that Natalie would be doing with Roxie because she'd be here and I'd be there and unable to fully immerse.

Fully immerse in the wedding?

Fuck it. No. I'll say it. Unable to fully immerse in this life, the life that the universe was picking up by the fistful and flinging toward me with a metric ton of squealing and stressing and laughing and crying and Archie.

But I couldn't immerse. I had my own life, I couldn't just swoop in and piggyback off this one. I'd worked my ass off my entire adult life to make something of myself, to stand on my own and be really good at what I did. I didn't let anything stop me, or slow me down, or change who I was. I would be there for Roxie, and celebrate her and Leo and the life they'd chosen to live together. But I'd go back to mine at some point.

And suddenly, for the first time ever, I wasn't so thrilled at the prospect. And that was more dangerous than anything.

I swallowed hard, then forced a smile. "So wieners it is. Are we doing chicken wings too?"

Mud. Icy mud. Icy water. Freezing cold bits of grass and grubby things raining down and coating my skin, weighing it down, threatening to take me out like so many others. My legs were on fire, my thighs felt like molten lava, absolute burn and absolute quivery shaky exhaustion. But I pushed through.

The thing about a race like Tough Mudder is that it doesn't matter if you're there by yourself or with an entire group of friends. There are challenges you simply cannot do alone. Everest, a dead climb up a curved wall with a watery ditch at the bottom. Not possible to do unless someone is already up at the top waiting to grab your hand and pull your ass over. Or at the bottom, sacrificing themselves to stand in the mud and muck and let people climb all over them, standing on their shoulders, your shoes dripping all over them, as they boost you up to waiting hands.

We lost Oscar at Everest. The tallest one of all, he let every single one of us crawl up his ridiculous body to get up and over. Once we were all at the top, we turned to help him up, but he stayed behind, the line of people behind us asking if he could help them as well. A teammate his entire life, he'd grinned bigger than I'd ever seen him, waved us on, and continued to boost strangers up the wall.

We lost Natalie at the Arctic Enema, where Dumpsters full of water and ice cubes waited. She took one look at the people cannonballing into the water, then popping up cold to the bone, their muscles locked and barely moving, a silent scream lodged in their throats, and said, "Fuck this shit," and headed for the beer truck. Always a wise one, that Natalie.

Leo and Roxie stayed with Archie and me until Fire in the Hole, an obstacle where you literally go down a waterslide to a ring of fire waiting at the bottom. A mind-fucker if ever there was one, you can't think about this too long or you'll never do it. Covered in mud and on the verge of tears, Roxie balked at the top and couldn't talk herself into going any farther. Leo stayed with her. Logan and Chad both took the opportunity to call it a day, realizing that if they were also helping to "comfort" Roxie they could comfort themselves right into some dry clothes and hot toddy.

Archie and I stuck it out, and he gave as good as he got. I

was used to doing these races on my own, relying on strangers to help me out, to give me a hand when I needed it. I'd never been through this with someone, and it was a totally different experience. Good . . . and bad.

I spent the entire race looking over my shoulder, making sure he was okay. Which was ludicrous, because the man's strength and overall athleticism were remarkable. He didn't need anyone making sure he was okay. But I felt like I needed to watch out, to make sure, and that took me out of my game entirely. I had to work harder on this course, go faster, push further, than I'd ever had before. And mentally, I was exhausted.

Do you have any idea how hard it is to let someone help you when you've spent a lifetime making sure people know you don't need them? Strangers could help me, that was part of it. But Archie trying to help me? It pissed me off royally, and what the hell kind of a person gets mad at their boyfriend for helping them?

The kind who'd rather go down a waterslide into a ring of fire than admit she just called someone her boyfriend.

I didn't feel the whispers of flame kiss my skin as I rocketed down the mud-laced slide. Didn't feel the icy water at the bottom, splashing over me, filling my eyes with muck and goo. Didn't feel the rocks digging into my kneecaps, or the plastic scraping my elbow, but fuck me if I didn't feel his hand on mine, asking me if I was okay and did I want to finish.

Did I want to finish?

I looked up at Archie's sweet face, covered in the same mud as I was covered in, and I glared. "Of course I do," I heard myself bark, and then I was off again. I pretended not to see his hurt face, the freckles I love so much now indistinguishable from the dirt he'd—we'd—been peppered with since beginning this endurance race.

I ran faster, moved quicker, splashed through puddles and conquered hills. I saw obstacles and quickly assessed the best way through, never around because around was weak. I celebrated with strangers, watched them battle their own personal trials and overcome them. But when Archie offered me his hand going over the last obstacle, The Wall, I averted my eyes, pretended I didn't see it, and grabbed hold of someone else who was dangling over the top, helping everyone up and over just like Oscar had done at the beginning of the race.

When I say pretended not to see his hand, I mean pretend in the most generous sense of the word. Because there wasn't anyone on the wall who didn't see exactly what I'd done. When given the chance to reach for someone who loved me, I deliberately chose a hand I'd likely never see again.

Again, I say, what the hell does that say about me?

I jumped down from The Wall, now just fifty yards from the finish line. There was a crowd gathered there made up of everyone who had already finished, everyone who had gotten out of the race early, but was still delirious with excitement and pride that they'd managed any of the course, and the people who had come to cheer on their loved ones as they navigated through this most difficult of activities.

I took one last look over my shoulder, almost without meaning to—it had just become natural at this point. And there he was. Archie. Running just as fast as I was but letting me lead. He didn't look hurt, even though he had a nasty goose egg already forming on his forehead from a bad fall off a rope bridge. He didn't look tired, even though the frown lines that'd been there when I'd first met him and had seemed to have disappeared recently were back and looking deeper by the second as the dirt and mud settled.

If I were a grown-up, I'd reach back for his hand this time, acknowledge that we'd done this together and accomplished something tangible and incredible, and cross the finish line together.

If I were a stubborn asshole child, I'd face forward, run like hell, and beat him to the finish line, then turn around and pretend I hadn't pretended and hope to God he'd buy it, embrace me anyway, and we'd continue on fucking but not feeling.

I wanted to run. Jesus Christ, I wanted to run. Which is why I knew that was the absolute wrong thing to do.

I reached back, took his hand, and we crossed the finish line together.

The sun was shining. But it was nothing compared with the ear-to-ear smile on his face when I held his hand. And I couldn't help but smile back.

We finished strong, his long legs and my short ones somehow matching stride for stride as we pushed ourselves to the limit, adrenaline kicking into overdrive as we passed under the arch.

"That was amazing," Archie cried, tugging me against him as we melted into the crowd of other tough mudders. "Incredible!"

Giddy, I laughed along with him as I felt our sloppy sweaty bodies crush together, happy to have finished, happy to have reached out for him, happy to have taken that small step that, although seemingly easy as pie, was impossibly hard for me to do. I grinned up at him, reaching to smooth back his messy hair.

Grinning, he gazed down at me, a sense of deep and pure satisfaction apparent in his expression.

"Aren't you glad you did it?" I asked, panting from exertion but feeling that crazy high that came when you pushed your body further than you thought was possible.

He nodded as someone popped a bottle of champagne and sprayed it down over the lot of us, smelly and disgusting and awesome. "I love you."

I froze. He felt it. The world went away. Everything went away. It was me and Archie standing together in a vacuum of white noise and static. My heart stopped, my lungs stopped, and I became aware that the grin on my face began to feel painted on.

But before I could respond, before I could even think how I could respond, the world crashed back in.

"You filthy motherfuckers, I knew you'd finish!"

Natalie, running full tilt and smashing into both of us, picked me up and congratulated me on being the toughest asshole she'd ever known.

Yep. I really was.

Once again I was riding home with Archie, avoiding meeting his eyes or talking about anything of substance beyond how well everyone did in the race. We'd stayed for a while, celebrating with all the other participants, drinking a few beers, enjoying a few actual hot dogs after all that wiener talk. Leo volunteered to drive back so Archie could have a beer or two, but that made it all the more difficult to continually keep someone else inside our conversation, preventing an actual conversation where I'd be in over my head and completely out of my depth.

No one in my entire life had ever told me they loved me. And I didn't really know quite how to take it in. Roxie and Natalie loved me, this I knew. Technically they'd told me, but usually in the vein of I love you but you cannot wear those pants, or I love you but quit stealing all the popcorn, or I love you but there's no way on earth Henry Cavill isn't the sexiest man on the planet. All joking aside, no one had ever looked into my eyes, punched through my chest and wrapped their hands around my heart and said I love you.

But then what happens next? I know the romance-novel version. I say it back, there are two or three more paragraphs of schmaltz and then poof, the end. I know the rom-com version, usually starring a Julia or a Sandra. The music swells, very often a song written expressly for the movie, there's some laughing followed by some kissing and very often every single problem these two people have been experiencing for the last ninety minutes is blasted away by love conquering all blah blah blah feelings.

What the hell are you supposed to do when you hear these words for the first time and your first instinct is to vomit? This is why romance heroines were never as fucked up as I was, because, my God, what a terrible story that would make.

The bottom line was I was terrified to get off this bus when we got back to the Mountain House because then I'd be alone with Archie and this time there was no way he was going to let me off the hook. I'd avoided Archie the entire way back, sitting with my girls or with everyone in a big group, drinking beer out of the pony keg Oscar had thoughtfully provided, passing around sloppy Solo cups and congratulating ourselves on being tough mudders. But now it was getting quiet. Everyone was pairing off, taking a nap or playing games on their phones, the interference our friends had been unknowingly running was disappearing. And here he comes, sitting down across from me at the back of the bus, alone at last.

Would he want to talk about what he said? Would I need to say it back? Could I say it back?

"Hey, Clara, quit working yourself over so much, you're off the hook, okay?"

Whoa. What?

I blinked and looked up at Archie, smiling ruefully.

"How'd you do that?" I asked, eyes wide and more than a little terrified. Was I cracking up?

"Not hard to tell what's going on in there," he said, tapping my temple. "Just don't let it freak you out too much, okay?"

"Okay?" I squeaked. "I can't, you know, I mean . . . I—"

He shrugged. "I said what I needed to say. You can say nothing. For now. Okay?"

I shook my head. "I don't get it. What's the catch?"

"Silly girl," he murmured, scooching across the aisle and sitting with me in my seat. "No catch. Just sort through whatever is going on in there, and we can talk later."

I didn't deserve this guy. I mean it, I really didn't deserve someone this understanding. And actually, not to put too fine a point on it, but how in the hell could he understand me so well when for the first time, I didn't even understand me?

Chapter 20

The email came in at 4:37 p.m. on a Friday with a company-wide header. "Excited to announce blah blah blah merging with The Empire Group blah blah blah leading the industry in blah blah blah a partnership for the ages blah blah blah some senior-level positions have been combined blah blah blah . . ."

Wait a minute. What senior-level positions? With my heart stuck in my throat, my eyes scanned the rest of the email quickly, searching for information that would tell me whether or not Barbara had been—

My phone rang. Her name popped up on the screen.

"Not you," I said, by way of greeting.

"Yes, me," she answered with a watery sigh.

"The hell?" I sat down hard on the chair I was near, not caring that I was in the middle of the lobby or that a few guests walking by heard me and raised an eyebrow. I was ready to raze this mountain if what I was afraid of was really true. "They can't do this! How could anyone ever think you of all people are replaceable?"

"It's already done, kiddo. Technically I wasn't fired, my job was eliminated and I was given the option of either taking a step down with a significant salary decrease or taking the severance package and going on my way."

"What great choices."

"That's what I said, right before I took the severance and told them to shove it."

"You didn't," I replied, not shocked at all.

"I sure did," she fired back. "I helped build this place, brought in half the clients and more than half the staff. Truth is, I was thinking about retiring in a few years anyway, but it just boils my water that I'm not going out on my own terms."

"Well, if you told them to shove it, you kind of are, right?"

She huffed out a chuckle.

"So . . ."

"So what does this mean for you?" she asked, knowing where I was going.

"Is it terrible that that's my next question?" I asked, wincing.

"No, it's exactly what I would ask. In fact, it is what I asked, after I got over the shock of their offer. All positions are frozen right now, wage increases frozen—"

"Promotions frozen?" I interrupted.

"You guessed it," she said. "You should be getting an email shortly explaining who you'll be reporting to once I'm gone, which is in two weeks."

"Two weeks," I breathed. "I don't even know what to say."

"Well, for now don't say anything, just listen. You've got to be in the office on Monday to meet with your new boss. He's bringing in all of the field teams except for those that are overseas. He wants to meet you all face-to-face. And let me tell you, he's a real jackass."

"Great," I said, leaning my head on my hand. "Just great."

"You'll be fine," she replied. "You're great at your job, you've always done incredible work, and your references are impeccable.

Just don't set fire to Bryant Mountain House or do anything to make a spectacle of yourself and everything will be okay."

"Mm-hmm," I said, not wanting to comment directly on the whole spectacle thing. "But, Barbara, what are you going to do?"

"Who knows, kiddo. I've been working since I was fifteen years old. Might be nice to take some time to decide. Hey, maybe I'll get one of those herb gardens everyone's always talking about."

"You should come up here, we're installing a new herb garden outside the kitchens so the chefs have access to fresh herbs all season long. Remember my friend Roxie, the chef? Her boyfriend, well, fiancé now, runs one of the biggest organic farms on the East Coast and it's just about ten miles down the road from here. Anyway, they're helping us reboot the gardens up here, beyond the already incredible flower gardens they have, they're taking a dormant field down past the croquet lawn and growing all kinds of crazy stuff. Archie was the first person to suggest it, actually, he really loves the idea of taking the Mountain House back a few pegs to what it used to be. Of course, he wants everything done within budget, but oh my goodness, you should've seen his face when Oscar, that's the dairy farmer in town who's dating my friend Natalie, you remember Natalie, anyway when he brought his cows up and they started running toward the lake Archie nearly split his pants racing after them and—" I stopped, listening to myself prattle on.

"Well, listen to you," she marveled.

Time to wrap it up. "Anyway, since you'll have some time off, you unemployed person, you should come up and relax a bit. Let a supercute farmer teach you how to grow basil."

"I'll think about it," she mused, but her tone told me she was done thinking about her predicament and already wondering what I might be up to.

"So, if I'm coming in on Monday, will you have time for lunch? If I'm fired too we can buy each other martinis."

"You're not fired. But I won't say no to the martinis, or the lunch. I'd love to see you, kiddo, let's get caught up. And remember, just stand your ground with this guy, let your work speak for itself."

"Mm-hmm." I nodded. Just like Barbara to be giving me advice during the call she had to make about her own job being eliminated. "I'm so sorry about this."

She huffed once more, chirped out a good-bye, and hung up.

I set my phone down, sank back into the chair and stared out the big picture window at the lake. I ended up sitting there for the next three hours, watching as the sun moved across the sky and set behind the mountains. Only when the room was so dark that the lanterns flickered on did I get up and walk back to my room.

I got a text from Archie around eight thirty. Did I want to meet him up on the roof? I'd been sad sacking for several hours now, I needed something to cheer me up. A quick tussle up top should be exactly the right thing to send me off to sleep tonight.

I hurried toward the staircase, smiling to myself when I saw that the door was already cracked open, letting me know he was up there. I climbed the stairs quickly, suddenly wanting nothing in the world more than to slip into his arms and snuggle into his chest.

When did you get so schmaltzy?

Just now, when I realized that there are benefits to not being alone every night, especially the night after you just got some bad news.

"Hey," he said, after I pushed open the door and let myself out onto the rooftop.

"Hey yourself." I sighed, so many emotions running through me at the sight of him. Relief, gratitude, contentment, shot through with pure unadulterated lust. End of the day Archie was my favorite Archie, when the tie had been loosened and the jacket was off and hello what's this, his shirtsleeves were even rolled up.

It was a far cry from Mr. Buttoned-Up Hotel Boss I'd seen those first days after I'd arrived up here.

I crossed the rooftop to him, a slight breeze ruffling the edge of my skirt. It had been the first really warm day so far this year, and the rooftop retained some of the heat. The air felt warm and soft and comforting, and when I reached him I slipped eagerly into his arms.

"I feel like I haven't seen you all day." He sighed into my hair.

"I've been a bit in hiding," I admitted, loving the feel of his hands on my lower back.

"Oh boy, that's never a good thing." He chuckled, stepping backward to perch on the edge of the railing. He pulled me in between his knees, positioning me so that he could look into my eyes. "What's up, Bossy?"

I debated telling him, what was the point? It's not like he could do anything. But I wanted to tell him, wanted to engage in this end-of-the-day ritual called How Was Your Day, Dear, and be inside this ritual for the first time.

"Well, I talked to Barbara this afternoon."

"Who's Barbara?"

"Seriously?" I asked, crinkling my nose.

"I've never heard you mention her before."

"That doesn't even seem possible," I mused, thinking back to all the conversations we'd had. Surely I'd mentioned her?

"You're not really what we'd call fond of sharing." He chuckled, grasping my hands and holding them in between us. "So who's Barbara?"

"Huh," I replied, still surprised that I'd never mentioned her. "Anyway, she's my boss."

"Got it, Barbara the boss."

"But she's more than that, she hired me, taught me everything I know, she basically groomed me and created this bossy hotel wunderkind you see before you today."

"So she's who I'd thank for your incredible sense of humility?"

"You'd have to do it fast, because she just told me she's leaving. A bunch of people are leaving. Ever heard of The Empire Group?"

I told him everything. Who Barbara was, what she'd meant to me, how she'd literally put me on the path that I was on today. And then all about The Empire Group, the merger, and what it might mean for me.

"So you know some of the details but not all of the details, it sounds like, right?" he asked when I'd finished.

"Yeah, I don't know too much. But I know enough to be nervous about what this means for me and my job. My partnership is essentially gone, that's for sure."

"Well, I think until you know all the details, you shouldn't worry."

"Shouldn't worry?" I asked.

He shook his head. "I've never seen the point in worrying until there's a reason to worry. This could all work out for the best, you never know."

"But Barbara basically got kicked to the curb," I said, frowning.

"Well, that's obviously terrible, but you said yourself she's looking forward to starting an herb garden."

"That's not really the point, Archie."

He clasped my hands together once more, brought them to his mouth, and kissed them. "All I'm saying is let's worry about this when the time comes."

"That time is kind of now. I've got to go into Boston on Monday to meet my new boss."

"Perfect, you'll get the chance to show him how fantastic you are. I'll tell him myself, as the client you're currently working with I can testify to how great you are." He turned my hands over and left lingering kisses in the center of my palms. "And when I say great, I really mean great."

He was teasing, but just the idea of him talking to my new boss, possibly somehow spilling the beans about what we'd been doing up here outside of working . . . it sent a shiver through me.

He noticed, and pulled me back into his arms. "Don't worry about this, Bossy. I promise it'll all work out."

"But you don't know that," I told his shoulder.

"I wouldn't spend any more time thinking about this until you know more."

I insisted. "But what if—"

"What if Martians showed up tomorrow, Clara, and decided to blow us all away? How would you feel if that happened and you spent your last night on earth worrying over something you had no control over, instead of spending that time with me, letting me do things to you."

I smiled in spite of myself. "Letting you do things to me?"

"Preferably things where we're both way more naked. Although I'm not picky, I bet I could work wonders even with your skirt still on," he said seriously, one of his hands dropping down my leg and sliding up and under my skirt.

"Oh, Mr. Bryant," I sighed, trying like hell to let go like he asked, to not worry.

Admittedly, it was easier to let go when he put his mouth on me underneath the night sky.

But I didn't really stop worrying.

Chapter 21

"Clara Morgan? Nice to meet you, I'm Dick Stevee."

Dick Stevee. Best name ever.

"Nice to meet you, Mr. Stevee," I replied, shaking his hand as I walked into the conference room. "How are things going for you so far?" The management team had taken over two of our conference rooms while they "transitioned" into this new arrangement. Dick Stevee would be my new supervisor, and he was the one meeting with the entire field team to appraise, adjust, and make any changes as he saw fit regarding the way we ran our operations.

Here's what I knew about Dick so far. He was efficient, clever, and made split-second decisions—not only on policy but on people. The kind of guy who if you were on his good side, then you saw him as a leader, but if you were on his bad side, then you just saw him as a—

"Call me Dick," he said, gesturing to the chair on the other side of the table. "Things are moving quickly, Clara, which is why it was so important for me to meet with you today."

I didn't say call me Clara, but . . .

"See, I've been reviewing your files, I've been reviewing the files of all my new employees, and I must say, very impressive."

"Well, thank you, I try and—"

"But you take too damn long."

I swallowed. "Excuse me?"

"You take too damn long. All of you do. Some of the changes you've made at these places, and the results you've been able to achieve, are incredible. No one is denying that."

"Okay?" I asked.

"But we need to start achieving those results in half the time."

"Impossible," I said, without missing a beat.

"That's interesting you said that, Clara, because some of the other people in your position said no problem."

"My colleagues do good work, great work in fact, but no one has the track record I do. My success rate is flawless, the returns made on my clients' investments are a windfall in each case, and every single one of them would hire me again."

"And yet you take longer on every project than anyone else in this firm."

"Some would argue that's exactly why I have the success rate I do. I take my time." I held my ground. I was all for making nice with my new boss, but I knew guys like this, and if they sensed a weakness, any weakness at all, you were done for.

"Take the . . . what's the name . . ." He shuffled through his papers. "Bigelow Mountain House?"

"Bryant Mountain House," I corrected, and he looked up at me over his glasses.

"Yes, the Bryant Mountain House. According to your initial plan you're spending the better part of the spring up there, but based on your projections you should be practically done by now." He slid the paperwork toward me.

"Practically done and done are two different things," I said, not looking at the paperwork. I knew what it said, I'd drawn up the plan myself. "This is a unique property, with unique concerns. They've agreed to more changes than I initially anticipated, and they're significant. To abandon them now would be to do exactly that, abandon."

"But surely you'd circle back to check in on progress?"

"Of course. After the initial phase is complete. Which we are still weeks away from, not to mention they're going into their busiest time of the year."

"One week."

"I'm sorry?" I shook my head, not understanding.

"One week, Clara, you have one week to wrap things up at the Bigelow project."

"Bryant Mountain House, but sir, with all due respect, that's simply not possible."

He looked at me keenly. "I've chatted with three other employees today, all of whom share the same job title as you. All of whom produce not nearly the results that you do. All of whom said they can bring their projects in early. Now, I have no doubt that whatever it is you're doing up there is incredible, but now is the time for efficiency. Did Barbara tell you about the hiring freeze? The promotion freeze?"

"She did, Dick," I said icily, locking eyes with him, not daring to look away.

"I know she talked to you about a promotion, making you a partner. I know you're likely the only person on staff right now who is even remotely qualified for such a position, but I also know that right now we don't need another partner. But next year, after things have settled down?" He closed his file. "There will most certainly be an opening inside The Empire Group. Provided that employee has proven she can be a team player. Embrace the changes we're asking everyone to make. Sacrifice now, and be rewarded down the line."

I said nothing. I could say nothing.

"One week, Clara. Then I want you bidding for that Oakmont job down South, and I expect you to get it. We can talk details after that."

He rose up out of his chair, and shook my hand, hard. "Nice to have met you, welcome to The Empire Group."

Sonofabitch.

My mind was reeling the entire drive back to Bailey Falls. My stomach, however, started reeling right about the time I pulled onto I-90 West. I'd felt a little off while I was meeting with Dick Stevee, felt a little more off while I was navigating the parking lot that was driving in downtown Boston, but by the time I hit the turnpike I was just hoping to make it back to Bailey Falls before all hell broke loose.

But apparently luck wasn't on my side today. All hell broke loose at a truck stop somewhere between Ludlow and Chicopee when I vomited everything on my shoes in the ladies' room. I threw up so loudly that when I came out there was a little old lady with a sympathetic look who handed me a bottle of water, which I took gratefully. It'd been ages since I'd had the flu, and for one brief and terrifying moment my brain galloped away with the idea that I was pregnant and that life as I knew it would forever be changed. I was halfway to the feminine care aisle to pee on a stick when my brain galloped back with the news that I'd started my period two days ago and was still currently enjoying the miracle of womanhood, so no, that wasn't it.

Luckily I was only halfway to the aisle, so it was only twenty steps or so back to the ladies' room when another round of let's-reexamine-your-breakfast hit.

I was blazing hot yet freezing cold, I was shaky yet my back seemed locked in place, and my hands were dry while my elbows, somehow my elbows were impossibly sweating. But if I was dying, there was no way I was doing so in a bathroom at Stuckey's. I splashed some water on my face, stumbled out to the store, bought Gatorade and a bottle of Pepto, climbed back into my stupid red convertible that I just had to have all those weeks ago, and pointed my car in the direction of Bailey Falls.

It took me another three hours to drive what should've taken me ninety minutes. I'd had to pull over two more times to throw up, and by the time I saw the crenellated stone roofline of Bryant Mountain House, I was pretty sure I had a fever that was high enough to concern the legions of leprechauns that had invaded my car.

I left the keys in the ignition, nodding weakly at the valet guy, took three steps inside the lobby and realized that I really didn't need to go any farther, the sofa just to the left of reception was a lovely place to take a nap if I could just lay my head down for a . . .

I've been told that I face-planted on a hundred-year-old fainting couch. You couldn't write this stuff, honestly, and that's where Beverly from the front desk found me before my shoes had even fallen off my feet. Beverly called Jonathan, who called Archie, who whisked me away to my room like Prince Charming while I moaned and groaned wildly about red convertibles and a boss named Dick.

Bryant Mountain House is like *The Love Boat*. And like *The Love Boat*, they have an in-house doctor. Kind of. They've got Dr. Carlisle, a retired internist who comes up to the hotel every afternoon to play pinochle and steal tea cookies when he thinks no one is looking. He was there, in the middle of pinochle, when I face-planted, and followed Archie and a boneless me up to my room to make sure everything was okay. I don't remember much of the conversation, but when he heard I'd been vomiting for about four hours, and other issues we do not discuss, then heard me vomiting once more when I made a run for the bathroom, he pronounced me down with a rather violent strain of the stomach flu that had been popping up all over the area, recommended rest and fluids and a bucket within splattering distance of the bed, and to let my body heal on its own.

For the record, vomiting in front of anyone is embarrassing. Vomiting in front of your kind-of boyfriend as he holds that damn bucket gallantly while whispering soothing words of encouragement is a fresh kind of hell.

Archie wouldn't leave. He refused to. He put me to bed, he took me out of that bed when necessary, called down for extra pillows, extra blankets, a portable heater and an oscillating fan, three different kinds of chicken broth and four different kinds of Popsicles. And at least a gallon of Lysol, which gave the room a nice hospital scent but was undoubtedly better than the smell of sick.

I couldn't fathom ingesting even a thimbleful of chicken broth, and when he tried to tempt me with a cherry Popsicle I vaguely remember telling him a very particular place he could hold it while I made yet another mad dash to the bathroom. I ended up curled up on the cool tile, convinced that I was going to die and that the last thing I was ever going to see were tiny bottles of shampoo lined up like soldiers and launching an attack on a stack of defenseless washcloths.

That bathroom floor delirium led to a confusing episode where I was convinced Archie was walking on the ceiling and had been sent by Jesus Christ himself to deliver the message that Mars could be made hospitable for human life if only Matt Damon could get the plants to grow.

Sometime around three thirty in the morning my fever broke, and I can remember a man with wonderfully cool hands tucking the comforter tightly around my shoulders and smoothing back my sweaty hair, the weight of his hand a lovely thing as it rested just above my closed eyelids. I remember the faint scent of pancake syrup and the tiniest freckles dancing just in front of my eyes before I slipped blessedly into an unbroken sleep.

Chapter 22

Birds chirped. A newspaper rustled. Then a low intermittent hum began . . . maybe a tune from *South Pacific*? Whatever it was, it only made the pounding in my temples worse. I tried to open my eyes, but they felt like sandpaper. Thumbing one eyelid open, I winced at the bright sunlight pouring through the wooden blinds. As the world slowly came into view, I put together the sounds I'd heard with the pictures I was now seeing and began to realize a few things:

1. I'd lived. I didn't die on that bathroom tile after vomiting up my kneecaps.
2. It had been Archie who took care of me for the last however many hours as I puked and cried and whined and . . . oh boy.
3. I was sore.
4. I was cranky.
5. I smelled.
6. Archie was still here.

Oh dear God, Archie was still here. He'd seen it all, been there for all my gross, literally seen me at my worst. I'd been gross, but more than that, I'd been weak. And he'd seen it all. Dammit.

Groaning, I rolled over. This action alone causing every muscle in my body, especially those in my tummy, to tense.

My groan alerted Archie, who turned in his chair where he was reading the paper, sipping coffee, and nibbling on a cinnamon roll. He smiled in my direction.

"How're you feeling?"

"Depends." I grimaced, struggling to sit up. "When did you park a truck in my mouth?"

"I'm afraid a particularly strong case of the stomach flu did that," he said, setting down his coffee to quickly move to prop a pillow behind me.

I looked around the room. Half-full glasses of ginger ale, saltine cracker sleeves still mostly full, a now-clean wastebasket next to the bed and . . . flowers? "Where'd the tulips come from?"

"I had them sent up, wanted you to have something pretty to look at when you finally woke up," he said, stroking my hair and smoothing it back from my forehead.

"That was nice," I said, trying to smile, but Jesus fuck, even my face hurt. "You shouldn't get too close to me, I stink."

"You don't stink."

"Well, my hair must be gross, then, seriously, you don't have to do that," I said, shrugging him off a little bit. The room felt overly warm. "Would you mind opening the window, let a little fresh air in here?"

He frowned. "I wouldn't do that yet, you don't want to get too cold, your poor body has been through a lot these last couple of days."

"Oh, I think I'll be okay."

"Maybe later," he said, closing the subject. "Are you feeling hungry yet?"

I winced. "Good God, no, I'm not eating for the rest of the year."

"You've hardly eaten anything since Monday, you need to get your strength back. Here, why don't you lie back and I'll have them bring up some chicken soup." He started to pull the covers back up around me when I processed, really processed, what he said.

"Since Monday, wait, what the hell day is it?" I asked, suddenly remembering my meeting in Boston and my conversation with Dick and—

"It's Wednesday, sweetheart, you were pretty out of it," he soothed, once more brushing my hair back.

"I was out for two days?" I cried, pushing back the covers and trying to climb out of bed. I'd only been given a week to finish this hotel, now I had even less time. What a nightmare.

"Clara, get back in bed, you need to rest." He tugged gently on my elbow, but I was almost out of bed now and I wanted that fresh air. Ugh, and a shower.

"I'm fine, really, let's get that window open and air this place out a bit," I said, slipping into my slippers and only wobbling a little on legs that felt like they hadn't stood up in months. "I'm just going to check my email real quick and then take a shower. Where's my phone?"

"I'm not sure," he said, looking around. "I haven't seen it since we brought you up here the other day."

"Oh man," I groaned, crossing quickly to my purse, trying not to notice that my head was still a little swimmy. I tore through it, looking. "Dammit, not there. Where's my tote bag?"

"Over by the desk, I'll get it for you."

"I got it," I said, already on my way, my mind trying to piece together what had happened once I'd made it back here after the trip to Boston. "My phone never rang, not that whole time?"

"I didn't hear it, but I wasn't really paying attention to anything except what was going on with you. You were really sick."

"I'm so sorry, I can't imagine how awful it was to listen to," I said, looking up at him from my tote bag. "*Please* tell me I didn't throw up on you."

"Okay," he said, shrugging.

"Oh God, that's disgusting," I cried, taking everything out of my bag, still no phone. "I'm so embarrassed."

"Nothing to be embarrassed about." He smiled, walking over to where I was standing, now turning my tote bag upside down and shaking it out. "It was the shower curtain that caught the brunt of it."

Where the hell was my phone? "Mm-hmm, shower curtain." Had Barbara tried to call? Had Dick tried to call? Jesus, what if they'd called the hotel and let slip that I'd be leaving here in just a few days? "Wait, what shower curtain?"

"You don't remember?" Archie grinned, reaching out to rub my shoulders. "You kept saying you were fine, you were done throwing up, and then you took off running to the bathroom and didn't quite make it."

Now that he mentioned it . . . "Archie, seriously, I owe you big-time. I can't believe you stayed here through all that, I could've managed and then you wouldn't have had to see all that. No mysteries left, I guess."

"You don't owe me anything, and you needed me, so I was here."

"Well, I'm not saying I don't appreciate it, but good God, I wouldn't expect anyone to stick around for that, I wouldn't even have asked Roxie to stay." I tried to think back through the muddled memories from that drive on Monday. I remembered using my phone in the car to call and leave Barbara a message. Was it still in my car?

I spied my tennis shoes in the corner, but before I could grab them to head down to the parking lot I noticed Archie standing there, a little too quiet.

"What's up?" I asked.

"You didn't have to ask me to stay, Clara, of course I stayed. Where else do you think I'd be if you're sick?" He looked a little puzzled, a little hurt almost.

"I'm sorry, I didn't mean it that way, I just . . . you're very sweet to have made sure I was okay, but I'm fine. All better. You can go back to work now." I sat down in the corner chair and started to lace up my sneakers, ignoring the thundering headache that kept building behind my eyes.

"Relationships aren't all fun, Bossy, sometimes when one half is down it's the other half who helps them back up again, you know?" I glanced up from my laces and he was there, looking thoughtfully down at me. "Why on earth are you putting on your shoes?"

I stood up. "I gotta run down to my car, I think I left my phone in the front seat, that's the only other place it could be and—"

"Oh no," he said, taking me by the shoulders and leading me toward the bathroom. "You said you wanted to take a shower, but I'm thinking a nice long bath would be perfect, not so much standing up. I'll get that chicken soup we talked about, and then if you absolutely need it, I can run down to your car . . . later."

"That all sounds amazing, Archie, really, it does. But I need my phone—merger stuff—so just let me run down there real quick and then I'll be right back to clean up."

"Clara, you're barely standing as it is. You threw up for two days straight and had a fever of 104. You're not going anywhere. If you need your phone that badly, I'll go get it. But after you take a bath and get back in bed."

I shrugged his hands off my shoulders. "Archie, I need my

phone. *Now*. I can't afford to be out of pocket for even an hour, much less forty-eight. I need to check my emails, check my voice mails, put out fires. I don't have time to still be sick."

"That's ridiculous. If you're sick, you're sick. You don't just get to declare you're not."

I pushed my hair back from my forehead. "Actually, I do. And I appreciate the hell out of everything you've done for me, but now I have to get back to work, simple as that."

"I think that's a terrible idea," he said, standing in front of the door.

My headache bloomed large and in charge, clouding my vision but changing what I could see to full-on red. "I need my phone. I'm getting my phone. Whether or not you think it's a terrible idea is irrelevant." I stood in front of him, hands on my hips, expectantly.

"I don't understand," he said. "Are you mad at me for taking care of you?"

"Is that what this is? Because right now it looks a lot like you trying to make decisions for me based on what you think I should be doing, and let me tell you, that's never a great idea."

"Holy shit," he muttered, running his hands through his hair. "You're picking a fight with me. I can't believe this."

"I'm trying like hell not to, Archie, so here's the part where you realize I am more than capable of taking care of myself."

"Is that what this is about?" he asked, incredulous.

"Goddammit!" I yelled. "This isn't anything other than me getting my stupid phone and you thinking you somehow have the right to try and stop me."

"I will get you your fucking phone if it's so important to you," he yelled back.

"God, you don't get it," I snapped. "It's not just the phone, it's trying to order me soup when I said I didn't want it, and telling me to keep the windows shut when I specifically wanted them open, and telling me I should be taking a bath instead of a shower."

"You're mad at me because I want to *help you?* To take care of you?"

"Yes!" I threw the shoe I hadn't yet put on, shattering a lamp on the nightstand. "I don't need anyone helping me, and I don't need anyone taking care of me. I have always taken care of myself, I've never needed anyone, and I can't afford to start needing that now. I will always make my own decisions, do what *I* want to do and when *I* want to do it because that's just the way I was made. I know you're used to taking care of people, I know what you went through with your wife, but let's get this straight now, I won't ever be *that* girl, okay? I will never get used to relying on other people, because do you know what that gets you? Left alone, fucking broken, fucking unwanted. So I don't need someone's help, in fact I prefer the opposite. It's easier that way, when you don't expect anything from anyone."

He was silent. The only sound in the room was my breathing, which was labored.

"Oh man," he breathed, finally speaking. "This was never going to work, was it?"

My labored breathing stopped altogether.

We never even had a chance.

"I'm leaving in five days," I managed.

I made sure of it.

"My new boss gave me a week to finish up here, before I have to be back in Boston to bid on my next project."

I'd cut this off at every single pass until there was no possible way through.

"Maybe it's better this way, Archie."

Maybe I made sure it was this way, Archie.

"I'll be back up here from time to time, over the next year or so, to check on the progress you and your team have made."

Your team. Not our team. It was never going to be our anything.

"Maybe someday, we can try and—"

"What I said, what I told you. Those words . . . " He swallowed, and I ached. "That doesn't mean anything?"

His expression begged me to tell him that wasn't true.

I took a breath, held it, then let it out.

"If you leave, that's it," he said, his eyes so icy blue. "I'm done."

"I have to leave. It's my job."

I am my job.

"You're very good at your job," he said, nodding. "Which is why I don't believe for a second that you *have* to leave. You just got finished telling me that no one makes you do anything you don't want to do."

"This is different."

No, it isn't.

"No," he said sadly. "It isn't."

He turned to go.

"I'm so sorry, Archie. I really am."

He stopped, speaking over his shoulder but refusing to look at me. "The worst part, Clara?" *Oh God, don't say my name, I can't do this if you say my name.* "I *know* you're sorry."

He left. I finished putting on my shoes and went down to find my phone. It was sitting in the passenger seat where I'd left it.

Couldn't you have just let him get your damn phone?

If I could have, I would have.

"No way."

"Fuck that."

"Guys, come on."

"Nuh-uh."

"Fuck. That."

"Thanks, really, thanks for being understanding about this." I tossed the fork onto my plate with a clatter, the piece of cake forgotten.

I'd met Roxie and Natalie at the diner to tell them my news, that I'd be leaving sooner than I'd thought and to keep me up-to-date on all the wedding planning so I could make sure to be in town for any bridesmaids' responsibilities. I'd no sooner broken it to them and taken a bite of Roxie's Lemon Dream Poundcake when I was assaulted from both sides about what an ass I was being and how dare I leave town like this.

It had been a hellacious few days. I'd spent all day Wednesday still trying to rally from being sick while simultaneously wrangling my email back under control and trying to cram literally weeks and weeks of work I'd yet to do into the five days I had left.

I hadn't been alone with Archie since that morning. Whether by coincidence or design, the only glimpse I'd had of him was during one very quick and terse exchange with him and his father about details on the summer season.

He'd refused to look at me at first, and when he did it was with none of the warmth and comfort I'd grown far too accustomed to seeing. His slow grin, his quick humor, the way his deep-blue eyes would twinkle when I was being naughty . . . or deepen when I was being truly naughty. This was all lost to me now, hidden behind a mask of strictly business and business only.

What did I expect? I'd broken his heart. I'd broken my own heart, if I had one. And I was no longer sure that I did.

My best friends were also convinced this was the case.

"I just, I don't fucking get it," Natalie protested, holding her fork in her fist and punctuating each word with a table pound. "You guys were so good together, like, really good together! What the hell, Clara?"

"Look, you knew this wasn't going to last. It couldn't. I was always leaving. He knew this. I knew this. Fucking hell, *you* guys knew this, so quit busting my balls."

Natalie pointed her fork at me. "I will fucking bust your balls all I want, Morgan, because you're acting like a real ass here. This is literally the worst decision you could make, you cannot leave. You just can't!"

"Clara, honey," Roxie said, always the voice of reason. She knew me better than anyone, she was always the mediator, the one who could tamp Natalie down when she was getting too out there. She would calm this down, she'd be able to articulate to Natalie what was really going on here, that it was just simply impossible for me to stay. Roxie would make it make sense. "This is some kind of bullshit."

"Wait, what?" I asked, my head swiveling toward her in surprise.

"I love you," she said, her eyes sad, "but this is the very worst kind of bullshit. And you know I don't push you very often because I know that's hard for you. I know you hate it when you think someone is trying to tell you what to do, but in this case, I don't care. Unequivocally and without question, this is a mistake. You do this, you leave this man who loves you, you'll regret it the rest of your life."

Tears, hot and wild, burned behind my eyelids. But I wouldn't let them fall. I couldn't let them fall.

"Has everyone gone crazy? This isn't about me, and it's not even really about Archie." A lump the size of an orange swelled up in my throat from saying his name out loud. "For God's sake, it's not like I have a choice. This is my job, in case anyone has forgotten, and my job means I'm in a different place all the fucking time." I swallowed hard, the orange growing to a grapefruit. "It's been fun, really fun, being here with you guys and meeting everyone and getting to know Leo and Oscar, and even Chad and Logan, and seeing Trudy again, and yes, of course, Archie." The grapefruit was now a pineapple. "I have loved the time I got to spend with Archie, and it was incredible and wonderful and fucking hell he's . . . Jesus, he's everything . . . but that doesn't matter because I have to go. And I can't be here. So that's just . . ." I sighed, so deep that every part of me down to my toes suddenly felt exhausted. "It's just the way it goes." I looked at them both through heavy lids. Everything felt heavy, every part of me just felt weighed down and so very sad. "Okay?"

Roxie shook her head, pursing her lips and looking for all the world like she had so many things to say but knowing innately that none of them would work. "Okay."

"Not okay, but okay," Natalie agreed, her normally loud and full voice no more than a whisper.

I picked up my fork, not hungry at all but needing something to do. "Okay."

Chapter 23

Two months later . . .

"Two hundred thread count is too low."

"It's what we've always used."

"I realize that, but it's still too low."

"I don't think guests really care what the thread count is when they're on vacation."

"Well, that's exactly where you're wrong." I sighed. "People want to feel taken care of when they're at a hotel of this magnitude, sometimes in ways they didn't even know they needed. They want to feel comforted, and looked after, and when they slip into their bed at the end of a long day they want to look at each other and say, 'Wow, this is seriously the most comfortable bed I have ever slept in.'" I picked up the old sheet and rubbed it between my fingers. "Believe me, the last thing you want anyone saying when they slip into bed is 'Holy shit, can you believe we're spending eight hundred dollars a night and they can't even spring for some nice sheets?'"

I was sitting in the Charleston Conference Room at the Oakmont Resort and Golf Club in Buford, South Carolina, in a meeting with their director of operations, their VP of sales, and the housekeeping supervisor. Trying to explain to them why their shitty scratchy sheets had to be replaced. As expected, they were fighting me. As expected, I was fighting back.

Not expected? I couldn't give a shit whether I won this argument or not.

I'd been at the Oakmont for less than two weeks and had already identified their staffing issues, noticed new branding opportunities, and pitched several severe cost-cutting initiatives as well as an entirely new recreation program. Before that I'd been at The Lantern Inn in Stowe, Vermont, The Red Hill Farm Bed & Breakfast on Mackinac Island, Michigan, and a whirlwind but highly productive visit to The Sea Grass Hotel and Tennis Club in Mendocino, California. Same issues, same troubles, basically the same solutions. I'd saved the day, righted the ship, and went on my merry way. And now here I was, in South Carolina.

Forty-five minutes in and we hadn't even addressed the new duvet I was suggesting. I'd shoot myself in the face, but I was tough on gun control.

I was suddenly exhausted. "You know what, let's table this. I know you're all anxious to get done and get home before the holiday weekend, so let's just all think about what I've proposed, and then when we come back we'll figure out a way through this, okay?" I waved them out with a tired smile.

Everyone, as anxious as I was to get home for the holiday weekend, agreed, thanked me for my time, and exited the grand conference room. I closed the door, and on second thought, locked it. I went back to the table where my materials were all in neat, tidy stacks. Ideas well researched and fully thought out, how-tos and to-dos and this-will-helps and these have-to-gos.

I sat in my chair, looked at everything, and laid my head down on the table. My boss, Dick Stevee, heavy on the dick, although in reality, I doubted it somewhat, had been right about one thing. When you don't give a shit about the job you're doing, you can bang it out pretty fast.

I'd become a machine. I breathed, slept, and ate cost analysis, staffing spreadsheets, booking projections, target sales goals. My schedule had been so busy I hadn't even competed in a marathon or a triathlon, and the exercise I did get was all inside a gym on a treadmill, usually with my iPad open so I could get more work done.

My boss was fucking dazzled. "You keep this up, Morgan, when it comes time, that partnership is yours."

I should be ecstatic. I should be over the moon. I should be . . . fuck me, I should be *happy*.

I was miserable. I'd only managed to sneak in one weekend to New York City to help Roxie shop for her wedding dress, and spent much of that weekend tripping over my own words to make sure no one mentioned the one person I was dying to ask about.

Archie.

Just thinking about his name made me want to sigh and cry and smile and frown all at the same time.

I'd never even said good-bye. What kind of a person does that? That last day had been so busy—trying to squeeze so much into so little time—and there'd always been other people around, buffering, keeping us separated, that when it came time for me to actually leave, I turned to see where he was only to find him walking back inside the hotel, head down. And I didn't go after him.

Shame burned hot in my cheeks, and I banged my head against the table, trying to block out the light streaming through the beautiful old leaded glass windows. The smell of old, rare wood brought me back to the present. I gradually became aware of my surroundings. This hotel, like so many others, was full of true old beauty. It had seen wars, the Great Depression, the moon landing, families beginning and growing and changing and aging and dying. Throughout many lifetimes it had stood strong, sheltering those who came to find something old and beautiful and comforting. The traditions housed within these old walls were worth saving, they always would be. This was my passion. But this kind of passion couldn't be hurried, it couldn't be shoe-horned into an already overworked and jam-packed schedule. I needed the freedom to do what I do best. But I needed to find the magic again.

I caught the last flight from Charleston back to Boston late that same night, sitting in the middle seat, last row next to the stopped-up lavatory. I sat in traffic when I stupidly grabbed a cab instead of the Silver Line, and to make matters worse, the cab's AC was broken so I sat in my own sweat. By the time I made it back to my apartment I was a haggard mess, and I was starving. I quickly dialed up my go-to Chinese delivery and placed an order for . . . well . . . everything.

I didn't need to come home over the weekend, but I was restless. Normally I enjoyed spending my weekends traveling throughout whatever part of the country I was working in. I could have driven down to Gulf Shores and spent a few nights on the beach. I could have driven over to Savannah and stayed in a grand old plantation house. I could have stayed at the Oakmont and holed up in my room, ordering room service and binge-watching pay-per-view.

On my TV. In my room.

But I was restless. So I went home. And here I sat on the couch in my apartment, surrounded by mei fun and chow fun and wonton. And one, no, two empty bottles of wine. I could hear my neighborhood bustling with pre-Fourth activities, kids laughing and a few stray bottle rockets going off here and there.

But I stayed inside, with my wonton and wine, and sat on my couch.

I was still restless. But now I was bloated and restless. And my eyeballs were somehow leaking. What??

I looked around my apartment that I was almost never in. In fact, when I counted up the days I was on the road versus the days I was home, it was no contest. This was a place to store the little bit of stuff I had. I looked around as I sat on my couch, saw the mismatched chairs that I'd liberated and had shipped home when The Graceful Palms Hotel closed up shop in Miami five years ago. I saw the end tables that used to grace the entryway at The Heights Resort and Spa in Vail, Colorado, which they got rid of when I convinced them to remodel four years ago. Even the couch I was sitting on, a fantastic green velvet Art Deco piece I picked up while consulting at Tucker Home in Rhode Island three years ago. Everything in my apartment was from someone else's home.

My apartment. Jesus, in my head I couldn't even call it my home. And dammit, why the hell were my eyeballs leaking again? Did I get some hot mustard in them?

Without much thought, I picked up the phone and dialed. I called Roxie, and she called Natalie. And we had a three-way.

"You guys, something's wrong with my eyes," I said, my voice gruff.

"How much wine?" Natalie asked.

"Two bottles." I sniffled. "But I didn't pour either in my eyeballs."

"Well, that's good," Roxie said, chuckling lightly. "What's going on?"

"I don't know," I answered, and never in my entire life had I ever meant it more. "I literally don't know."

"Well, for starters, have you talked to Archie?" Natalie asked, and I immediately bristled.

"Why in the world would me talking to Archie have anything to do with anything?" I asked, my fists balling up. "Have I talked to Archie, have you talked to Archie?"

"I have, actually," Natalie said. "And—"

"Natalie, shut up," Roxie interjected, and for once Natalie listened. "Where are you, Clara?"

"Home." I sniffed. "Well, my apartment."

"Boston? How long are you in town?"

I calculated, which was tricky because wine. "I'm here for a few days, the staff at the Oakmont rotates their holidays, so when I realized they weren't all working and that I'd get a few days off I figured I'd just bum around down there, but I just . . . dammit." I had no words, no words to explain how I was feeling, and it was frustrating as hell. "I don't know!" I repeated.

"Clara, sweetie, just come here. Just get on a train and come up here, we can pick you up at the station in Poughkeepsie."

"I can't." I sighed. "I can't do that."

"Hell yes, you can," Natalie said, having remained silent for all of thirty seconds. "Get your ass on a train and come home."

"Home?" I asked. "I thought Manhattan was home."

"Listen to me, you crazy person, and if you ever repeat this inside of the five boroughs I will beat you up with your own hands, but my home is here now. Goddammit, I can't believe I'm saying this, and I will never give up my brownstone, but"—she paused, and neither Roxie nor I even breathed—"fucking hell, my home is wherever Oscar is. And he's where his cows are. So . . . there. Bailey Falls is home. And if I can say that, Jesus, would you just get on a train and get your ass up here?"

"I can't, I really can't," I said. "I left so quickly, and I didn't . . . oh God, you guys I didn't . . . ." And then I started to full-on donkey cry. "I didn't even say good-bye!"

They were quiet while I worked it out. While the wine and

the wonton did their job and allowed tears that I didn't even think my ducts knew how to make flowed fast and hot.

"I love him," I finally managed to hiccup out. "I love him and I broke his heart, and now I'm trying so hard to go back to what I do best and it's just not the same, you know? I work and I work and . . . oh, everything just sucks right now." I sighed a big, blubbery sigh.

But then I heard Leo in the background, asking if she'd picked up milk on the way home, and it just all hit me like a ton of bricks. Roxie and Natalie had those conversations all the time. *Hey, did you pick up milk on the way home,* or *honey, is that faucet in the kitchen still dripping,* and *do you know if the gas bill got paid yet,* or *does this mole look funny to you?* All those random stupid questions that fill a day end up filling a lifetime. With memories. And traditions.

"You know what, guys," I said, suddenly feeling stupid-tired. "I'm gonna go, I've got to get some sleep. I'll call you tomorrow."

"No no, Clara, you're upset, let's talk this out," Roxie started to say, but I was already shaking my head.

"It's okay, really, I'm sorry I flipped out tonight. I just need to get some sleep."

"I can be in Boston in four hours," Natalie said, and I smiled in spite of the tears that still coursed in absolute rivers down my cheeks.

"I know you can. I'm okay, though, seriously."

"I don't believe you for a second," Roxie said, her voice sad. "Not for a second."

"It's okay, I've got tons of work to do this weekend. I'll sleep tonight and tomorrow, I'll be back to normal. I'll go for a run, trust me, it's all good." And before they could try to keep me on the phone any longer, I said good night and hung up.

I lay down right there on the couch, surrounded by

hot-mustard packets that had in no way caused this outburst, and looked at my ceiling. The ceiling I'd lived under for years now, and had never really bothered to look at.

And for the first time, I realized I wanted my own traditions. It wasn't enough to simply archive and treasure and try to save someone else's. I wanted my own stories to tell.

My traditions were small, but they were everything. I knew how to dye Easter eggs. I knew which radiator to fiddle with when the steam whistle began to blow in the Lakeside Lounge. I knew you could see the Milky Way from the roof on a clear night.

And I knew that running no longer gave me the static I craved. I craved quiet, but the kind of quiet that only comes after the love, after the sighs and cries, when his hands roamed freely across my naked body, no longer frantic but touching just for the sake of it. Just for the pure reason of skin touching skin with nothing in between, of communicating on a cellular level, you're here and I'm here and we're here and this is so much more than enough because it's everything.

I fell asleep that night dreaming of mountaintops and ice skates. And when I woke up the next morning I knew what I had to do. Or at least, what I needed to try to do.

But first, I needed to buy my first car.

Green. Everything was so green. The last time I'd driven up this mountain, it had barely been spring and anything even close to green was only timidly peeking out. But now? The whole world was green.

I turned right just before the exit into town, but even from here I could see that Bailey Falls was ready for the Fourth of July. Red, white, and blue bunting hung from every balcony, crisscrossed the light posts on Main Street, and, beside every front door, the American flag proudly flew.

I drove along the riverfront on the south side of town, the Hudson River sparkling to my left in the afternoon sun. It was warm, but after the humidity and close, hot heat of South Carolina, a summer day in the Catskills brought a pleasant breeze and a welcome break. That pleasant breeze ruffled my hair as I drove with the top down, heading for the turnoff for Bryant Mountain House.

Ever since I'd made the spur-of-the-moment decision to leave Boston this morning, I'd literally been flying by the seat of my pants. There was a car dealer around the corner that specialized in classic cars, and when they were offering a Fourth of July sale on a little cherry-red, wholly unnecessary convertible sports car, I took it as a sign that the universe was endorsing my Hail Fucking Mary pass to beg Mr. Archibald Bryant into being my feller.

I smothered a laugh, then decided against it, letting my laughter ring out loud and proud against the quiet country air as I raced up the mountain, determined to go get my man. No one knew I was coming, not even the girls. I didn't want to talk, I just wanted to *do*. I did well when I followed my instincts, and I knew I needed to follow them right now. I laughed to myself when I thought about what my friends would say when they found out what I was up to.

I let out another laugh when I thought about the likely look on Dick Stevee's face when he got my email that I was, essentially effective immediately, terminating my employment with The Empire Group. Something surely he never saw coming.

Dear Dick,

I am writing to tell you, this Fourth of July, that I'm announcing my own independence and tendering my

*resignation. While there may not be actual fireworks ac-
companying this actual email, please know that in my head,
they're going off like gangbusters right now. You see, I love
my job. Or I should say, I did love my job, until you and The
Empire Group came along and changed everything. Now,
change is good, and I've never been one to fear change, but
at this point in my life . . . yeah, no.*

*I'll be staying on to finish up the Oakmont project, but
consider that my final contribution. I don't know where my
life is about to take me, but I am comforted in the knowledge that I will not be, and will never be, your partner.*

*Regards,
Clara Morgan*

Yeah, he definitely didn't see that coming. And frankly, I
didn't see it coming either. But when everything that mattered
weighed in the balance, it was time. Time to stretch my wings a
bit, see what else might be out there. Time to stretch my Rolo-
dex too—I had contacts and references going back for years,
and all those hotel owners and managers wouldn't hesitate
to recommend me to others who needed help restoring their
brand. I'd find work, I wasn't worried about that. Work that I
could be proud of, could do on my own time and at my own
pace and actually carry through to fruition rather than finishing
piecemeal because I had to race to my next gig.

My next gig, however, I was hoping, was going to be working
at Bryant Mountain House, to finish up the job I'd started. *If* the
owner would have me.

A nervous giggle flew out of my mouth at the thought of
being had by this particular owner.

Would he still want me? Could I make him want me again?
Was it too late?

Maybe not. Maybe not. Maybe so. But I wasn't going to back down and walk away this time, I was going for it full steam.

I pushed my foot down on the gas pedal a little harder, climbing higher into the Catskills, searching out the sign that said the turnoff for Bryant Mountain House was just around the bend.

❧

"No, I don't have a reservation. But Bert, you know me, it's Clara. Clara Morgan, I was here for weeks and weeks this spring."

"I do know you, Ms. Morgan, which is why I know you know the rules. No one goes up who doesn't have a reservation." Bert the security guard frowned at me over his clipboard. "Unless you have a day pass. Do you have a day pass?"

Bert was killing my buzz. "No, but if I need to buy one, I'll buy one."

"Does anyone know you're coming?" He looked at me pointedly. I knew what he was asking. Did Archie know?

"No," I said, swallowing. "It was kind of a spur-of-the-moment thing."

"Uh-huh," he said, frowning. "I thought that might be the case."

"I'm here for a good reason, though, I promise," I said, trying my best to look contrite and deserving.

"You're not planning on making some kind of scene, are you?" he asked, looking dubious.

I swallowed hard once more. "No." I certainly wasn't *planning* on it.

"You want to buy a day pass, huh? The day's almost over." He looked at his watch.

"Bert, I'm literally begging you. Just give me the day pass, and I promise you, you won't be sorry."

"I can't give you a day pass." Dammit. I mentally began wondering whether I could hike through the woods up the side of the mountain without getting lost. "I can sell you a day pass, though."

"Bert. I love you."

"You better keep those words handy, Ms. Morgan," he replied, blushing a little as I handed over my credit card.

"You don't have to, you know"—I looked up at him with a pleading look—"call up there and tell certain people I'm on my way, do you?"

He looked at me with an amused look, then handed me the tag and my credit card. "I don't suppose I do."

I let out a sigh of relief. "Thank you, Bert." I started to roll up the window when he waved at me.

"I went ahead and gave you a guest parking pass on there, even though you're not technically a guest. That way you can park at the main house in case you're trying to get up there quickly and all." He winked.

"Thank you, thank you so much!"

"Good luck," he called out as I drove away.

"Hopefully I won't need it, otherwise I'm coming back for you, Bert!" I yelled back.

I looked quickly at the clock on the dashboard. Four thirty. I wracked my brain trying to remember what the hell they did up here on Fourth of July. I'd gone over this with recreation, I knew this. I knew there was a lobster bake for dinner, I knew there were campfires and s'mores, I knew there were eventual fireworks over the lake . . . but there was something else special they did during the day. Watermelon races? Egg toss? Probably, likely, but no, there was something else. A big tradition, something they'd always done, but for the life of me I couldn't remember!

I made the last turn, and there it was. Stretching out over the entire horizon, the hotel was grand, so very grand. And in the warm summer glow, it was a night and day difference from the still grand but somehow almost bleak first impression I'd gotten when I saw it for the first time that freezing cold afternoon so many months ago.

Now the hotel was shining in all its summer finery. Balconies filled with flower boxes bursting with a riot of summer reds and oranges, rocking chairs filled with people of all ages, and American flags flying from atop the parapets along the roofline.

The front lawn where I'd watched kids hunt for Easter eggs was bright green and trimmed neatly, kids playing croquet with the same mallets as their parents did when they'd learned. More rocking chairs lined the Sunset Porch, which faced the mountains, these filled with guests having an afternoon cocktail before heading up to the big barbecue.

And something else . . . dammit, why couldn't I remember?

No matter, the hotel looked incredible and inviting. I drove around to the parking lot quickly, skipping the valet and swinging into the first open slot I saw. I ran my hands through my hair, tweaked my cheeks like a good Scarlett, and started off for the main house.

Two steps into the lobby and I ran into Mrs. Banning and Mrs. Toomey.

"Hello, ladies! How are you, I've missed you!" I cried out, stepping quickly over to embrace them. I was just all full of the love today.

"Well, I never," huffed Mrs. Banning.

"I also never," Mrs. Toomey chimed in, equally huffy.

"What's the matter," I asked, looking down to see if I'd spilled something on my sundress, wondering why in the world they didn't want to hug me. Unless . . .

"You have some nerve, showing up here," Mrs. Banning scolded, looking at me like she'd sooner see me strung up on the flagpole than Old Glory.

Mrs. Toomey nodded fiercely in agreement. "I should say, coming up here, on a holiday no less. I certainly hope you're not here to cause trouble for him, young lady."

"Ahhh," I sighed, understanding. "And the him you're talking about would be Archie?"

"Oh, so you remember his name, do you?" Mrs. Banning said, raising her eyebrows so high I was surprised her forehead didn't split open.

"I see, so I take it everyone knew that we were—"

"Yes, exactly," Mrs. Toomey hissed. "Everyone knew that *you were*. And if you've come back to break his heart again, just know that we're not going to let you do it, right, Hilda?"

"That's right, Prudence."

"In fact, one of those new industrial linen manglers just arrived. Would you like a demonstration?"

"Well, now, Prudence, that's a little bit much, don't you think?"

"Hilda, don't you try and rein me back in, I'm good and mad at this little hussy and I—"

"I'm a hussy now?" I asked, grinning in spite of my death literally being planned right in front of me.

"You motherfucker!" I heard ring out across the lobby, and saw several actual mothers clap their hands over their kids' ears and scurry them away.

"Oh man," I groaned, turning to see not only Natalie, but Roxie, Leo, Oscar, Polly, Chad, Logan, Trudy, and her new boyfriend, Wayne Tuesday. "*Of course* the peanut gallery would be here for this."

"I'm allergic to peanuts," Polly said.

"You're not allergic to peanuts," Leo replied.

"But everyone in my class is, why can't I be?"

"You're not allergic to peanuts, Pork Chop, get over it," Leo said.

"I'm lactose intolerant," Logan said.

"Only when you eat an entire pint of ice cream," Chad added. "Which you should stop doing."

"I'm starting a line of ice cream at the creamery," Oscar said.

"Oh, that's great," Trudy said, "if it's any good I'll use it at the diner."

"Of course it'll be good," Oscar huffed.

"No one is saying it wouldn't be good, I was just saying that—"

"You motherfuckers!" Natalie shouted, turning to everyone. "Shut up, and you, motherfucker"—she pointed at me—"what the hell are you doing here? And Polly, here, take ten dollars and we'll call it done for the day." She shoved a fistful of cash at Polly and her swear jar, which she carried everywhere nowadays. Kid was going to be able to pay for her own college at this rate.

"Clara." Roxie smiled. "Are you here for . . . ?"

"Yes, yes, I am." I nodded happily. "Do you know where he is?"

"He's down by the mangler," Mrs. Toomey interjected, and Mrs. Banning told her to hush up.

"He's up on the third-floor balcony," Roxie said, beaming. "They're about to do the Fourth of July Porch Jump."

Yes! That's it! That's the tradition I couldn't remember, the Porch Jump. Since the hotel had been built, guests and staff alike had been jumping from the third-floor balcony into the lake below to celebrate our country's birthday. It was the oldest and most beloved tradition. Short of the hot cross buns. And they jumped promptly at 5 p.m.

I looked at the grandfather clock across the lobby just as it started to chime.

Bong . . .

My heart leapt into my throat. I took off running for the staircase. I took the first three steps in one leap, taking the next few entirely in double time. Behind me, I heard my gaggle of people give chase, crashing into each other as they tried to follow me up the stairs, but I had a huge head start.

"Where are we going?"

"Weren't you listening? The third floor, come on!"

"This is so exciting!"

"I'm so glad I already have popcorn!"

Bong . . .

I was on the second-floor landing, striding fast and passing guests on the left and right. Even though I was running, even though I was racing to find the man I loved more than anything on this planet, I couldn't help but notice they'd removed the carpet and the fucking wood floors underneath were incredible.

Bong . . .

My feet hit the first step to the third floor, and I nearly took out a potted palm tree—hey, that was new.

I hit the fifth step. I wished I had time, more time, to think about what to say now that I was here, now that I'd be seeing him again. What could I say to make him hear me and know how sorry I was that I left the way I did? Could I make him see me, hear me, love me again? What if he didn't love me anymore? Oh shit.

Bong . . .

"Can you see her? Where is she?"

"Pinup, quit hitting me, that doesn't make me go faster."

"Sorry, sorry, so sorry, excuse us, pardon us, so sorry, excuse us."

"Mangler, I'm telling you, the mangler will take care of her."

"I'm worried about you, Prudence."

"Why would anyone jump off a porch?"

306   ALICE CLAYTON

"Why wouldn't *everyone* jump off a porch?"

I cleared the last step, looked around wildly. There was a crowd of people all gathered around the balcony, some in bathing suits and some still in their summer dresses and Bermuda shorts, all teetering on the edge of the wooden railing, poised and waiting for something, some kind of signal, to jump into the lake below.

I burst into the room, my peanut gallery less than ten feet behind me, pushing my way toward the front, elbowing like a groupie at a concert, trying to get up to the front before—

Bong . . .

Five p.m.

There. Standing dead center in the middle of the railing, perched and ready to jump. He turned around with a whistle in his mouth, ready to sound off and let everyone know it was time.

I pushed through the crowd, one particularly robust man throwing a wide arm and almost causing me to hit the deck, but as I gave one more strong push with my runner's legs, he saw me.

His eyes met mine and my eyes met his and in his surprise and shock and my delight and happy kicky balloon lovestruck . . . well. The world just plain faded away.

But my forward momentum was still kicking.

And just as he blew on his little whistle I crashed through the last string of cheerleaders and leapt up onto the railing, smashing into his chest as I threw my arms around his neck . . . and carried us both right off the ledge.

He tweeted his whistle the entire way down.

They say time is elastic. Sometimes an hour passes in an instant while you scratch and cling at every second as they go by, willing them to slow down. Sometimes, an instant stretches out to an hour, when everything runs in super slow-mo, time itself elongated as the edges blur and the colors run.

I fell three stories with Archie Bryant, and it was a lifetime. I knew he was blowing his whistle, there was a part of me that could even hear it, shrill and pitchy as we plunged toward the lake below. But inside that bubble, the part of me that was inside that space where time stood still, I knew nothing except what it felt like to feel his skin under my touch and to be able to just stare into his eyes, searching for a hint of anything, anything that might tell me where I stood.

In those three stories, his eyes spoke to me, volumes and volumes of words and sentences and paragraphs collected into pure raw emotion.

Hurt.

Sorrow.

Fear.

Passion.

Heat.

Anger.

Disappointment.

Elation.

Joy.

Hunger.

Need.

Hope.

And finally, just before we hit the water . . . once more, hurt.

We splashed down, hitting the glacial lake as one, plunging under the cold, clear water, descending down into the watery depths, the chill taking my breath away.

Also, to be clear, he tweeted his whistle the entire way down.

Once underwater, I let go of him, and upon surfacing we were several feet away from each other. He surfaced . . . angry.

"What the hell is wrong with you?" he huffed, brushing his hair out of his face. "Who does something like that?"

"I didn't plan to do that, I just got excited when I saw you and I didn't want you to jump without me so—"

"So you threw us both off a balcony?" he sputtered. I tried to swim closer, but he paddled away.

"Technically, I did the Porch Jump. I just didn't know I was going to do it or I would have taken a moment to take off my aspirational sandals."

"*In*spirational sandals?"

"*As*pirational, as in, I bought them before I could afford them, years ago, when I was trying to show the world what I was aspiring to be. You know, it's like dressing for the job you want instead of the job you have? Anyway, I saw these expensive Kate Spade sandals in the window at Saks one time and I just knew I needed to have them. Yellow and turquoise with a peep toe and a kitten heel, they looked like exactly the person I wanted to be. And eventually, they became like my good-luck shoes."

"I can't believe I'm having this conversation," he mumbled, paddling away from me.

I flipped over a little to stick one foot in the air, a naked foot. "But see, I lost them both, they're at the bottom of the lake now, which I really didn't think about ahead of time, had I paused for even five seconds before slamming into you I would have taken them off." I stuck my foot back underwater and swam a little closer. "They're my aspirational shoes, after all."

"I don't give a damn about your shoes," he said, turning his back to me and stroking toward the boat dock. But he hadn't gone very far when he suddenly turned around, the water swirling with him. "What the hell are you doing here?"

Just then, an enormous round of applause erupted from above, and as we looked skyward we saw three levels of the hotel, crammed onto their porches and balconies, watching us and cheering. The cheering, of course, led by my peanut gallery.

"For God's sake," he grunted, turning away from me once more and swimming away.

"Hey, hey!" I shouted, stroking smoothly through the water. "Where are you going, come back here!"

He swam faster, I swam faster. He headed for the boat dock, but when he saw the recreation guys and not a small amount of guests now crowding in between the canoes to watch what was happening, he made a sharp right turn and headed out into the middle of the lake.

Toward the swimming platform.

I'd been right about Archie all along. He *was* a swimmer. And right now he was like a wet blur, he was moving so fast through the water. For every two strokes I was giving it, he was giving it four. He was gliding smoothly, clipping along at a ridiculous pace, but I wasn't giving up. Fuck that.

I put on a burst of speed, eye on the prize.

"Stop chasing me," he called back.

"Stop swimming, then," I shouted, not pausing at all.

"This is insane! You're insane!" he yelled back, flipping easily over onto his back and not even losing a stroke.

"Says the guy making me chase him!"

"Unbelievable," I heard him say as he reached the platform and hauled himself up effortlessly. I put my head down and made like a torpedo, swimming straight for him.

When I got there, he was standing at the edge, water dripping off his glorious body. For a split second, he stood between me and the sun. I stayed in the water, in his shadow, his silhouette painted across my wet skin. I could see his face now, so beautiful, so angry. His eyes were like two iced blueberries. Fuck, I love this man.

I pulled myself out of the water, my dress sticking to me everywhere, and stood next to him.

"You want to explain to me exactly what the hell is going on here?"

"Yes. I love you."

"I mean, what kind of a stunt was that, you threw us off a balcony, for God's sake, Clara, you could have gotten hurt!"

"Worth it. I love you."

"What the hell kind of a person does something like that?"

"This person. I love you."

He started to ask me another question, but I stopped him with my mouth. I launched myself once more at him, jumping into his arms whether he was ready for me or not and kissed him square on the lips. He fell backward onto the platform, taking me with him, and I landed on his whistle.

"I can't believe you're still wearing this."

"I can't believe you're talking about my whistle."

"I can't believe you blew that thing all the way down."

"I can't believe that you— Goddammit, no! No, you don't get to do this again, you don't get to one-up me in the middle of a lake." He tried to sit up, but I pulled him back down.

"Too late, I love you."

"Stop saying that," he yelled, leaning up on his elbows, bracing himself over me.

"I can't. I love you. I love you. I love you." He tried to sit up once more, but I wrapped my feet around his thighs and tugged him back down. "I've never said that to anyone in my entire life, and I'm finding that I love saying I love you to you."

"You don't know what you're saying," he said, his face still full of exasperation, but his voice was somehow softer now, somehow not as angry. "Please don't say it again."

"Archie," I said, as the water from his auburn hair dripped down onto me, "I can't stop saying it because I do. And I came here today expressly to tell you that I do. I was a stupid jerk who left because I couldn't handle what I was feeling. I loved you then, of course I did, but I couldn't say it. I've loved you every day since I left and I *love you* right now. I feel better when I'm around you, I *am* better when I'm around you. I don't like my life without you in it. I quit my job. I bought a stupid car. I jumped off a fucking porch on the Fourth of July because I love you and I couldn't stand one more second on this earth without your arms around me."

He was silent. I still had my ankles locked around him, not letting him go.

"And something else." I took a breath, but found that my chest didn't hurt so much, not like it used to. "My mother went to prison when I was six years old. Before that happened, I'd been taken away from her three times because of her drug use. When she finally went to prison, I went back into foster care because there was literally no one else who wanted me. I never knew my father, her parents were dead, I had no uncles or aunts or cousins or anything. There was nowhere for me to go. And when she got out of prison, she never came back for me. She overdosed a year later, I didn't find out until I was thirteen. I was with seven different foster families before I turned eighteen and was then on my own. I never looked back. I've spent my life knowing that no one ever wanted me, and that was how I made sure my life stayed. No attachments, no roots, no real home, no real traditions. I took care of myself, and that was it. The idea of depending on someone else, of having to need someone else, was nothing I ever allowed myself to do, because if someone else walked away from me, I would break."

"Clara," he said, his eyes full.

"But it's okay," I said, reaching up and swooping his hair back. "I can tell you all of this now because I'm not embarrassed anymore. I'm not my past, I'm my present. And my future is wide fucking open. I can make whatever kind of life I want for myself, and the life that I want for myself is with you, only with you. Everything, all of it, right down to your antiques and your Archie Special and your freckles and your stupid pointy whistle, I want it. Because I love you, I love you so much, I love you with my entire heart. And until you, there was nothing in it. You've literally filled up my *entire heart*." I held his face in my hands. "My heart, if you want it, is yours."

He was silent once more. I barely breathed. Would he? Could he?

Finally, his eyes closed. And he lowered his forehead to mine. "I can't believe you threw us off a balcony."

"I can't believe you made me chase you across a lake."

He opened his eyes. "I can't believe I've got such a bossy girl to love me so much."

"I love you."

"So I've heard."

"Now you say it too."

He kissed my nose, my eyelids, each cheek, then my chin. And then he whispered, "I love you."

My toes pointed. "Kiss me, Hotel Boy."

He really just did.

The peanut gallery, an entire hotel full, cheered.

We swam back to shore. Our friends were waiting for us on the dock.

"I mean, when you go big, you fucking go big," Natalie cried, throwing a towel around my shoulders.

"I love him," I said, beaming up at my guy.

"C'mere, Bossy." He laughed, tucking me under his arm. He looked up at the third-floor balcony. "Did no one else jump?"

"No way, man, everyone just watched to see what was going to happen," Leo replied, clapping Archie on the back. "Maybe you can do a Labor Day Porch Jump instead."

"I might sit that one out." I looked up and saw how high that balcony really was. "Good lord, that's high."

"Esther Williams over here." Roxie laughed. "But you weren't going to miss out on your man."

"I love him," I repeated. It didn't get old, hearing those words coming out of my mouth. Thrilling.

"I know you do, sweetie." She laughed, then waved at someone in the crowd. "Hey, I've got someone for you to meet."

"Can it wait? I kind of want to go kiss on Archie a little bit." And without waiting, I reached up and tugged his very willing mouth down to mine, not caring a bit who was watching or who I was supposed to be meeting.

"Ahem, uh, Clara?" I heard Roxie say.

"Yeah yeah, in a minute." I sighed as Archie's hands snuck around to the small of my back and pulled me closer.

"No worries, Rox, we'll meet up with her later, they both look a bit busy, yeah?" I heard an oddly familiar voice with a distinct British accent say.

My eyes blinked open even though I was still kissing Archie. I looked to my left even though I was still kissing Archie. And saw none other than Jack Hamilton standing there, looking a bit embarrassed . . . while I was still kissing Archie.

"I love you," I said to him, while still kissing Archie. "I mean—"

"Ow!" Archie said. "You bit my lip!"

"Why is Jack Hamilton standing there looking at me?" I asked Archie out of the corner of my mouth. I looked at the gorgeous redhead standing next to Jack. "Shit, and Grace Sheridan is looking at me too, what is happening?"

"We caught your porch jump, brilliant, wasn't it Crazy?" Jack asked Grace, wrapping his arm around her shoulder.

"If I hadn't seen it, I wouldn't have believed it," Grace replied with a naturally warm smile.

"Someone tell me what's happening," I said, not able to take my eyes off the Hollywood royalty standing in front of me. "Also, Jack, I love you."

"Okay, quit it," Roxie said, jumping in. "Remember how you were talking about trying to drum up some celebrity clientele here, bringing some new blood to Bryant Mountain House? Well, I mentioned to Archie that I might have a couple that would fit that bill exactly, and he invited them up for the weekend, isn't it great?" She linked arms with the two of them. "I haven't seen these two since I left Los Angeles last year."

"She said she'd be back to cook for us, but she stayed away forever," Jack said.

"And now that I've met Leo, I can see why," Grace said, flashing another movie-star grin in Leo's direction.

"Grace is doing a show in New York for a few weeks so we thought we'd pop up here, see Rox, and check out this hotel she's been raving about. Which is great by the way, cheers, mate," Jack said, reaching out to shake Archie's hand.

"We're glad to have you here," Archie said, and I suddenly realized I was meeting the star of *Time,* one of my favorite movie franchises ever, while wearing a soaking wet dress after throwing myself into a lake to kiss the man I loved.

Best. Day. Ever.

"I just wish someone would have told me, is all I'm saying," I said again, from underneath the towel. Archie and I had finally managed to step away from the gaggle of well-wishers, guests and staff alike, who'd been gathered around us down by the lake and escape to one of the rooms to clean up a bit. I was scrubbing at my hair, trying to get most of the wet out, and when I emerged from underneath, it stood out around my face in spikes. "I mean, it's Jack Fucking Hamilton. That's like not telling someone, hey, by the way, Robert Pattinson is picking apples in your front yard, no big deal."

Suddenly, warm hands slipped around my waist and tugged me back against a warm body. "They've been here for a few days already, Bossy. It's not really a big deal anymore. Remember, royalty has stayed here. You get used to it."

"Royalty," I scoffed, turning around in his arms. "They're Hollywood royalty, and I still think someone could have told me. I looked like a fool."

"You looked amazing," he replied, kissing me on the nose. "Especially when you were telling him you loved him."

"I do." I grinned. "But not like I love you."

"Let's hope not," he warned, lifting my chin with his hand. "How much time do you think we have up here before they come looking for us?"

"Fuck 'em," I said, reaching up and taking his hand in mine. Turning the palm up I pressed a kiss in the center. "They don't know what room we're in, and I have no idea where my phone is so they can't call me and . . ." My voice trailed off as I stopped cold, looking at his hand.

"Clara?"

I held his hand in mine. "Your ring. You're not wearing it."

"No."

My heart beat faster. "When did you take it off?"

He lifted my chin once more so he could look into my eyes. "The day you left. I haven't worn it since."

"Oh."

"I've only loved two women in my entire life, Clara." Those indigo eyes, feathered with the most beautiful auburn lashes, began to deepen.

"To be clear, I'm one of them, right?"

"Ridiculous," he murmured, softly brushing my cheek with his fingertips.

I reached up on my tiptoes to kiss him. "Want to stay here and not watch TV?"

He lifted me up off my tiptoes. "I thought you'd never ask."

He had me naked in seconds. And the way he looked at me told me we weren't going anywhere anytime soon. "We're going to miss the fireworks," I said as he carried me to the bed.

"We can watch them from the balcony."

"Sort of like a new tradition, huh?" I threw my arms over my head as he began to kiss down my body.

"Exactly what I was thinking," he told my belly button.

"I love you."

He lifted my leg over his shoulder. "Never stop saying that."

"I love you. I love you. I love you. I . . .

"Oh,

"Oh,

"Oh,

". . . loooooove you!"

Epilogue

I watched her from across the dining room. She hadn't noticed me yet, but when my girl was focused on something it was tough to get her to look away. Which was okay by me, because I loved to watch her work.

She looked down at the new menu cards through her new eyeglasses, the ones she insisted she didn't need but finally got. She looked adorable when she was wearing them, especially when I came to bed to find her still awake and reading. Perched on top of the thousand pillows she liked to have stacked around her at night, she'd sit primly on a mountain of white, wearing her glasses and one of my old T-shirts, spreadsheets and trade magazines spread out all around her. Sometimes when she read, the tip of her tongue would stick out. Did she know she did that? Did she know it drove me wild?

Sometimes she knew. Like when I was buried deep inside of her and she was hot and wet all around me and she'd dig her nails into my backside, just past the point of pain, knowing I'd fuck her faster and harder if she did it. Drove me wild.

My girl was wild. And loud. And obnoxious. And irritating. And bossy as all get out. And I wouldn't have her any other way.

"Hey, Hotel Boy," she called from across the room, and I grinned just hearing her voice. "Get over here and proof these with me."

"Coming, Bossy."

And she had been. This morning. All morning. *Every* morning. When she was in town, that is.

Clara had quit her job, and while her boss tried like hell to get her to come back she was steadfast in her decision. And while she did spend the rest of the summer with me, helping our team to implement all the changes she'd initially gotten started back in the spring, by September I could tell she was getting antsy.

"So I'd get to pick and choose the jobs I do, when I want to do them. I mean, I'd have real freedom to set things up exactly the way I want."

"Sounds great."

"No really, what do you think?" she asked, chewing on her thumbnail nervously. She'd approached me with the idea of going back to work in a freelance capacity. Simply put, my girl had made such a name for herself in our industry that she literally had owners beating down her door to work with her. Even with the hit job The Empire Group had tried to put out on her, her work spoke for itself. But she didn't want to make that decision without me.

It wasn't easy for my girl to loop people in, she was so used to doing things her way and her way alone. She'd made decisions for years based solely on her own needs, but she was trying like hell to include me in everything now, and I loved her even more for it.

"I think it sounds great, really I do," I said, leaning over to kiss her soundly. *"I'll miss seeing your face first thing every morning, but this sounds like a great opportunity."*

"And my boobs second thing," she said, leaning over to kiss me back just as soundly.

"If you'd just sleep naked, then I could sometimes see those even before I see your face," I growled, pulling her down onto my lap.

That discussion had ended a few seconds after that. But she went back out onto the road a few weeks later, and so far it was working out pretty great.

Bryant Mountain House was slowly and surely making headway. We'd implemented almost every change Clara had recommended and it was coming along nicely. We were closing down part of the hotel after the holidays and we only had to make minimal adjustments to the staff. Caroline and her team had already begun the room renovations and even I had to admit they were looking great. And just a few tweets from someone like Jack Hamilton had put our hotel on the map for an entirely new group of travelers. Who knew?

And here we were, a week before Christmas. Holidays were still difficult for Clara, but she was trying really hard. We spent Thanksgiving together in Manhattan with Natalie's family (a fight that Trudy was still sore over), and Clara did okay. Slowly but surely, we were making new memories together to replace the ones she'd missed out on for so many years. And we made sure to celebrate each and every holiday so far with as many I love yous as we could say.

I missed Ashley. Of course I missed Ashley. She'd been a part of my life longer than she hadn't been. But where our relationship had seemed easy and almost fated, my love for Clara was work, but the very best kind. We challenged each other, we fought hard, but we loved harder. And the payoff? Christ, she was worth everything.

"Did I tell you Roxie and I found some old menu cards from the twenties? We used them as the base for these, but just as a base. We weren't going to start serving grapefruit and tomato juice at dinner, I mean, who does that?"

"The Bryants did, that's who," I said, looking over her shoulder at the menu cards. "Grapefruit juice was a great palate cleanser."

"That doesn't explain the tomato juice." She looked critically at me, one eyebrow raised, like she was ready to start an argument. I was ready if she was.

"It was Prohibition, the tomato juice was likely laced with basement hooch."

"Speaking of the basement, we gotta get back down to that boiler room sometime, Hotel Boy." She grinned. "I love the way you look when you're holding your wrench." Then she leaned over the table, pretending to fiddle with the placement of the salt and pepper shakers but really, she was just making sure I saw her ass in that tiny pencil skirt she was wearing. And speaking of the twenties, were those stockings she was wearing?

My girl, she drove me wild.

"Meet you there in twenty minutes."

She turned around, heat flashing in her eyes, and shook her head. "Make it fifteen."

Can't argue with that.